MENDING

MENDING

T. A. PARRISH

MOUNTAIN ARBOR
PRESS

Mountain Arbor
Press
Alpharetta, GA

ISBN: 978-1-6653-0102-2 - Paperback
eISBN: 978-1-6653-0103-9 - ePub
eISBN: 978-1-6653-0104-6 – Mobi

Library of Congress Control Number: 2021910584

Printed in the United States of America   0 6 2 2 2 1

♾This paper meets the requirements of ANSI/NISO Z39.48-1992 (Permanence of Paper)

PROLOGUE

Jane Hansen, nee Henderson, was a generous, caring, gentle woman who nurtured her children—Helene and Horace—to the best of her capability. She fully intended them to become clones of her virtues.

For no good reason, she failed, according to some because she turned out to be a lesbian.

This was a mysterious turn of events in Jane's life since she had shown no predisposition toward her own sex while growing up. The trait surfaced after she endured repeated beatings by her East Texas lumberjack husband, in between the spells of drunkenness he imposed on their domestic condition. Jane was praised for her stoicism and her subsequent devotion to her beleaguered children. Since they were only one year apart in age, they jointly suffered through these experiences, developing an unusually close bond, which seemed to evolve into shared bitterness, erratic behavior, and, later, generalized hatred of quite nearly everyone with whom they came in contact.

It was not clear to those who knew the family how Jane's daughter, Helene, ever involved herself with a man sufficiently to actually become pregnant and give birth to her son, Henry.

According to all reasonable assessments, Henry managed to shed the negativity of his childhood and matriculate to manhood in fairly good psychological and emotional shape.

His mother, Helene, had managed to care adequately for him in the formative years, although with a certain emotional distance that assured he would never be handicapped by irrational ideals stemming from a loving childhood. Henry managed to sublimate the missing emotional content of normal life, plunging into sports, music, philosophy, literature, math, and politics with little capacity for anything else in his daily life.

His uncle Horace spent a great deal of time with Henry overseeing his education in the manly arts. He taught Henry the ins and outs of basketball, baseball, golf, bird hunting, riding, and bass fishing. Henry, as a man, would be nothing less than well-rounded. He was, thanks to Horace, well-schooled in sports and outdoors activities to an extreme degree, even though his participation was limited by circumstances.

Baseball, golf, and riding got most of Henry's attention and he was talented enough at each. Less so with basketball, as the team responsibilities eluded him in competition. He was much more comfortable relying on himself for competitive success—he was never selfish enough to develop into a great shooter, taking on the responsibility of scoring for his team. Baseball, as a slower combination of individual and team efforts, was more manageable for him. As a position player (outfield and third base), the team cooperation requirements were infrequent, and all out individual efforts were the big drivers of success. In the batter's box, the only team sacrifices required were true sacrifices—bunts and hitting deep fly balls, or to the right side of the infield with a runner on third and nobody (or one) out—and generally taking the signs from the third base coach faithfully. Baseball also created myriad opportunities for an outrageous variety of statistics, which played into Henry's passions and abilities well.

Horace's involvement with the institutions of horse

racing, developed quickly over a short time span due to a "lucky investment," enabled Henry to learn to ride according to proper equestrian traditions and principles. And, as he became competent, he learned how to ride thoroughbreds for speed and endurance, although he was too large for proper jockeyhood. He also developed a solid understanding of the noble sport's history and practices — including more than a passing knowledge of the sleazier aspects of racing as well as the vagaries of parimutuel wagering.

Horace ensured that Henry would be equipped to be successful in gentlemanly circles, whether astride a horse or working a grain field for pheasants behind a good gun dog. Henry would always be aware of his gun, and would carry his over and under open (but loaded) until the dogs went on point.

Horace worked diligently to help Henry become academically capable too. He made sure that Henry was exposed to the humanities and arts, but especially to math, science, and numbers. Through his involvement with horseracing, Horace was extremely qualified to provide many "teachable moments" utilizing the genetics of breeding, the physiology of equine musculature, and, naturally, the numerous examples of betting odds and their impact of risk management (bet hedging), and the profitability of bringing a good horse to the starting gate. Henry took this all in with joy and wonder, and, as he grew, became known for precocious skills unfamiliar to most teens.

He also grew into a strong, fit, and well-groomed specimen of emerging, genteel, upper-middle-class manhood. Six-foot-two, sandy hair, piercing blue eyes that saw everything, and an affable sense of humor that made him acceptable company for almost anyone. His body was strong, supple, and agile, with a grace of movement that provided him success in his chosen avocations. His outgoing personality was constrained by his focus on in-dividual sports and disciplines—but this appearance of introversion was not sufficient to cause concern in those that knew him. His lack of confidence in the areas that he did not intentionally develop—and his lack of type-A personality characteristics—actually, and accidentally, positioned him well to become a collaborative manager and possible leader, even though he never gave that role much conscious thought.

As Horace's success in racing improved, and his pros-perity accordingly, he involved Henry in the bewildering art of golf, teaching him expertly from the fundamentals to the advanced and sophisticated skills of shaping shots, reading greens, and course management. As it turned out, Henry was particularly adept and embraced the ul-timate individual challenges, both physical and psycho-logical, that the game imposed. These abilities were to stand him in very good stead as he grew and attended a college with a national tradition in the sport, yielding him several conference championships and a means to generate small bits of off-books income as an adult.

Today—in spite of the perversity of ancestry—in his own mind, Henry was the picture of well-adjusted, upper-middle-class achievement. Full scholarships, fellowships, and graduate grants to notable Ivy League universities had certainly played a leading role in his success and well-earned self-confidence. He was definitely not Holden Caulfield, nor Theophilus North, but he probably knew them both in college, and made the decision that Henry Hansen would be different.

It had always been terribly important to Henry that he never be judged unworthy because he became a narrow person. He was quite keen on expertly navigating the broad "myths" of human existence, undistracted and unfazed by predicaments and entanglements.

There had been a few girlfriends, but not often for more than one or two dates. Attachment had just never attracted him … nor, as he became aware, *them*.

CHAPTER 1

Baseball used to be so much fun when I first discovered it. It was about being smarter, in better physical shape, running faster, throwing straighter—or not straight, if you were a pitcher—and hitting the ball harder and more frequently "where they ain't." Five-tool guys were the heroes, and guys who could do it all had their faces on bubble gum cards, enjoying the adoration of kids and adults all over the country.

It was beautiful. Fifteen thousand dollars was a huge salary. There were no unions, no collective bargaining agreements on salary caps, no luxury taxes to govern which team traded for which player. Yankee Stadium was old, Shea Stadium was relatively new, there was little artificial grass, and no sliding roofs with climate control to ease the summer heat or the autumn chill. The minor leagues provided a romantic playground for kids to develop into baseball's version of men, and the grizzled old guys who ran minor league teams were actually focused on making young players good enough to move up to The Show.

But Dylan—Bob, not Thomas—got it right, "The Times, They are a Changin'." Ever since that guy discovered that baseball metrics were all wrong, and began to dominate the majors with a cast of underpaid and anonymous players, it has all been downhill. He figured out what really mattered and how to use data to enhance run production. Over the course of a ridiculously long season, runs win games—not pitching, stolen bases, strong outfield arms, or great fielding. But those skillsets all have a major impact on the other team's ability to score runs, and preventing that scoring is an important, though secondary, objective. Why did anyone need new truths to figure out the obvious truth of the old sacred metrics?

And I, Henry Hansen, have built my career on becoming the best "metrician" in the minor leagues. My lifelong love of the game, combined with my statistics-heavy mathematics education, has given me a natural entrée into the game ... and a decent, if not extravagant, lifestyle.

So, why ain't I happier?

Hell, I don't even know for sure what it means to be happy. Is that political idea of the "inalienable right" to the pursuit of happiness a real thing? Maybe it's just something old-fashioned that is good for history class or political science but irrelevant in real life.

Why even waste time thinking about BS like that? Apparently, nobody who actually makes laws thinks about it.

Henry! Stay focused. You just quit a good job for reasons you really can't see, and you may be dangerously close to homeless in a couple of months.

Like Apollo 13, "We've got a problem." Except they never actually said that. Yeah, like a lot of crap, legends grow up feeding on popular fantasies and then drive current and future realities that change history but that didn't really happen. Thousands of examples, one of the few valuable lessons emerging from an extensive acquaintance with post-Renaissance history. Would've been nice if that history had taught something that would help get a job. Have to rely on the spine-tingling field of statistics for that. Seems to be the only thing anybody is willing to pay for.

Why did you make some of the decisions that you have? Would life have been different if you had become a music teacher? Or a literature professor? Certainly, you are intellectually qualified for those.

Focus! Where do you go now? Your resume is full of degrees and certificates from prestigious universities. You are the one percent of almost any measure of men your age. You have a deep well of knowledge and cerebral process at your disposal to learn and master a world of varied disciplines. You may not be Superman, but maybe Sherlock Holmes. You can figure things out because you pay attention to detail. How do you get paid for that? It's time to figure it out, Doofus, quick. When your better angels talk to you, their disrespect is not always helpful in providing answers to tough questions.

Shit! It's late, I'd better get going. A guy on a job hunt can't afford to miss that Ursa, Stearns, and Giacana soirée tonight. Their reputation as investment bankers is legendary. And my rep as a dazzling stats whiz has earned me an invitation to the event of the season.

Move your butt, Cinderella. You need to tell your story to these folks.

CHAPTER 2

Henry was not unacquainted with the excesses of the privileged classes, but also not accustomed to acting as a beneficiary of their courtesies. Upon entering the gigantic ballroom, he nearly swooned at the magnificence and carefully engineered comfort of the setting. Bars at both ends of the large space, stand up tables, sit down tables, spacious areas for mingling on foot and moving from benefactor to benefactor, and a spectacular buffet of exotic nibbles to assure that the participants need not embarrass themselves through overindulgence without protection from food calorie consumption. Live music in the far corner on a small stage.

This sure beats hell out of free beer in the locker room after winning a home series with a league rival.

At least he had the benefit of knowing some of the more technical practitioners of the arcane art of statistics in town, whom he spotted in the corners of the room. Spreadsheet jockeys seem to find each other no matter what the function. Variables, formulae, and algorithms always lead to joyful discussions and assure that one does not get into any trouble with loose women, or even nice women. The atmosphere was perfect for Henry since he had long mastered the art of non-involvement while maintaining a polite demeanor. He was well at home here.

He was at home, that is, until he was struck by a red-headed bolt of lightning in a burgundy cocktail dress, slit up the left leg, and showing enough cleavage to be quite interesting, perhaps provocative. Henry was not familiar with the tight collar reaction he experienced from this particular lightning storm.

He leaned over to his conversational friend, Ari, a young grad student working part time for a mid-sized insurance company trying to devise favorable actuarial tables for senior-citizen life insurance.

"Who the hell is that?" Henry asked, with more than a usual sense of wonderment.

"Oh, that's Amanda. Don't know much about her. But she shows up from time to time at some of our Statistical Society networkers. Always draws a crowd at cocktail hour."

"Yeah, I can see how that could happen. Introduce me?"

"Sure. This way." Ari moved toward Amanda with all the confidence of a new colt five minutes after a difficult birth.

"Hi, Amanda. You look great tonight."

"Thanks, Ari. Who is your friend?"

Not a time-waster, thought Henry.

Ari graciously introduced Henry, "This is Henry Hansen. He is the AI and stat guy for the Pirates. And a highly respected number cruncher in local performance-metric circles."

"Sounds exhilarating," smiled Amanda without a trace of sarcasm.

Henry was smitten by the broad, sincere smile and her perfectly straight, shining teeth.

Ari excused himself and wandered off to mix with some other insurance guys.

"So, how are you holding up with the Pirates? That .218 team batting average certainly is not worth getting excited about, nor is that 6.50 ERA." *Surprising command of relevant baseball stats, for a girl.*

"It has not been an exciting season to date," mumbled Henry. "But the second half of the season should prove better."

"Like hell," she snorted. "Those guys are not talented. None of them will ever see The Show. They will spend the rest of their four-year careers in Double-A."

"You have some strong opinions about baseball, at least here. And you are acquainted with some meaningful data. How did you develop that?"

She smiled that smile again. "Brothers. All of them played on select teams and traveled around the country trying to make the family great again. As the youngest, I got dragged around until I actually learned the game."

"Trying to make the family great again?"

That smile. "Yeah, Dad played Triple-A. Got called up to The Show and tore his knee up in a collision with the left field wall in a game where his team was up five runs in the bottom of the ninth with two out. He was due to leave the next morning. End of dream."

"Oh, I bet I know that history. Who is your Dad?"

"Maurice, 'Mo' ... Stearns."

"Hmmm, so you are Amanda ... Stearns."

"Yeah, doesn't it show?" A self-deprecating small laugh to go along with the smile.

"Um, yeah, the dress gives it away." They shared a genuine laugh, and she took his arm.

"Why don't you help me refresh my drink?"

"Deal!"

He didn't want to think he could actually be having an enjoyable, relaxed conversation with a spectacular redhead who was an elevated member of the class of wretched excess.

New experience, and a pleasant one at that. Even though maintaining the façade of the sophisticated man of the world was challenging his available resources to the max.

The bartender asked what they wanted and Henry inquired about craft beers. Amanda jumped in, "Screw the craft beer. Two very dry English gin martinis, up, extra olives."

Henry, suitably impressed, sipped the drink slowly when it came. He was already intoxicated.

"So, what about you?" purred the ravishing and attentive Queen of the nobility. "How did you get where you are today?"

"Sort of the long way around," he said. "Eight years of the finest universities that scholarships and fellowships could buy. And some key thesis projects in areas unexamined by previous students. Degrees in history, literature, and mathematics. Then tripped over the job with the Pirates reading *The Baseball News*. Been with them four years."

She gasped. "I don't think we've ever had anyone that deep in our proud little commercial community. Aren't you a little bored surrounded by such plebes?"

He parried, "Without ignoring the obvious, how'd you get where you are?"

She horse-laughed, "Well, ignoring the obvious, I finished top of my class at NYU Business School in marketing."

"Isn't that the Stearns School?" he asked.

"No," she sheepishly grinned, "it's the Stern School, not even a misspelled relation."

"Nice, you could have been angry at my smartassed question."

"Not a chance," smiling again. "And by the way, the red hair is natural."

"I never had a doubt." He replied, trying to keep his cool sophistication, completely missing the point of reference.

"Not even curious about carpets and drapes?" The smile was turning lascivious.

"Hunh?" He was a bit bewildered and sensed he was out of his league.

"Never mind," she smiled. "Not a deal breaker."

Henry silently instructed himself to look that one up when he had a chance.

Back in her official voice, "We should trade cards. It might be mutually helpful if we get engaged as an advisor to sell the Pirates. Hold on! Just kidding. Nothing like that in the works, cross my heart." Smile.

Henry, in his most gravitas-style voice, "Of course, I'd be pleased to trade cards. I need to be going, though. I've got a major job search to start tomorrow morning."

"Oh, you didn't tell me that. Maybe I can make some introductions for you."

"Yeah, I don't like to rely on connections, and I don't know quite which direction this thing is going to take. But I'd love to tell you about it sometime."

"Anytime. Call me. G'night."

"G'night."

He left the hotel with a lilt in his step that was like a loss of virginity. Nothing in his experience gave him any clue why he felt that way. He began to wonder if there might be investment banking in his future, but then rejected that insane idea as putting the cart way out in front of the horse. Not a practical consideration or desire. But Amanda stuck in his mind.

Holy shit! What just happened? She was alright! Not stuck up, not arrogant, great laugh, and gorgeous beyond any woman I have ever talked to. And I actually cared that the conversation was great. What the hell is that all about? Won't forget her for quite a while. Maybe that job with the Pirates wasn't what happiness is supposed to be ... if anyone can figure that out anyway.

CHAPTER 3

"Henry Hansen to see Mr. Stearns."

"Come right in, Mr. Hansen. Mo is expecting you." Her demeanor was almost unbearably formal, cheerful, engaging, and casual, all at the same time. It cast the impression of encountering greatness and humility wrapped up in one corporate personality.

As the door opened, a six-foot-six giant rose from behind the elegant mahogany desk and came to greet Henry, covering the twenty-foot distance in four graceful, athletic strides. It was almost frightening the way the room shrank as he came closer. *Gigantic man, even larger personality.*

How had this happened? What ethereal influences have guided these people to be in this place at this time? It made no sense. *Where was all this headed?*

The best Henry could remember, it had moved to Phase Two three days after the thrilling conversation with Amanda at the event. Phase One was *the dress.* His phone had rung about nine-thirty that morning. He was not yet realizing all the benefits of his second cup of coffee and was still a bit slow on the uptake.

"H'lo," he had mumbled.

"Hey, Hotshot. How the hell come you haven't called me and asked me out? Don't you remember *the dress*? We even traded cards, so I know you have my number." The voice of royalty ... on the prowl.

"Uh, I have been busy getting things in shape for my job search. I haven't really talked to anyone," he stammered defensively.

"Well, stats guy, I am not just anyone, and you would do well to keep that and the dress image in mind. Henry ... Henry ... hey, I'm just yankin' your chain. No big deal. I just wanted to call and see if you would be interested in meeting my Dad at his office ... tomorrow, at 10:00 a.m.," she not-so-subtly offered.

Temporarily floored by the suggestion of her "yankin'" his chain, Henry managed to respond, "Yeah, that's great. But why?"

Amanda was smiling but perhaps losing a tad of her patience with him. "Because he has an open job that would be perfect for you, and we need it badly—*very* badly." She hinted that it could be quite lucrative for the job holder.

"Sure, but what makes you so certain it's perfect for me? We don't really know anything about each other ... except that you looked great in that dress."

"Don't take this wrong, but I vetted you."

"Vetted me? What, do I need a security clearance?"

"Sort of, but not actually. Our business is fraught with commercial espionage and we need to know about our staff. Dad has sort of delegated that to me, in addition to my marketing responsibilities." She sounded very CIA-like.

He wasn't clear whether to be insulted, afraid, or flattered. What did she/they have in mind that could require a humanities-educated number cruncher? *And, oh lordy, what did the vetting discover?* There was lots of "stuff" back there that he was not ready to have anyone else know.

"And?"

She backed off the CIA voice a bit, "My Father, the founder of the firm, would like to meet you for a friendly cup of coffee in his office. C'mon, couldn't hurt."

"You know how I feel about connections and using them to replace skills and merit."

"Oh, bullshit Henry! You have to have both connections and skills in order to accomplish anything today. Grow a pair and come into the real world. It might also score you a lot of points with me ... remember *the dress*?"

"Okay." Point well and memorably made. "I'll meet Mr. Stearns at ten tomorrow."

He wasn't all that clear which point was well made but he conceded both were reasonable.

"It's 'Mo,' by the way," Amanda cautioned.

And that's how we got here. *OMG, I am here because of the boss's daughter. What does he think is going on? What if he finds out that she is outrageously flirting with me? And what if she gets pissed and doesn't want to have anything to do with me? Can I keep the job? Will I be blackballed around town and have no friends, if friends actually matter? A professional and social outcast, not even welcome at the ballpark? This is dangerous. Focus, Henry. One small step for numbercrunchingkind at a time. Apologies to Mr. Armstrong.*

The handshake was intimidating. Using the old European two-hand approach, Mo's huge hand engulfed Henry's right hand in warm sincerity while his left hand came up to Henry's elbow in a reassuring embrace that Henry was certain could snap his arm on a whim. But the smile was broad and genuine. Henry knew where Amanda got her perfect teeth.

Henry allowed himself to be drawn into this web of good will to hear what the giant had to say.

"Amanda tells me you are *the* guy to help us with a need we have in our deal team. Have you ever done any merger and acquisition advisory work?"

"Well, honestly sir, no. I am a good analyst, and can string data processes and structures together to discover some interesting information, but mostly I am good at performance-type statistical analysis, defining metrics that are true indicators of future performance." Henry was proud of his skills but somewhat tentative in front of the great man.

"Well, Henry, that is exactly what I am looking for. I need someone smart enough and bold enough to go beyond traditional financial analysis. Traditional business models capture operating data and build good financial models, but they are not all that good at seeing and measuring the true traits of a winner. They are based on backwards-looking data and are difficult to extrapolate into true information. That extrapolation requires someone to identify future trends, possibilities, variables, and the like, and translate them into value-weighted performance factors, then to model a wide range of operating and financial scenarios and results. The next trick is to figure out how those measurements will motivate an investor to pay a top valuation for the company and convince the client to hire us to improve his chances of a top-end sale. That requires still another multivariable and multi-scenario model, behaviorally-based, and separate from company operations. Not a simple nor a straightforward set of tasks."

"Sir, I don't know that that has ever been done—by anyone. Has something happened here that leads you to believe that it can be done?" Now Henry was beginning to understand expectation anxiety.

"No, Henry, I don't accept 'can' and 'can't' ... I identify

what *needs* to be done and find a way. Just like baseball—no risk management, no 'safe play,' no backing off a big lead. Make every play and win 'em all. If you can do that, you'll win a lot of pennants."

"I would be misleading you, sir, if I unequivocally claimed to be able to do that. I have an idea about some approaches, but you are looking for the holy grail of analytics."

"OK. I accept your disclaimer as evidence of your modesty. I like that. Arrogance is a prized characteristic in investment bankers and M&A advisors, but we have no appetite for it. We like to speak with results. Now tell me something that shows me your spirit and your 'can do.'"

Henry stiffened. *What a great locker room speech. It was actually confidence-building and maybe even inspiring.* It made him want to try.

"I can envision a multi-step, multi-process approach. We'd need a team of five at least—finance, sales, logistics, marketing, technology. They would evaluate, industry-by-industry, the needs, customer desires, available technologies, capital costs vs operating costs, potential profit margins—and then model outcomes based on a number of customer behavior curves, political environments, economic cycles, and national liquidity scenarios. It's probably two and a half years of data gathering, impact mapping, variable weighting, and coding to get the first model built, then maybe a year to get the next two. And, honestly, that is a SWAG. Lots could go wrong."

"OK. Got it. What would be the ultimate value of the competitive advantage—over a seven-year period—of the capitalized costs, discounted at seven per cent to today's dollars?" Mo probed to explore Henry's ability to mix concepts and numbers.

"I can't give you an intelligent number with any certainty, but I would estimate a couple of billion, given the inability of anyone else to match an accurate model. All depends on the size of the clients and what they are willing to pay, of course." Henry took a deep breath.

"Yeah, I got that number, too," sighed Mo. "You wanna give it a try?"

"It would be the project of a lifetime. Harvard would build case studies on it for decades." *Professorships, lecture tours, book revenues. Even aside from the trading and client income values, it would be an income stream capable of supporting a separate large company.* "What about comp?"

"One hundred and eighty-five thousand dollars, exec-level bennies, access to the company jet and ski lodge, golf club." Then he threw in, "You're a four, aren't you? Also, options and stock awards for milestones," Mo barked.

Henry nearly choked. He hadn't been a true four in years, and he had never heard of such compensation. Struggling mightily to keep his sophistication intact, he asked, "Can I have a couple of days to think about it?"

"Sure, call me by Friday lunch. But don't bring any of that weak-assed cheese, rookie," Mo chuckled.

Henry got the baseball reference, and, with a small smile, bid his astonished farewell.

How did he know I was a four?

CHAPTER 4

As he left Mo's office, Henry found it taxing to walk a straight line. His elation was only matched by the wondrous images of executive power, comfortable cars, nice clothes, status, and wealth—all new experiences for him, ever in his life. The little boy growing up in the social outcast environment of his mother's home never anticipated that these advantages might accrue to him.

Even though he lacked background—technical or personal—to conduct business from this elevation, Mo had assured him he was on the way there. Looking back on the talk, Henry realized that Mo had done a perfect job of subliminal advertising on him, and he had bought the popcorn.

It was only a matter of time and a couple of high-profile projects where he could demonstrate his technical immortality. The spreadsheet jockey was destined to become the "Master of the Universe" of analysis and future modeling for the best investment advisory firm in town. Ah! The magnificence and glory!

In a more concrete expression of Henry's status, Mo had promised resources in the form of the team that Henry had suggested, and all the backup that any team leader in the history of the world could ask for. Henry was having trouble separating Mo's enthusiasm and hyperbole from the reality of actually being a team leader. It wouldn't be the last time.

His pulse raced, and energy arced out of him like a Tesla tower. He was giddy, but electric, and eager to explore his self-satisfaction. *Hmm, noon, don't feel like eating, too early for cocktails, but need to celebrate, let off some steam, go for a run ... then it's time for cocktails. Maybe three miles or so will do the trick. Why does everyone complain about how difficult and humiliating a job hunt is?*

Home to change, an hour to run, an hour to wash up and recover, and it's time to party! Get in the bar at four, in front of the crowd, and then I don't have to stay up until midnight or one to have my fun—and I'll be of sound mind when I call Mo.

As he left his apartment to head for the trail head where he usually got his outdoor exercise, he was already behind schedule. It wasn't a big deal, he had plenty of time, and he decided that, maybe, in honor of great achievement, he should do an extra mile. For now, at least, time was the least of his concerns. He was walking new ground and was going to smell the dollar trees and enjoy the path.

In the parking lot he took some time to do his usual stretching routine—certainly didn't want to risk a pulled muscle or other injury on the threshold of greatness. It did seem that the crowd was unusually large for a Wednesday afternoon. Lots of suburban moms and dads, lots of labs and golden retrievers, lots of three-wheeled baby carts being pushed by joggers (as opposed to real runners). Oh well, no problem for an experienced athlete; just have to make sure that those rookies were warned that he was coming and moved of the way.

So, two loops would be right at four miles. He had done four loops when doing max training a couple of years ago, and two wouldn't be a problem—not with all the adrenalin coursing through him right now. The first mile was downhill, and the second mostly flat, with a challenging uphill finishing stretch. The sand-pebble paved path ran alongside a very pleasant small stream, crossed over a bridge at about one mile, and came back along the other side, which was the downhill side of a canyon. All in all, it was an enjoyable run without stressing his abilities to dangerous levels.

He plunged into the start a bit ahead of his usual pace in order to create a little space between himself and some lesser runners. He passed a fit-looking blonde woman who was also just starting and warned, "On your left!" as he motored past. After he fit himself into an opening in the jogging-running-walking parade, he settled into a quick but comfortable running tempo that rewarded him with a feeling of ease and achievement, all at the same time. He was home.

At about three-quarters of a mile, he noticed that he was coming up on a jogger-stroller combo a little faster than he liked. So, he politely called out, "On the left!" and proceeded to move around the slower traffic. Precisely as he took his second accelerated step, he was bowled over by either a pickup truck or a middle linebacker—hard to tell which—and took a tumble, sending him ass-over-teakettle for about ten yards before he rolled to a stop. He was dazed and felt a twinge in his old baseball-injured left ankle. "Dammit," he cried out. "That hurts."

"Are you OK?" he heard through the fog of pain that had suddenly engulfed him when he figured out what had happened. It was coming from that blonde he had passed when starting his run.

"Not really," he groaned. "Some giant guy just ran

right over me and I think my old baseball injury is acting up pretty bad as a result."

"Actually," she said sheepishly, "the giant guy was me. I'm terribly sorry."

"You are telling me that you couldn't see me?" he mocked.

"I'm telling you that you should look in your rear-view mirror and signal when you change lanes, Doofus. I was almost right beside you when you just pulled out right into me and tripped over your own feet," she shot back.

Hmmm. A little spirited and hostile for my taste. But she could be right. I am a bit distracted by other events.

"You just had to hit me? No other alternative?"

"No, I chose to hit you because you are so unaware and piggish that you have no idea of what's going around directly around you. Of *course*, I had to hit you. There was nowhere to go, especially with that tank coming up the path from the wrong direction. I tried to stop but I had no place to go, and I probably would've pulled a hamstring anyway.

"Can you walk? Do you need help getting back to your car? And can you drive when you get there?"

"How do you know that I have a car?"

"I saw you stretching beside that ancient Econoline van. I figured that you were too broke to have a real car, and too green to have it tricked out as a seduction wagon. I can see I was right."

"How so?"

"Just the way you handle yourself. More like a displaced jock—a doer not a lover. I can always spot 'em."

"You might be surprised," he chortled, remembering his smooth moves with Amanda.

"No way. I am sure of this one. Here, lean into me and

put your arm around my shoulder. I'll get you back to your car, and then be out of your life."

"Gee, thanks for the in-depth emotional support to go along with the physical injury. Not often you get everything in one package like that."

"Just be thankful that I didn't throw you over the edge of the cliff and walk away smiling. Now let's go back to your car ... such as it is."

Things were slightly more civil on the long-assisted hike back to the parking lot. Henry discovered that Harper Philips was an avid activist for all causes outdoors and natural, without being a classic "tree hugger." She was practical, and only dedicated to having a place to go for the ordinary person that allowed respite from the city. Hence, she was a fly-fisher, and valued the solitude and peace of free-flowing streams and wild fish with insect hatches rising out of clean water. It was all practical to her.

Harper found out that Henry was about to enter an exciting new phase of his life and gain access to a world that neither of them knew from experience. His new job did not impress her, per se, because she had no idea what he would do. This they shared. So, they could laugh a little about that mystery. He did not seem to be a bad guy. There was just a lot of stuff that he apparently had never thought about—but what he knew, he was good at. And she could certainly admire that.

They both discovered that being very close and dependent on each other physically was not an unpleasant feeling. The thirty-minute trip was enjoyable, and a little ... stimulating.

When she deposited him back at the van, they traded cards. Henry was genuinely surprised that she had cards.

Harper's proclaimed, "Activist for outdoor causes, fly-fishing guide, part time poet, and author." An eclectic mix, if nothing else. There seemed to be some character and depth here, even if he did not fully grasp its breadth or value. But at least he had her phone number if it should prove useful in the future.

Henry cautioned that his cards were no longer accurate since he had just walked away from the Pirates. But he promised to provide her with one of his new cards as soon as they were available, probably sometime next week.

She smiled suspiciously, "Sure, whatever."

She climbed into her '57 Jeep, meticulously restored with her own hands, and waved cheerfully as she exited the parking lot. And so they parted on pleasant terms.

Henry, a little confused, struggled to get into his van and navigate back to his apartment. It had certainly been an eventful day, and, like all days, good news and bad news. He wondered just how badly the ankle was injured. It would really tick him off if the injury interfered with his new job.

And he wondered what it would take to recover.

When he got home, he managed to shower and change into some comfortable clothes ... and get an elastic wrap on the ankle to keep the swelling down. A couple of local IPAs eased the stress and the mild pain that had begun creeping up his leg. He felt more relaxed, but unsettled, and apprehensive. But thank God this day was over.

CHAPTER 5

Wrong! Over was not happening. The doorbell was ringing. The absolute last thing he wanted or needed.

As he opened the door, he was blinded by the most electric red hair and the brightest yellow sundress he could remember. Once the original flash from the dress subsided, freeing his eyes from temporary blindness, it was very obvious that the dress was cut low on the top and high on the bottom. The legs ended in feet with exquisitely pedicured toenails painted bright red and encased in the most elegant sandals this side of Beverly Hills.

"Hey!" grinned Amanda. "Thought you might like some company to consider big decisions tonight. I come as the bringer of inside knowledge and the best wishes of the tallest man to ever play left field in Triple-A baseball. I also have some very expensive gin, a very fine mellow vermouth, and enough olives to keep us busy for a while, if you have ice that is." The queen was on the prowl again ... still.

Stupefied, Henry invited her in. In the tiny sundress, every movement was provocative and clearly directed to Henry's clouded gaze. Not that Henry had any idea of what was happening. Amanda coyly inquired about the elastic wrap on his ankle, making some elusive allusion to something swelling. Henry stumbled through an explanation of his running incident, omitting the details about Harper and the lengthy, physically close rescue trudge back to the car. He wasn't sure why he didn't mention that.

As Amanda made the martinis, she asked about the conversation with Mo. Henry enlightened her.

"Your Dad is a convincing, energetic guy and he paints nice pictures of the future. It's difficult to imagine any way to turn him down. And, of course, it is incredibly exciting. I've never been involved with anything like what he is doing, ever in my life. He seems to think, though, that I have experience and skills that I haven't really demonstrated yet, like team leadership."

Amanda's sly smile returned, "I may have argued that your natural intelligence and high-profile educational background make you a strong guy to be out in front of a team effort."

"Thanks, but you're taking a credibility risk for both of us."

"No credibility risk for me. My Dad owns the place. Your ass, however, is on the line big-time."

"Again, thanks."

"Relax and enjoy it, Dad will give you air cover and you will be great. I am never wrong on these things; that's why I have this job. Now let's talk about something other than work."

"And that would be … ?"

"When are you taking me out and where are we going?"

"Honestly, I have thought about you quite a bit but I haven't thought about that specifically. Wouldn't that be a problem at the office?"

The sly smile returned, "As long as I am not working directly under you, at the office, it isn't."

As usual, Henry completely missed the signal. "Yeah, not sure about that. It would sort of undermine the credibility that I don't have yet. I don't want anyone thinking the only reason I have the job is because I am dating the boss's gorgeous daughter. Although it would be fun to be envied."

Amanda was getting slightly annoyed, "Henry, for God's sake. Grow up. I am not used to throwing myself at anyone and getting rejected. You never had an offer like this, either in the job or personally. What the hell are you thinking?"

The light dawned. "Oh ... you are correct! I never had an offer like either one of these and I am not adept at dealing with them. I may need a lot of patience from Mo and you. I sense that I have a better chance with Mo on that score."

"It's not a score," she muttered, "and it never will be if you don't wake up."

"I'm awake, I'm awake. But I am also incapacitated by this ankle and not concentrating at my best. Maybe one more martini and we take this up again at a more appropriate place and with me more fully alert?"

"I don't like getting brushed off," she pouted, "but I'll give you the benefit of the dubious doubt. Don't make me wait too long." She leaned in and placed a huge, deep French kiss on his astonished lips while assuring that the tiny yellow dress made all the right moves. "Talk to you tomorrow." And she left. The gin, vermouth, and olives stayed.

The effect of the martini and the kiss suddenly reappeared in the radiating pain moving up from his ankle.

Surprisingly, he was not aware so much of hurting as he was of how he got the injury. His mind retraced the journey back to the parking lot with his arm over Harper's shoulder and the friendly banter of their talk. It struck him as odd that he remembered her at all, but the ankle pain was undeniable.

An omen of things to come? Is Harper going to be a source of pain in my life? Or maybe Amanda?

CHAPTER 6

Mo called the meeting to order. "You are all probably wondering why I asked you here this morning. We have a couple of purposes. First, I want to introduce our firm's newest senior member, Henry Hansen. Henry is going to be doing something for us that we have never had before. As you may know, Henry is an expert on performance metrics and the statistical methodologies used in designing them, implementing them, and then using them to produce improvement in various types of behaviors and performance. He has established his reputation in sports performance—a subject dear to my heart—but after considerable research and conversation with Henry, I think there is heavy-duty application to some of the things we do at Ursa, Stearns, and Giacana that will benefit significantly from Henry's insights."

At the side of the room Henry was uncertain if that intro made him feel good or not. He was being forced onto a well-functioning organization in a capacity not necessarily understood nor accepted. He would have to establish his credibility and prove his worth in order to be able to deliver those "significant benefits" Mo referred to and earn his very comfortable salary. This could be a daunting situation if it were to go the wrong way.

Mo continued, "His first assignment will be to coordinate

and lead a cross-functional team formed to support the development efforts of a potential project at Parsons Point. As some of you know, I have acquired an option on 100 acres there for a year to explore that area as a possible technology campus to attract a new group of companies to our local business community. Such a development could bring modern stability to our workforce, our financial base, and the tax base, providing revenue for our local essential service funding. This is a civic benefit project, and a profitable one for the firm, if we do it right. We need to put together a case for the development, get the appropriate approvals, secure political support, and find funding from investors and lenders. Our work is cut out for us, and we need to begin with a serious study built on favorable available data and models that Henry can guide us through building.

"Henry requested a team of specialists comprising both industry and functional knowledge. At the time, we were talking about supporting the firm as a whole, but the approach makes sense for this project." Then, speaking to Henry, "So, to get the ball rolling, we have our technology industry expert, Martin Jamison, our 2IC in finance, Hanna Melancon, and our number two in marketing and PR, behind Amanda, whom you have met, Charles Cameron. At some point, the team will be expanded to include a logistics function to help with the construction schedule and budget, and a sales team when we are ready to present to investors and lenders for our client and their investment bank. Henry, your team."

"Thanks, Mo. I am not a heavy-handed team leader. To me, the most important thing we can contribute to this project is a very solid analysis of the risks, the time, the regulatory issues to be accommodated, the available resources, and the money to get this one across home plate.

We won't do it by hitting home runs; it will require meticulous situational awareness and being willing to do what we can, when we can, one base hit at a time. Sorry for the heavy baseball similes, but baseball and stats are pretty much what I'm good at. And there actually is a lot of similarity in this project and a nine-inning game.

"So, here is your program. In this booklet is the concept of the project as it now stands, primarily in Mo's mind and some of his potential partners. It's a detailed document but requires still more detail. Please take the next three hours to digest it as much as possible and let's gather back in here at 2:30 p.m. to get started. I know we won't be able to get a complete picture today, probably not even in two weeks, but we can think through an overall critical path and process map to get down on paper some representation of what has to get done first, and by when in the timeline. And that's a good place to get started. We'll make a list of critical questions and identify short term impediments that have to be cleared immediately in order for us to proceed and then we'll keep going in that manner until we have a much more complete project plan from start to finish."

Hanna's finance focused frown attracted the group's attention. "You sound like a consultant. We need to know what concrete steps and costs will be necessary to get this baby born."

Henry flinched a bit but responded coolly and with a smile, "Hanna, you could not be more correct. I truly am a consultant and this discipline is one I have found useful to get your arms around a huge set of tasks when it's too early to have concrete knowledge. But that's why we have a cross-functional team. The specialists, like you, will help the consultant and stats guy keep his foot out of his mouth and help keep the team protected from self-imposed embarrassment. Everybody shares that responsibility.

"If there are no other questions or comments, let's start familiarizing ourselves with Parsons Point and how we can successfully execute this vision. See you here at 2:30 p.m. Thanks."

Henry returned to his corner office to focus on the project booklet. He liked his office. Even though it was not the ultra-luxurious corner variety, it was far more than anything he had ever had previously—enough room for a small conference table and chairs, a small sofa, and two chairs in front of the desk. One wall was a whiteboard and it was very large, sufficient to scribble, diagram, visualize and outline the most complex ideas that he was likely to generate. The office was Junior Exec certainly, but exec nonetheless. He felt as much at home as he could, given the spiral of events around him since last week.

CHAPTER 7

As he was settling in to devour the project book, a flash of brilliant red hair appeared in his door. Accompanying the red hair came the expensively suited, beautifully shod, stunning and intimidating form of US&G's head of Marketing, HR and Admin, as Amanda stepped in.

And the niggling pain of his ankle returned ... momentarily.

"Hey! Lunch? It's my job to take the newbies out on their first day."

"All the newbies?"

"No, just the special ones."

"I really need to get into this project book."

"No prob. Bring it along. I can fill you in. I've been on this with Dad since day one."

"Looks like you have rank on this. I'll get my jacket. Where we going?"

"Yes, I do have rank and we are not going anyplace fancy. I'm saving that for a more private occasion. We'll just run to the sandwich shop next door. You can be back in forty-five and ready to go with your intrepid team into the great void of the Parsons Point Project. Fully informed, I might add."

"After you," said Henry, limping slightly, trying to keep up with Amanda's commanding strides.

They entered Sweeny's and found a quiet booth.

Amanda ordered coffee and a croissant club sandwich, Henry went for iced tea and pastrami on sourdough with a slice of Swiss cheese.

"So why is Mo hell-bent on doing this real estate thing? He's an investment advisor; raw land development is a different horse."

Amanda considered her answer carefully. "Daddy is concerned about the future of this area. He is convinced it needs a shot of the twenty-first century in its arm. Our current employment base is much too closely tied to the aluminum plant and the suppliers and service companies that keep it going. He is not confident that the aluminum industry has much of a future—primarily due to the increasing cost of power. So, in the spirit of community support, he wants to move the employment base toward emerging technologies. They're clean, no manufacturing waste or exhausts, no toxic raw materials, no labor unions, and a steady inflow of classy professionals who draw and spend high salaries and can afford to pay higher than usual taxes to protect their little slice of heaven. Presto! A fresh community with a future stretching to the seeable horizon."

"Sounds honorable and positive," offered Henry. "What is the community's take on this plan?"

"They don't really know about it yet," whispered Amanda. "Dad wants to get it rolling so that it will sound more appealing as a work in progress rather than a pipe dream before getting it out in the open. There is a lot of preliminary work to be done before it can even look like a doable project. But he is committed to a full community examination of the merits, and a debate in an open atmosphere as to how to make it effective for community goals and desires. That'll be the tough part."

"How come?" he asked.

"There is a large naturalist element in the community—mostly young, outdoorsy, unattached—that just don't want to see that kind of change. They feel like development is an evil in spite of its honorable goals and they like things as is. Their opposition to an electric power plant and dam years ago is one reason that our local aluminum plant is at a cost disadvantage in the industry. No cheap power nearby. The opposition is adamant. Especially as it regards Parsons Point. That is hallowed ground for them."

"So they will protest and try to delay the EIS and all the zoning hearings, construction permits, completion permits, use permits, etc., right up until move-in day?"

"Correct."

"And that's why Charles is on my team, huh? 'Cause this one is going to need a lot of PR?"

"Correct again. One more correct and you win the grand prize." The smile returned.

Henry ignored her flippancy. "So is Charles up to this? This could be a tough one to cut his teeth on."

"Yeah, he can do this. BUT it will be uphill. He is a bit fragile and unsure. And, a tip, don't ever call him Chuck. He withdraws and becomes very passive aggressive. His Dad was Chuck, and Charles doesn't want the hint of a connection."

"Got it. Thanks for the heads up. What about Hanna and Martin?"

"Solid skills but green. They both need mentorship and support. Hanna is a great technician but is not comfortable with the ... compromises ... necessary in business finance. Martin is a dynamo for pure information and stats, but is still growing into the guy who can put it all together and define a trend or a change of direction in an industry's structure or behavior. Again, mentorship and support."

"Hmmm. Sounds like I need to be about fifty-five and on the downhill side of a long and distinguished career to get these guys going and keep them going."

"So, you're thirty-six and on the upside of a long and distinguished career. No biggie."

Henry didn't bother to correct her, and he was encouraged with the sincere support. He liked the apparent approaching challenge, but that didn't offset the sense of intimidation that it brought. They finished their sandwiches in silence and contemplation, and Amanda paid the check with a generous tip when they left.

"Forward, the Light Brigade ... into the Valley of Death rode the six hundred," Henry thought.

CHAPTER 8

Upon returning from the lunchtime break, the team did not look refreshed and energized to take on the new challenge. Browbeaten and discouraged would have been more accurate. When Henry joined them, he noticed, and registered his own surprise.

"Hey guys. I detect a lack of enthusiasm for the reading matter we digested over lunch. What are your Issues?" He asked.

Finance opened the discussion. "Henry, we are an advisory firm. We book things on our financials—like fees earned, commissions received, short-term investments and cash equivalents, and cash. We don't have a history or an understanding of things like EIS in progress for the costs of that study, or lab fees for soil testing, or land use consulting fees paid, or anything like that. This is totally new ground for this firm, and I have no idea how to track it in our current financial systems." Hanna was nearing apoplexy.

Martin chimed in, "I am a tech industry specialist, and I have no idea how real estate development works. Ask me about software, hardware, networks, devices, data organization, message transmission, and I can fill volumes for you. But I am not useful on this one."

Charles threw another stick on the fire, "Yeah, we

should mention that the public already thinks of us as crooks who practice deception, and then engage in insider trading. So far, we have managed to blunt that impression by being strong supporters of local worthy causes. I can't imagine what they will think and how they will respond if we come in with a huge development project which decimates their precious wild woods and could affect their precious stream. This is not a worthy cause in that light. There isn't enough good PR in the world to make that OK."

Henry immediately understood that this reaction was what Amanda was talking about. Reasonable and accurate in its assessment, but unmodified by knowledge of how to cope with problems and priorities. Technical skill without benefit of worldly experience.

"OK. I got it. This looks impossible. Let's write a report and sign it to tell Mo that it can't be done."

Greeted by stone silence, Henry continued.

"*Impossible* only means that it *can* be done, but we just haven't figured out *how* yet. Let's begin by identifying all those things that you are talking about that scare you about this project. Forget that is what a consultant would do. Remember, instead, that it is the *right* thing to do to create some realistic understanding of what we're facing. Then we can see what we need to make progress. After that, we have something to talk to Mo about, at least for the first stage."

Hanna took a task-driven approach, "We have a lot of preliminary work to be done that will cost money. I'm not sure how much latitude we have in reflecting those costs in our financial information, given the regulators and banks."

"How can you find out?" Henry pushed.

"It would have to be subtle, so I can't ask our auditors. Maybe the legal staff can do some quiet research on precedent and applicable statute. Morris Klein is Mo's nephew. He should be a trustworthy source. Then we would have to find a way to finance the EIS and contamination test studies on the QT."

Henry moved on to the next reluctant warrior, "Martin, what have other tech firms done when they moved into new HQ's or major office installations? Do you know anyone in the Silicon Valley firms, or Microsoft, or TI? They've all done this stuff. Maybe we can get some ideas of where to start and what makes it attractive for those kinds of firms."

Then, the next. "Charles, your points were certainly accurate. If you had to, how would you go about putting lipstick on this pig?"

Charles mused, "Well, I suppose we could look for good points and benefits of the project and show the daisy chain of benefits that would flow out into the hands and pockets of the average city and county dwellers. We would have to be careful not to exaggerate, though. They would be on that like white on rice. Would kill our credibility for good."

Henry thought a moment, "How could we build that into a preliminary presentation to get first-level approval for all the studies and research we need? Can we make a credible case for the county board in charge of the permit process?"

"Let me do some PowerPoint magic for a sample and run it past you, see if it makes sense. I won't show it to Amanda or Mo until you and I are comfortable with it."

"Go. Make it so, Number One," in his best command voice.

Henry shifted gears, "One other thing. I want all of you to do some thinking about stuff that absolutely has to happen and what has to happen first, second, etc. Let's map how all these requirements impact each other. That'll lead us to what resources we need and when. This is serious, needs some time. Let's meet in here again in, say, four days, with your ideas, findings, and results of our decisions today. Everybody good with that? OK. Do it."

Hanna piped in, "Oh, you mean like a critical path plan?"

"See?" Henry teased. "You sound like a development guy already." And the team filed out to go conquer worlds they knew absolutely nothing about.

Whew. 'No idea if they would come around. They were really scared to death of this thing. First barrier down. I wonder if that'll work all the time?

CHAPTER 9

As Henry sat in his office two doors down from Mo, he marveled at the seeming success of his efforts getting the team focused and committed to the outsized tasks at hand. *Maybe this positive leadership crap really works*, he thought. *Who woulda thought you would ever find anything from business school that would be useful in the real world? These kids. You just gotta reach 'em like they wanna be reached.*

Just as his self-satisfaction was reaching a peak, the door opened without a knock, and the Queen entered. Preceded by her perfect hands and nails and the scent of her very unique perfume, there was no doubt that the incredible red hair and something else special would be following quickly. Henry was not disappointed. The red hair draped down over the shoulders of a well-tailored and quite conservative black one-piece suit which, although quite suitable for work—it showed no skin at all above the elbow—still left no doubt that Amanda was the queen and perfectly capable of claiming her subjects at will.

Henry felt claimed. But he did notice a twinge in his ankle.

"Hey, tough week and big doin's. I'm having a few of the team over to my house for drinks and snacks after work. Given the buzz around the firm on our newest superstar, I thought you would like to come and build a few relationships as well as share some great company." Amanda sold hard. "No big deal, just a bunch of us relaxing and doing a bit of teambuilding while having fun. Personal invitation from the hostess."

Henry reveled in the glow of his self-generated back patting and responded, "That sounds like a great evening. I'd love to come and meet some more of the team. Where, what time, can I bring anything?"

"Here's the address and the code to the parking garage. Anywhere on the ground floor guest parking is fine. Time is seven-thirty and you don't need to bring anything. This is a company soirée. And there is a lot of important company business to be covered as well as just having a fun evening. I think you will find this a very enjoyable opportunity." And the Queen made her exit. Henry thought he heard Aida's Grand March playing somewhere.

Why would she give me the parking code? Especially if she knows what I drive. There's plenty of parking on the street.

Upon her majesty's departure, Henry had a meeting with Hanna to examine what she had learned on the key financial and regulatory issues relating to the proposed project. He was immediately aware that something was different.

Hanna was more relaxed. The top two buttons on her button-down oxford cloth shirt were undone and her knee length skirt seemed just a tiny bit shorter. But most of all, she was smiling and excited about the project. Everyone knew Hanna was brilliant, but now she seemed ... likable (in that way so often reserved for male colleagues) ... as well. Henry chalked it off to great project leadership.

"We've got a lot of hurdles to deal with here, "she began. "Basic site issues are going to take up to three quarters of a million to get handled. Soil studies, drainage maps and patterns, endangered species protection, water pollution scenarios, riparian vegetation impacts, stream bottom impacts, fish impacts. It may even be closer to a million, and that is not a dead certainty.

"Then, if we can manage all those, we need to deal with amendments to that data necessary due to construction plans and, of course, the remediation of any problems that may be caused by our activity. And that is just to get the site ready for sub-developers, builders, and tenants."

"Whoa, Hanna. Slow down. I'm having trouble keeping up, and I want to take some notes. But, good preparation, go on, just help me stay with you." Henry was secretly pleased at the enthusiasm.

"Next, we have interaction with the political units involved, the county (road impact, fire and police protection, emergency medical services), the city (transportation to and from for the workforce, traffic flows, funding the physical improvements needed to city infrastructure, fire, police, and first responder issues again), and, believe it or not, impact issues with surrounding school districts. Almost all of those entities get some benefits from the project resulting from increased tax revenues, but it is not clear which revenues should belong to which entities. Many potential legal fights and lawsuits are easily possible before we even get the first shovel in the ground. I'm thinking six years at the very best."

Henry was reeling. He shifted in his chair and tried to look scholarly and informed. This was all stuff that he was only remotely acquainted with. He quickly realized that he was totally out of his depth. "Wow! Very thorough preliminary analysis Hanna. I am blown away. Whaddaya think we should do?" *When in doubt, deflect. Ask a question.*

Hanna was waiting for that specific question. "I've got a project pre-check list with the boys in legal ticking these off as they get a firm idea of what is necessary, who would be involved outside the firm, and what the most likely barriers will be. When I get something back from them, I can give you more precise numbers and a better timeline. They have suggested that we may have to get the governor involved and they have ideas how to do that, maybe even legally. I should have better information from legal by a week from Wednesday."

"Great. Will we know enough to begin to estimate the necessary scale of the project and then assess and cost out the whole thing?" Henry was pushing a bit, but he knew this was the very fulcrum of the decision to go or not go.

Hanna, a bit shocked at Henry's insight responded, "We'll need another week after I hear from legal to be able to do Kentucky windage on that, and there are a million things that could change what we estimate, but by the end of the month, we should have a handle on feasibility."

"I like it. Git 'er done," sneered Henry, with a smile, in his best hillbilly.

Charles and Martin were next. "Hey, guys," Henry stressed the collegial informality. "How're we doin'? Any new information or thoughts on how to deal with the start of the project?"

Charles began, "We have some unplowed ground that needs developing, literally and figuratively. We don't know how the public really feels on something of this magnitude here in this location. So, I put together a little fun project for a couple of our interns to make a chart of winners and losers with this project in place. The w/l chart should help us identify preliminarily who will support and who will oppose."

Henry had heard this kind of analysis before, and it always rang a bit hollow with him. Carefully shifting the position of the virgin ashtray on his desk, he asked Charles, "So what does that do for us that is really actionable?"

Charles hesitated slightly, "It will allow us to put demographic characteristics on the w's and l's. Then we can use some good data from our ad agency to map by zip code where those folks are and see how opinion maps out. When we know those centers of influence, we can tailor media and messaging for each group in each location to garner support across all the issues affecting the project. With that in hand, we have a great piece of knowledge to share with the politicians for next year's election. And we can get their support. We can even model probability of our winning or losing those zips and groups to tell us where to spend our money most effectively. I don't have an estimate yet for the budget, but think six zeroes after the first two numbers and before the decimal."

"Charles, your boss will be proud. I am familiar with the w/l chart technique, but I had no idea we could model the rest of that stuff given the politics. I have actually been involved, to a small extent, with a similar but simpler model on the ball park location issue for the Pirates a few years ago. If your interns need help with the algorithms, have them come see me." Henry hoped to hell they did not need help. He had visions of being lost in the conversations with a couple of whiz kids.

Martin spoke up next. "I have rattled cages wherever I can in the tech community to see what we might use as an example to start from. Nobody has considered anything like this. Silicon Valley has some possible use for us but that is mostly urban or suburban, no 'wilderness' development. But a couple of buddies have introduced me to their law firms who may have done research on the basics. Austin and Seattle have some history but, again, mostly suburban, no pure, clean, wild land.

"The construction issues shouldn't be difficult, assuming we can solve the environmental mitigation issues economically. There are plenty of people who know how to design and build these structures; the land and its eccentricities are the main drivers here. It looks to me like Charles' progress will be important to what I can open up on the construction side."

Henry felt the rising flush of ego in his cheeks. "Good job, guys. Good solid thinking and research. I don't know what conclusions we are reaching but this team is putting good information on the table for the firm to base decisions on. This is going to be fun as well as useful. I'll send everyone a memo for a meeting next Tuesday, and we'll pull what we have together so that I can give Mo a prelim. I think he'll be pleased with this level of quality.

"See you guys tonight at Amanda's."

Charles and Martin glanced at each other with bewildered glances.

CHAPTER 10

After dismissing Charles and Martin, Henry allowed himself some time to admire his new status.

He had a great office with all the space and appointments he could want, at least for now. He had unfettered access to the leader, Mo, and probably good access to Amanda, the heir apparent. Maybe better access than he thought, or needed, or wanted.

He was privileged to have a solid, enthusiastic, and energetic young team working with him, and they seemed to respond well to him and his style. And, best of all, he was making a shitload of money for the first time in his life. Things could be a helluva lot worse.

He was so high and pleased that he had lost track of time. It was six-thirty. Barely time to get home, cleaned up, and ready for Amanda's party.

He charged out of his office and into the garage where the old Econoline clattered to life and he began to limp the van home.

Crashing through the door to his flat, he automatically hit the "play" button on the message machine. He still believed in land lines and VM machines and used them faithfully. There was one message.

"Hey, it's Harper. My client cancelled for tomorrow, and I am stuck with these great deli sandwiches and some great craft beers for a shore side lunch. Thought you might enjoy getting initiated into the sorority of fly-fishers. It's five-fifteen now. If I don't hear no from you in thirty minutes, I'll pick you up at six-thirty tomorrow morning. Yes, I know where you live, so don't embarrass yourself. We will have time to get some breakfast before heading for the water. It's going to be a lovely day and I think you will actually have fun. The company isn't bad either. So, here's hoping you don't call."

Henry was rushing to get ready and since he didn't hear any requirement for action on his part, he basically ignored the message, taking only vague notice that it was even there. He was focused on looking good but not dressy, sort of business casual with an air of recent success, which, of course, was quite accurate. Pressed grey flannels, his best Titleist red golf shirt, blue blazer, frat boy loafers, no socks. He looked like a poster guy for the U.S. Golf Association—a good looking, capable young executive off to have fun on a Friday night.

Arriving at Amanda's was an experience in itself. He used the parking code, getting a very disapproving look from the on-duty guard. And when he parked in the guest area on the ground floor, he noticed a lot of late model SUV's, a few British roadsters and sport coupes, several German sedans and saloons, but only one of the famous German brands. None of the other two models of German luxury cars were in evidence. *And these were just the guests.* He wondered if any of these were from the firm. And he decided that maybe he should reconsider his personal transport, given his rise to successful senior exec.

At the twenty-seventh floor, the elevator opened directly into Amanda's home. "Home" because it was way too nice and way too large to be just a flat or apartment. It was very spacious, very tastefully decorated, and very comfortable. Everything a home should be. And the party was in full swing.

Mo grabbed him as soon as he entered and began introducing him around with great glee. The firm's chief in-house counsel, Hanna's boss, the CFO, the IT guy, the trading supervisor, and head underwriter—more firm big shots than Henry realized existed. He saw his team over in a corner and they came over to join him—smiling, happy, motivated, and enthusiastic. They never seemed to change. It made Henry feel good, separate from the rest of the crowd. Hanna looked especially bright and perky. Charles clued Henry that, after their meeting, he and Martin went into Amanda's office and browbeat her into inviting them to join the illustrious persons on the original guest list, employing Henry's name as justification for the demand. Amanda agreed, further enhancing Henry's status in the firm.

Henry saw Amanda across the room and sucked in his breath. Conservative (but short) dress, sleeveless and up to the neck, but extremely shape hugging. Not vulgar, but leaving little to be imagined. She saw him and gave him her most radiant smile and then turned her back to him. He thought that very strange until ... he saw that the beautiful, tasteful emerald dress had no back—none. It tied at the neck and then plunged down to what he would politely call the area of "plumber's cleavage" without revealing anything but her gorgeous back. After a moment she turned back around and gave Henry a wink over the rim of her martini.

It was not clear who else may have noticed the wink, but it buckled Henry's knees.

As the evening progressed, it became clear that Amanda had been right. It was loads of fun and Henry met some very influential people, some of whom he even liked. And his team acquitted itself proudly. They shuffled and mingled like the pros they were becoming. Hanna seemed to be growing up and she and Charles appeared to be very comfortable, even taken, with each other. They both glowed, while maintaining very professional demeanors, of course.

Toward the end of the event, Amanda came over to Henry, whom she had studiously avoided. "Don't be in a hurry to leave. I have some things we should discuss." The smile was shining even more than usual. Thirty minutes later everyone else had left, and Mo was the only one who noticed that Henry remained.

Amanda poured two brandies and sat down, kicking off her expensive, strappy slings as she did. Her feet were just as seductive as the rest of her.

She curled up against Henry and extended her long shapely legs out to the end of the sofa. Then she grabbed Henry's right arm and brought it across her waist. Nothing aggressive or blatant, just personal, comfortable, and intimate. Henry was not so sure about the comfortable and intimate part; he was scared to death. But in Amanda's home, she's in charge. He did think that hundreds, thousands of men would trade places with him right now in a heartbeat.

She began. "You know, Dad wants to retire in five or six years and just play golf. He is worn out. But he has no candidate for a successor. He looks to me but I am only good for about forty percent of what the firm needs. I can be a great operations and admin leader, Chief operations officer, number two in the company. Dad needs a number one."

Henry nodded, nervously, "I can see that, but you could learn the rest. You'd be great."

"Thanks," Amanda returned, "But you're just saying

that because you're nervous. And you are not really correct. Henry, Dad loves the way you have taken over a difficult situation and inspired your team to do a good job so far. He thinks you have what it takes to carry his legacy forward. You could run this firm very well."

"Uhhhhh . . ."

"And let me sweeten the pot," she continued. "I *also* want you to be the guy to do that. I trust you to care for this firm and make it a strong presence in the future. And I have some personal reasons for that, too.

"I have never been around a man who could keep up with me. They all just wanted to conquer me, to take me as a trophy. To be known as the man who tamed the office bitch and brought her to heel. Actually, I took a bunch of them, and it was good fun, no complaints. But it gets to be a boring game."

"And?" Henry cautiously ventured.

"You, Henry, have not tried to conquer me. In fact, you have rejected me twice. No other man has ever done that and lived to tell the tale. You have something that the rest of them sorely lack. You have substance—and for the first time in my life that is important to me. I want you, Mister Substance."

Henry had no clue where to go next. So, he made the fatal mistake and decided to be perfectly honest. "Amanda, I have no idea what to say to you. You are an incredible woman and I do enjoy your company, your intelligence, and certainly your style. How you can be so competent and so sensuous at the same time is beyond my limited comprehension."

"But?" she offered.

"But you are way out of my league. Hell, this firm is even out of my league, although I am doing OK in the current capacity. There is so much for me to learn that it is almost overwhelming."

Amanda pierced his eyes and his soul saying, "What better way to learn it than with a hot, smart, dedicated woman who adores you at your side?"

Henry had no answer, nothing. He was running on fumes. And she wasn't wrong. This really could be his chance, their chance, to do something significant and meaningful. They would have the power to do that together.

"Henry, I know things about you that no one else does. And I don't care. They could ruin you forever. But with me by you, no one will ever find out. I'll make sure of that. We will be absolutely undefeatable in anything we undertake." She was gently pressuring him, not quite threatening him, but he wondered.

It was still enticing, seducing, just what you would expect from Amanda. And a guy could be real happy ... not all bad or any bad by any stretch.

"Amanda, no person in a state of sanity would walk away from you right now. I need time to try to get my mind around what you've planted in it. I can't say right now that I love you because that just hasn't been on my radar for anyone. But I do have a hard time imagining a more desirable partner for great things than you. That is sincere. I need to go home, and understand what is happening."

Amanda's obsession with Henry's desirable character trait became clear as she raised her voice a bit, "So, a third rejection, eh, Judas? I told you that two was the limit on life. But substance, damn substance is enough to make me forget my principles and actually do the right thing. Disgusting! I have never had that experience. Go, think, exercise that substance, and we will figure out where this is going. Who would have thought substance justified loving?"

At four o'clock in the morning, who could possibly figure anything out? thought Henry.

CHAPTER 11

Somewhere in the fog of the previous night's festivities, a horn was honking ... loudly. Not fully aware of the situation, Henry reacted violently, or at least as close to violently as he ever did. Ripping off the bedcovers and discovering his utter nudity, he sneaked over to the bedroom window and peeked outside through the curtains.

To his surprise, a red jeep driven by a very attractive blonde was making all the noise, and right in front of his sidewalk. Henry, in his condition, recognized neither the little wartime vehicle nor the driver, but his attention was fixed. The driver dismounted and approached his door. Henry immediately panicked. The doorbell rang and rang again.

Still flustered, if not terrified, Henry found a small robe and jumped in, not quite as modestly as he would have preferred, and answered the persistent doorbell. Although he did not recognize Harper, he couldn't help but be distracted by this wholesome, fit, and altogether beautiful woman in his door.

"If I'd known you were having a party, I'da been here sooner," she said in her best Mae West. Henry, obviously at sea, blushed and betrayed his confusion.

With instantaneous perception, Harper realized he didn't have a clue as to what was going on or with whom.

"Hey," she said, "It's okay to be confused and hungover, but it's really bad form to not recognize a great fisherperson who has come, as promised a week ago, to take you out and educate you as to the finer points of the world's most rewarding pastime."

Then it clicked. Henry rushed to apologize. "God, I'm sorry Harper. Little celebration at the office last night and I completely forgot that we had a date today."

"No date, Doofus. A major turning point in your education as a man and a human being. But you'll recover and thank me later. Now get that cute ass of yours into some outdoor clothes and let's get a cup of coffee on the way to the river."

Realizing that the robe was not quite large enough for proper company, Henry smiled sheepishly, invited Harper in, and scooted off to make himself more presentable, but making some imaginative connections while he did. He had never noticed just how attractive Harper was and the reality hit him hard, although pleasantly.

"I have no idea what proper fly-fishing attire is," Henry shouted through the hallway door. "What do I need?"

Appearing quietly in the bedroom door, Harper clarified, "I've got pretty much everything you need. Just some sturdy shorts and good walking shoes, a hat and some sunscreen. Long sleeves are not a bad idea either."

"Uh, don't you knock? I could be naked."

"Yeah, big family, four brothers. Nothing I haven't seen before," Harper chuckled.

Surprisingly, Henry felt at ease with the familiarity. It somehow seemed natural and no big deal for this confident and collected woman.

"But I'm going to want more than just a cup of coffee. I'm starved. Breakfast is on me."

"Sounds great," she said, "But we've got a hatch about ten-thirty, and you have a lot to learn before that. So, get a move on. We do have time for breakfast and can still be on the water by nine forty-five."

Henry had no idea what all that gibberish meant but he was certainly in need of breakfast and some wake up caffeine. So, he smiled, and they took off on a great adventure, at least for Henry.

On the way to the Pancake Emporium, Harper, inspired by the open-air configuration of her pride and joy, sought to probe this strange Henry Hansen she had encountered and who was becoming interesting to her.

"Hank, how is it that you are here in this space going fishing with me today? The beginning, please."

Slightly put off by the familiar version of his dignified name, Henry responded, "It was a dark and stormy night. . ."

Harper laughed so hard that she twisted the Jeep into the next lane over and received a very loud honk from a trailing driver. "OK. I earned that. But seriously, here I am going off to the woods with a guy I know nothing about. A girl deserves a little reassurance, don't you think?"

Henry smiled. He was enjoying the banter. "Fair enough. I don't really know where to start. I always enjoyed learning new things ... so long as they involved sports, history, science, or math. Those seemed sort of 'decided,' y'know? Not subject to a lot of debate. Proven, if you will, and therefore, clean. I was always uncomfortable with having to see two sides of a question. Made me feel wishy washy. So I learned all I could about facts, opinions, data, and information which could be applied looking forward. Stuff that could add stability to an uncertain situation. Learned modeling and a bit of data analysis and finance to go along with it. Not so much accounting, mind you; that is way too subject to crazy interpretation and even legal issues, way too unstable. But finance is different; it results from real world situations. A manufacturing company or a baseball club makes decisions on how it uses its resources, money, and people, and gets certain observable and measurable outcomes. Those can be modeled for the future. I enjoy that."

Harper thought a moment and responded, "I come from a bit different place, but I can certainly respect your desire to find knowledge amidst chaos. You make it sound almost noble. That can't be all bad."

Henry figured that was as good as he was going to get from this introverted and introspective woman, and, strangely enough, it was sufficient to spark his curiosity further, for the moment. As they pulled into the drive-through window of the breakfast place, he was jolted back to the present by his hunger. "Hey I thought we were going to have a real breakfast, my treat. What's happnin'?"

"Ah … we don't have as much time as I thought, so let's just get a couple of sausage and biscuits to go with our coffee. I promise you won't be hungry later. I've got some great and large sandwiches along with some cold beers in the cooler. If you're a good student, I'll host you to a great streamside lunch, but only if you're good."

For no good reason, Henry sensed a slight double entendre in Harper's remark. Or maybe it was the sly smile. Not being very good in these situations, Henry was not sure how to process this "data."

Breakfast sandwiches and coffee in hand, they headed for the woods. "We'll start small today so as not to overwhelm you with technical details. You won't even need waders, just good non-slip boots and fishing gear."

"Non-slip?" inquired Henry.

"Yeah, first critical issue. Rocks in the creek are slippery with moss and, if you fall, you could conceivably get washed downstream. That could be dangerous, so you have to be able to keep your feet. I'll show you how." She reached into the CJ and pulled out a pair of size eleven clodhoppers with sticky rubber soles and small cleats sticking out through the bottom of the soles.

"Try these for size," she instructed.

Henry found them to be comfortable, although a bit pinched at the heavily reinforced toes.

"We have to hike about a half-mile to get to the stream, but it's an easy walk. You up to that?"

Mildly insulted, Henry snapped, "Been walking golf courses and carrying my own clubs since I was six. Of course I'm up to it."

Grinning, Harper demurred, "Ok, ok. You'd be surprised how many of my clients can't keep up on the walk to the stream."

"Clients?" Asked Henry.

"Yeah, don't you remember my card? I'm a fly-fishing guide."

"You can make a living doing that?" said Henry, slightly astonished.

"Sometimes," smiled Harper. "But not all the time."

Henry decided a bit more deference was due Harper. *Maybe this was a truly formidable woman.*

The anticipation built up and, when they reached the stream bank, Harper asked if he had ever cast a fly.

"Nope," Replied Henry. "Done a lot of bass fishing and some salt water for tarpon and snook, but no flies."

"Okay, prepare for a new experience." Harper put the rod together, an eight-foot, three-piece, five weight with a weight-forward floating line.

Henry Immediately reacted, "Hey, how come such a puny rod? It looks like a small stick with a cork handle."

"Calm down he-man. It's a great rod for learning how to cast. This is not like a bass rod where you cast the lure. With this, you cast the weight of the line. You see how the line is bigger at the front than the back? That makes it easier for a beginner to feel the rod working and it makes it easier to cast in the wind." Harper clearly knew what she was doing, obvious even to Henry's uninformed eye.

"You going to tie a hook onto that thick line?" he mocked.

"We'll get to that part in a bit. First, I want you to learn to feel the rod and line working together. This demands timing and coordination more than strength. It's not that different from the golf swing."

"How so?" He aggressively pursued. "This doesn't look strong enough to stand much of a load."

Harper patiently shifted into teacher mode. "Imagine that you are leaning against the face of a clock on your right side. As you face forward, you are going to start the rod at ten o'clock, lifting the rod tip fairly sharply until you have reached back to two o'clock, and that is where you stop the rod. Ten, two, ten, two. Try it."

Henry did the drill, and fairly successfully.

Harper gently corrected. "You're overpowering it a bit, as many athletes do. It is a gentle movement, so that you can feel the rod bending behind you, just like a golf club at the top of the backswing. When you feel the rod fully loaded, then you can bring the rod back to ten and stop until the line straightens out in front and then gently lower the tip so the line settles on the water."

Henry thought that sounded easy enough. Again, he did the drill, and it worked fine.

"Nice job," assured Harper. "Your chances for that fancy lunch are improving steadily. But there is a complication. Remember you asked about the hook? Well you are casting the weight of the line but you need something smaller between the end of the line and the smallish fly that will be eaten by the trout. That's called a leader, and it comes in various lengths and diameters. Most of them are tapered so that it is smaller near the fish and thicker at the end of the fly line. And they break easily if you mistreat them.

"When the line straightens out on the forward part of the cast, you have to be strong enough to make it extend but not so strong as to overpower it and get it all tangled. Tangled leaders do not catch trout." She tied on a nine-foot leader tapering down to about three pounds of strength. And tied a size fourteen dry fly on to the end of the leader.

"Now try it again."

Henry lifted the rod tip and was surprised how easily the fly rose off the water and extended behind him. Feeling the increase in pressure as the weight forward line loaded the rod, he gently pushed the rod forward with his wrist and was again pleasantly surprised to see just what Harper predicted actually happen. The line straightened out and the leader straightened out and as he lowered the rod tip slowly, the entire rig touched the water at precisely the right time.

Harper was amazed. "You're a natural. I have never seen a beginner do that on the first cast."

"Great instruction," he beamed. "All that golf comparison really helped. Where did you learn all that?"

"Happy to tell you over lunch, but first let me have the rod for a bit, I want to make a few casts into this hatch."

"Hatch?" Henry asked in confusion.

"Yeah, see all those bugs fluttering around? Not long ago they were nymphs on the bottom of the stream. Then, as the sun warmed the water, they began to emerge from their nymphal husks and 'hatch.' As they sit on the water drying their wings, the trout eat 'em up. If your fly looks like the bug, and if you put it in the right place, with the right drift, you catch fish. Voila."

Henry's amazement accelerated as he watched Harper wade into the edge of the stream in water up to her knees. An expert cast put her fly just upstream of a small dimple on the surface of the stream. It drifted for a couple of seconds and then disappeared in a subtle splash. She lifted the rod tip, and had a shapely two-pound rainbow in her net within seconds. Henry was speechless, and he was hooked on this new form of adventure.

Four more Harper casts yielded two more fish of the same size, and one tug of war with what appeared to be a much heavier fish. It ran up and down the stream for a few seconds, then the rod tip jumped back to straight as the fine leader broke, and the fish and fly disappeared beneath the surface.

"Damn," she complained, "that was a nice one, maybe a big brown trout."

Slack-jawed, Henry sat dumbfounded on the bank, totally enamored of what he had seen, and pretty enamored of his very capable guide as well. "What about that lunch? I have so many questions, and I am excited to learn how to do this."

"Lunch it is," she playfully shot back, "and I am only too happy to answer all questions." There seemed to be an invitation in the "all questions" part that excited Henry.

CHAPTER 12

As they walked back to toy jeep to retrieve lunch, Henry was tongue-tied. He was having trouble forming words. He did not know if his amazement was centered on the fishing he had just seen or the fisherperson. Probably both.

Finally, he mumbled a conversation starter, realizing that it was not really what he wanted to ask. "So, how did you learn all this stuff? Is it easy? Do most people know about this? Do girls know about this?"

Harper flashed a stunning grin and responded, "Lots of practice. No. No. And only very special ones."

"Details please, from the beginning."

The grin returned, "It was a bright and sunny day."

"Touché!" offered Henry. "Now that we are on equal ground, give me the real skinny."

Grabbing the cooler with the food and craft beer, Harper opened up. "I was the youngest. Four bros. My Dad and Granddad were disappointed that the boys did not share interest in the manly pursuits. They were interested in more cerebral and intellectual paths. Mark, the oldest, is a lit professor and part time poet; James is an interior designer in LA; Scotty is a concert cellist in Minneapolis, and Andrew designs sets for Broadway musicals. So, I was the only sporty, outdoorsy option

available. Pop and Gramps taught me everything they
knew: hunting, fishing, volleyball—I was a great libero
for my early years—La Crosse, golf, tennis, and an attempt
at basketball (too short). Softball never really connected
with me but I liked all the others.

"My favorite was anything that I was invited to do
with them. Golf was the first thing, and by age ten I was
an eight handicap, a real prodigy. Vball and La Crosse
were good, tennis—a bit stodgy and stiff, pre-Martina
and the Williams sisters—but anything that confined me
to a court or a gym was too restrictive. I wanted to be
outdoors in an environment that allowed and required
me to move around a lot. Even on the golf course I was
more interested in the critters that lived around the lakes
and ponds and at the edges of the rough than on break-
ing par.

"Then one time, when I was fourteen, Gramps
sneaked a fly rod onto the course in his bag when we
were the only ones playing. We stopped at my favorite
lake and he rigged the rod for bass. I made two casts,
hooked a three-pound largemouth, and the rest is 'her-
story.' Game over."

"Harper, that is a great story, even without all the details. You're amazing. And what has happened since
fourteen? It's not that long ago."

The smile flashed again, this time even broader. "Not
too many years, but an eternity of experiences," she said.

"Finished high school at seventeen with enough advanced placement to be admitted to State as a soph.
Etymology major and loved it. Four-point-oh GPA with
minimal effort and lots of enthusiasm. Then the brown
stuff hit the fan. Met a guy. Never had done that before,
and, of course, I fell in lust thinking it was love.

"He was the quarterback and everyone's dream. Pre-med. Stop me if you have heard this one before. He thought I should work so we could save money for home, hearth, and family. And he, of course, would get rich in the NFL after three years in school. I didn't respond all that well to the family part, and the momentum of the game changed quickly in favor of a hot, red-headed cheerleader who was ready to do the master's bidding ... often. So, after we had been married for a year, I found myself on my own from a quickie divorce. I just said 'screw it' and finished my undergrad degree—and then kept going until I had my PhD. So, there I was at twenty-four, with a fancy resume, and nothing to do with it.

"Naturally, I thought that I should write a book, and so I did. Very scholarly and very scientific. It sold relatively well as a university text, but not enough so as to make any real money. And besides, I really wanted to write that book about fly-fishing. It seems to be a rule that the best bug writers all want to be famous fly-fishing writers. And they often are."

Henry was swirling, not ever having met any person as compelling as this lovely woman. He just wanted to keep her talking. "So that brings us up to what, three years ago? How did you end up here fishing with me?" (He thought that was clever on his part.)

She continued, "I didn't know what to do for certain, and I lived for a while on the money from the book. My family has some connections to this area, and it gets some attention in the fly-fishing magazines, so I thought I'd come here and be a guide. There aren't too many, and there are a few women, so I wouldn't be too much of an outlier.

"I've done OK. Got a truck for clients, a drift boat,

own my small house, got a little money in the bank, and I love what I do. That puts me one up on most everybody else. And I get to fish one of the most beautiful, challenging, productive, and magnificent little spots in the history of the sport of fly-fishing. Kids fish it from the bank; fishermen can wade it close in or fish it from a drift boat. It's shady and cool, and it always holds big browns and active rainbows. It is a little slice of fly-fishing heaven."

Henry's stomach was shaken with a small knot that appeared in response to Harper's passion. "What's it called and where is it?"

"I'll show it to you when you have earned the privilege. It's called Parsons Point."

Henry choked on his sandwich and had to take a long swallow of craft beer to keep from losing his composure. "I'll look forward to that."

CHAPTER 13

As they gathered up the remains of the lunch, Henry's foreboding about Parsons Point couldn't dislodge the experience of a very successful and thoroughly intriguing day. The fishing grabbed his interest and demanded a commitment to it that he had never experienced in any of his recreational pursuits.

His time with Harper screamed, *"More!"* Not just because she was so competent and knowledgeable, but also because she was so pleasant and unassuming. She had a knack for reading between the lines and understanding why, not just how, about anything. The setting was healthy and pure, beautiful in its own right—and the emotions and feelings were of well-being, self-generated contentment, unmatched by sports of the traditional style.

Harper said, "I hope you don't mind, but I need to make a quick stop by my place on our way home to drop you. I need to take care of my real fishing buddy, Rex."

Henry was a little put off. He wasn't expecting to have to share his time with Harper's significant other.

Harper picked up on the momentary tension and teased, "Yeah, Rex is my one true love. He is the best male I have ever known and treats me so well ... except when I leave him cooped up in the house all day and don't let him out to pee and chase squirrels around the yard … gotcha, didn't I?"

Henry howled at his own way-too-premature envy of Rex and grinned at Harper, "Yep, score one for you. What breed is Rex? Wait, let me guess, Silver Lab?"

Harper grinned back, "I wanted a silver, but they are rarer, so I settled for just a big ol' black Lab with a huge heart and large paws. He weighs 118 pounds, so he is a handful. Rex is short for T Rex because of his size."

"Somehow that all fits," pronounced Henry. "I wouldn't have expected anything else."

As they rode back, Henry was contemplative. He wondered what Harper's home would be like, although he suspected he knew. He anticipated the exact opposite of Amanda's penthouse. It caused him to remember the homes he had known growing up, and what those homes meant to the people who lived there, and to him when he was in them.

"Hey! Harper interjected. "Where are you? I've been talking for five minutes straight and you haven't said a word. Are you OK?"

"Fine, in spades," said Henry. "Just remembering some things from my grandparents and childhood."

"That sounds like a story I need to hear," she said.

"Yeah, no problem. We can discuss that when we are sitting down in a quiet spot telling fish lies or other fairy tales," chortled Henry.

Henry settled into the Harper's jeep surprisingly comfortable seat and thought some more ... maybe a bit too much more.

Harper raised her voice, "Man you sure know how to insult a girl who just treated you to a new hobby and a great lunch and great conversation. What in hell is going on with you?"

Henry, only partially aware of the neglect paid to Harper, responded, "Just some introspection, brought on by a wonderful day and an enchanting teacher."

"Great save on that one, "Harper grinned. "I was about to get pissed. Here we are at the Harper cave. Let me introduce you to Rex."

As she opened the door to her house, she was assaulted by a small black horse who immediately put his front feet on Harper's shoulders and licked her nose eyeball to eyeball. She giggled at the aggressive but affectionate greeting, turned to Henry, and laughed, "See what I mean?" Then she opened the door to the back yard and Rex bounded outside in search of squirrels to harass. He never caught them, but it was good fun and great exercise to chase them.

Harper, obviously pleased that Rex had not destroyed the house, suggested that Henry stay a while, share a good small batch bourbon, and tell the story that Harper was questioning. Henry, still somewhat besotted, and in reverie from his initiation into the sorority, thought that was a great idea. He recounted to Harper what he had remembered on the ride home and then continued to the next phase of the history.

This was a strange sensation for Henry. Given his manly protection of all that he held dear, and all the stats he liked to collect and manage, he had never had to deal with this soothing feeling of being content with his day.

And here he was pouring his innermost thoughts out to Harper, a remarkable person, but one he hardly knew, and the only measurable he could determine in this process was that it felt good, and he liked her. As he looked around the house, he was surprised at how emotionally comfortable it seemed. Harper's sense of precision, so evident in her fishing habits, carried over into her home.

She wasn't a neat freak, but things were where they needed to be, where they were used, and made sense. The walls were decorated with fishing art, including several framed collections of exquisitely tied flies in various collections—mayflies, caddis, terrestrials, streamers, and baitfish imitations—and, the most beautiful, the Atlantic Salmon flies. *Those collections must be worth significant money.* Some pictures, several classic fly-fishing first editions. And photographs of the young athlete Harper in several sports. Cozy, inviting, not in the least pretentious, but a place where you could always feel good about yourself and your life. A real home.

Harper came back with refills for both of them.

Henry smiled, "Hey, what are you trying to do? Get us both sloshed?"

Harper retorted, "How'd you guess? No, really, it's just so relaxing sitting and hearing someone else's tales of woe that I am just enjoying the company. And you have to admit, the bourbon is damn good."

"Agreed and agreed," mumbled Henry. "But I am not an experienced hard spirits drinker. You probably need to get me home."

Yes, I definitely do. Harper sneaked a knowing smile for her own slightly naughty pleasure.

Henry left half of his second bourbon in the glass—for which he received proper chastisement from Harper—and they piled into the "Officer's limousine" to get him *home.* When they arrived, Henry fumbled around awkwardly with his seat belt trying to get out. Harper leaned over to help, and they "accidently" kissed. Not a long passionate lip press, but better than a second cousin hello kiss. Henry tingled. Another first for today. Harper smiled and they said polite goodbyes, Henry wondering who might have seen the seat belt incident.

Henry dragged himself through the front door as Harper sped merrily away, and was still a bit foggy as to the significance of everything that had happened. He immediately noticed that his flat lacked the cozy invitation to serenity that Harper's home had extended to him. *How come some homes do that?* he wondered. *That is really a nice thing.*

The idea rolled around in his addled brain for a moment, and he began to remember the homes he had experienced in his family. Grandma Jane came to mind first. She had kept a "proper" home which she learned from her Alabama upbringing. She had grown up there, and played piano and organ in the local Baptist church for fifteen years, before leaving to find her future in the woods of Wisconsin. She met Lars at a dance in Wisconsin, and his stories and physique convinced her that he was the future.

Jane married Lars Hansen in the place where he was a local hero lumberjack. He had saved thirteen men from a crowning fire at great risk to himself. Everybody knew him and respected him; he was welcomed at any logging job in the state. His ability and stamina with a crosscut saw were legendary.

As the industry developed and mechanized, Lars was alienated from the new processes which he felt devalued the efforts of men like himself and emphasized daily production. No one seemed to care anymore that a tree was felled well so as not to damage future harvesting of younger trees around it. The point was to get as many cuts as possible and then manage the damage by replanting the cuts with baby trees. Mechanical saws and chain saws were replacing the traditional, long, two-man crosscut saws, and the noise was hostile to a real lumberjack's ears. When he was drunk, Lars would often bellow, "Fy don dey yust make a big per of mechanical sissers unt cut de trees like flowrs!"

So, Lars decided to pick up the family (Jane, their little girl Helene, and baby boy Horace) and move south for a new start. Yellow pine was quickly emerging as an alternative for the fir and spruce of the northern forests, and lumberjacks could still make a go of it there. He decided that East Texas was the booming place to be. Jane was happy with this move as it brought her back closer to her childhood roots.

East Texas turned out not to be the promised land, and this small band of wanderers was caught up again in the teeth of the industrial revolution, as the industry continued to mechanize. Lars' drinking increased to an unendurable level, and Jane always paid the price, physically. When he was sober, Lars was always sorry and apologized profusely, further eroding his self-esteem, and his image of proper manliness.

As her children grew, Jane withdrew entirely from Lars, and another log was thrown on the fire of his fury. The violence grew worse, and everyone around them knew it. Jane hid from Lars and tried to renew her participation in church activities. That was where she met Margaret Elliason, a calm, peaceful woman, full of acceptable Christian virtues, and affectionate toward Jane in Jane's time of need. Very affectionate. Friendship with Margaret had a visible impact on Jane, and she hardened her attitude toward Lars' behavior. And she became fiercely protective of Helene and Horace.

According to what Henry's mother, Helene, had always told him, Margaret's entry into Jane's home was a major turning point. Lars was ballistic, and Jane was resolved that her relationship with Margaret—which offered comfort, support, and affection—would not be threatened by Lars' outbursts. Jane was aware that the community was raising eyebrows at the Hansens, but just interpreted that as sympathy for her situation with Lars. She wasn't incorrect.

But people were also apprehensive about Margaret's role in the hierarchy. Margaret was so submissive, and Jane so forceful, that Margaret soon acquired the sobriquet "Jane's doe"—and most of the small town was certain they knew what was "really' going on.

Lars, however, had still to be reckoned with.

One day, Lars failed to return home from a day of cutting large yellow pines under a short-term contract. No one really noticed ... until the next morning's newspaper showed the horrific pictures of Lars hanging backward over an exposed blade, the big crosscut saw embedded in his leg across his femoral artery. The scene, when examined post-mortem, revealed heavy alcohol content in his blood, and the conclusion was quickly reached that he fell into the saw blade—which was stuck half-way through the tree—cut himself deeply, and bled to death, because he was too drunk to get help. Indeed, there was clear evidence suggesting that was the case.

The church ladies of the town, however—taking particular note of Jane and Margaret—subscribed to another theory which was never proven by anyone. They surmised that, since Jane and Margaret were unnaturally affectionate, and since Lars was very angry about that, and since Jane was very assertive, and since Margaret would do anything that Jane told her to, the two women had schemed to ambush the drunken Lars in the woods at work, emasculate him, and leave him to suffer his own consequences of Jane's mistreatment. The theory explained that the big saw was just too much weight for the two women—both diminutive souls—to handle, and they botched the surgery, and Lars bled to death as a result. This was, of course, a totally preposterous idea ... most thought.

While most of the town was content to leave Jane and her doe alone, the church ladies chose to exact an eye for an eye through their children. They carefully indoctrinated their kids at elementary school that evil things were happening at Jane's house, and that those poor kids, Helene and Horace, were unfortunate victims, contaminated by the two women. The CLK (church lady kids) were not to be friends with the two children, not to have them over for play, and certainly not to associate with them where the public could see and identify that the CLK were supporting the devil's work. Jane and Margaret's proper, organized home provided little shelter and no solace to the troubled pair.

Helene and Horace were ostracized with little or no understanding as to why, and were persecuted for the rest of their preteen and teen lives. A certain amount of natural bitterness and resentment toward everyone in the world resulted, and the social development of the two was arrested, to say the least.

"Maladjusted" is a kind description associated with the penances imposed on Horace and Helene as they grew up. They were expelled from school multiple times for being unruly and noncompliant with various rules that no one had ever heard of before. They were sent to the school psychologist for "help." Under normal circumstances, that would have been a good thing. They were separated from other students as much as possible in a public school in order to contain the spread of the radioactivity that seemed to emanate from them.

No clubs, no friends, no boyfriends or girlfriends—zip, nada, zilch. Loneliness defined, and anger beyond comprehension. When senior prom came around, Helene coerced Horace into being her date so she could go. Neither had ever been to a party, and neither knew how to dance. But they knew that a lot of the couples were going to "party" afterwards. Much alcohol would be consumed, and a lot of virginities would be lost. But Helene and Horace had little understanding of the reasons any of that happened.

According to what few records Henry had seen, he was born late in the spring of the year following Helene's graduation from high school. His father, if known, had apparently disappeared into the ether. Henry could not shed any light on this situation, as his only memory was that his mom was always younger than those of his friends. He thought a single parent mom was the norm, and that his dual parent friends lived in a fantasy world. But he was never close enough to his mom to get answers to any questions.

His mom's home was disorganized, uninviting, and generally hostile to outsiders. Grandma's home was neat and organized, but fortified against the hostilities around it, and the people who predicated them. There seemed to be no possibility that would ever change. Nothing in Henry's early memories suggested that home was anything special, nor worthy of any special regard.

Helene never showed him a lot of attention, or love, since she regarded that as a false promise and a guarantee of failure later in life. "Make it on your own," she had always told him. "That way you never have to depend on anyone else, and you don't have to share with anyone else."

That always struck Henry as odd, since he had some experience in team sports, and saw firsthand how teammates work together. But he always had an indistinct knowledge that Mom was not totally wrong about that. So, he tempered his "investment" in others carefully, never overcommitting or over-trusting. He determined to be his own best protection just by being good at whatever he undertook, and being educated enough that he could figure anything out, given a little time and room to think. He was never going to be surprised by factors he had not considered.

And that was how Henry got to his own personal pinnacle. He was smart, knew how to work hard, didn't form emotional attachments, and focused on letting the numbers tell the story. Measurables were everything, and they couldn't screw you if you had the numbers.

As Henry stumbled into his "minimalist" bedroom, he wondered why the feeling in Harper's home was so different from any of his experience. He was lost in that thought for about fifteen minutes—before conscious thought vacated his brain, and he crashed into sleep.

CHAPTER 14

Sunday morning, bright, sunny, and beautiful. But Henry was filled with a strange sense of foreboding. He had experienced a wonderful, enlightening Saturday (even considering the disturbing Friday night with Amanda), and should still be floating. But Harper's emotional attachment to Parsons Point, which he did not yet fully comprehend, could be a difficult thing to deal with when she found out just what Henry's job entailed. He had no idea how he would explain that one, and he sure as hell wasn't looking forward to *that* conversation.

In his best analytical mindset, Henry resolved that the only realistic thing to do was to get some firsthand data on Parsons Point.

The Point was famous in local fly-fishing circles because of a young man named Craig Parsons. He was a fishing nerd, years ago, who had made himself completely obnoxious hanging around fly shops asking questions, and looking at all the flies to see how they were tied—and the compound leaders, and the hand-made fly rods, and the gear and equipment essential to the art of fly-fishing ... but never buying anything. Lovable, but obnoxious.

In a couple of years, and with an eight-inch growth

spurt, Craig began to show up with stories and the occasional picture of himself with some very handsome brown and rainbow trout, caught within an easy walk of the various fly shops. The obnoxious kid was winning credibility, and people were suddenly eager to pay him real money to act as their guide when fishing the river. It took him a spell to get used to helping other people catch fish, since his fishing skills far exceeded his interpersonal skills. But after the first year, he came to be known as gracious, informative, and entertaining—always having his clients' interest in mind—and the chef of some really amazing shore-side lunches. When he was old enough to include a good bottle of wine or some cold craft beer to the lunches, the demand for his services—and his fees— rose impressively. The fly shops that booked his time with clients liked that part, as their share of his fees climbed impressively also.

Most noteworthy, however, was his discovery of a richly fish-populated spot that became known as Parsons Point, or "Craig's Cast." The distinction was awarded to the place because only Craig Parsons, among all the locals, could trick its persnickety trout into taking a fly. It required a special rig, a truly unique cast, a very careful drift, and a couple of specialized mends to get the fly presentation just right.

"The Point," its short nickname, was the result of a rock formation left over from an earthquake several thousand years ago. From the bank, an underwater ledge curved out for some twenty-five yards, about two-and-a-half feet under the surface. The ledge could not be seen from the bank due to the grit in the water stirred up by the current over the ledge. But for the bold and knowledgeable it was wadable, and very fishable.

Henry had heard the history but was too inexperienced to try to fish The Point seriously. And Harper had told him he had to earn the introduction to The Point. Just casting from the bank wouldn't produce the necessary drift, and the currents would swallow a fly on the rocks and weeds and moss. It had to be fished from the river, and the wading could be treacherous. Today, he wanted to look at The Point through the eyes of an investor/developer.

What he saw was breathtaking. Large old fir trees, medium-sized cottonwoods, which shielded the ground from sunlight and spread a cool, comfortable blanket of shade during the hottest days. Still waters in eddies and small coves close to the bank with irrepressible currents in the middle, swirling around the rock outcroppings, that added visual character and physical shelter for large trout. The view and the reality of the river at Parsons encouraged fishermen, landlocked hikers, and picnickers to become enamored of the place's beauty forever. A natural haven from the nastiness of a city and its amalgamated corporate nests, and only twenty-seven minutes from the heart of the nastiness at that—what a magnificent development opportunity.

A little further upstream he saw a group of people crowded into a small flat spot on the riverbank. They were listening to someone actually in the river, wearing waders and boots, and carrying a short, lightweight bamboo fly rod gingerly in the crook of his arm. Henry moved up quietly to join the gathering.

The tone was respectful and attentive. The shore group was awestruck by the man in the water. Henry expected a baptism to follow. He quietly inquired of one of the group at the back what was happening.

"Oh, didn't you know?" the man responded. "That's

Bob Dorffman. He's in town to film his fly-fishing show, and he volunteered to host a clinic on fishing Parsons Point. Imagine, the most famous fly fisherman alive, right here in our little town, with our little fishing club, showing us the secrets of our little legendary spot.

"Something not quite right about it, him bein' a furriner and all. But he knows his stuff, and he used to fish with Parsons back in the day."

Henry took note. He had listened to Harper waxing eloquent on how The Point was the most under-rated and misunderstood fishing spot in North America, as if she would know. But she did get his curiosity up, and so, he listened intently as Dorffman droned on.

"Last time I was here with Craig, I fished it for an hour—never got a hint of a take. Then I gave the spot to him. 'Bob,' he says, 'Ya gotta think outside your normal way of fishin'. Gotta focus on getting that fly deep to get in the fish's line of sight. He's down there at least four, five feet. So ya gotta have a long drift to give that tiny little fly time to sink to the fish. Mebbe help it a bit with a tiny split shot.

"'Ya fish a double-fly rig. Floater on the line, sinker on the dropper. I use a size fourteen goofus, bright green on top, then about an arm's length of dropper with a size twenty olive scud or chironomid on the dropper fly. Shot about twelve inches above the fly, like a super-mini Carolina rig for a bass fisherman. Leader tippet needs ta be about five feet, and no biggern' six-x. Five-x too easy to see.

"'Just hafta stand in the river, 'bout ten yards out, no more. Cast upstream fifteen yards, and let the fly sink as it comes down. Double mend—first one upstream to get the dropper into the second level current, and the second mend, about twelve seconds later, downstream to catch the swirl made by the big rocks down deep. Only way to have a prayer of getting to a fish. But if you get good at this, there's a couple ten-pound browns livin' down there where it's safe. Ya might get one.'"

Dorffman tied the tiny chironomid on below the green goofus and made the cast. He emphasized that it was a different cast, made with a wider arm swing to produce a wide loop so the dropper fly didn't get tangled with the leader, and so that you could make the dropper hit the water first to begin sinking before the goofus started its float. He tossed the first gentle upstream mend, waited twelve seconds, and then threw a more aggressive downstream mend. Three more seconds, and the goofus twitched imperceptibly while the little bamboo rod bent gently, then more sharply. Dorffman set the hook with just a gentle raise of the rod tip so as not to break the delicate tippet, made a couple of turns of the reel handle, (he always played the fish from the reel if possible instead of the hand-strip retrieve), and a pound-and-a-half rainbow broke the water surface, struggling against the pressure exerted by the line, leader, rod, and fisherman. A couple of short leaps, and Dorffman had him in the net—to the amazement of the crowd.

"That's the only fish I have ever seen caught here," said one.

"He sure makes it look easy," said another. "And he ain't even from here."

Henry was quickly developing an understanding of Harper's reverence for this place.

CHAPTER 15

Sunday morning! Amazing what you can do on your own when you are a grownup. Hanna had not seen her apartment since she left for work Friday morning. She had vivid memories of Amanda's party Friday night, the enjoyable conversations with Henry, and the emergence of Charles as someone special whom she had not really noticed previously.

Whatever possessed her to go to Charles's house Friday night? Never in her life had she contemplated this—and with a colleague, no less. What eternal hell awaited her for such a lapse in judgment? It is almost unforgivable for a talented, dedicated, disciplined, and focused person like herself to be distracted by a pleasant personality, a handsome face, and a sculpted body. But right now, she was ecstatic that she had allowed herself to succumb.

Friday night was a borderline psychedelic experience. Hanna could not imagine such sensations unaided by drugs or alcohol. She had been uninhibited and open and had realized the miracle of multiple orgasms, the holy grail of womankind. She and Charles had experimented in ways that Hanna did not even know were possible, and apparently neither did Charles. They were both floating.

As Charles awoke, it was clear to Hanna that he did not immediately recognize her or the circumstances that led to her presence in his bed ... for a second night in a row. "Morning Sunshine," she giggled.

"Mmphf." Charles managed to mumble into his pillow. Then, comprehending the situation more completely, he kissed Hanna affectionately, and snuggled against her comfortable body. He was greeted by another giggle as she wrapped her arms around his head and shoulders and returned the snuggle passionately.

"We probably will both get fired, you know," Charles grinned ruefully.

"Yeah, but we can live off your trust fund, and the baby will be happy," laughed Hanna.

Charles laughed also, though uncertain about the humor. Admittedly, there could be worse lives. He was totally besotted with Hanna, the woman he had always known was smart, but was really only a mousy, rigid little accountant ... NOT!

Charles got up, and, from a drawer, produced a t-shirt which he tossed to Hanna.

"Throwing me out?" She asked.

"Nah, just don't want you scaring the neighbors if they peek in." He teased.

She teased him back by bending over and making sure he got a full view of what the neighbors would enjoy. They both laughed and he kissed her deeply again. She neither struggled nor giggled.

In the kitchen they peered inside the fridge to see what was available. They had already used up the omelet fixings on Saturday, when taking a brief respite. So, the only thing left was a cut-up chicken, some broccoli, potatoes, and yeast rolls. "OK," proclaimed Charles. "Sunday dinner at Grandma's house. Apologies to Grandma for the dress code. She would be a bit shocked."

So, as Charles floured, egged, and re-floured the pieces of chicken, Hanna busied herself with prepping the broccoli and cutting chunks of potatoes to be boiled and mashed. They didn't speak except when they both turned and, in surprise, said simultaneously, "And you cook?"

Hanna playfully coquetted, "Yes, in the kitchen, too."

And they both howled.

An hour later, as they sat contentedly after "lunch at Granny's," Hanna asked if Charles was really concerned about word getting around the office. He answered cautiously, "Well, on the one hand, I would be proud that I discovered a Hanna that nobody would believe exists. But, on the other hand, I would also be concerned about how people might see you as Charles's girlfriend and make some stinky assumptions. And, we might both get fired."

Hanna assured him that the secret was safe with her, but she was curious as to why being Charles's girlfriend would be such a badge of dishonor. The fired part they both took as a possible given.

Charles cautiously opened up. "Hanna, it's tough out there in the real world to make a reputation on your own for the right reasons. You've done that, and I don't want to be any part of undoing that. Especially now that we know so much more about each other."

"Is that code for 'now that we are a couple'?" she teased.

"If you think we are, yeah."

"Why don't we just let this play out before we get all the way to the conclusions," she wisely advised.

"I can live with that, but I am going to have to be careful in meetings with you and other people to make sure that I don't let my thoughts give me away," he said.

"I'll help," she countered. "Long skirts."

He changed the subject. "You know, we might not be the only ones."

"How so?"

"Did you notice that Henry left the party awfully late Friday?" Charles offered. "I think Amanda has the hots for him."

"Would that be such a bad thing?" Hanna probed.

"It would sure alter Amanda's image, and it might affect her dragon-lady approach to colleagues. She might lose the fear factor and just have to rely on being the boss' daughter. Not sure how that would work."

Hanna was doubtful. "I don't think Henry would bite on that one. First, he doesn't have a clue about women, and especially hot ones, and especially in the office. Second, he really admires Mo, and doesn't want to piss him off with an office romance."

"I'm gonna withhold judgment on that one. I don't think Mo would mind a bit. He really likes Henry's style and mind. And If Henry needs to learn about hot women in the office, can you think of a better professor than Amanda?"

"Point made," agreed Hanna.

"C'mon." Charles reached for Hanna's hand and started to pull her up from the table. "Time for dessert."

"Why are you pulling me away?" she asked in mock panic.

"Dessert is not to be found in the kitchen," Charles informed her.

Hanna giggled ... again.

CHAPTER 16

Promptly at 9:00 a.m. on Monday morning Henry was surprised by a knock on his office door. As he allowed entrance into the lair, Hanna greeted him in her usual grey knee-length skirt with a button-down oxford-cloth shirt. Something was different though. The shirt was unbuttoned down two buttons and Hanna was smiling from ear to ear, very relaxed, and confident with her understanding of herself and her world. Henry was actually glad to see her.

It didn't last long.

"Hey boss," she cheerfully intoned. "I've got an update on some of the prelim work on the project. Got your morning coffee yet?

"Not yet." He grumbled.

"Well here, I took the liberty. Milk and two yellow sweeteners. Your favorite."

"Hanna, what are you up to? You are far too happy, sunshiny, and smiley. If you are not careful your reputation as dragon lady number two will be endangered. And people may even come to like you, which means they will actually seek out your company and interfere with your ability to accomplish your monumental task lists on time."

"Well, their problem, not mine. I am discovering the joy of doing something important (*and some **one** important*, she thought to herself). And I am enjoying being something more than a bookkeeper managing debits and credits."

"A worthy outlook!" allowed Henry. "You are becoming a pro and increasing your value to everybody around you."

You have no idea, she quietly mused.

"Anyway, there is an issue which indicates some attention is needed. I don't know how significant it is, but I see a wide range of possibilities, not all of them good. So, I thought we should be looking a good distance ahead, since we already have a lot of money on the line here."

She continued, "There is an old mine back in the hills above Red Rock Creek that has a settling pond full of arsenic sludge on the bottom. It has never been a problem because it has never overflowed, and the two dams confining it in have held. Sometimes the summer heat even dries up the water, and the sludge sits there until it gets water from the winter rain."

"And this is an issue because …?"

"If the pond fills up and overflows, or one of the dams breaks, the outflow goes right into Red Rock Creek, and then into the Hattawoc River, which drains into *our* river, one point five miles above … Parsons Point. We don't yet know how toxic the outflow would be, but there are a number of possible impacts." Hanna was very precise.

"Educate me," Henry nervously said.

"None of the possibilities are very good," she stated matter-of-factly. "At maximum, the outflow would kill everything downstream of Parsons Point for fifty miles. At a minimum, if it can be fixed, the cost of doing so would require such a sizable investment that the project could become financially unfeasible."

"Isn't there EPA Superfund money available for a situation like this?"

Hanna hesitated, "Not clear. We talked—through intermediaries of course, so as not to tip our hand—with the people in Anaconda, Montana. Some time back, they had a humongous problem with tailings from an old Anaconda mine and smelter. The EPA and the state fashioned a major agreement and project to mitigate the mess, and there is now a magnificent golf course with black sand in the bunkers from the tailings, and a number of other procedures for the benefit of the surrounding landowners. It was hailed as a landmark settlement of a serious issue. Recently, however, there has been stirring among the landowners that the settlement did not go far enough, and additional measures are merited. The courts are now being asked to decide if the landowners and the state have the standing to alter the agreement and go further than the original EPA deal. It is not certain that anything will happen, except that some lawyers will make a lot of money creating documents."

Henry moved around to sit on the same side of the desk as Hanna. "How does that relate to our situation?" Henry was very cautious now. He was having bad images of delivering this information to Mo.

"It certainly is not a direct parallel. But there are enough similarities, especially with the surrounding land ownership situation, that we are treading very thin ice, given that we don't yet know the true extent of the problem."

"Okay. Recommendation?" Ever the good leader, Henry wanted his team to come with solutions, not just problems.

"We can get the dimensions of the pond, volume, topo maps to examine the drainage and all that, and model the possibilities at various levels of toxicity in the sludge. We can't get exact data on that without raising a lot of eyebrows on what our plans might be, but we do have excellent modeling capabilities," Hanna informed.

"Do it," Henry stated decisively. "I'll work with the modelers to get it right if you need me."

"It's 'modeler,' and we do need you on this one," she said. "I'll send him up to see you this afternoon."

"Thank you, Hanna. You are giving me good data and very professional options. Great work for the team."

To himself, Henry was not quite so confident. *Oh, man. Shit's about to hit the fan and it won't stop for a long time.*

As he was about to go on a lunchtime walk to think about how to pursue this latest information, and how to deal with Mo, there was a knock on his door. A bit ominous at that …

Earlier, while Henry and Hanna had been slicing and dicing the options for the abandoned mine in Red Rock Creek, Charles had knocked on Amanda's door for their customary Monday 9:15 a.m. meeting. It had to be precisely at 9:15 so that Amanda could properly orchestrate her meeting. Charles entered, bringing the requisite vanilla latte with a half shot of two-percent.

Amanda opened, "Bring me up to date on the project."

'Well," Charles replied, "There is not much new. Hanna has the troops spread out looking at a dozen different aspects of the prelim preparation and reports, but no one has really come back with anything meaningful yet."

"Are we on track and on time?" Amanda asked a bit icily as she rotated her swivel chair toward the window.

"As well as we can tell for now. But nothing is really rolling yet; it is still all starting to make sense, but we are a long way from any conclusions." Charles felt he was being pushed and pumped — perhaps for Mo's benefit?

"Well," Amanda ordered, "don't let any grass grow

under this one. Dad is antsy because it is so large and we are first in the field for now. We don't want to lose our advantage because we didn't move quickly enough."

Charles replied confidently but deferentially, "Got it. I'm on it." He knew there was very little he could do without Hanna's troops getting their tasks accomplished. But he had to put on a good face. He got up to go.

"Charles," came the sharp address. "One more thing. I noticed that you and Hanna were getting chummy at my party. Something going on there?"

"Yeah, but it's just that I have discovered that Hanna is much better than a mousy accountant. She is very capable and quite excited to be working on the project. She, as the finance guy, can coordinate a lot of different activities, and be a good focus point to know where the entire thing stands at any given minute. And beneath that ultraconservative façade she has always maintained, she is nice, fun, and very pleasant."

"OK. She is a great resource, as you say," Amanda cautioned. "But be very careful about getting involved with the 'resource.' We really don't need that kind of distraction around the firm."

"Right," Charles answered obediently. "Got it." This time he did actually leave.

I guess what's good for the goose is not necessarily good for the gander, he thought walking out Amanda's door.

After two more meetings and a report from the audit compliance team, Amanda was ready for lunch. She had an uncomfortable feeling she should have lunch with Henry.

So, she went down the corridor to his office and knocked gently on his door, permission to enter was given, and Amanda decided to tone down her entrance this time. Best to be a friend and colleague rather than the queen and heir apparent.

"Hey," she smiled. "Lunch? I'm buying."

"Well as you know, I never knew my father, but I'm sure he would have taught me to never turn down lunch with a beautiful woman when she is buying," Henry joked.

"Careful," Amanda warned playfully. "In some places that could be considered as a hostile workplace statement and you could be brought up on harassment charges."

Henry wasn't sure that she was joking after their conversation Friday night, but thought that lunch was minimally dangerous. "OK, let's go."

The air was full of foreboding to Henry as the memory of Friday night was still fresh on his impressionable mind.

As they took their seats, Amanda offered, "Have you given any further thought to our conversation last Friday?"

The foreboding was right, and the knot that Henry developed immediately in his stomach rendered lunch impossible. "Amanda, I don't know how to respond to this. I told you that it makes me very uncomfortable; I'm not one of those guys who get to the top by using the boss's daughter. Hell, I'm not even one of those guys who get to the top, so far as I know right now. An office romance with you would kill any cred I have with anyone at the firm, and I like having cred that I earned."

"I'm proud that you feel that way Henry. You a man of considerable honor, as I said." Amanda was almost pleading again. "But you have to realize that Mo wants this to happen; he wants you to be my teammate, and inherit the firm. He thinks you are a natural leader. I guess he thinks I am the natural policeperson to keep things in order. There are no problems here."

Henry was on the defensive now, and feeling his options evaporating. "Amanda, this is not me, so not me. I am totally at sea here."

"Henry, you need me! Like I told you, I can keep you safe from the stuff that could come out that would ruin you ... and Mo is planning to make you CEO."

Henry flinched, partly in confusion and partly in anger. "What could possibly come out that would damage me? I am a pretty straightforward guy, a known quantity with skills and degrees. What you see is what you get."

"You mean you don't know?" Amanda was horrified. "You don't have a clue, do you?"

"About what?"

"Henry ... your 'uncle' is your 'father'—you were born out of incest!"

Struggling to keep some composure, Henry retorted, "Well, I wouldn't be the first son-of-a-bitch bastard to become a CEO, *would I?*"

Amanda collapsed, "How is it possible that you don't get it?"

Henry's stomach tightened still further, and he took his leave of the table. "Sorry Amanda, I'd rather not eat anything right now."

CHAPTER 17

When Henry returned to his sanctuary, he was marginally calmer—bolstered by his contention that Amanda was using the unpleasant connotations of his ancestry to somehow build a case that he could never be considered for any position of responsibility or leadership.

But the calm demeanor was temporary. As he considered the ramifications of Amanda's revelation, he quickly approached rage.

"Screw *that!*" he snorted. "That's just total BS." *It sure as hell ain't my fault if my parents were perverts. I turned out fine ... I'm not deformed, I'm not deranged, I'm not crazy ... I'm a great human being. What freakin' difference does it make if Helene and Horace got ... off-center—given their weird childhood and the narrow-minded people in that crummy town, it's almost understandable. And I got out of there, built a respectable life, a record of success—I have done everything possible to make myself a valuable person ... done anything I have ever been asked to do, and risen to the top. My crummy uncle and ditzy mother cannot ruin me. My "lineage" will NOT hold me back—anyone can see the quality in Henry Hansen!*

The silent rant had raised Henry's ire to a level he had not experienced in recent memory. And, as he became aware of his anger, he began to take a few deep breaths.

In the middle of his pressure-valve-release exercise, a knock at the door announced his first afternoon meeting.

As the door opened, Henry was immediately awed by a presence of power and sheer size.

"Hi, I'm DeMarius Moffat. Hanna said we need to talk and to get up here as soon after lunch as I could."

Fascinated, and recovering quickly, Henry asked, "And where do I know you from, DeMarius? I know I have seen you before, and not in this building."

"Well, I do *belong* in this building," snapped DeMarius, a little defensively Henry thought. "I am Hanna's financial modeling intern. But you may well recognize me from other venues," he admitted.

"I'm guessing basketball, Big East, Marquette, all-conference your first two years, and All America three years ago—and then you disappeared." Henry had a phenomenal memory for anything sports.

"You are correct. Most people get the basketball part right off. Six-foot-eight black man in good shape seems to suggest basketball for some strange, widely-accepted reason." They shared a laugh. "But you are right on the rest. Not one person in 500 could do that."

Henry smiled, "I am a huge basketball fan, and I saw you play several times, twice in the Garden. I had you as a second-round pick with a good bonus. And now you're here building financial models as an intern? How does that happen?"

"Actually, the draft service said I could have been late-first, but I really got tired of the stereotypes. You know, quick to the rim, forty-two percent from the trey line, and a forty-two-inch vertical. I wanted to be something else, to my parents' dismay. Most people never get far enough down in my resume to see the Stanford MBA and the PhD from Columbia in statistics and computer science."

Henry was very curious by now. "So, what the hell are you doing here making next to nothing when you could be doing seven figures even with a Development League contract or in Europe? Even if you had pursued normal MBA and advanced degree recruitment processes, you should be somewhere at one-sixty just for starters."

"Mr. Hansen, I have been one of the chosen for most of my life, due to my forty-two-inch vertical, et cetera. I recognize privilege, white or black, when I see it. I decided that I need to learn how to do something on my own based on smarts and some creative, challenging work. I chose the road less travelled. And it didn't hurt that Mr. Stearns is as big a fan as you are. You use what you got to get where you want."

"It's Henry, by the way, and that is an astonishing answer. Congratulations on your maturity and your thirst for masochism." Another hearty laugh shared. "Do you go by DeMarius?"

"People who want to be cool call me D Mar. My Friends just call me D. I'd be pleased if you would use D."

"Deal. Now let's get down to the little challenge we face. There is a lot of money at stake, and we need to make some order out of chaos. Actually, there is not even enough data to call it chaos. We are dealing with a lot of unknowns."

"Unknown can be a good thing. Just ask any six-eight black man."

Henry was developing a healthy respect and a sincere liking for this extroverted, confident, and capable young man. "What did Hanna tell you?"

D spewed the preliminary details as he knew them.

"Old mine, probably very toxic, arsenic and other heavy metals which could leach into the drainage affecting a major development for us. Don't know anything but size of the settling pond and the topo features of the landscape. We could get access to details but that would tip our hand to regulators and opponents. So, we need to make models incorporating a wide range of known and unknown variables to establish some limits that we can be confident will accurately describe the situation, and allow us to develop some alternatives that can be executed in order to assure a safe development."

"No hill for a climber, huh? Especially with a forty-two-inch vertical. Right? Please tell me," Henry pleaded. "Where the hell do we start?"

D was calm and focused. "Let me get the pond dimensions from Hanna and the topo data. We can make a series of assumptions on the thickness and toxicity of the sludge layer, and organize the data into a table that anyone can understand. Then we have to figure out how fast the layer will dissolve and increase in toxicity, given the amount of water in the pond. There is going to be a lot of 'averaging' involved here, so everything will be approximate. Then we calculate speed of runoff for the various levels of overflow and various levels of toxicity, measure the overflow down the drainage, and calculate the amounts of toxic water that reach various key points along the full drainage, and finally the amount that flows into the Blaine River above Parsons Point. Then the real work starts."

"What do you mean?" inquired Henry, genuinely amazed.

D began cautiously, "When the runoff overflow hits the Blaine, it will disperse and sort of spread out—that means it will be reduced slightly in spot specific toxicity—*but*, it will be pushed over a wider area due to the currents that move toward Parsons Point and on downstream. We will have to estimate various levels of damage, based on various levels of pollutants, based on various speeds of flow in the stream, and so on. You can see the layered risk in the calculations, with no real way—that we yet know of—to hedge our estimates."

"D, you scare the hell out of me, for any number of reasons. You seem to have a good understanding of the complexities here, what do you need to get started?" Henry was genuinely concerned. He could see no good outcomes to this exercise, given his limited knowledge of mines and leachings that pollute streams.

"For now, Henry, I just need you to talk to Hanna and let her know that this is critical and it will become my first priority. That shouldn't be a problem, because she is excited about this project, and is really into it. She will be pleased to provide an important resource, if I don't miss my guess."

"I'll give her a call today and let her know. Now go forth and work modeling miracles. Let's find out what we are dealing with here."

The two shook hands—a fast new friendship formed—and set about doing the impossible.

Henry also paused to consider that Hanna might be the most undervalued resource in the firm. She was taking charge of a difficult set of tasks: she had the loyalty of a very strong, independent resource; she spoke authoritatively, and was not afraid to let you know that she may not know; and, she was very enjoyable to work with and be around. And people used to be afraid of the stern, conservative, by-the-book, number two in finance.

The knot in his stomach eased ever so slightly.

CHAPTER 18

Even the ring of the phone sounded ominous.

Henry was not expecting any calls, and his two-day old conversation with Amanda still sat in his stomach in the form of a knot. He did not want the phone to ring at all, and he wanted even less to answer it.

"Hansen," was the false bravado response.

"Henry, Mo. Can you join me in my office for a few minutes?"

"Sure, Mo, be right down."

Creeping dread crawled up Henry's spine as he reached for the handle to Mo's office, visions of a chainsaw massacre flipped through Henry's mind.

"Henry! Glad you're available, really good to get a chance to talk," boomed Mo. Henry couldn't help but wonder about the degree of sincerity in Mo's enthusiasm. "Nothing really important, I just wanted to get an update on our project and pass along something I heard."

Henry was not reassured.

"Sure thing, Mo. I haven't got a lot to tell you because I've got the team fanned out pursuing a list of preliminary issues that we have identified. But I can tell you that all of them are picking up a shovel and digging in with energy and commitment. They are all smart and focused and giving me a great effort. We won't have any specifics until late this week, or early next, but I can give you a summary of what we've started if you like."

"Not necessary. But if you have anything that I truly need to know, I want you to regard my door as always open and you come talk to me ASAP ... always. But I did want to mention that I am getting great feedback on you and your leadership in getting this thing going. Most of my division heads who have given you resources tell me they have not seen their young charges so well focused, and doing such a good job—and actually liking it—in a long time. This firm has a sore need for that kind of leadership in the mid-term future."

Henry flinched a bit at that one. Sounds like some father/daughter conversations going on.

"And in that regard ... I'm sure you know that I place a lot of confidence in Amanda on the operations side of this business. She is crackerjack, and knows what we do and how best to do it. But she will need support and even some strong direction (without showing her up, you understand) on certain issues. She is the future of this firm, but she is going to need the help of a well-liked peer. You could be that person, Henry. I am seeing the light at the end of the tunnel, and it is not a train where you are concerned."

"Well, thanks for your confidence, Mo. It's been a long time since I had a boss be so frank and so positive with me. It is refreshing and inspiring." Henry was being a little obsequious but the occasion seemed to call for it.

Mo continued, "And I can see that you and Amanda may have a little something going. I approve, totally. We don't need any office romance drama, but I know I can trust the two of you to be very discreet. You are made for each other, and provide complementary skills which can only be great for the firm. Just remember discretion is the better part ... "

"Right, Mo. Got it." Obsequence ran amuck.

As Henry shakily strolled back to his own office, he had a sense of being trapped in a Hapsburgian succession drama. He was quite dismayed that he might end up playing Archduke Ferdinand.

His sense of possible doom was not helped by the insistent beeping of his office phone as soon as he opened the door. "Just what I don't need right now," he griped to himself out loud. "More crises."

His vision of the future proved to be acute. "Hansen. Oh, good morning, Amanda."

The sweetness dripped out of the earpiece. "You talk with Dad? See? I told you what the true story is. Any Impressions?"

Henry was put off by Amanda's bombardment at the precise moment when he was realizing what a mess he was potentially immersed in. He hesitated before answering.

"Uhhh. I was happy to get Mo's support for the project and the progress of my team. He was very complimentary."

"And ... "

"He had some remarks about the succession of management and leadership in the firm."

"Just like I told you," Amanda purred.

The kitten sounded more like a predator to Henry. "Yes, but as I told you, I am not real comfortable with all that right now. I didn't say no to Mo, but I still have a long way to go."

"And did Daddy tell you that he knows about us?"

Henry nearly exploded. "What the hell do you mean 'us'? We are not *us*. We don't even know each other. You are the queen of the firm and I am the chief minion.

There is no story here, Cleopatra. I am neither Caesar . . .
nor Antony. I am just trying to lead a complex project and
do a good job."

"That's admirable Henry, but you need to be looking
ahead for your future. If you don't, nobody will. Except
me. Don't you get it? I am all in on you. You're 'the one,'
chorusmaster. I have dabbled with dozens of guys from
my red-headed bombshell cheerleader days at State up to
just two months ago before you joined the firm. I won a
lot more than I lost, and then tossed them away when I
saw what they were made of. You are different. And believe it or not, I never said that before to any man."

Henry was on the verge of full body muscle spasms at
this point. "Amanda. I like you. I respect you. You do a
great job, and are great for this firm. Your Dad clearly
knows how important you are to the firm's future. You
are gorgeous, intelligent, shrewd, and desirable by any
definition. I am just not in a position to be what you want
me to be right now."

"But maybe soon, huh?"

"I've got to go; I have a critical meeting in five
minutes, and I have not looked at the information."

"Okay. Progress. We'll take this further soon. Bye."
Amanda sounded like she thought she had won round
three. Henry's frustration pushed the limits of his safety
valve, and he was straining to resist blowing the valve
wide open.

The phone rang again. The valve blew. Infuriated, expecting it to be Amanda, Henry angrily grabbed the in-
strument and snapped, "Hansen, what do you need?"

A silvery, pleasant voice came back through the
phone, "Whoa, Cowboy. This is a friend. Your fly-fishing
instructor, remember me?"

Embarrassed at his temper, Henry shifted tones. "Oh, god. Harper, I apologize. Bad day at Black Rock here. I'm a bit edgy. You have no idea how good it is to hear from you."

"Well, that's a lot better. I might even not be sorry I called now. I have an open date for Sunday. Wanna take your fly-fishing experience to the next level? I would suggest that I bring the drift boat this time, and we float a stretch of the Blaine so you can see how the rich guys fish."

"Harper, that sounds wonderful. I can't think of anything that would be nicer. Are we supposed to have good weather?"

"Yep. A little warm late in the morning, but that will be good for hatches, and we should have a lot of activity. And being on the river is a lot different than being in the river wading. Both very good things but distinctly different. You'll see."

Henry relaxed, "Great, same time in the morning? I'll try to be out of my coma by then."

Harper laughed a knowing laugh. "Six-thirty sharp. Be prepared to buy breakfast."

The knot was shrinking and sanity was finding a way home. Henry couldn't wait for Sunday morning.

CHAPTER 19

The week had crawled by like an inchworm race, and Henry had done everything in his power to avoid Amanda and Mo. Fortunately, he was getting good feedback from Hanna and Charles; Martin had picked up some interesting ideas from some friends of his in the industry, and D was making sense of the unknowable with some shrewd sorting of available data and some insightful assumptions. All in all, it would be difficult to improve the progress the team was making. But Henry did not want to have to go to Mo yet for fear that the conversation would drift away from the project and toward the future of the firm.

On Friday afternoon, he could see the finish line. In this case, the finish line was actually Sunday when he got to go out in a drift boat with Harper. He had no earthly concept of what a drift boat was, but he knew it was going to be fun and would deepen his understanding of the "manly" art of fly-fishing—manly in spite of the fact that he was learning its intimacies from a not terribly manly but attractively feminine practitioner of the art. It would be relaxing to be on the water, and fun to talk with Harper away from the madding crowd.

But, just as he thought he could sneak through and escape the corporate world, the door burst open and D absorbed all the spare space in his office. "Hey, let's have a beer, I've got something to discuss with you and we need some privacy, some shelter from prying eyes and ears. You make the big bucks, so you can buy."

"Well D, that's a hell of an offer. Didn't they teach you anything about sales at Stanford? Usually when you're trying to sell something, *you* buy the drinks," chortled Henry.

"Yeah, but you're the big shot with all the power and access to high places. I am just the innocent six- eight basketball player/intern trying to learn my way around the complex world of corporate politics and economics. Besides, you don't pay me enough to buy you a beer."

"Point made," countered Henry. "Let's go. Where to?"

D suggested Murphy's.

"They have a great craft Porter there and it's far enough away from the office that we should have some space to ourselves."

When they were seated at a table in the back, they looked around to make sure that no one else from the firm had trekked across town for a Friday afternooner. It appeared they were safe, and their spy craft was adequate.

"Whacha got?" asked Henry.

"Long story short, it ain't good. We managed to get sat pics, topo info, maps, even some photographs which carried infrared information that allowed us to measure the thickness of the sludge layer in the ponds—about eighteen to twenty-four inches—and we also got some basic info on the composition of the sludge."

Even though the information was not positive, D was clearly proud of what he had learned.

"Can I ask how the hell you found all that out without me finding myself on the CIA termination list?" In spite of his jocularity, Henry was suddenly concerned.

"Well, if you know too much, I do have to kill you," solemnly intoned D. "But I can tell you that a lot of it came from an old buddy of mine from AAU and Marquette days. White guy, but he had a lot of street cred with all the brothers, and he was tough under the boards with never a whimper about all the physicality. Held his own very well. He went on to Wharton and then to MIT where he became an expert on space communications and data interpretation. He was a big help, and he won't give us away. He actually does work for the CIA now."

Henry swallowed hard. "You are dangerous. So, aside from this excitement, what did you find out that is so bad?"

"The sludge has all the wrong stuff in it, in all the wrong proportions. It could be mitigated through some creative chemistry but it would cost upwards of ten mill and take three to five years. No superfund money available. "

Henry didn't understand. "Why hasn't this come up before in some EPA study or someone's political campaign?"

D patiently reverted to professorial mode, "The ponds have dried up and the sludge is solid. There hasn't been sufficient rain or snowmelt to loosen or dissolve the sludge. It has just been sitting there, getting a little wet in the winter and drying up in the summer. Never created a problem because no one was interested in developing anything around the ponds. And they never created a runoff problem because they never filled. So, the problem is an unexploded bomb that nobody wanted to talk about. As a result, it is now pretty much forgotten."

Henry ruminated over his dwindling beer. "I don't know whether you are a devious genius for getting such valuable info, or whether you are a bringer of bad news and bad luck. Looks to me like our options are severely constrained from the get-go."

D agreed, 'Yeah, probably so, but that is not a decision that can be made on one beer. We need at least one more round."

Henry signaled the waitress. "And we haven't even begun to consider the overflow/broken dam/runoff-in-the-drainage scenario, have we?"

"Nope. But it will be scary." D clearly did not want to kill the project at this early stage, but he didn't want himself and Henry to be hanging high and dry either.

"Okay, First Round, what do you recommend?" Henry asked.

"I don't have a lot of hope at this point, but let's at least do a full worst-case analysis. You know, broken dam, two broken dams, enormous rainfall, drainage analysis, and simulations of the effect on the Hattawoc and the Blaine. At least we would know what the total downside is so that we can give Mo a fair picture."

Henry agreed but worried about this added cost for potentially no benefit. But he figured that he and Hanna could work something out on that which would be acceptable.

Not a great way to end the week, in spite of D and his help.

CHAPTER 20

Henry had spent the week avoiding Amanda and Mo successfully. That was a huge relief. The beers with D Friday afternoon were fun but frightening, given the possible consequences that leapt out of the conversation. Henry was becoming less certain of the project, his role, the outcome, and his future in a position and firm that he really was beginning to like, in spite of the obstacles that Amanda was intent on creating.

But, in truth, he couldn't wait for Sunday morning. The freedom, the excitement of fishing, and learning all the techniques and the small pieces of the art that made one knowledgeable, and, ultimately, successful ... and the time with Harper.

She was a terrific, calming influence in what was becoming a chaotic world for Henry. Her competence and confidence were reassuring, especially when she was in teacher mode. Henry felt no risk, and only the possibility of success, in whatever she was trying to teach him. He figured out that is what made her fun. She not only taught him good stuff, but she taught him how to be confident, how to believe in his own ability to produce a good result. That was a rare quality in any human being, based on Henry's experience. Imagine, discovering a whole new fishing experience, far superior to the others he had tried, and acquiring an amazing fishing buddy at the same time.

But, for the moment, it was still Saturday, and fishing was tomorrow. Something had been nagging at Henry, an itch that he was feeling an increasingly urgent need to scratch.

In spite of the uncertainty surrounding the project, and the wobbly relationship with Amanda which could affect his status with the firm, Henry was worried about the old Econoline. He loved the beast, but he was well aware that she was long past her sell-by date. She had served him well, but he was feeling past the teenage need for a van—which he had never taken advantage of any-way—and, instead, feeling the need for an adult car.

The car should have utility, but should express the sat-isfaction that Henry was feeling for his work, his knowledge, his apparent appeal to sexy women, and newfound leadership capacity. Money was not really a problem. Given his new job and his abstemious spending habits, he had saved enough money to pay cash for what he wanted, provided he did not let his self-image run roughshod over his good sense.

It needed to be nice, but not pretentious; unique but not flashy; and different, appropriate to Henry Hansen's style and manner. No Cadillac, Mercedes, Beemer, or Lexus would work for him. And he was not at all clear what his requirements demanded. So, he climbed into the Econoline, perhaps for the last time, and started cruising and looking.

What about a truck? Lots of pickups on the road; everybody seems to want one. Not bad, would even come in handy for fishing adventures. And camping; I've never really tried camp-ing. Yeah, nice but not really right for me.

He saw lots of minivans. They had advantages, lots of

room to haul people and gear. But not much pizazz from his point of view. He was not ready to become a soccer Mom.

Lots of high-end compacts with all the luxuries of a bigger, fancier car, but good mileage and easy maintenance schedules. *Practical except for the fact that I'm six-foot-two and would not fit easily into those cars, and their trunks are too small to accommodate golf clubs.*

He was inevitably forced to focus on SUV's. They seemed to be practical, comfortable, had acceptable mileage for the most part, and were even sufficiently luxurious to merit being driven by a personage of Henry's stature and status. But there were so many—foreign made, domestic, big ones, little ones, mid-sized ones, five-passenger, seven-passenger, big engines, small engines, diesel engines—the choices were overwhelming. And they were not bargains in terms of price. Fortunately, Henry could afford the top of the line in whatever he chose.

And top of the line was where he wanted to go.

He looked at—and rejected—American and Japanese SUV's of all sizws and pursuasions, and a few British and German ones also. The British and German vehicles were just too expensive (and pretentious to his way of thinking) and the Japanese and American ones were just not satisfactory for a variety of unspoken reasons. At the end of a long afternoon, he discovered a dealership selling the American descendant of the wartime transport that Harper drove for fun.

He knew that Harper loved her jeep and it was decades old. But he wanted something enclosed for a start, and something a little less in-your-face than her hand made CJ. As he approached the dealership door, he was accosted by three "friendly" sales persons. They seemed to spar momentarily over who would win the right to cajole

Henry into spending way more than he planned, and finance it on terms very favorable to the dealership through the captive finance company that shared fees and income with the dealer. According to some coded signal between the three, one rep won the competition and escorted Henry inside out of the heat and glaring sunlight.

Once inside, the rep launched into the normal tire-kicker routine.

"What are you looking for? I can get you into a nice basic all-wheel drive or I can put together a sweet deal on our top line, full-featured model. You look like you would like to start with something more mid-line. Am I right?"

Henry didn't know whether to smile or grimace at the contrived pitch. Not a single serious question asked, except for the obligatory greeting. But he decided that he was going to go in a different direction than he usually did. He was going to be the hard-headed customer who knew what he wanted, and negotiated very little to get it. He wasn't going to be nasty, but no-nonsense, and make a deal quickly on his terms, and finish the transaction.

"Actually, no. I want the top line, full-featured one. Tell me about that."

The rep swallowed hard. He had found a unicorn. A big dollar buyer, maybe.

"Well, I assume you are looking for an SUV rather than a truck. So, let's look at the deluxe models. This car has defined the best of the best for decades in versatile SUV-type transport. Go ahead and have a seat inside this one, and we can talk about features, and I'll answer questions."

Henry slid into the luxurious, soft leather interior, and was pleasantly surprised by the quality of materials, fit, and finish. It was as good as anything he had seen.

"What makes this car better than the competition?" he asked.

"Well, first, This car has a lot of history." The rep seemed relieved that he could finally launch into the pitch he had been trained in. "The only company in the world with hands-on experience in rugged, utilitarian, off-road, durable vehicles dating back to World War II. Now it is the leader in luxury, four-wheel drive systems, electronics, interior comfort and safety, good mileage, low emissions, and value holders, par excellence" — that last part he added himself.

"I don't believe a word of that pitch," snickered Henry, "but I have always liked these cars. I trust them."

The rep caught his breath. This was just too good to be true. "Let's take a test drive, and if you like it, and if you are prepared to buy today, I can make you a very special deal."

Henry responded, "Don't need a test drive. I like the car. I like the features. I want the deep burgundy with a tan leather interior and the full tech package, including the full safety package and all-wheel drive. Throw in a roof rack and I will write you a check right now if the price is right."

"We have this car in the burgundy and tan, and the price is sixty-six thousand and fifty-three dollars, all in, plus tax and license."

"My check will be for fifty-eight nine, all in, and you get my classic Econoline," countered Henry.

"I need to talk to my manager on that one. Let me introduce you to our owner while I go talk to the manager."

Henry was enthusiastic, "Fine. Here's my business card. Go do what you need to do, but that's my deal."

"Yessir, Mr. Hansen. Be back shortly."

Presently, Henry was joined by a portly gentleman, holding Henry's business card, well suited, and smiling.

"So, you are the new guy with Mo who he is so proud of. He mentioned you to me at Rotary last week. He seems to feel like you add something important to the firm. It's an unexpected pleasure to see you in here so soon."

"Thank you for passing that on to me Mr. ... Morris. I am really enjoying working with Mo. And I have been a fan of your product since I was in high school."

They were joined by another man, not nearly so well suited, but clearly in charge of sales. Morris introduced him. "Mr. Hansen, allow me to introduce Jimmy Bell, our sales manager. Jimmy, can we make a deal with Mr. Hansen here?"

"Sure Mr. Morris, his offer is aggressive, and we need a bit more than that. As always, there is a deal to be made. But I need more than fifty-eight nine to come out on this one."

Morris took over the conversation. "Let's the three of us go into my office and talk about this. Mr. Hansen, bring your check book."

An hour later, after interminable paperwork, Henry drove his new off/on road combo, luxury, upper middle class outdoorsy SUV out of the lot. The final deal was fifty-nine nine, including tax and license, with a year of free scheduled maintenance thrown in for good measure. A better deal than Henry had offered, and very far short of what the sales manager would have liked.

Henry began to appreciate Amanda more. He had a new understanding of what she had told him. You need skills *and* connections. Maybe she deserved more credit than he had given so far. He also thought about Mo's reaction when he found out that he bought the car from Mo's buddy. And what Mo would think about his choice, in view of all the fancy European sedans and coupes in the firm parking lot. It had never occurred to him that a choice car could actually be so important to his status, career, and future.

And then, inevitably, *I wonder what Harper will think?*

CHAPTER 21

Sunday morning came at its own decrepit pace, but it arrived. The truck appeared followed by the strangest looking boat Henry had ever seen. And, as expected, out popped Harper, clearly ready for a day on the water in her official capacity as guide, teacher, and grand poohbah. Smiling.

Henry opened the door before she could ring the bell. "G'morning. Welcome to Hansen House, your Sunday morning breakfast host." Harper registered shock and Henry was delighted to have put one over on her with the surprise. "We have a hearty buffet with scrambled eggs, homemade buttermilk biscuits (out of a frozen bag), bacon or sausage, artisan bread toast, three kinds of cheese, sliced tomatoes, fresh fruits, and the finest coffee this side fresh brewed from home ground beans."

Harper was ushered into the small kitchen and sat at the bar. "What's up? Too cheap to buy a real breakfast?"

"Real breakfast? Did you not hear the menu?" responded Henry in disbelief. "There is no better breakfast available in this hamlet than at Chez Henry. It's just not very well known."

"Yeah, I suppose that not enough of the local ladies have tried the fare here to have its eminence spread," jabbed Harper.

"Geez, you know how to hit where it hurts," Henry uttered in mock pain. "But look at it this way. Breakfast at Chez Henry will certainly not stain your reputation as other more well-acknowledged establishments might. No walk of shame here."

"Fair enough," smiled Harper. "Let's have the full menu with link sausage; I'm hungry, and the boat will require me to have had some nourishment."

"Yeah, I noticed the boat when you walked up. Funny looking contraption."

Harper seemed a bit hurt by the comment. "Listen, there is no better purpose-built piece of gear in all fishing than the river drift boat, a lesson you will learn quite soon. So, don't insult my baby.

In fact," she continued, "I have a question. Where is Eco the van? I didn't see her out front. And some wise guy with a pretty new SUV is parked in your place."

"Strange, huh?" said Henry. "Actually, that's mine. I bit the bullet yesterday and stepped up to an adult car in celebration of my new job and my newfound interest in fly-fishing. It's got everything to carry gear to remote sites and get prepared to fish, and it is very luxurious and comfortable when I am carrying guides around but not fishing."

Harper got sly, "And that happens often?"

Henry answered in kind, "Dunno. We'll see."

They both laughed comfortably and attacked the sumptuous breakfast. It was delicious and filling. Harper conceded that she had plenty of strength to handle the boat since the breakfast was so good. They finished, loaded the dishwasher, and then headed for Harper's truck to go to the river. It was only about twenty-five minutes to the launch site on the Blaine, and Henry recognized that it was downstream from Parsons Point. He hadn't earned that privilege yet.

No one else was around, so Harper backed the trailer right up to the edge of the river and hopped out of the truck. As she set about undoing the restraints that held the boat on the trailer, she asked Henry to get the cooler and some gear out of the back of the truck. By the time he got back, the boat was in the water, tied to a log on the shore so it wouldn't drift away. Henry was asked to pull the truck and trailer up into an open spot and lock the truck. He did.

"But … if you leave the locked truck here and we drift downstream, how do we get back to the truck?" Henry cautiously inquired.

"Rookie question, Hansen," she answered. "There is a service to come get the truck and move it to the take-out point. I book them ahead of a trip; they have a key to my truck, and they are as reliable as rain on a picnic. 'Never fail."

Harper put the oars in the oarlocks, blades back, while Henry was loading the cooler and gear in the mid-section under the rowing seat, and then she bounced nimbly into the rowing seat. Holding the boat steady against the bank, bow downstream, she invited Henry into the front of the boat (the pointy end) and began the orientation tour.

"First things first," she began. "Life jackets are under the seats in the compartment. Wear one if you feel the need, or have it close at hand, but it has to be accessible quickly. Stay seated on the seat if you feel unsure about the boat in moving water. It's quite stable but it may take some getting used to. When you are fishing, you can do that sitting down, but usually only very good casters can be effective that way. Most anglers stand up with their knees locked into those curved things sticking out in front of you. Those are knee braces specifically for fishing on the move—again, very stable, you are perfectly safe even in class two water. And you can probably cast much more accurately when standing. It is certainly easier to fight a fish and land it from a standing position.

"We need to talk about mending line, but let's get into the stream a bit first. We can pull up on a sandbar a little bit down the way here and get you educated about mending and some other casting stuff."

Henry asked, "Harper, why does the boat look so funny? It is very curved from front to back."

She responded like the pro she was, "Yes, It's like a dory. The curve is for buoyancy and to help the boat bob along in choppy water without plunging and diving into waves. It can get a bit splashy, but it won't throw you into the water unless you make a mistake. The boat protects you."

She went on, "You notice that it's flat on the bottom from side to side. That enables the boat to slide over sand and gravel, even logs and rocks sometimes. But with no keel, the boat requires a special technique for steering it in the current. There's no rudder, so you have to steer it with the oars, and it takes some time to understand the dynamics."

"Is it something that anybody can learn?" asked Henry. "Could you teach me how to do it?"

"Yes, I could, it's not hard, but you have to do it enough so that it's instinctive. If you have to think about it, you could be in trouble. Things happen fast in moving water."

"How does it work?"

Professor Harper took over. "Since there is no rudder or keel, you actually steer with the stern of the boat. And that is done by pointing the stern in the direction you want to go, pulling on the oar on that side of the boat, and then pulling until the boat actually slips over the top of the water in the right direction. You'll see me pulling on both oars frequently. That's to allow me to slow the boat relative to the speed of the flow and then position the stern to allow me to move the boat. This steering makes the process a bit slow, so you have to be very aware of what is coming up from downstream to avoid nasty surprises that might trap the boat. A lot like life, I guess. I usually look at least three hundred yards downstream when I can. As far as possible when I can't."

"Wow. This is amazing ... and slightly frightening," said Henry.

"You get used to it; like I said, this whole drift boat thing has to become instinctive. One more thing. We will spend most of our moving time in the middle of the stream. There is a lot less trouble in the middle than the sides of the stream. Logs, rocks, obstacles tend to pop up on the edges. Of course, there are some good fish holding spots to be found there also. Since I am the guide, it is my job to find the right spots to anchor the boat so you can fish those spots safely, and not get us hung up and tipped over. I've been pretty good at that so far."

Harper spotted a sand bar in mid-stream and gave Henry a heads up. "I'm going to drop anchor on that sand bar, and we are going to get out of the boat and work on a couple of techniques you need to become good at." As the boat stopped on top of the sand bar, and they exited, there was a lot of splashing. Henry got wet, and the water made Harper's nylon guide shirt cling close to her fit body.

She paid no attention, but Henry did not fail to notice.

CHAPTER 22

As they stood on the sandbar drying off, Harper picked up a rod and worked out a short cast of line, handing it to Henry.

"Make a cast over to that big rock on the left," she directed.

Henry made a good cast to the rock, and immediately the mid-section of his line began to drift faster than the fly, causing it to drag and look unnatural. Henry asked, "And you are trying to make an instructional point here?"

"Exactly," Harper replied. "You'll never catch a fish on that cast, will you? The drift is all wrong and no self-respecting trout would ever think that was a natural meal for him or her to eat."

"So," she continued. "Let's discuss the fine art of mending—in my opinion, the most necessary skill in presenting a fly that a trout will actually take. Make another cast to that same rock."

Henry complied and as soon as the mid-line belly started to accelerate, Harper said." Now lift the rod tip and gently toss the close part of the line back upstream. Not too hard because you don't want to move the fly if you can help it."

Once again Henry complied, or at least he thought he did.

"That was a little strong," Harper injected. "You see

how everything moved, all the way out to the fly? Just toss it a bit less. It's a matter of feel that you just have to learn by making a lot of casts."

Henry cast and mended again and it worked better this time. "There, all you need is practice," proudly claimed Harper. "You just need to get the touch."

She continued, "Even though you need to work on mending a bit, let's move on to the roll cast. It comes in very handy when you don't have enough room to make a proper back cast. And if you can combine it with the proper mend, you can fish moving water without worrying about getting hung up behind you. It is also useful in still water and wind under certain circumstances.

"So, you see that your line is fully extended. Now just raise your rod time to about two o'clock and then accelerate it forward to ten and stop."

Henry did so and was surprised at the result. The line shaped itself into a loop that traveled all the way down the line and as it got to the end, lifted the fly up off the water only to deposit it back gently. Never a back cast was made, and the fly line was at full cast.

"I never would've guessed that was possible," said Henry in amazement.

"Yes, and you can do it across the current if you combine it with a good mend. It simplifies fly presentation, especially when you don't have a lot of casting room." Harper was clearly in her element. "For instance, if we are on the side of the river and need to cast back to the middle for a rock or a shallow riffle, you can do a roll cast and won't lose your fly, or make your guide do something superhuman to try and save it after it gets hung on a tree."

"Got it."

"Now, one more thing," she went on. "Wind. Wind

can make it difficult to get a fly line to go where you want it to. If the wind is blowing across, you can correct mostly by mending, even though we will have to teach you a sidearm curl cast for some conditions. But if you are casting into the wind, the line may just be too resistant to the wind to go far enough to reach your target. So, there is a trick called a double-haul cast that is very useful in those times. It is a little advanced for a beginner, but you're doing pretty well, so I think we should try to get this in your repertoire."

"Show me how, professor."

Harper laughed a bit at that. "The point is to get the line moving faster so that it has momentum to combat the wind. If it is moving faster, it will also travel farther when you accelerate forward. So, make a cast. Now when you pick the cast up for the next cast, just pull the line quickly back with your free hand, almost an arm's length. Then let it go back immediately. Just release the line, but keep your hand close. When you start the rod forward, do the little tug again just like before. Now you will have accelerated the line twice and it will carry a lot farther faster … but the timing is critical. Too soon, and the line will fly in a big loop and the wind will get it. Too late, and it will crumple in a tangle. Try it."

Henry's first attempt was a disaster, and he had to spend some time untangling his line, leader, tippet and fly. The next time, he got the pickup tug correct but flubbed the forward tug. The third time, he got them both approximately right and said to Harper, "Yeah, I can actually feel the line tighten when I do that. And especially if I do it right on the forward cast, I can actually feel the rod load just before I tug."

Harper's broad grin betrayed her approval. "Bingo,

you are now an advanced caster. So, let's put this baby back in moving water and see if you can catch a fish."

As they got back in the boat and pushed back into the current, they got splashed again and Henry sneaked a look to see if the splash managed to provide him a thrill with Harper's wet shirt again.

It did.

Harper, apparently unaware of Henry's pleasure, instructed him to cast toward a line of what looked to be foam on the water, and mend upstream. This he accomplished with a decent degree of skill and was rewarded by a splash where his fly was floating. He was so surprised that he had no idea what to do, and the fish swam away unharmed … and Henry recovered his fly, also unharmed.

Harper was pleased that the strike had come quickly, but cautioned Henry, "Next time, when you see the splash, count to one and then just lift the rod tip gently. That should push the fly into the corner of the fish's mouth, and when you get it in the boat, it will be easy to release him."

Henry nodded and cast again. Nothing. Again, and nothing again. His cast was in a good spot and the drift was acceptable, but no action. Harper saw his disappointment. "Hey, you don't catch a fish every time, y'know."

"On a good day, how often does a fisherman catch a fish?" he asked.

Harper thought a moment and replied, "If we cover ten miles in a day, you will make several hundred, maybe a thousand, casts. And if you catch ten to fifteen fish, you have had a helluva trip."

"So, my baseball stats mind tells me that if I make five hundred casts and catch ten fish, my batting average is .020.

In baseball, even the batboy hits better than that. That kind of 'success' would have you looking for a new profession."

"In fly-fishing," smiled Harper, "that success rate—if they are ten good fish—could make you famous, especially if you can write a couple of good articles or a book that tells the story well. I guess it just depends on whether you are a quantity or a quality guy. Again, just like life."

Henry surprised himself by embracing that idea. He understood quickly that his chances of hitting .300 while fishing were quite slim.

They floated another two hours and Henry did manage to get two fish in the boat. But he lost four more. He was exhausted, partly from excitement and partly just from being out in the sun and wind on the water for the better part of a day. And he was deeply satisfied.

Henry put his rod away as Harper pointed the stern of the boat to the takeout location and expertly pulled into a small notch that allowed her to ship oars and get the boat right next to the bank. No playful splash for Henry's benefit this time. Henry climbed out and Harper asked if he could back the truck down to the edge of the launch area.

Henry wasn't sure he knew how to do that, but felt he would lose a lot of face with Harper if he said so. Swallowing hard, he took his pride in his gut and moved toward the truck. When he got in and got his bearings, he figured that if he just moved slowly and didn't panic, he would be okay.

So, he started the pickup and began to back slowly. He turned the wheel slowly and only slightly, and figured out the relationship between wheel movement and trailer movement, and began to feel a bit more confident. A few course corrections, and a couple of backup and re-center operations, and he had the trailer in place. He stepped out, beaming at his success.

"Never done that before, huh?" questioned Harper.

Henry was crestfallen and showed it.

Harper quickly corrected, "No, it was fine. Just looked like you weren't real confident about how the truck would react. She does have a mind of her own sometimes, especially in reverse."

Henry felt good that Harper was alert to his sensitivity and protected his fragile ego.

As they got the boat over the roller and onto the trailer bed, and then got the straps fastened, gear put away, and bow and stern tie downs tightened, Harper suggested, "This is the point where I usually get $500 and a nice tip for a great day on the water. But since you are a special student, I would settle for a good dinner and some good wine."

Henry swallowed hard, but had no trouble taking the second suggestion as the preferred one. They jumped into the truck and proceeded down the highway to a small (possibly intimate) little Italian place that was a favorite of Henry's. Henry wore an exhausted smile, and Harper wore a joyous grin. Good day on the water for both of them.

CHAPTER 23

As they pulled into the parking lot, Harper was suddenly concerned. "Aren't we a tad underdressed?"

"Nah, not really," assured Henry. "The owner is a buddy of mine from my days with the Pirates, and he has no problems with dress codes. And he always gives me a special table back in a quiet corner."

"Henry, is this a date?"

"Would you like it to be?"

"Probably."

"Well then, it probably is. But I never dated a guide before."

"Don't worry. They're just like real girls."

"Yeah, Harper, that's not a lot of help here."

A comfortable laugh and the "date" was off to a great start.

Ralph, the owner, greeted them immediately on their entry, chastising Henry for not coming around more often. Ralph led them to Henry's favorite table and took their drink orders. "How about a nice Barolo?" Henry asked authoritatively.

"Got just the thing, Mr. Hansen," replied Ralph. He left and returned moments later with the wine and menus. As he opened the wine, Harper offered, "Since we are drinking Barolo, I'll have the veal scaloppini."

"Henry, your lady knows what she is doing. The scaloppini is our specialty, and it is best with the Barolo."

Henry chimed in, "I'll have Ossobuco. That should hold us for a while."

And the first glass of the Barolo was poured.

As they sat in the quiet comfort of the upholstered booth, Henry couldn't help but lose himself a bit in the reverie of the day's memories: the boat, the water, the fish, the learning, the sunshine, the splashes—which revealed a new side of Harper. It blurred together, but it was grand.

"Hey! You're developing a pattern. After a day of fishing, you seem to drift to someplace else and leave your guide alone. That is not good for a guide's confidence ... or a girl's."

"Oh, no, Harper—I am just remembering all the wonderful stuff I have experienced today. I have learned so much, and you are so good at what you do. Thanks for taking me on and educating me. I think I may be hooked for life."

"That's the idea. We guides have to keep growing our markets by adding new fly-fishers."

A couple of sips and the quality of the Barolo was well established. Henry was impressed that Harper knew about Barolo and veal, and Harper was impressed that Henry knew about Barolo at all. They talked about travels and experiences. Henry had spent a summer in Italy in the Piedmont and become very familiar with inexpensive Barolos. Harper had never traveled outside of the US, but certainly knew a lot about where the good fishing was. Henry figured that was an even trade; he even thought that knowing the fishing might be slightly more important than knowing wines.

They were getting really *really* comfortable as the food

arrived. As Ralph promised, both dishes were superb, and fit the wine perfectly. It was easy to slide into a quiet, sated zone where nothing mattered except this dinner and these two. As they were debating dessert, Harper suddenly came to a realization. "Henry, here we are getting all dreamy eyed with all this good food and wine, and I don't know a damn thing about what you do. I certainly didn't learn anything about you on our very first encounter, and not much last week either. What do they pay you for?"

Henry began cautiously, "Well, I am a stats guy, remember? I worked for the Pirates for four years, looking at all their performance metrics, and my main job was to identify what metrics really predicted good future performance ... for an individual, for the team, in a situation, for a left-handed pitcher, or a right-handed first baseman. Anything that could be quantified, we looked at. And then I was responsible for building statistical models with variables that could be tweaked and used to see what would happen in a given situation for a given player according to the historical model."

"Order out of chaos, huh? But there is only one professional baseball team here, who else needs that kind of experience and expertise?"

Henry continued," Well, it turns out that merger advisors like models too. Financial models, sales models, economic models, fee structure models linked to investment performance, predictors of individual analyst performance, even models of what kind of PR and advertising are most successful in given economic conditions and markets. It appears to be a lot like baseball. So, I am modeling for an investment banker now ... mathematically, that is."

"Sounds impressive. Slain any dragons with those models?"

"Not really. I have just been at this a few weeks. I just barely know where the men's room is. It isn't nearly as invigorating or as pleasant as your profession, but It allows me to live well and get addicted to costly hobbies like fly-fishing. Man, guides are expensive."

Harper laughed again. She seemed to do that a lot with Henry, and she realized she hadn't done that in a long time. "I've got a regular client like you. He has a big-time investment portfolio but loves to fish. He owns a bunch of land on the Hattawoc where it meets the Blaine and doesn't know what to do with it. He is not a great caster or fisherman except that he absolutely loves it. He says it is cathartic. He can't think about anything that bothers him when he is fishing, He says that is when he is 'home'."

"Have you decided about dessert?" Henry asked.

"Not tonight, Henry," Harper teased. "I am a contented guide right now. Anything more and I would pop."

"Well, given your hospitality last weekend, I feel I must return your kindness and offer you a fine fifty-year-old single malt scotch when we get to my house. It's only fair."

"If you treat me nicely, I might be able to handle one wee dram to cap off a great day."

"Let's roll," ordered Henry.

As they pulled Harper's boat and truck out of the restaurant parking lot, Henry was totally unaware of where this was headed. He just knew that he was more comfortable with this woman than any he had known, and she appeared to like him too. Strange feeling, given his history, but oh-so-nice.

CHAPTER 24

As they pulled up in front of Henry's place, Harper asked how he was enjoying the new wheels.

"Kinda hard to tell. It's only got five miles on it—from the dealership home, yesterday. But I think I am going to enjoy it. It's really nice."

Harper chimed in, "And you know, you can pull a drift boat with it very easily. It's good for towing, especially the all-wheel drive."

"How convenient," joked Henry. "And I do have all-wheel drive. I can go anywhere in my new truck."

They went inside the Henry den, and it had not deteriorated since breakfast. While Harper sat down on the sofa, Henry found the fifty-year-old and two small tasting glasses. He poured a dram for each of them. As they slowly savored the rare scotch, they shared a glance and a contented smile. It was very nice, but with a bit of really good peaty edge to it.

"Not exactly like your small batch bourbon, but comparable in terms of quality and unique flavor," pontificated an expansive Henry.

"It is very nice and warming. Just right for those cold Scottish nights," agreed Harper.

Henry smoothly shifted gears and subjects. "So, when do I get to fish Parsons Point?"

Harper was a bit coy. "You're almost worthy, but we

have a couple of skill-building exercises that we need to do first. Casting and mending there are difficult, not to mention possible complications in wading, depending on the river flow and the current. But you're close. And having a guide to recommend you to the fly-fishing gods will help you."

Henry ventured into some more detail, very carefully. "Y'know, I went out there the other day. You have said so much about it, I thought I would see for myself."

The scotch was settling in as Harper asked," Yeah? What did you find out?"

Henry went on, "Well I looked around for a bit, and I decided it was a beautiful place, very calming and soothing, bordering on spiritual. I see why you like it so much. There were a bunch of people there talking with some guy in the water who was fishing, along with talking. Bob Dorfinger or something. Fly-fishing TV personality or something."

"I was there, up front, but I didn't see you—I would've remembered. And, by the way, it's Bob Dorffman, and he is quite possibly the best living fly fisherman. 'Uncle Bob.'"

"Uncle Bob?" asked Henry. "How so?"

"It's 'Uncle Bob' because he is an old friend of the family and we have known each other for years. I have even fished with him some."

Henry was very wary with his next question. "So, if he is an old friend of the family, who is the family?"

"Craig Parsons was my grandfather."

The answer pierced Henry's heart like a cold steel knife. He stopped breathing for a moment. Luckily Harper did not notice. "Wow, so you are fly-fishing royalty," Henry recovered quickly. "Why didn't you tell me that I was learning from the heir to the throne? I would have been more respectful and attentive."

"You have been very respectful and attentive, especially when my shirt got wet today. And you are a terrific student. You are going to be a fine fly fisherman, and I am going to have a great time fishing with you and teaching you all the tricks."

Henry was speechless. He had no idea what to say, so he wisely opted for silence.

"And, I'll tell you something else Hank Hansen, I think you are pretty terrific in a bunch of ways."

With that comment, Harper threw her arms around Henry's neck, running one hand up behind his head and planted the most passionate kiss on him that he had ever contemplated … and it was very sincere. Once again, Henry was completely at sea, but floating high. He had some inkling of the brewing storm here, but, at this moment, he didn't care. Nothing like this had ever come his way from any woman he had ever known. This could be … very nice … if he could rescue it from the jaws of hell.

Harper suddenly turned shy. "Oops, surprise. Not sure where that came from. Must have been the scotch … but … I sure liked it. Maybe I should get home while I can. And maybe we can figure this out on our next fishing trip."

She got up to go, and Henry suddenly felt empty—not knowing what to do if she stayed or if she went. But she went.

With a smile and clear, honest affection she walked out to her truck, and, looking wistfully back for a few moments, drove off.

If it had been a war, Henry would've been shellshocked. And he had no idea where the front lines were. Hell, he didn't even know the enemy troops from the friendlies. But for right now he didn't care. The feeling was just too new. He was … happy.

CHAPTER 25

Monday morning and the office was in a mild panic. The Queen had called a special meeting of the Parsons Point task force—without consulting Henry. It was set for 9:30 a.m.

Hana, Charles, Martin, and Dr. D were in Henry's office and infuriated, confused, unfocused, and a bit concerned all at the same time. Hanna spoke for the group. "Henry, did you know anything about this? What the hell is going on? Can she even do that? We all work for you—and our respective bosses; she is crossing over a lot of organizational lines here. Are we in trouble?"

Trying his best to maintain a demeanor of calm and command, Henry responded, "Whoa, slow down and let's look at what we are facing. If Amanda is calling this meeting, I would guess that she has gotten some static from your bosses that your time is being sucked away from other important tasks. Make sense? If that is the case, then we have to make the point that we are chartered by the big boss, Mo, and given limited time to get things done. If the company wants to change the priority of the project, that is Mo's prerogative. But we don't know any of that for a certainty. So, let's just be confident in the good work we have done and be comfortable in knowing that the worst that can happen is that we go back to doing non-project stuff, if that is what Mo wants. We are all enjoying this project, and each other, but that is not a terrible outcome. Certainly no cause for panic. Take a deep breath, and let's just be the pros that we are all becoming."

The tension eased palpably. Charles spoke up. "I haven't heard Amanda or anybody else say a single negative word about any of us or about the project, so maybe we just need to get prepared to do a large-scale update to keep the momentum going. If there were serious problems, I think I could have gotten that out of Amanda."

"Thank you, Charles," Henry replied in a soothing voice. "That makes a lot of sense."

D and Martin had nothing to add, so Henry asked the team to go back to their desks and make sure they were up to speed on every detail within their respective areas. As usual, he believed that if you have the data, you are not vulnerable.

At 0930, everyone appeared in Amanda's office as requested. The Queen did not appear to be distressed, so it was generally assumed that no heads would roll this morning.

But Amanda was completely aware that she had created some drama, and she was determined not to let the opportunity to flash a bit of power go unused.

She opened her remarks relatively safely, "I just want you to know that you are all scoring big points with your bosses and with Dad for the way you are digging into the Parsons Point thing. You are serving the firm and your own credibility well."

Multiple sighs of relief. Henry had to give her credit for picking up on the anxiety in the group and relieving it humanely. "Dad has picked up some scuttlebutt that may change a few priorities as we are beginning to get into the meat of the project.

"At his Rotary Club lunch on Friday, Dad was told that there is a new partnership that has been formed which is composed of all the landowners of the area affected by our project. I don't know if they are aware of our plans or if they just coincidentally see an opportunity like we do. We don't need competition, and, if you remember, we only have an option for a year before we have to put some real money into this thing and take fee ownership of the land, or tie it up some other way. I don't think we know if we can get all the work done that we need to do in the course of that year. If we have to fight a competing group, it could well diffuse our efforts and spread us too thin to make the one-year deadline," she continued.

"So, here's the deal. Dad asked me as the de facto chief operating officer to work with Henry and you guys to make sure we have all the resources we need—and to get a hard, formal timeline in place for all the steps we need—to execute to best use the time we have. I apologize for calling this meeting on short notice, and especially to you, Henry. You are the leader here, and these guys have been working their butts off to follow that lead. Dad has noticed, as have others. I am not going to interfere with your direction, but I do need to emphasize the time pressure we are facing. Tell me what resources you need to accelerate the progress."

Henry was quick to recognize the opportunity. "Thank you for that support Amanda. There is a way to do this more effectively and be a more efficient team. We need exclusive access to a mid-sized conference room for our use only, a sort of war room, keys for all team members.

The room needs to have lots of whiteboard space, a projector, and a dedicated, off-network printer that we can all hook into and have privacy from the rest of the firm. That should give us a good base to start from, but there may well be more, including some additional people for some tasks yet to be determined. Just a future heads-up. Is any of that a problem?"

"Not a bit," Amanda's enthusiasm was quite clear. "That is a great can-do attitude from this team. I'll arrange what you need and you can have it right after lunch today."

"Thank you. And, team, until lunch, let's squeeze ourselves into my office and start setting up some time sensitive priorities so we can hit the ground running after lunch. Everybody on board?"

They all were on board and jumped up immediately to carry the great adventure to the next milestone.

As they stopped for coffee refills, Henry noticed that Hanna was smiling to herself. "Hanna, not a word until we get into the privacy of my office." The smile got even broader. D picked up on it and smirked a bit himself.

Safely ensconced in Henry's office, Hanna burst out, "The threat that Mo is concerned about involves that car dealer, Jack Morris. Henry, you probably know him; he is in Rotary with Mo. He controls the land north of where the Hattawoc joins the Blaine, all the way up to Parsons Point. He wants to make some money off it but he is also an avid fly fisherman and well acquainted with the legend of Parsons Point. He reveres it. He is in the investment group Amanda referred to, but he is very cautious, and will move slowly to protect the land and the fishing. He could be a big thorn in the side of a project."

Amazed, as always, with Hanna's access to information, Henry incredulously asked, "Hanna, that is a potential blockbuster. Where did you get this from?"

"Well, a girl has her ways and doesn't reveal her secrets until she has to. But you can take this one to the bank. It is a dead cert."

"So, what does it mean for us?" retorted Henry.

D chimed in. "Jack Morris has the most to lose if there is an accident, overflow, or seepage issue with the ponds at the old mine. According to the maps that Hanna and I looked at, and the modeling I have done, all the heavy metals could seep into the drainage and even the ground water of Morris's property—and that is a key piece in the scope of the development. That land, made available to big tech companies for their grand HQ's or regional offices, would bring the most money and create the most value in the entire project. So, our friendly car dealer swings a very big stick here. Nothing is going to happen unless he is disposed to help it happen."

Henry shifted in his chair and frowned. "If Morris is a part of a partnership, why does he have the most to lose? Wouldn't all the partners have a lot on the line?"

D responded, "Yes, of course. But Morris could develop his property successfully without the other partners if he chose to get out of the partnership. His property is the keystone in any development effort. And it might even be more valuable if he did something on his own without all the regs and pressures of a project like we are exploring."

"Let's re-center to see where we are," said Henry. "We have a shaky landowner group who could split up at any moment, depending on the perceptions of individual owners, particularly Mr. Morris. We have a high uncertainty of the stability of the old mine and its ponds, and we have a highly vulnerable drainage that could threaten a highly valued piece of ground—both financially and ecologically—if anything doesn't work exactly right. And nobody knows that we are thinking of starting this project. Have I got it all?"

Martin spoke, "Not entirely, Henry. I spoke with some good friends who have built parks like this in urban locations, and they enlightened me on the vagaries of getting investors, debt financing, architects, builders, and then tenants for the buildings. There is a lot of preplanning and design work to be done, and even some prelim stage sales work early on in the project. That means large-dollar investment by the developer, which at present is only us. If we want to enlarge the developer/investor group, we will need to have some meetings and make some serious money pitches to key players in the next month or six weeks, given the one-year option. I'm not sure that we even know who the key players are at this point. That news will spread quickly, and we will have to deal with a whole new series of issues, perhaps even crises. Everybody will want in. Competing investor groups, regulators, politicians, local business leaders, architects, builders, not to mention the average citizens who may not be very supportive of a big development on this site."

That statement froze Henry's blood as he thought about how Harper would react to the plan, and to his involvement. Suddenly that took on importance for him in a very personal way.

"Thanks, Martin. That shows me a lot of research and thinking, and we are going to need all that we can get if this thing is going to work."

After a deep breath, Henry suggested lunch. "We can adjourn for lunch or get something in," he said. What's your pleasure team?"

Hanna piped up, "Boss, I took the liberty of ordering sandwiches and soup from the deli. It should all be here any minute. We can just go on from where we are and we will be ready for anything that comes up this afternoon."

Once again, Henry thought Hanna was developing some insights no one had given her credit for before. "Great, let's get on with it."

CHAPTER 26

When the team reassembled in the now dedicated conference room, Amanda was there with a small surprise. "New developments from Dad. We need to have a public informational meeting within ten days. Word is getting out, although we have no idea how, and we need to be able to get investors interested while placating the tree huggers that we are not ruining the world. So, the urgency is up a notch from this morning, and it was high then."

Henry responded for the team, "How will the meeting work? We don't have a lot of firm data, and most of what we have is just not suitable for such a public forum."

Amanda made it clear, "I'll handle the meeting. It will mostly be a PR and marketing type gathering, and we want people to like the idea without having to explain a lot of the possible complications. Your team should be there, but we need to keep them out of the spotlight since we don't want the attendees to know the technical details as well as the project team. It is too early.

"So, give me lots of pretty pictures and thoughts to share with them that will make this project look like a civic dream and not a worrisome ecological challenge. But don't mislead anyone. That is sure and certain death at this stage."

Henry wasn't sure he knew how to do that, but Amanda

assured him that Charles knew the ropes and could meet those requirements for the meeting materials. So, on they went to put lipstick on a pig that did not yet exist.

Henry wanted to start the remaining work with some energy, so he asked urgently, "What needs to be done first before we can even take a second step? Any thoughts?"

D offered that they needed to know what the composition of the sludge layer in the settling ponds was, and how or if it could be treated or removed without ecological harm to the site and the drainage. Charles suggested that it would be important to get a feel for the level of comfort or discomfort among attending voters as to the risk in such a project. It would probably come to their attention sooner rather than later and all the politicians involved would want to see that barometer reading early on before taking a stance.

Hanna was focused on the costs of remediation in the development plan and how much would need to be invested on the front end before any money could be recovered from the project. Martin just listened and wondered aloud how the developer would entice major tech companies to participate in what was an unproven project and one which might generate a lot of public animosity toward their brand if it went astray.

Henry was having a difficult time figuring out how they could discuss this project with the public and avoid these highly controversial subjects. Furthermore, he was beginning to wonder if they *should*. If those settling ponds were the least bit unstable, the lawsuits could go on for years. Talk about liability with a tail.

"Okay," he started, "what've we got? Dr. D, anything? "

"Yeah, good news and bad news. Which do you want first?"

Henry smiled ruefully, "The good of course. The bad news will always show up sometime."

D laughed almost sincerely, "The problem with the settling ponds can be fixed. They can be stabilized by covering the sludge layer with eighteen to twenty-four inches of good soil, overlaying that with an impermeable layer of material designed just for this purpose and then overlaying that with another two feet or so of soil. Then you revegetate the soil with appropriate plants and grasses. At that point the whole thing is stabilized and won't move or flow out, at least as far as we have seen … so far. This method has been in use for quite a while; it is very similar to what was used in the copper mining region in Montana. Now they have vastly improved streams and beautiful golf courses growing out of the former contaminated tailings and leach ponds. Very successful."

"Great! What is the bad news?"

"This method has only been in use a few years. There still could be some long-term surprises that occur with age. But, overall, the risk appears to be quite favorable for a landowner or user and the technique is considered to be proven."

"Hanna, I assume that you have some bad news on the money front for this fix of D's."

"It's a bunch, but not prohibitive. I figure six to eight million to stabilize both ponds. The big variable is the cost of moving fresh soil up that puny road to the mines by truck. If the road is not in good enough shape, then more money would be needed to bring it up to standard. And, of course, that small project would have its own environmental and prep costs added to the overall costs of the bigger project. If the road investment is large, it would probably kill the project. The base costs would just push the sale—and, ultimately, the space rental prices— too high. The liability is manageable but the risk of an eco-problem is still out there to some degree."

Henry looked at Charles, "What is the public perception of this thing?"

"Not bad. They like the idea of a load of big tech salaries coming into town and the resultant spending that will benefit everyone. But there is a sizable opposition from the people who just don't like big corporate development. And Parsons Point is regarded as a place of natural beauty; therefore, not a good development choice. This is a strong community and they are well organized. I'm sure we'll hear from them in the public meeting."

And Henry knew just who would be heard the most. "Okay, let's get to work on Amanda's materials. PowerPoint slides emphasizing those tech wages and local benefits, emphasizing the unique project which will make this place a magnet for more money in the future. A concept-type site map could be useful with all the futuristic future HQ's of big tech operators. Remember to make them well spaced with lots of green belt room between. Lots of trails for walkers and bikers."

Henry pursued another topic with Hanna, "What more do we know about this ownership group partnership that Mo got the option from?"

Hanna lit up. "They are shaky. Very different people in the group. A couple of hard-core corporate types, a couple of family landholders, and one guy who isn't sure what role he plays, Jack Morris."

"Could he make or break the whole deal?" Henry wanted to know.

"Yes, he's stubborn and irascible. Does pretty much

what he feels like at the time. And if he feels like he is getting crossed, he will definitely do his own thing, to the detriment of all the others."

"No wonder it was so easy to make a car deal with him."

"And, he is an avid fly fisherman. He may well have plans of his own for the land he owns and is just testing the group to see which deal makes the most sense," finished Hanna.

Henry hit the save button on that thought.

Hanna crept off and started putting rough financials together for the presentation. D was making a summary model of the costs and risks of mitigation, and Martin was sketching out a tech campus for the site which would make young techies swoon at its care and precision. Charles was working on the slides so that Amanda would have polished and classy visuals for the crowd of supporters and critics she was bound to face.

In spite of the available remedy for the pond problem, Henry was seeing aspects of this project he never imagined and difficulties he could not have conceived. It was not at all a certainty that the project could be executed, and it was not even certain that the landowner group would hold together for the challenging prep period required to get a solid start.

He was not sure where he should stand as a project leader or as a citizen rapidly becoming a fly fisherman and environmentalist. And he was totally unsure about how he would explain to Harper that he was not only involved in this project but the key leader in making it feasible.

His stomach knot and the cold steel knife returned with a vengeance ...

CHAPTER 27

As Henry left the team to work their magic and return to his office, he encountered Amanda in the hallway. "Strategy meeting with Mo at three," she announced matter-of-factly. "Just the three of us."

"What aspect of strategy?" Henry asked.

"Dunno, but I'm sure he'll tell us."

At the appointed hour, Mo's door opened and the three of them gathered around the conference table in Mo's office.

Mo began in his normal, expansive style. "I'm sure you both understand how important this Parsons Point thing is to the firm. It will establish us as the premier IB in this whole region as well as delivering a ton of important benefits to this community. That scores well with the politicians and will stand us in good stead for the future. Not to mention, we will make a ton of money on our fees, money-finding consultancy, and related services."

"How so?" inquired Henry.

"Well," replied Mo. "Good work in the community is its own reward. Plus, it puts us in good shape with regulators and politicians when we need their help. And, on top of all that, you never know when someone, recently retired, might want to run for office—say, governor."

Henry's eyes widened slightly, "Got it."

Amanda's knowing smile suggested more than Mo was

saying, and Henry began to understand her aggressive approach on him as a life partner. She was planning the near-term future for the both of them. He didn't like the feeling of being played at all, even in such favorable circumstances. *Foreknowledge is forewarning.*

Mo restarted, "Where do we stand on Parsons?"

Henry stepped up. "We have identified that we can deal with the potential eco problems of the old mine up in the drainage to the Hattawoc. That was a big worry, but we looked at what they did in Montana, and it seems like we can make that work here. It's not fool-proof, but it is reasonably reliable ... though costly. Looks like it could add another ten million in upfront costs, worst case. That's not fatal, but it sure screws up our financial modeling by lengthening the payback on initial capital and possible pushing up of sale prices, and, at the end of the chain, tenant rental prices."

"What about the tree huggers?" continued Mo. "Will they have anything to hang onto that would slow things up and cost us still more?"

"As I said, the eco risk mitigation procedures could have a limited life. They have only been in use two decades or so, and could fail at some point out in the unforeseeable future. They have worked well in Montana so far. If there were to be a failure after the development was completed, it would be fought out in the courts for years, and the liability could carry a lot of additional charges and costs. But that is only a 'could.' We don't have any reason to think that will happen anytime soon. Naturally, the biggest opposition we will face will probably just be from people who don't want to see bulldozers growling around Parsons Point, ruining the beauty of the place for commercial purposes." Henry sounded more authoritative than he felt on these points.

Amanda jumped into the discussion.

"We'll deal with the potential eco opposition in the public meeting with an overwhelming presentation of the economic benefits to the community. You know, growth in high wage jobs, bigger tax base, ability to finance more community services, reduced pressure on individual homeowners to pay for stuff they don't directly use or need, better schools, better roads, parks, et cetera. You get the picture. Martin has done a site map of the place that is almost obscenely beautiful. It's enough to make a banker cry."

She continued, "We won't make any direct investment pitches because we don't know who in the crowd will be a 'qualified investor' according to law, but we do intend to stimulate a lot of interest. And, of course, we will avoid technical detail on the land, the soil, and the potential issues with the mine. I'll present to the crowd as the voice of the firm. Henry's team will be there but unobtrusive in the corners of the room, in case I get trapped into answering some questions that only they know the answers for."

Mo beamed.

"Sounds like you got it covered. What do we know about the landowner group, the ones I have the option with?"

Amanda repeated what she had heard Hanna report earlier, "They are a squirrelly group. Not unified at all. They represent different interests and different points of view. They gave us the option to create an opportunity to generate some value and some money from the holdings, but they all have their own agendas, especially your Rotary buddy Jack Morris. We are pretty sure that they will hold together as long as everything moves like it is supposed to. But if we need to modify the option or change the timetable or anything like that, it could be a major negotiation. We're just not real sure for now."

Mo addressed Henry, "Is there anything that you can see that would cause us to not be on the timeline or need a modification to the option agreement?"

"Yes, of course, we have a lot of work to do in all the environmental areas and then we have to get some financial support lined up. Those two priorities alone could take us past our timeline if we hit any snags. If we don't have any problems, we are probably alright. Then there is the problem of the mitigation at the mine. That could end up taking a long time. We might need to get some cooperation from the EPA to get that one in place. Those things can always stretch out. Charles is working the political front in case we need some help from the regulators. Other than that, we are in great shape."

Mo frowned, "Henry, I can't tell if that was supposed to make me smile or make me scared."

"Neither, Mo, just an honest appraisal of our situation."

"If Jack is a possible monkey wrench in the machinery, maybe you should get better acquainted with him and develop a relationship. He is a sports nut and would enjoy your knowledge and stats approach. He is actually very knowledgeable and very opinionated. Loves to trout fish, too."

"I'll look for a chance to get to know him," said Henry.

Mo's parting shot involved Martin, "Make sure that Martin is actively chasing his contacts in the industry on this thing, He tends to want to talk about techie stuff and software. Doesn't see himself as a real estate guy at all."

"Will do, Mo."

As they left Mo's office, Amanda tugged Henry's sleeve, "Can I see you for a moment ... in my office?"

They entered and Amanda closed the door. She didn't lock it, so Henry felt relatively safe. A fleeting sensation which turned out to be totally unwarranted.

"Did you pick up on what Dad said about 'someone' running for governor? That election is in two years. That means that there are a lot of things that need to be put in order at the firm if he is going to do that. Get my drift? That is what I have been talking about when we are together. You have any thoughts about that?"

"Amanda, we have talked and I have told you. That is not something that I am in a position to even think about for now. I am the new guy in the firm … with a big-assed responsibility. I am not going to poison the well by consorting with the queen. I have to make my own way here."

In her best demure ingénue look and voice Amanda purred, "I know that Henry. That's why I like, even love, you. You have character and substance. You are the right guy for all of these roles at the firm and at our house. I am not desperate. I am making choices and I choose you."

Henry laughed modestly, "I might have reason to question your judgment in this case. I am flattered, and it is even possibly exciting, but not yet. I'm too wrapped up in learning how to be the boss and a leader people look up to for the right reasons."

"Just don't lose sight of the golden ring as the merry-go-round circles back," she said with a bit less patience and less demure than before.

"Got it," he said.

Then he slithered away, making his escape back to his team for a moment, and then back to his office to contemplate how he could have fallen into so many messes at once.

Some guys are just lucky.

While he sat and considered the options that he was facing, Henry's phone rang. It was Mo.

"Say, I meant to talk to you about something else. DeMarius Moffin."

"Mo, his name is DeMarius Moffat. I know he is only a low-paid intern, but he is top notch, one of the brightest guys I know, and a guy who will do a lot for this firm."

"Fine, fine," muttered Mo. "I suspect the kid is a decent basketball player, and I thought if I could get him to play for our rec league team, we could dominate the standings. With me at six-six and him at, what, six-ten? … nobody could keep us off the boards."

"Mo, he was all Big East for two years, All America as a junior. He can go to the rim with anybody, he is six-eight, shoots forty-two percent from the three-point line, has a forty-two-inch vertical, and a seven-foot wingspan. He is more player than anyone in the rec league has ever been or ever will see. Not only that, he is smart. Two PhD's, incredible modeling skills, and a terrific team member to work with. I have no idea if he would even be interested in the rec league. He seems to have priorities outside of basketball."

Mo was flabbergasted. "How did we ever get him in here? This is phenomenal! We wouldn't need anyone else on the court, just him and me. We could beat the rest of the league just the two of us. League champions, here we come."

Henry tried to soften Mo's enthusiasm, "Calm down, Mo. Neither you nor I even know if he still plays or is interested. All you can do is ask him. But please, for me, don't make any assumptions about him and his history. Don't embarrass me. He is quite valuable to the firm if he never touches another basketball. I need him on this project.

And by the way, he is the biggest bargain you ever acquired. He could be making four times as much money almost anywhere else."

"Thanks, Henry." Moe hung up.

Henry shuddered.

CHAPTER 28

At the end of a trying day, Henry rushed for the comfort and protection of his new Grand Cherokee (still less than 50 miles on the odometer) and turned on the big Bose sound system for some relief. *Some light, uncomplicated baroque music would be nice.* And so it was, all the way for the three miles home. And when he arrived at the safe haven of the Henry Den, he immediately sought the solace of his favorite craft beer. He could've gone for the bourbon, but if he decided to go ahead and pursue alcoholic relief up to the state of tipsiness, the craft beer was a more economical alternative.

If you have the data, no one can argue with you ... as always.

As he sipped the sweet tasting porter, he contemplated the events of the day. If he hadn't miscounted, he'd had four or five new problems dropped on him today, and that did not include the ones that he could foresee based on the four or five—probably ten to fifteen in all.

Mo was clearly anxious about the project. There was no easily discernible reason, but he was definitely uneasy. Maybe Mo's issues were compound and complex. Perhaps he was looking at the possible failure of the project and the impact that could have on his run for governor. Maybe just the sheer weight of so many heavy intellectual, ethical, and financial concerns was outside Mo's capacity to manage and stay calm. Maybe he was worried about Amanda and whether she would be able to ascend to the leadership of the firm ... and what she would need to do that ... *like, for example, me.*

And there was that silly episode about the company basketball team. This was out of all proportion to its real relevance to anything, but Mo was openly excited and even concerned about it. He didn't want to look like he had stocked up on ringers, but he didn't want to allow any possibility of a non-championship season either. And none of that basketball stuff would have any bearing whatsoever on US&G now or anytime in the future.

Henry twisted open the second bottle of porter and began to feel less apprehensive about the world in general.

The next large category of complications occupying Henry's now limited capacity was Her Majesty, Queen of the firm, and Future Ruler of the Empire. Amanda was a real opportunity, surrounded by problems, and defended by an army of enigmas. At times she almost seemed psychopathic. At others, she seemed real and even likable; lovable was not a certainty. And she was always spectacular.

She was probably correct that she and Henry would make a dynamic and very qualified team to lead the firm, although Henry had strong suspicions that there might well be some infighting about who controlled the firm's steering wheel inside the royal bedroom. If the mental gymnastics were expanded to consider matters of personal happiness, added to the obvious corporate advantages, the value of such a match became more clouded and difficult to evaluate. Perhaps even frightening.

Henry thought back to some of his university courses in disciplines that he had pretty much rejected, philosophy particularly. Hegel came to mind—thesis, antithesis, with no clue to synthesis in sight. That pretty well defined his vague relationship with Amanda.

And then there was D, Dr. D, DeMarius Moffat, a truly unique individual, aching to get his teeth into something meaningful and away from basketball. Henry respected D enormously, based on his experience to date, and if he had to pick a most trusted colleague in the firm it certainly would be D. Even though he worked for Hanna—second most trusted colleague—D and Henry formed a formidable team and the relationship was underscored by strong personal bonding. D created confidence in anything he undertook, and communicated with the clarity and authority of a much older, wiser man. Henry envied and respected him in many ways—ways that were far away from his basketball successes.

Speaking of the project, that was turning into something that Henry had never dealt with in his short career. He had always just worked the problem. Not much ethical or ecological question about how a left-handed batter performed against right-handed pitching, or with runners in scoring position. It was always very clear what percentage of three and two pitches were in the strike zone, and how many turned into outs versus a man on base. Pure numbers were a wonderful challenge to manage. Actually, you didn't manage them, you just collected them. You might analyze them or compare them or even try to project them, but mostly it was reasonably cut and dried. The fun was in the gathering and calculating ... and one needn't worry about the ethical choices involved with who to use as a pinch hitter against a curve ball lefty with runners on second and third. *Well, not unless you could steal the catcher's signals anyway.*

But the Parsons Point project was not at all that easy nor clear. It had elements that were not even measurable … yet. It required projections and surmises and assumptions that were two sandwiches short of a full picnic in terms of their reliability. And the potential liability was enormous. Who would be responsible if the old mines settling ponds turned out to be non-responsive to the Montana method treatments proposed? If the down drainage land was to be sold and developed, and then built out and leased, what would happen if an eco-accident ruined the land and negated all that value-added put into the land through the development, building, leasing, and usage chain? How would the court system ever deal with all that?

And what role would he personally play in the event of such a disaster? Aye, there's the rub.

The second porter was not helping Henry escape the turmoil in his head resulting from the events of the day … or week. He was feeling the need for rejuvenation that could be sated by a third. As he reached into the fridge to rescue the third from its prison of cardboard, he became aware of a strange buzzing. *It's way too soon for my head to be buzzing; I've only had two. What is going on here?* After a moment, he realized that his phone was buzzing in his pocket and he rushed to get it answered before the buzzing stopped.

"Hey, Hottie," intoned a playful female voice.

Aw, shit. I don't need any more of Amanda's world domination theories tonight.

"Time for the third date," the voice continued. *Just what you would expect from Amanda after a drink or two.*

"And you know what happens if the first two dates have gone well?"

Henry was not aware that the first two "dates" with Amanda had gone well at all. "You mean ..."

The voice responded, "Right, you get the grand prize, that which all men strive for but few are fortunate enough to receive."

Henry was thinking, *I really don't need Amanda's bullshit right now.*

"You get to experience Parsons Point."

Henry was stunned for the second that it took him to figure out that this was not Amanda, but Harper. He was relieved, excited, and terrified at the same time.

"Harper, you little devilress, are you leading me on?" With only a slight slur in his words.

She said, "Yeah, a little bit. But who knows what it might lead to?"

Recalling the finale to their last fishing trip, Henry choked on his porter momentarily, and continued, "What do you have in mind?"

"How about you pick me up this time? We'll break the new ride in on how to take two people wade-fishing — lots of gear, no boat. And I will introduce you to the mysteries and the seduction of Parsons Point. I will show you why it is one of the most fun and challenging places in all of fly-fishing. By the way, in accord with the rules of the third date, you're buying dinner."

Henry's relief had peaked out at twelve on a ten-scale, but the excitement and terror both notched up two points.

Harper continued "We'll fish our way down to Parsons, and along the way you can pick up a few small-er fish just to get a feel for the river, the currents, and the lies that ordinary fisherpeople can enjoy. Then we will climax by taking some shots at the point itself, and you can learn the famous 'Craig's cast' that Dorffman was talking about the day you were there."

Henry wondered if Harper were choosing her words for maximum effect and double entendre. But even if she weren't, it sounded like a very worthwhile day. "What time shall the student call at the professor's office?"

"Nine-thirty should do the trick. We aren't fishing to a specific hatch or anything, so we can just take our time and fish our way down to the Point. That's where we will want to spend the most time. And where we can have the most rewarding experience if the fish gods are with us."

"Oh, man, I am looking forward to seeing the professor in action on the Point," Henry laughed. He wasn't sure that he really felt like laughing but, politically, it was the most favorable reaction. He would have thought that the invitation from Harper would have raised his excitement at the end of the day, but it had also heightened his anxiety, as he could imagine the risks that went along with any discussion of Parsons with Harper.

CHAPTER 29

As he awoke the morning after Harper's invitation on a "third date" of fishing, Henry walked into his office thinking that he needed to clean things up before the pending storm reached its full fury. Probably the least obnoxious of those tasks was introducing Dr. D to Mo. Even though that chore carried its own possibilities of embarrassment and chagrin—for both D and Henry—it was the least difficult to correct if some iota of unawareness got in the way ... *like, say, Mo's general cultural unawareness regarding black people, and basketball players in particular, including Dr. DeMarius Moffat.*

Mo invited them in for a morning coffee, which they both accepted cheerfully. Henry was dreading Mo's opening line of conversation, but was pleasantly surprised.

"Dr. Moffat, Henry tells me you are quickly making yourself indispensable in our firm. He extolls your skills as a statistical modeler, and seems to think that you have a sense for what makes a business proposition hang together."

"Thanks to both of you. I am flattered. And to make it simpler, my friends call me D. I'd be honored if you were comfortable with that yourself," smiled DeMarius, the tall and socially agile.

Mo nodded, "Likewise honored, D. Welcome to our

team, and thank you for what you have already contributed. Henry says it's plenty, and he would have a much harder job without you around."

D was genuinely embarrassed to be the target of such praise off the court, but felt reaffirmed that it was happening. Maybe this business and this firm held something special for him that would allow him to escape so many stereotypes that had surrounded him since his childhood.

Mo rambled on, "Everybody here seems to enjoy working with you. They like you, but more than that, they believe they can count on you to give them your best and work with them on reducing complexity and confusion. In this business, that quality is golden. There is never enough of it to go around for the number of crises that need it.

"And, in case you might think that I have lived under a rock, I am aware of your incredible basketball career. Maybe not for the reasons you think. I saw that Big East Tourney Championship in the garden when you played 'Nova. The last five seconds of that game are the best and smartest basketball I have ever witnessed.

"When that big brute of a center from 'Nova clobbered you at the rim, it was clearly a flagrant one at a minimum. You should have had two free throws and the ball out of bounds. But the dumb zebra called a shooting foul and gave you two shots. You were down three. I have to ask, what was going through your mind at the line?"

D smiled. He had never been asked that question by anyone, even though he had been interviewed hundreds of times on the game. "When I got the ball with seven seconds left, we were down three, so I looked for the three to tie and get to overtime. It wasn't available, so I drove hoping to get the 'and one'... and go to overtime. Didn't happen. Got the foul, but not the bucket. So, I had two shots and not much time. I looked at our post guy, the only white guy on our team—he now works for the CIA by the way—and nodded at him. I made the first freebie, so now we are down two. When I nodded, he knew I was going to miss intentionally to his side and his job was to get the 'bound. He did, but couldn't get the ball back to me inside. So, I dropped out behind the three line and he got me a pass, I got the shot off just before the buzzer sounded, and it caught nuthin' but net ... for three. Put us up by one, if it stood.

"Refs said it was a good bucket, before the buzzer, and, Bob's your uncle, we won the tourney. Most exciting game ever in my life for sure. But you are the only guy that I've met who ever credited smart basketball for that one. Most just think that it was effort and luck."

Mo smiled, "Nope. I saw you nod at your guy and figured that something was up. It was obvious to me that the miss was intentional. It was the only option available to you and you made it work. Brilliant, smart ball. And you appear to be doing it off the court too. D, you have a very bright future, anywhere."

Henry exhaled slowly. Mo had gone through the whole routine exactly as Henry had coached him. Mo had seen the game and the nod, but he didn't know the whole story. Give him credit though, he had asked the right questions and allowed D to take him through the whole fantastic finish. And then, Mo had said the right things to encourage D that basketball was not the only skill set he could use successfully. *Maybe Mo gets it after all.*

Mo moved to the clincher, "So what I need from you both is twofold. First, the Parsons Point landowner group is a shaky partnership. They are seeing the potential of a big profit maker but they are afraid in the extreme of the liability posed by that old mine up in the hills.

"I know that the two of you have found a soil treatment for that place that has worked in other sites in other states. I need a way to express that positive possibility to the partnership. I need a model that can quantify the risk and the probability of success and come up with a present value dollar number for the liability. I know that is a lot of speculation and assumptions, but you two can make it realistic if anyone can. We really have to be able to give some comfort to these nervous nellies that this will work and make us all a lot of money."

Henry jumped in, "Mo, you know that is virtually impossible. There is no way to give any certainty to those numbers."

Mo answered, "Henry, you remember the first conversation we had in this office? I talked to you about 'impossible.' And we agreed that only means we haven't figured it out yet. This is what is needed; let's find the way to measure it and present it ... fairly ... so as to create confidence in our ideas."

Henry realized that there was no turning Mo away from this point, so he asked, "And what is the twofold part?"

Mo laughed, "Oh, the twofold part is easy. Jack Morris is the fulcrum of the partnership group; he has the most important land in the scope of the project. But he is the most vacillating member of the group. He thinks he could do something with the land that is simpler, safer, and more beneficial than our 'grandiose' project—his word. And he is not looking for the biggest dollar return on his investment to influence his thinking. I don't really know what motivates him.

"So, I want you two to establish a good solid friendship with him. Become guys that he trusts. He will love meeting D, since Jack is the most avid college basketball fan in this town. Hell, he was probably at that 'Nova game too, D. And Henry, you already have a bit of a relationship with him since you bought his premium car. He remembers you well. I might mention that Jack is an excellent golfer, single digit handicap, and he is also a dedicated fly fisherman. So, you have plenty of 'manly' pursuits to utilize in building this friendship. We want him to be on our side when the key issues come up for discussion and decision. Can you guys do that?"

Henry, recognizing inevitability when it jumped into his face, quickly put an arm on D's sleeve and answered for the both of them, "Sure thing, Mo, piece of cake." Now all he had to do was convince both D and himself that it really could be done, and that it was the right thing to do. *No problem for a four handicap and a guy with a forty-two-inch vertical.*

As they exited Mo's office, Amanda met them in the hallway. "Got a minute?" she asked.

"Not really Amanda," Henry answered. "Mo just dropped a big one on us, and we have a lot of planning to do to get started."

"Well," Amanda said, "I've got a big one for you, too."

D noted the sly smile.

"We have our public meeting tentatively scheduled for a week from tomorrow and I need to get that whole enchilada ready for public consumption … and it has to be great. When can we polish it up and get it finalized?"

Henry cautiously responded, "I should have something prelim by tomorrow afternoon. I'll call you around three-thirty and we can review it."

Amanda is feeling the pressure and panicking. She is way too far out in front of this.

"And not a minute later," she insisted.

D could not constrain his curiosity as they moved around the corner toward Henry's office.

"What was that all about? Unless I miss my very educated guess, there was a lot more than a meeting under consideration from her."

Henry tried to diffuse the question with nonchalance, "Oh, you know Amanda. She can make a ham sandwich seem mysterious and loaded with double meanings."

D was not so sure. "Henry, dammit, you be careful around her. I like working with you, and I don't want to see you incinerated when the barbarians burn the city."

Henry said thoughtfully, "Point taken."

CHAPTER 30

Henry arrived home from a typical day at US&G feeling a need for a good craft brew. As he opened the fridge, his eyes fell on the last bottle of a rich Oregon craft stout, and his taste buds imagined the heavy, chocolaty, black barley sensations as it rolled down his parched gullet. Decision made. The bottle was opened, and the first sip totally appreciated, when the phone rang. Thankfully, it was Harper.

She crooned, "Hey, when are you picking me up for our third date Saturday morning?"

Henry, demonstrating his quick learning capabilities, retorted, "You said we didn't have a hatch to match. What time would be best?"

Harper smiled over the phone at her pupil, "Actually, there is the green drake hatch at noon, but I would rather show you the wonderful world of streamers as we fish down to Parsons Point. The Blaine is full of small baitfish and the brown trout get real fat on them. If you fish a sculpin just right, you might net a three- or four-pound brownie before we get to PP and make a few casts for the giants."

Henry laughed, "Okay, how about ten o'clock? That way we can both be awake and on our game for the streamer lesson. Deal?"

"Deal," Harper agreed. "We'll have a bit of gear, so make sure you have the back seats of the SUV down so that we can pack it in without any risk to the rods. A good guide thinks of everything."

"Great, see you then."

As he left the phone and went to sit down on his sofa, Henry contemplated how to best cultivate Jack Morris. It seemed like a good possibility that Jack would like to meet D in a casual setting, perhaps beers after work, and Henry could certainly set that up. He was sure they would hit it off and build a comfortable relationship.

As for himself, he wasn't sure how to proceed. He had a natural in because of the car. And they could talk fishing. But maybe his best chance would come with Jack on the golf course. *Maybe a friendly challenge with a comfortable wager to spice it up?* That made a lot of sense, and Henry was quite confident that he could be at his best on any course that Jack might come up with. He probably was a member at one of the better clubs and might even enjoy having Henry as his guest … until Henry took his money.

The more he thought about it the better he liked the golf idea. Henry had played so much golf that he was always at his social best on the course. He was knowledgeable and proficient, always the proper guest, never an embarrassment. That would give him solid cred with Jack on the course and in the men's grill afterward.

No reason why he shouldn't have some fun while furthering the company cause. The idea of taking Jack's money, in a friendly game of course, brought a familiar smile to Henry's face. It was a smile he had not experienced since he was medalist in the conference championship in college.

The phone call to Jack was pleasant and Jack quickly

invited Henry for a game on Sunday at his club. He fell asleep with a warm glow of satisfaction. Sunday was going to be a fun day. But first, Saturday on the river fishing Parsons Point with Harper.

CHAPTER 31

After a quick cup of coffee to assure he was awake when he met Harper, Henry fired up the new ride and headed out on the fifteen-minute drive to Harper's house. When he pulled up in front, he was greeted by a galloping Rex who promptly jumped and slobbered all over Henry's face. Harper came to the door laughing and happy to have Henry at her home again. This time she had cooked breakfast so that they could get some nourishment before fishing the exciting part of the Blaine, Parsons Point. It was as good as Henry's breakfast, although not as elaborate. Harper felt less need to impress.

While they ate, Harper gave a summary of the day's planned fishing activities. They would start fishing at a nice, easily wadable point upstream of Parsons Point, about a mile and a half. There was plenty of parking and the brush had been cut back so Henry's new pride and joy would be in no danger of scratches. The water between there and Parsons Point consisted of riffles followed by curving pools with undercut banks across from the shallow inside of the curves. Easy to wade, and yielding lots of safe lies for big browns. It would take a little artful casting, mending, and drifting to get a fly in front of a fish—but, after all, that's what guides are for.

There were a few straight pools where the deepest part

was in the middle of the stream; but again, the wading made it straightforward to get a fly in the right place. Those they would fish from above and across, letting the weighted streamers swing with the current like a baitfish being pulled by the current. Usually at the tail end of the swing, a good sculpin would interest a trout and there would be a twitch in the line. These were difficult to see or feel for the novice, so Harper told Henry they would rig "strike indicators" (bobbers) so that he could more readily see the takes from the holding fish. Not a normal thing to do with streamers, but as a teaching device, quite valuable.

Harper had decided not to rig double-fly set-ups with an indicator-type dry fly on the surface. She wanted to concentrate completely on getting the sculpin imitations in front of hungry fish without dry imitations to distract them. Probably not a big deal, but she had made up her mind that Henry would not be distracted and would learn how to make good big loop casts with the streamers and not have to worry about getting his dropper tangled. This was advanced course stuff.

Professor Harper explained as she set up the rods and leader rigs for the day. "We are going to use seven-weight lines, weight-forward taper, to help get the heavier flies to cast in the wind. Make lots of shorter casts, and save the long ones and the double hauls for when the wind demands it, or when you can't get close enough to make the controlled short cast. The main thing we need to concentrate on is the mend and the drift. And by the way, the drift is not the same as a dry fly. It is not a matter of getting the fly to move at exactly the same pace as the water. We want these flies to look like they are swimming, not floating: these 'flies' imitate baitfish, not insects."

She continued, "You notice there is no split shot on

these lines. The flies are tied with lead wire around the hook shank, and so the weight is integral to the fly itself. We want the line and leader to be rather straight in the water. We swim these flies to the fish. And when you get a take, it is not just a gentle lift of the rod tip. But it is not like setting the hook on a bass, either. It is a firm raise of the tip, and then maintaining pressure on the fish with a tight line while you try to move it toward a bank. You'll have a leader with eight to ten pounds of strength, and the tippet will be four to five pounds—just enough strength that you can "horse" most fish, but will have to be artful if you get a big one."

Henry's head was swimming like the streamers. That was a lot for him to digest, but as Harper had said, *that's what guides are for.*

They waded into the river at a shallow rocky beach on the inside of a bend, the water just over their boot tops. Harper took the lead to demonstrate before subjecting Henry to the trial by fire. She waded down a few steps, false cast out some line, and threw a big wide loop with the weighted streamer coming close to her ear (not a recommended technique), and settling on the other side of the stream. She immediately made an upstream mend to get the fly well ahead of the trailing line, and Henry could actually see where the fly was by virtue of the bright orange strike indicator. The indicator continued to drift close to the bank which was undercut on the outside of the bend, then it disappeared close to a rock that stuck out of the water. Harper's rod came up firmly and she pulled the line that was off the reel to tighten it all the way to the fly.

Two seconds, and a bright rainbow leapt from the water about four feet. Henry was gobsmacked. It was magnificent, an emotional experience as well as physical. In about a minute and a half, Harper had the fifteen-inch 'bow in her net, the sculpin lodged squarely in the corner of its mouth. Harper lifted the net, but did not take it out of the water, and she kept her hand on the bottom of the net without touching the trout. The fly was gently removed from the fish's mouth, and then Harper lowered the net, allowing the fish to swim free.

Henry did not fully comprehend what he had just seen. He had caught fish with Harper before, but had not paid attention to what happened after Harper netted the fish and then released it. He had been too caught up in the euphoria of just having caught a fish on a hook with feathers and hair tied on it. Now he began to see that there was a logic and a method to this art that he wanted to understand.

"Harper, "he cautiously inquired, "There's more going on here than I had realized. Educate me as to why you handled the fish the way you did, and what benefits come out of all that trouble."

"Thought you'd never ask," she smiled. "Fly-fishing is not just a way to catch fish; it is a way to treat the outdoors, the fish, the streams, and other people, with care and concern. Admittedly, it is done for pleasure and not so much for altruism. But the pursuit of this particular pleasure demands a bit of altruism to be successful. Where do you want me to start?"

"Start with landing the fish. Why so careful and never touching the fish, and getting it out of the net so quickly? Shouldn't we have taken a picture or something? The bass guys insist on that ritual as homage to their manhood."

Patiently Harper explained, "The fish are coated with a slime that is protective for them. If you touch them with dry hands, you remove the slime, and it is not healthy for them. So, I try to just do the handling with the net whenever possible. And by the way, the net is special material that does not put undue pressure on the fish; it is soft and pliable so as not to get caught on a gill plate and damage the fish's ability to breathe."

She continued, "And you noticed that the fly was in the corner of the fish's mouth? That comes from a proper hookset. Since the hook is barbless, it comes out easily. It comes out easily from humans too, in case the fly catches a person on the way to the water. Barbless is good. Releasing the fish quickly is to prevent damaging the slime or mishandling the fish in some detrimental way. It's all about taking care of the resource. And it is all selfish, because I like to catch wild trout. And if I want the trout to make more wild trouts, I have to care for them and assure that they live to fight and breed another day."

"It's really simple, huh?" said Henry. "If you want to have wild trout in the future, take care of them in the present."

"Yes, and that also goes for protecting habitat so they have places to hide and ambush food. And the food has to be cared for too, like these little baitfish we are imitating today. It means making sure the water is clean so they can grow and reach a mature, healthy size and strength, and making sure the trout don't get overfished. So, catch limits, slot size limits, and sometimes closed seasons. It's all important."

Henry was getting a vision of how this ecologic system actually worked, and how far reaching its requirements and impacts were. *It was all obvious*, he supposed, *if one had ever taken the time to really think about it*. Harper clearly had. She deserved a lot of respect for that, especially since she was a bug person. She had started at the minute level and built her understanding up to the top of the food chain. *A woman and outdoorsman commanding respect.*

They moved down to the next pool. (Harper had said, "Don't over fish the pool. Give it a rest and then maybe catch it later in the day if you think there is a bigger fish, or if there is a hatch."

This situation was a bit different. The stream was relatively straight here, and the deep spots were in the middle of the streamflow. Harper cast about two-thirds of the way down, threw a downstream mend, and let the fly swing into the heart of the tail end of the pool. Nothing. Rather than pick up and make a new cast, she twitched the tip of her rod, jigging the fly and pulling it toward her slightly. The strike indicator disappeared but no fish came up out of the water when she raised the rod tip. So, she let the fly drift back to the tail of the pool.

Then she did something else that amazed Henry.

Rather than pick the fly up and make false casts to work out line, she just picked the line up when the rod tip bent and allowed the fly to recoil back behind her, just like a back cast, but with no casting motion in her arm. When she felt the rod load behind her, she pushed it aggressively forward, dropping her elbow slightly to widen the loop. The sculpin fell into the water before the line touched the surface and began its drift. This time when the indicator disappeared below the surface and Harper set the hook, a strong, scrappy brown trout showed just under the surface. It ran and tugged rather than leaping dramatically, but there was no doubt that a very hearty fish was on the line.

The fight took longer than before, and when Harper brought the fish to net, it measured nineteen inches. She guessed that it weighed between three and three-and-a-half pounds. Again, she worked very hard to avoid touching the fish. But it became obvious that the brownie was not going to let her win without picking it up to release the fly. So, she put her hands in the water and grabbed the trout gently behind the gills, lifting it up and carefully removing the hook. Harper was wet from the splashing and Henry thought he noticed that, under her wet guide shirt, she wore no bra. Smiling, he cautioned himself to focus on the fish.

Professor Harper returned, "If you do have to touch the fish, if it is unavoidable, wet your hands first. It protects the slime. Then pick the fish up around its body gently so as not to squeeze it too hard. Get the fly out quickly, and then let the fish go, facing upstream into the current, so the water moves across its gills faster and provides more reoxygenation."

Henry thought, this fly-fishing stuff has a lot of depth. It's not just another way to catch fish. And Harper gets it.

As they approached the next pool downstream, Harper turned it over to Henry. "Okay, Hoss, your turn. Tell me what you see, and how you are going to fish this pool."

Henry considered his options, wanting very much to impress Harper with his learning capacity. "I see two things. I see depth in the middle and along that undercut bank. I think both could hold fish and can be fished without overfishing the pool. So, I am going to fish the near portion first. There is a foam seam at the top of the pool that disappears about half way down, so I am going to swim a fly down that foam seam, let it swing to the middle and see what might be there."

"Very astute for a rookie. Fire away, and let's see what happens," she advised.

Henry made a short cast to the foam line and let out

line to let the sculpin swim down the side of the pool. About fifteen feet down the side of the pool the indicator disappeared and Henry raised the tip. The line straightened, but Henry could feel no real resistance or tug on the line. Faithfully however, he stripped line in, and in a matter of seconds, he had a juvenile brown trout of about ten inches flopping in the net. He released it as Harper had instructed him, taking care of the young fish, and was rewarded with a big smile from the professor.

He took a step downstream to better prepare himself for the next cast and tried further over the pool to the opposite side. Throwing the upstream mend, he let the fly drift into the undercut and toward the bottom of the pool. No take. But at the bottom of the pool where the stream came out of the undercut, the indicator disappeared violently. Henry was surprised but remembered to set the hook firmly, but not viciously, and began stripping to tighten the line. He realized that stripping was not going to be a good way to fight this fish, so he got to the reel to get the excess line taken up. His rod tip bent precariously. He knew he had something bigger than he had ever even seen, and was very glad Harper was there to help him.

The fish was running all over the pool and required Henry to follow it, moving several times. Henry actually sensed that the fish might be too much for even the relatively strong leader-tippet combination, and Harper cautioned him to let the fish run at times, keeping side pressure on it by holding his rod to the side. That would encourage the fish to move the direction Henry wanted it to rather than move where the fish wanted to.

This give and take lasted a good ten minutes. Henry had no idea that a fish could fight that long, but this one sure did. Slowly the tide was turning, and Henry was gaining control over the big brown. He could see it as a shadow in the water, and it was moving slowly in his direction. Harper was getting excited.

"Don't horse him too much!" she shouted. "He will break you off. Just try to be patient and gently tease him toward the net. I'll help with that; you need both hands to fight this fish."

Ever so slowly the fish was giving in and coming to the net in Harper's hand, agonizingly slowly. It was in shallow water now, shallow enough that Harper yelled, "That fish is at least six pounds. You have got a monster, Henry!"

Henry smiled and continued his careful pressure with the rod, pulling the fish to the net. He could see Harper prepared to net the fish when it got close. As the fish came closer, Henry kept reeling slowly to gain line and the fish reluctantly followed. Harper gently extended the net … and the movement spooked the big trout. It raised up exposing half its body, tossed its head to the side, and Henry's line went limp as the fly sailed past his head. The trout swam away calmly, just another day in the life of the king of the pool.

Harper almost cried. Henry almost cried. Then they laughed out loud for ten minutes. Henry's adrenaline was flowing at a supercharged pace, and he experienced a clarity he had never felt in his life. Harper came close, hugged him, and then kissed him passionately. "You did everything right," she said. "Sometimes at the net, they just get away. You just passed into fishing manhood. That was a magnificent fish, and you fought him as well as anyone could. You should be proud."

He was proud, but he was even prouder of the bond that was building with Harper, especially that kiss. *Who knew that fly-fishing carried such possibilities?*

Exhausted, they decided to walk downstream to Parsons. It was about a half mile, and easy walking. They walked close together, rods in outside hands. Inside hands were holding each other in a very natural, comfortable way of two people who shared a history of special moments. There was not a lot of conversation.

CHAPTER 32

As they approached Parsons Point, it was clear they had it to themselves. No one was in sight. That would allow them to fish leisurely and explore all that the point offered. It was not an easy place to fish, and Harper secretly celebrated that she would be able to fish, and teach Henry to fish the Point, at her own speed.

"Let's sit down over there on that log and take a look at what we have here. This is a lot to take in at once. Lots of opportunities and lots of unique situations that demand some attention before jumping in the water." The professor was in full analysis and instruction mode. "Tell me what you see."

Henry looked around. "I see slow currents back there to the left where the river enters this little bay. And swift currents a bit farther out where the river is in its main flow. It's shallow here on this point but the water gets darker about twenty-five yards out; I suspect that means that there is a drop-off and it gets deep. Lots of vegetation back in the slow bays. That means lots of insects, frogs, probably some freshwater shrimp, and lots of baitfish. The main river looks pretty clean; I suspect some nice mayfly hatches and (showing off his research into fly-fishing) caddis in season. Movement in the river tells me that the bottom is uneven and could be hard to fish deep because you just don't know where your fly is unless you pay very close attention. How'd I do?"

Harper smiled again—that radiant, "I'm happy" smile. "Very well. You missed a couple of important details, though. You correctly identified the drop-off, but I hope you realize how dangerous it could be. It drops straight down, and if you slipped while wading near it, you could be swept into water that is way over your head. If you are wearing waders, they could fill with water and you are a goner. So be super aware of that drop-off, always. Second point, the main flow can be fished from a boat, and you're correct it is tough because of the uneven bottom. But as attractive as it looks, the best fish are not out there. The current requires too much energy for the fish to hold in place. The best and biggest fish are right out here about five yards over where the currents converge and then diverge. Those currents bring a lot of trout food to the waiting mouths of big trout who choose to hang out in a small twenty-five-square-foot area. This is the heart of Parsons Point. "

Henry nodded dutifully, and Harper continued, "But it is important that everything else you saw contributes to the fish-holding capacity of this small area. That slow water generates lots of insect life, much of which drifts into the holding area. There are lots of scuds in that vegetation and they drift into the holding area. Getting the pattern?

"That's why Dorffman spent so much time on the special cast that Grandad used to get a fly into the small place where the big'uns hide. The upstream mend is to get the fly in front of the line, and the downstream mend is to get the fly swimming across the current so that it looks like food. And the timing is essential so that the fly gets down to the best holding lies."

Henry felt the light go on. "I am now understanding all that stuff that I thought was mumbo jumbo. It all has a purpose."

Harper nodded, "Pretty much like everything else. There's always a cause and effect."

"Now, watch and learn, Rookie. I think our best chance is with the rig we have been fishing, the number six sculpin with an indicator. No need to make it more complicated."

She got up from the log and walked to the edge of the river at the precise edge of Parsons Point. Carefully, she stepped into the slow current and moved gingerly over the mossy rocks to the famous point, about twenty-five feet out on the ledge. A short cast upstream, upstream mend, then the downstream mend, and then the wait for the completion of the drift. When the line was even with her in the water, she picked up and cast again. This time there was a little tic on the indicator just before the line drew even, but no substantial take. Clearly disappointed, she cast a third time. No take. And a fourth, and a fifth.

Harper glanced at Henry with a quizzical look and said, "So much for the legend of the invincible guide. Sometimes they just don't bite."

Henry teased her, "Yeah, looks like your success metrics will be in thousandths of a point at this rate."

She stuck out her tongue playfully and continued casting. On about the sixteenth cast, she got a big movement of the indicator, but no fish when she lifted the rod tip. "Okay," she said, "five more casts and it's yours." After five casts, she retired to the bank, defeated but beaming.

As Henry stepped into the stream, Harper tossed him something from her wading belt. It was a bunch of aluminum tubes held together by a Velcro strap. She told him to take off the cord and hold the tubes in his right hand at shoulder height. He did so, and, aided by an internal bungee cord, the tubes magically jumped into an aluminum stick about five feet long that was rigid enough to lean on.

Professor Harper instructed, "What you have there is a wading staff. Use it as a third leg and you can help yourself stay upright if your feet slip some on the rocks. Remember high school geometry, three points define a plane? That's the idea."

Henry liked the idea of some added stability, and he used the staff as a feeler to reach out in front and test the footing going forward. That helped his confidence, although he seemed in no danger of falling on the small-rock bottom. He unstrung his rod and prepared to cast as he reached the magic spot.

Looking upstream, he envisioned the place where he saw Harper's fly fall into the water, and decided to cast a bit farther upstream to give his fly some time to sink, and to give him some time to execute the tricky mends to position the sinking fly properly. He cast, waited a few seconds, upstream, waited a few seconds, downstream, then let it swim for a few seconds. As the line drew even with him, it suddenly straightened, but nothing else happened. There was no movement. Henry thought he was hung up on a rock or a log.

Harper screamed at the top of her voice, "Set the hook, Rookie!" And he did. Firm raise of the rod tip, and stripping quickly to get the excess line tight with the fly, wherever it was. And he waited for something to happen. He raised the tip again and, suddenly, the top of the water exploded with spray flying every direction. Henry was looking up at a huge rainbow trout, at least two feet over his head, its beautiful colors flashing in the afternoon sun and shadow mixture. It was humbling, exciting, scary, and totally marvelous at once.

Harper ran to the edge of the water with a net, and Henry tried to wade to her. She was leaning into the river but not jumping into the water—too many fishermen spoil the landing. Henry was hanging on for dear life, and remembering what happened just a little while earlier when he lost the big brown. He was surprised at how patient he had become as the giant rainbow began jumping. He applied sideways pressure to move the fish gently, and Harper was yelling encouragement as the fish neared the net. The bow didn't feel as strong as the big brown, but it was more athletic, jumping and wriggling all over the water surface. Henry focused on moving the fish to Harper, then he saw Harper extend her arms with the net in her hands … and the fish was in the net. Harper raised the net to keep the fish from jumping out and they both admired their trophy.

Harper admitted, "This one is worth a picture. It'll run seven pounds at least. I bet it measures twenty-seven inches." As Henry held the net carefully, Harper took a snap with her small guide special camera. They lowered the net and the fish back into the water, and it swam away gleefully. Both fisherpeople just smiled and laughed … a lot. "You deserve a huge reward," Harper joked.

"What did you have in mind?" Henry asked coyly.

"I don't know right now," she said, "but I bet I can figure it out by the time we finish a good Italian dinner with some quantity of cheap Chianti."

"Deal," agreed Henry, and they began the stroll back to the car to get out of their fishing gear and ready for dinner. Holding hands again (a delightful habit developing here), they walked in very knowing silence.

When they got to the car, Harper spoke, "You know, you are something special. I have never seen anybody take to this sport like you have. You have an instinct, and you learn quickly. You're just a natural."

"You can use my picture in your ads if you like," said Henry, "and I won't even charge you. It'll play well in the local stats nerd market."

They left for Ralph's Italian, now "their" place, and hoped Ralph had something interesting for a special tonight. Ralph did not disappoint. He led them to the usual table and immediately suggested the "knife and fork special" dinner pizza. Handmade dough, pepperoncini, sausage, peppers, mushrooms, olives, onions, four cheeses, and diced tomatoes. He guaranteed they could not eat it all, and it came with a bottle of inexpensive Chianti—countryside wine without vintage, but full and flavorful. They agreed.

As they sipped the first glass of Chianti, Harper mentioned that she had only ever seen eight fish caught at the Point. One each by her grandfather and Bob Dorffman, two by her, and four by clients of hers, one of whom sold Henry his car. And Henry's was probably the fourth biggest, but that didn't count because it was a rainbow and therefore easier to catch than the elusive brown trout that sulked deep at the edge of the ledge. She was still basking in her own amazement at Henry's success and his astonishingly solid skills. He actually seemed to know what he was doing.

Henry was still high from the thrilling fight with the big rainbow, but he was slowly being overtaken by another strange feeling that he could not recognize. This time, over dinner with Harper, was even more important to him than the wonder of the fish catch. He absolutely glowed in being with her, and seeing her in her element.

What the hell is that all about? Just one completely new experience after another.

Conversation at dinner was light and easy. Truth was, they were both high from the excitement of the day, and from the long strolls holding hands. Both knew that something was changing in their lives. And they were going with it, joyfully. Totally new for Henry, thought lost forever by Harper. It had only been what, three weeks? four? since Harper had crushed his ankle on the trail. Well, maybe not crushed—but she had run him over. Not that it mattered one bit.

For her part, Harper quickly figured out that she was probably the more experienced of the two at matters of intimacy, and chuckled a bit at Henry's almost total lack of attention to those matters. But that probably made him a better partner in the long run, because it would be important to him to make intimacy work well. He had no idea that a disguised form of it might be available from a lot of women who had no better understanding of true intimacy than Henry.

As they filled up on pizza and Chianti, they both relaxed into a comfortable state of inaction that discouraged movement. When Ralph came to the table to ask if they needed anything else, they both picked up on the fact that they were the last customers and Ralph needed to close. They thanked him profusely and apologized for keeping him so late, and happily shuffled out to the car. Henry was sober enough to drive but Harper was a bit nervous that the local constabulary might not agree. They arrived at her home safely and she invited him in.

Rex greeted them with his customary enthusiasm, and they responded accordingly. Harper disappeared for a moment, and returned with two glasses of the same small batch bourbon they had enjoyed last time at her place. Henry accepted his and said, "Hey, we may have had enough already. And I still have to get home."

Harper smiled slyly, curled up under Henry's outstretched arm and cooed, "You know, you don't really have to go home tonight."

Lightning struck Henry right between the eyes ... and perhaps some other places. Oops. Life changing experience about to happen. Even though he did not expect this, and he didn't know how to best respond, he let it go, and kissed Harper fully and deeply. *Wow. Did that feel great!*

And just like the fish on the sculpin today, he was hooked. But then, so was she.

It was sinking in that this was serious. Henry was not inexperienced in the physical aspects of an intimate relationship, but he had never identified the emotional component of true intimacy. The realization came as a shock. Neither his mother, nor university, nor work had prepared him for the profound sense of calm, care, and tenderness which pervaded his senses right now.

They sat in comfort with each other, and mostly silence, until they finished sipping their bourbons. Then Harper rose and took Henry's hand, leading him to her bedroom.

The sensations of gently undressing each other, without hesitation or inhibition, startled Henry. He had no idea it could be so natural, so open, and honest. It wasn't a game played for one-upmanship—just a kind, slightly lustful way to make a statement of sincerity to the other person. It comprised an expression of vulnerability and trust unmatched by any words. Mutual consent—even mutual enthusiasm and mutual respect—dominated the process. Even though there were no performance metrics to be imposed, Henry was not intimidated. He felt at ease. Harper clearly was in the moment.

When their bodies pressed against each other, they simply molded to the available shape, and laid down in Harper's bed. The rest of the night was an exciting—though unfamiliar to Henry—and tender mixture of urgency, tranquility, and wonder. It seemed to continue unending until sunlight pierced the curtains the next morning. Both awoke smiling and happy. Harper rose to go make some coffee and Henry remained, his euphoria taking over and propelling him to a level of awareness previously unknown, and certainly unexperienced.

After coffee and affectionate goodbyes, as Henry left to meet Jack Morris for golf later at Jack's club, he became aware of a foreboding sense of impending conflict—which he would have to deal with when Harper found out about his professional interest in Parsons Point. The foreboding turned to dread, and he knew deeply that the piper would have to be paid. This conflict would not go away until Henry made perhaps the most important decision of his young, and, so far, uneventful life.

He was going to have to make some grownup decisions very soon. And it was not clear to him how Harper would respond.

CHAPTER 33

When Henry had talked to Jack about a round of golf, Jack had been a bit surprised. Although he could certainly justify golf with a customer who had just written a check for a very expensive purchase, he ordinarily did not do that. He had talked with Mo to get some insight, and Mo had enthusiastically endorsed Henry as a golf partner, and even suggested that he might soon be a member at Jack's club, the historic Cottonwood Springs Club.

Cottonwood, while not in the U.S. Open rota, had some history in the game. Fleck and Hogan had played an exhibition there in '56 after Fleck had taken the Open in a playoff at Olympic from "the wee ice mon" in '55. It had been epic, since Hogan was determined not to let the Olympic experience repeat itself on him. Hogan had holed a twenty-foot birdie on the eighteenth to win, one up, and the legends had begun to circulate in the club—and, naturally, grow over the years. Whenever Cottonwood had hosted a regional qualifier for the Open, the stories always came out about the exhibition and the fierceness that Hogan displayed. Cottonwood wore the stories as a badge of honor and a claim to historical significance in the game.

Henry was aware of the course history and the club

pride. He was flattered and honored to be Jack's guest on such a venue. He always played good courses, but playing a historic course was icing on a very tasty cake. He was looking forward to testing Jack's skills, as his guest, even though he was having a bit of concentration trouble, given the events of yesterday and last night with Harper.

He pulled into the parking lot and dropped his clubs at the attendant's kiosk. After parking in the guest spots, he entered the club and asked for Jack. Jack had arranged a locker for Henry to leave his street shoes and have a place to change if needed after the round. A shower and sauna might be welcomed. Surprised and pleased, Henry used the locker to change his shoes and went looking for Jack in the grill.

Jack greeted Henry warmly and offered a Danish and coffee to get the day started. They were both delicious. As Henry and Jack chatted, two other men walked up to their table and joined them. Jack introduced them as the remainder of the foursome today, and suggested a "friendly" game with Henry and himself as partners against the two of them. Knowing that Jack was an eight handicap, the two gentlemen immediately began to tease Jack that Henry would have to be a twenty to make a competitive team due to the difference in team handicaps. Jack smiled and proudly proclaimed, "No, he is a six." Henry gulped. (His last official handicap was four, but he had no idea if he could actually play to even the six.) He sensed a big money game with strangers, and he was not carrying a lot of cash with him, and he knew nothing about this course or these men.

Jack further offered that they play "Cottonwood Candy"—a club favorite format in which the two teams played eighteen holes, properly handicapped, in Ryder Cup combined format. That meant front nine in Foursomes (alternate shot), and back nine in Fourball (best ball). The handicapping consisted of adding the team members' handicaps to a total and then dividing the difference of the team totals by two. The higher team would get that many strokes spread over the most difficult holes. The difference between the team total handicaps was twelve, so Jack and Henry had to give their opponents six strokes—one each on the six hardest ranked holes. CCC had five really difficult holes and one not as difficult, where a one-stroke advantage could mean money at the end of the day.

This would be a challenging match, and Henry had no idea how he might make a contribution to a good team effort. As a matter of fact, Jack had quite surprised him with the offer to partner. *No pressure, huh?* Henry was reminded of Lee Trevino's famous opinion that pressure was playing for five dollars a hole when you only have two dollars in your pocket. Then, Jack proposed that they play a fifty-dollar Nassau. Fifty on the front nine, fifty on the back, and fifty for the match total. Henry realized that he had forty-five dollars on him, and immediately felt a kinship with Trevino.

As they walked to the first tee, Jack explained that the CCC layout allowed them to make some strategic decisions. If they chose for Henry to tee off first, that would position Jack to be making the tee shots on most of the par threes, and that was a strength of his game. Most of those holes did not fall into the seven stroke holes in the match today. With Jack's iron play and, hopefully, Henry's putting, they would have an advantage. It would also help that Henry would be positioned to boom the ball on the par fives and intimidate the opponents slightly.

The first hole was such a par five—561 yards, straight

away, with minimal fairway bunkers and a well-trapped green. Naturally, the pin was tucked in behind the trap on the right, making for a nervous second or third shot, depending on where it came from and who was hitting it.

Henry, as the guest, was awarded honors and teed first. He did not disappoint.

He and Jack had decided to play a tour model ball since it was one they were both comfortable with. Henry would have preferred to play his old life long favorite, but they were becoming harder and harder to find, so he had begun playing the tour models and was happy with them. The lower trajectory and slightly lower spin rate allowed him to hit shots that bored into the wind while still giving sufficient distance control to hit a variety of scoring shots inside seventy-five yards. Jack liked the Pro V1 because a lot of pros played it, and he wanted to play the same gear.

As Henry teed up, he was aware that they probably could not reach in two, so he decided to position Jack for a second shot that would not be threatening, and allow him to position Henry for a solid wedge for the third and most vital scoring shot. He made a good swing that started the ball slightly to the right, then drew it back slightly to the left-middle of the fairway. It looked to be about 260 yards. Not at all one of his longest, but a good opener. The opponents were impressed, but not overly. Their lead guy hit his drive about 245 on the right side of the short grass.

As they rode to the ball, Jack said, "Well done. Positions me perfectly to get you in position for us to score." Henry was pleasantly surprised to see that Jack understood exactly what had to happen. *Maybe he had underestimated Jack.*

He answered, "Right. What are you going to hit?"

Jack said, confidently, "I don't want to hit 3 wood. Not enough reward for the added risk. I'll play a hybrid and that should leave you an easy wedge pitch to the hole. If you can get it to five feet or less, I guarantee us a birdie."

Henry liked this confidence. It seemed real and not just bluster.

True to his word, Jack spanked a hybrid about 220 and left Henry eighty to the hole. "Nice work, well played. Just like you said."

Their opponents had mishit their second, left a 120 approach to the hole, right in between a wedge and a nine iron for them. The nine was bladed and flew over the green to lie three.

Henry confidently took his sixty-degree wedge and hit an almost full shot to four feet right of the hole, as good as one could ask. The opponents pitched back to the hole for their fourth and left a downhill six-footer for par. No strokes on this hole, number nine on the handicap ranking. They missed the six-footer, but Henry and Jack conceded the one-foot remaining putt for a six.

Now it was Jack's turn to deliver. He had promised a birdie. They both looked at the putt and it was not slippery, nor did it break a lot, but it was four feet, an easy distance to pull or mishit. Jack stepped up and with seemingly too little preparation stroked the ball into the middle of the hole as promised. Jack and Henry one up after one.

As they walked off the green Jack asked, "Feeling better about that Nassau now?" Henry just smiled.

Play continued in that vein on the front nine, with Jack and Henry demonstrating considerably more competence than the opposition. But because of the two strokes awarded by handicap on the front, Jack and Henry were only three up at the turn. Jack cautioned Henry that the rules of "Cottonwood Candy" allowed press bets at the conclusion of nine. The Cottonwood press added a new bet for the remaining nine holes at the same amount as the original bet. That would not have bothered Henry, given the obvious difference in the quality of the two teams' game, but those guys got four strokes on the back side. They didn't have to be better; they could just get a little lucky and turn the money around, big-time.

If Henry and Jack won the backside, then they won twice the original bet. If they lost the backside, but by less margin than their three up at the turn, then they would win a hundred bucks. If they lost big, they could lose the back and the match and would be out one-fifty. Trevino's comment was running around in Henry's head again. Jack just smiled.

A quick beer at the turn, and they were off to the tenth tee. Jack goaded his buddies, "You guys up for the Cottonwood press?"

A semi-surly response came back, "What, Jack, you bring a ringer into the club and want to double the bet? We get four on this side you know."

Jack smiled, "I know, just wanted to give you a fightin' chance to walk away with your wallets, if not your dignity, intact." Everybody laughed politely, but the tension was noticeable.

"Sure, why not?" they responded. "Let's make this interesting and put a little pressure on the good players."

Jack was still smiling. Henry was apprehensive. He felt a little like the ringers might be on the other team, and he was being sucked into a trap bet. Jack assured him not to worry.

Since it was still Jack and Henry's honor, Jack hit the tee shot on ten—a dogleg left par four and a stroke hole. Position off the tee was critical as the pin was on the left side of the green, close to a bend in a small creek that intimidated most players, even the good ones. The tee shot had to be on the right side of the fairway so that the second did not have to come in across the bunker, and there would be a little bail-out room to the right, but still on the green. Jack hit the ball in the perfect position. Since the game had changed to best ball at the turn, Henry could "let out the shaft" and crush one to see if he could get very close to the green. And he did. A birdie by either Jack or Henry seemed inevitable.

Properly intimidated, the opponents both pulled their tee shots down the left side. As a result, they were both blocked from an attacking second shot and had to lay up out to the right of the green. Two shots, and not yet putting.

Jack made a passable good shot to the green about thirty feet to the right, probably a good two-putt for par. Henry, with only about fifty yards to the middle of the green, played a very aggressive lob wedge behind the hole, and it backed up to eight feet. The putt was a little downhill and slick, but not unmanageable.

The other team had mixed results. One shot was completely useless, rolling over the green and into Cottonwood Creek. He was out of the hole, effectively. The other shot found the green, but eighty-five feet from the hole. If he could two-putt, then, with a stroke, they could win or tie. He putted first and rolled the ball up to four feet below the hole.

Jack putted next and slid his ball downhill to one foot. The par was conceded. Henry could now secure the win with a natural birdie, but the putt was tricky. Downhill, down-grain, with a slight bend to the right about nine inches out from the hole. It would take a steady nerve and a smooth stroke to get the ball rolling right and have a chance.

Pace was everything here. Henry's college coach appeared in front of his eyes: "Good putting is a combination of line and speed. The line is easy. Pay attention to the speed above all else." Henry backed off to look at the break once more, and then stepped to the ball—taking a deep breath, and holding it to minimize body movement. A smooth stroke that felt good … but looked like the ball was going to be a bit too high. Then the right leaning grain grabbed it and turned the ball back toward the hole. A solid rattle, rattle as the ball fell to the bottom of the cup. A big cheer from Jack, a moan from the other team, and Henry and Jack were up four with eight to play, having already assured fifty dollars for the front. A good day in the making.

Play continued without much drama, and Henry and Jack walked onto the seventeenth tee—up four on the match, up three on the front, and up one with two to go on the back. A potential two-hundred-and-fifty-dollar payoff for their team. The hole was a drivable par four but surrounded by loads of trouble. Bunkers both left and right in front with a narrow neck to get a drive through. The creek on the right of the green, and a pond on the left. There was a bunker in the center of the fairway that was more a visual hazard than a real one—at least for a strong player—but the hole demanded a combination of precision and power that eluded most golfers.

Jack teed a shot up the middle, short but reliable. He could easily play onto the green and probably make birdie. So, Henry's job became to go for the clincher. Drive the green and make eagle, a gutty strategy, but it could end the match and the press in Henry's and Jack's favor—a very profitable day.

Henry counted to ten, breathed slowly, visualized a slight draw landing between the two bunkers, and stepped up to the ball. A solid swing, not his fiercest, yielded exactly the shot he had visualized, and the ball rolled onto the green fifteen feet away from total victory.

The opponents both hit good shots in the middle of the fairway but short of the green. Easy pars, most likely, but Henry and Jack would, at worst, go to the eighteenth one up, with one to play on the back side. If Henry were a superstar, they could win everything outright.

Both opponents hit seconds to sixteen or eighteen feet. Jack played a short wedge to nine feet. The other team had not demonstrated any tendencies to make critical putts all day, and the tendency continued. They both two-putted, and that left it up to Henry and Jack. They elected to have Jack putt first with the idea that he could make birdie for the tie (the opponents had a stroke on this hole) and then Henry was free to go for the win with his eagle putt. If Jack missed, Henry could easily make birdie and they would halve the hole going to eighteen needing a halve or a win for the day.

Henry's putt was up hill, up grain, and the challenge would be to get it to the hole. He would have to hit it harder than the fast greens had suggested all day. Then there was the double break. It started to the right and came back to the left, and it was not clear where the directions changed. Henry took a long look and thought he had the picture. He needed controlled but precise aggression. It was not a scary putt, under ordinary circumstances, but there was money at stake here.

Henry moved into his stance, feeling like he knew the

line, and focused on the speed. His first feeling was that he had hit the ball too hard, but it was rolling on what he thought was the right line. At four feet from the hole, the ball caught the left turn and slowed down a bit. Now Henry wasn't sure the ball would reach the hole, but it kept moving. In the last six inches, Henry was sure the ball was short of the hole, but it kept moving. As it approached the lip of the cup, the ball appeared to stop turning, one half turn short of made. Henry let out a scream, which seemed to scare the ball into a final half turn, and it dropped into the cup.

Jack was jubilant. Henry was relieved. The opponents were amazed, and not in a good way.

Since the match was over, the eighteenth was drama free, and everyone adjourned to the bar for a celebratory or mournful drink. Checks and handshakes were exchanged and the opponents walked off into the rest of their day, while Jack and Henry ordered another drink.

Jack looked at Henry with a new respect, "Henry, that was a fabulous display of calm and cool under pressure. And I'm not talking about the money. You just did what needed to be done. Are you the same way at work? I see why Mo is so high on you. I think he even has eyes on you for Amanda. Tread carefully around that one."

Henry saw that Jack was a perceptive guy, "Yeah, I am treading carefully. Amanda is a very competent professional, and necessary to a lot of things we are doing at the firm. But she can be scary, just overpowering."

Jack laughed, "That's the way Mo raised her. But I have to tell you, I really enjoyed the golf today. I especially enjoyed taking those two to the cleaners. I can't tell you the amount of money they have won around this club because their handicaps are too high. They really know how to work that process. Like I always say, birdies are better than pars with strokes, and that's the way the game should be played. You did yourself proud today, son. Made me proud of my guest, too."

Henry blushed a little and quickly changed the subject, "What else do you do for fun, Jack? Mo tells me you are a real Renaissance guy."

"Oh, I play with my business. It's fun, but it is a clichéd trade. Been doing the same things for seventy-five years, and all the dealers think there is no other way to successfully sell automobiles. I like the personal dealing, like you and I had. I don't worry so much about the numbers when I can deal with someone I like and respect. And then I love to fish, fly-fish. It's the most absorbing thing I know. Impossible to think about troubles or worries when you are fly-fishing."

Henry took the bait, "I can agree on that. I am learning to fly-fish, and I am totally in love with it. Perfect combination of art and recreation. It is competitive, but not in the unhealthy way of team sports, and especially professional team sports."

Jack now picked up the drifting conversational fly, "If you're serious about fly-fishing, I should introduce you to a friend of mine. She is a guide and the best one I have ever known, but she is a very competent and interesting person as well. Long background in the sport, and a lot of formal education. Brilliant woman. Harper Philips. You should really get to know her."

Henry choked on his drink. The world was getting smaller by the day.

"Mo tells me that you are a big-time college basketball fan, too, Jack."

"Oh yeah. Nothing matches it for passion and athletic

action. I have been addicted to the game for decades. I see every big-time game I can. It's the best when everything's on the line, except maybe golf."

Henry countered, "In that case, I've got someone you should meet. How would you feel about a drink after work one day this coming week? This guy is someone you'll really enjoy."

"Sure, even tomorrow evening is good. Call the dealership and schedule with my assistant. I'll tell her to expect your call."

"By the way," said Henry, "I don't feel like I really deserve this money. Why don't you take this check and use it for the dealership Little League team? Get the kids some equipment they need, or throw them a big party. My contribution."

"Henry, that's really generous of you. As far as I am concerned, you earned every penny of this, but the kids will certainly love what it can do for the team. Thank you so much; you are a class guy."

As they left the men's bar, Henry felt that he had made a good new friend as well as advanced the interests of the firm. And the friend part seemed like the most important part of that, by far.

The developing friendship with Jack brought the developing relationship with Harper into sharp focus, Henry knew he was entering new territory, at least for him, and he reveled in the idea of having good friends and, perhaps, even a girlfriend.

Sorry, Mom, this actually feels good.

When he got home, he immediately reached for the phone to call Harper and tell her the story of his golf adventure. But when he dialed and there was no answer, Henry was overcome by another new feeling. He was disappointed that he couldn't talk with Harper, and he was just a bit curious (worried) that she might be with someone or something more interesting than him. That had certainly been his history with women.

Putting his primordial fears aside, he left a cheerful message so that Harper would know that he was not ignoring the significant events of the weekend between them, and hoping that she shared his growing feelings about pursuing a future.

CHAPTER 34

While Henry had spent an enjoyable weekend learning new skills, experiencing new sensations, and developing new friendships, in a dark warehouse several hundred miles away some sinister-looking characters were developing their own relationship. This one, however, was based on cold and rigid principles unencumbered by legalities. Some land was being bought and sold, and the terms and conditions under negotiation were heavily focused on the time and means of payment rather than the condition of the land.

The seller team was managed by a tough-looking but well-dressed thug named Granato. He fronted for a supporting cast of three equally tough-looking hoods dressed in black tactical fatigues and heavily armed with small submachine guns and sidearms that Henry had only read about in gun magazines, backed up by Americcan made 9mm military and police model side arms, hanging low in combat-style holsters.

The buyer, surprisingly unintimidated by this display of paramilitary force, was identified as Max Stendahl, a businessman from Kentucky with a track record of success in the horse racing and breeding business. Granato's team had thoroughly checked out Stehndal to assure that he was legitimate, at least in the meaning of that word in the dark circles in which they moved. His background was impeccable, again within the specific context.

Granato was responsible to his "corporate" bosses for selling the land for at least six-and-a-half million. That was the number they had identified in order to get a return on their fairly short-term investment and holding period. They provided Granato an incentive bonus—in addition to the ability to keep living—that he could keep anything over six and a half that he managed to get in a full, recorded closing, just as though the deal was real and conducted through clean channels. Granato was pushing for seven and a half, but since he knew things about the property that no one else knew—and which could affect its value dramatically—he was prepared to go down to seven. Half a mill "commission" for this piece of contaminated or potentially contaminated crap was a good deal for him and his boys.

Max was vague as to what his intended use of the land was, but he was firm on the seven million price, as he contended that the deal he was trying to pull off would not work if the land was too expensive. Max didn't know all the details of the land, but he suspected it was high-risk on ecological grounds and potential EPA problems if nothing else.

In truth, Max didn't really care about the actual economics of the land because he was acting in cooperation with a multi-agency government task force seeking a conviction of the leaders in Granato's organization for money laundering plus narcotics and illegal arms sales to powers hostile to the interests of the US.

The business practices of Max's own enterprise were not above reproach, but Max had been effectively cooperating with several government agencies since a change of conscience. His newly acquired ethics were inspired in large part by a potential fraud charge to which he had been introduced several years ago before he got into the racing and breeding business.

The FBI had graciously agreed to overlook the greater portion of his indiscretions in exchange for his help in closing the loop on Granato and friends.

Max and Granato sparred over the price, the closing date, who was authorized to conclude the arrangements, and who was authorized to actually make the transfer to facilitate final payment. The situation was quite tense—Uzis, Ingrahams, and Smiths notwithstanding—but Max negotiated confidently ... with more confidence than he actually felt.

Granato was intimidating and tough, but surprisingly skillful as well. The negotiations almost carried themselves out in an atmosphere of mere cutthroat business rather that mob-style extortion enforced by hitmen and guns.

After approximately twenty-nine minutes and fourteen seconds, the two men shook hands and the deal was agreed. Max didn't know how much a handshake was worth from such an individual as Granato, who Max knew would "eliminate" the last remaining scion of the Stendahl line immediately if it profited him to do so.

As they left, Granato and his guys slipped into the overstated comfort of a Maybach limo while Max got into his smaller but shinier orange Porsche 911. He unconsciously wiped perspiration from his only slightly furrowed brow and took a couple of deep breaths. He would really be glad when this operation concluded, as he intended to use it as leverage to gain his statement of satisfaction and release from the terms of cooperation with the government ... excepting of course the maintenance of his personal protection.

CHAPTER 35

Monday came all too quickly for Henry after the eventful weekend. Fishing with Harper, golf with Jack. Everything was a blur. And then there was after fishing with Harper. Henry still reeled from that one. He never thought he could be pulled into an emotional involvement like that. And then to have the serious and very predictable problems that would arise when he and Harper had to discuss his role in the Parsons Point project.

The terror of that confrontation was underscored when Henry arrived at the office. There was a message from Harper, left apparently while he was in transit to work. Harper was on her way out the door but sounded happy that Henry had called and promised that they would talk later when she was not working. Additional urgent messages from Hanna, D, and Amanda screamed for a callback and a conversation. Henry wondered what could be up that would involve all three and in such an immediate mode. There was only one possible answer.

Now he had to decide whether to call them back in chronological order, in the order of rank of the senders, or just according to his preference. He concluded that the latter would be the easiest to deal with. He would call D first, especially since he had a matter concerning Jack that involved D. And he would call Amanda last. He didn't know exactly why, but figured that Saturday night at Harper's house might have some influence on his feelings about that call.

D answered in something of a panic, at least as close to panic as Henry had ever seen or heard him.

"Have you talked to anybody yet?" D asked anxiously. "The brown stuff is about to be splattered all over."

"Fill me in." Henry replied.

"Mo called me direct this morning. Said he couldn't get hold of you yet and asked me to fill you in when you got to work. It seems the EPA has taken a hard line on any potential development of the land below the old mine, and especially where drainage into the Hattowoc and/or the Blaine is concerned. They are not saying no development, but they are imposing strict time limits on presenting the mitigation and prevention plans. It is not certain we can get them all done before Mo's option runs out.

"Mo got a note from Jack Morris late Friday informing him of the requirements. I guess Jack had been talking to a buddy of his at the agency and heard sort of off the record about the limits. The time the agency takes to review the proposed plans is the issue. They need a minimum of four months to review, possibly six. It will actually take about forty-five days to devise plans, since we plan to use the Montana model—that is, after we receive the necessary data. So, assume nine months total if we are lucky on the data."

Henry sipped his coffee and frowned, "So ten months at the very best. When does the option expire?"

D hesitated, "End of the year. So that leaves us eight-and-a-half months, nine at best."

Henry frowned again, "I have always been pretty good at math and those numbers do not make a solvable equation. We have eight-and-a-half months to solve a ten-month problem. What wiggle room do we have?"

"None that I can see," exhaled D.

"Interesting, but that leads us to why I wanted to see you today," said Henry. "Remember how Mo wanted us to develop a relationship with Jack? Well, he and I played golf yesterday. We took about $250 off a couple of sand-baggers who thought they had a sucker bet. Jack and I made a few shots and the 'baggers wrote checks. Jack was pretty pumped.

"Turns out that he is a huge college basketball fan. But he is also a decent guy. I thought it would be fun for the three of us to have drinks together and introduce you. He will certainly enjoy getting to know you and I think you might even enjoy him … if you don't mind playing the basketball card again. Whaddaya think?"

D smiled, "Yeah, I don't mind talking hoops to a true fan. Especially if he is a good business contact and might be able to help us with our project."

"Okay, I'll call him and see if we can have drinks to-night, since time appears to be of the essence, and we can make intros. Now get outta here and go build me a mod-el that says we can get all this done in the time we have. I'll let you know what Jack says about drinks."

"On it. Talk to you later."

Henry breathed a sort of sigh, indicating relief. He wasn't sure why. Next call was to Hanna. She appeared at his office door almost immediately after they hung up.

"So what crisis does my favorite finance guy bring to the machinery today?" he joked with Hanna.

"Not a crisis at all," she bantered. "But I did want to give you a heads up that no one else in the firm has been privy to."

She became serious but still smiled, "You know I have been feeling stagnant until I started working with you and this project. I now feel alive and valuable for the first time since I have been with this firm. This emergence has led me to believe that I can do better for myself as an independent than as a house finance donkey, and I plan to leave to start my own financial advisory company. I won't leave you high and dry on Parsons Point, since it will take me some time to make all the proper arrangements, and give the appropriate notices. But I will start the New Year as Melancon Advisory Services, LLC."

Henry's mixed reactions showed but he stifled them.

"Hanna, I think that is a wonderful plan. Let me know how I can help, confidentially or openly, however you need my help. You will do well, and I will be happy to reference you and send you potential clients. You have done a great job here, and you will be successful going forward. Congratulations, you have grown a lot in the time we have worked together. I'm proud to know you."

She blushed, "Thanks, Henry. You have been supportive, and that has helped me find my possibilities to pursue."

"Glad to help, Hanna."

As she turned to leave, Henry asked, "Does this have anything to do with Charles?"

Hanna stopped dead, turned around, and looked Henry straight in the eye with a very serious expression. "No," she proclaimed clearly. "I have found my own path here, and I am taking it. It makes sense for me."

Then a broad grin crossed her face, "But it will make it a lot easier to see if a relationship with him is going to be something that will make us both happy." She giggled as she left, confident of Henry's support in her choices.

Well, one blockbuster to go ... and he strode down the office three doors to Amanda's office. "You called?" he smiled.

Amanda responded pleasantly in kind, "Yes, we have some news that requires us to act fairly quickly. Jack talked with Dad late Friday and wants to have that public meeting this next week to explain Parsons Point, and start building some public enthusiasm for the project. We will be giving an overview of the plan and not actively seeking investors, so we don't have to meet regulatory requirements for investor disclosure, but the project has to look good. If we get the kind of response from the audience we need, the next step will be to get some legislators on our side to help with the burden of meeting the regulatory deadlines, and maybe getting some of the more onerous conditions softened. So, the team has to be in top form. There will be a presentation and Q & A, probably hour-and-a-half to two hours max. Can do?"

"No prob. What is the date?"

"Looks like a week from Wednesday. Can we have a run through on, say, Thursday of this week?"

Henry hesitated just the slightest, "Can do." And he went back to his office, resolving to get the team together ASAP to see where they really stood.

But first, he needed to call Jack about a meeting.

The dealership receptionist tried to take a message but Henry insisted, as a new owner of an expensive dealership offering, on speaking with the head guy. When Jack found out who was calling, he gladly took the call and greeted Henry cheerfully. "So, how's the best golf partner in the county this Monday morning?"

Henry chuckled, "Couldn't be better. And boy, have I got a proposition for you, the college basketball fan."

Jack perked up, "Yeah, How so?"

Henry followed on, "Did you ever hear of DeMarius Moffat?"

"Of course, one of the greatest finishes in MSG history. That Marquette win was one of the best ever. It ranks up there with the Kentucky-Duke game in the Elite Eight in '92."

"Well, Mr. Moffat is in our firm, and working closely with me on a major project. He has become a key guy for us, and I thought you might enjoy meeting him. How about a couple of good craft beers at the Riverbend Inn tonight, say six-thirty?"

Jack was nearly incredulous, "You mean *the* DeMarius Moffat? You're serious? I'd love to meet him. He is one of my all-time favorites, and he just disappeared after his junior year and the 'Nova game in the Big Dance."

"Yeah, said Henry, "There is a great story behind that. He is a class guy and loads of fun. You'll like him."

"See you at six-thirty."

Henry and Dr. D were in place at the Inn when Jack arrived, beaming. "Great to see you," he said. "Thanks for the invitation."

Henry shook his hand and introduced D.

Jack still beamed, "You are one of the greats in Big East History. It is a pleasure to meet you. And you don't even have to tell me any basketball stories. I am familiar with your career, and have always admired the intelligent and active way you played the game. But I am curious as to why you quit. You were clear first-round in the draft."

D explained his reasons, as he had told Henry and Mo, and Jack obviously respected the style and integrity of this young man. He had no idea that first-rounders had actual depth and values outside the game. His confidence in Henry, combined with his new confidence in D, gave him license to talk openly with them.

"You guys know that I am heavily involved with Parsons Point. My land is kind of key to the whole concept. And I have some concerns. The project, as I understand it, is a big one that will stretch resources in the firm and in the community. And it carries a high risk that could affect the landowner group members if anything were to happen down the road. I don't have a big argument with the project, but I do wonder if it is the best use of my land and the land belonging to the other owners. I talked with Mo Friday evening and voiced my concerns. He was surprised and a bit frantic. I know he wants to run for governor in a couple of years, and this project is to be his foundation for that campaign.

"So, I suggested that we measure the public reaction, and requested he put together a meeting for all interested parties. He tells me he had one planned but will move it back a bit and broaden it so that we can have a full discussion and do some kind of survey to see where we stand. I think that is the right thing to do, but I still have deep concerns. And I may want to talk with you guys to work through them and to get my opinions and feelings into consideration. I hope that doesn't put too much pressure on the two of you. Mo thinks the world of both of you, and I think he will listen to what you have to say."

Henry and D glanced at each other, thinking the same thing. *No pressure here, huh?*

But this is the relationship that Mo had wanted them to build.

"Sure Jack. Glad to help," Henry said.

CHAPTER 36

On Tuesday morning Henry joined the team in their allocated conference room for an all hands meeting of the group to assess progress and to prepare for the public meeting. They had made a lot of progress, but were still faced with a two day deadline..

Martin opened. He showed beautiful site plans with some suggested owners of buildings and tenants of other structures based on his talks with buddies in the tech sector. They had a good handle on who was looking for new physical facilities and what kind. While none of the names were commitments and were fully disclosed as only possibles, the names were impressive and the underlying G2 was impressive.

Hanna followed with a proposed summary of estimated costs, which was very extensive and well prepared. She had done her homework exceedingly well, and the only real risk in her numbers was the potential to spend more than estimated in rehabbing the land around the old mine—a significant, but not overwhelming, variance risk. D's models had established that—while the costs of ownership and, therefore, square footage leases would be slightly above average in the region—the project clearly commanded premium valuations and rents because of its quality, environmental management, and amenities.

Charles offered an approach to the public discussion which focused on the project quality, the nature of owners and tenants likely to be attracted to the site and the area, and the benefits to the public which would self-fund the infrastructural investments required, according to Hanna's financial models. It would be structured and financed in a manner which would be an example to other communities attempting to turn moribund economies around, and prepare themselves for the new industries of the twenty-first century. And the benefits, at least those presented to the public, were heavily weighted to citizen-realized ones. The astronomical levels of profits projected for developers, owners, and investment bankers involved in the project were not highlighted.

The presentation was tight, connected, and logical. The community would stand to benefit in a big way when it was built out, and the financial burdens on ordinary citizens were minimized. At this point, and on these considerations, Parsons Point had all the earmarks of a winner. Henry complimented the team.

Henry purposefully walked around the conference table to the large whiteboard on the wall and picked up a red marker. Requesting that his assistant take careful notes of the rest of the meeting, he stated, "You have all done a great job in getting this information ready for the planned meeting. The delay in the date from the original allows us to do a bit more homework. Since it is intended that Amanda will present most of the discussion points, we need to anticipate where things might come off the rails and come up with answers to all possible questions. Let's tear down everything you have done so we can prepare Amanda for the worst-case scenario.

"Have we taken all potential objections into consideration? Do we know who the people are that might be less
enthusiastic about this project, and what their concerns
are? Can we show them how they can be comfortable
with this development? Do we really know the possible
downside of the project and can we prevent it or mitigate
it? Let's take an hour and try to destroy this presentation
so that we know where it is weak as well as strong."
Henry was focused only on doing a good job of his assignment. *When you have the data, no one can argue.*

The first question came from Hanna, "Someone is
bound to ask where our assumptions on the costs and
values came from and does it really apply to PP."

Henry looked at her quizzically, "Well?"

Hanna rose to the challenge quickly, "We looked at all
the development projects for tech properties in the last
twenty years. We compared site costs, rental prices, environmental costs (including mitigation costs), infrastructure adequacy, community opposition/support (at least
as far as we could tell), timeline from start to finish, financing arrangements and financing costs, specific companies involved, and total economic benefit/problems
created in the various geographic areas. We looked specifically at Silicon Valley, Route 128, Seattle, Portland,
Austin, Research Triangle, and a couple of outlier projects not in any of those locations. Our data is based on
real life, of course adjusted by inflation, and by our best
judgment to fit local circumstances here. And, no rose-
colored glasses. We were tough on ourselves."

Henry looked around, "Martin, what is your take on
this approach?"

"I introduced Hanna and her team to my contacts who
had actually experienced projects like this, and Hanna's

guys did the rest. Looks to me like they are on top of everything my contacts said. Great job by Hanna's team."

Henry looked at Charles, "Any PR or political issues that you can see?"

"Certainly some will come up, but nothing is glaring as we get started. The only real bugaboo could be the reactions of the naturalist community and the conservation people."

Henry knew exactly who "they" were—at least the key one for him, and her predictably certain reaction sent chills down his spine.

Trying to distract himself, Henry instructed, "I want us to really work this hard. Tear into our plan and expose every weakness you can ... but don't let it out of this room or this team. We want to know everything that someone else might be able to discover or attack us on and be able to answer if we absolutely have to. But even if we know the answers, we want to remain very close-mouthed if no one asks. Confidentiality is very key at this point in the project. I'm going to deal with some other matters right now, but I want you all to continue this process and push it hard. Let's meet again tomorrow morning and prepare ourselves for a dry run tomorrow afternoon with Amanda. Then we will have the weekend and a couple of days to polish it up and get it right before we go public. Any questions?"

No questions, so the team skulked back to their respective caves to don the character of relentless skeptic and question everything about the concept and possible execution of the project. They were a formidable group, and their efforts to find holes in the firmament of this work would be good for the overall project in terms of prep for the public.

Henry, on the other hand, needed to talk to someone outside the boundaries of US&G to test some thinking/feeling and find some answers of his own. Given the tenor of the conversation last night with Jack, he picked up the phone and called the private number Jack had given him. He was sure that Jack would take the call.

The phone rang twice on Jack's private cell before he answered. Henry suggested they have a private meeting very soon, say breakfast tomorrow. Jack offered the buffet at Cottonwood Creek. That sounded acceptable, as anyone who saw them would assume that their conversation was golf related and maybe even membership related for Henry. Good cover for what Henry wanted to discuss.

Henry went home from work that evening feeling good that he had taken positive action to relieve his stress, but still knowing that after the talk with Jack, he would need to have an even more delicate one with Harper.

And he dreaded that.

CHAPTER 37

As Henry and Jack walked to the buffet table at CCC the next morning, Jack expressed surprise that Henry had called.

"What's on your mind, partner?"

The familiarity, in turn, surprised Henry, but in a pleasant and comfortable way. *Taking $250 from a couple of sandbaggers by virtue of good golf and a great team effort has its rewards on the relationship side, too.*

"Jack, I need some serious conversation on a sensitive topic or two, and I need it with someone I can trust. I don't know many people in the business community that fit the description. You and I have sort of begun to form that kind of bond, so I am asking you to be very discreet with what we discuss today," Henry began.

"Agreed and agreed," said Jack. "If you want an omelet, they are at the table just at the end of the line. He'll make it with anything you want thrown in. And they are great."

"Thanks, Jack, but I'll just stick with the scrambled eggs … and the biscuits and gravy … maybe with a big side of bacon added."

They took their meals to a table at the back of the big room so they could talk, confident they would not be overheard. Coffee was poured and orange juice served by the club staff. Henry opened up about his issues, "You mentioned last night over drinks that you had some concerns about the project, and the risks to your land, which would cast some doubt on the feasibility of the whole effort. Could you give me some specifics about those concerns? And when you have finished, I will share some thoughts with you that will explain my needing to talk today."

Jack let out a long sigh, "Henry, you cannot allow anybody to know what I am about to tell you. I have not shared a word with anyone, and it can't go further than the two of us for now. But it is a blockbuster.

"When the landowner investment group was first put together, it was composed of five of us who own most of the land in the lower flats where the Hattowoc meets the Blaine, and three owners who own land farther up the drainages who would benefit from the mitigation needed for the project. Those three are not well known to the five of us. They are corporate owners, and the corporations are neither public nor transparent. They are basically shells. Nothing illegal that we can tell, but just enough shadow and secrecy to make us uncomfortable. They have owned their land for several years, and that history is also unknown to the rest of us."

Henry inhaled slowly and nervously.

'Six months ago, through means I can't discuss right now, I became aware of sales of parcels of these lands to other shell corporations whose history also cannot be traced or verified. I have been unable to come up with any information that might bring these transactions into the sunlight, and, as a result, the other four legit owners and I are looking at our options carefully. We don't have a legal reason to pull the plug, nor do we have evidence of any wrongdoing. But we are not at all certain that we want to follow through with the Parsons Point Project to the end either."

"Wow, Jack. That is a mouthful. Have you discussed this with Mo? This could kill his whole dream, not to mention his run for governor."

"No, Henry, I haven't. If I create any movement to kill the project, I and the other four are possibly subject to a major lawsuit for breach of contract, and the suit would include massive damage claims. I have been quietly warned by the three corporations. Apparently, these are serious people, and, frankly, they scare me."

Henry took another deep breath. "Gee, Jack, that all makes my concerns sound a little lame. I have just been having second thoughts about the ethics of this whole deal for the tech campus development, and wanted to get your perspective on that."

Jack bellowed out a giant belly laugh, "You're telling me that you came to a car dealer for ethics advice? You may be the only human alive who can say that with a straight face." Laughing continued, and Henry picked up the irony too.

"Well, it made more sense than the Tom Clancy story you are telling me. But now, I'm not so sure," Henry chuckled. "Tell you what. I have some very secure connections to certain government agencies who are familiar with the dark side. Want me to see what I can find out? Extremely discreetly, of course."

Jack blanched, "Henry, I think this could get us killed. I am not just playing around here. There's lots of money involved, and heavy guys with hats pulled down over their eyes. We may be out of our league here."

Henry acknowledged Jack's point but added, 'You remember D's friend, the white guy center on his team?

He was a first-round draft guy too, and quit the game like D. He works for the CIA now and has been helpful in the past. Maybe ..."

"Geez, Henry," exclaimed Jack, "Are you some kind of spy? I didn't know Jack Ryan was a fly fisherman, *and* a golfer, *and* a baseball guy. I'm laughing, but I may have dirty laundry to deal with here. This is not what I signed up for when I bought that land."

"Jack, wait, wait ... you haven't even heard the best part yet."

"Dunno how it could get any better."

Henry smiled, "I understand that you have a great relationship with Harper Philips, fly fisherman to fly fisherman, of course."

"Absolutely! She is the best. And a real jewel of a person also. I hear from Ralph that you and she have been spending a lot of time at his special table after days of fishing. He only knows that because you pulled Harper's boat into his parking lot once."

"Oops, outed. Well, I may need your help with Harper, although I'm not sure how. My involvement with Parsons Point is not going to go over well with her. I haven't told her yet, and this is going to cause me some pain ... probably her, too."

Jack asked cautiously, "How far along is this relationship?"

Henry grinned, "It started when she ran over me on the trail after my interview with Mo for my job. Then she has been teaching me to fly-fish, and one thing has led to another, and another. I am getting more serious about her than any woman I have known 'cause she seems like the first one to be worth the trouble ... and, boy, she is worth it."

"You haven't told her anything? Partner, you are in

deep shit. There is nothing more hateful to her than willful dishonesty. You may be swimming downstream with waders full of water and lead-soled boots. I am not sure how to help you fix this one. All I can say is you need to be honest ... and contrite ... with her. When all else fails, try honesty, y'know? She's not unreasonable. If you are a straight shooter with her, she will listen, and she will be fair. That is her touchstone, fairness. Maybe it will work to your benefit.

"And I hafta tell ya, any man who comes to a car dealer looking for love advice and ethics advice is either crazy or very naïve. In your case, I am praying for naïve. But I love you for tryin'. And it would be nice if we were around to tell this story to our grandkids."

Henry and Jack parted company with a solid handshake, having crossed a bridge not often built in such a short time. Henry certainly had no life experience that would suggest a friendship like Jack's, and Jack, a naturally suspicious business guy, was not in the habit of placing confidence so quickly and completely with a young man he had only gotten to know in the last couple of weeks. But then, they were both committed to finding a solution to the PP problem that would keep them both alive to play golf another day.

Upon returning to the office, Henry's first call was to Hanna, "I need to see you immediately, and bring Dr. D with you. We just had a serious out-of-body experience that you two don't even know about yet."

"On the way," she replied cheerfully.

Hanna and D arrived in minutes bringing coffee for the three of them, and carrying worried expressions. "What's up, boss?" Hanna inquired. "Your call sounded ominous."

"Ominous may be the simple version," Henry responded. "I have come across some information about the ownership group of our project land that needs some serious analysis and knowledge. I can't tell you the source, and we can't tell anyone what we find out. As a matter of fact, we can't even tell anyone what we are looking for. It is not just business confidential, it is potentially physically dangerous—to us and some other people. If you don't want to be involved, I understand, and you can distance yourselves from this activity."

Hanna, rather than flash her familiar caution, actually flashed a keen interest in Henry's summary. "You mean we might have to be secretive like spies?" She was alive with energy and eager to know more. D was likewise attentive.

"Yes," said Henry. "Like very accomplished spies. Here is the deal. The land ownership group is composed of eight entities. There are five individuals whom we know and have known for years in the local community. But there are three shell corporations who also own land in the project scope and are part of the group. We know nothing of them. There has been some buying and selling of pieces of parcels to other shadowy entities, of whom we know nothing. This all sounds very suspicious and risky.

"Add to that fact that there have been 'warnings' given to certain owners in the group to avoid learning anything about these shell owners, and/or exposing any of them to public scrutiny. All under the guise of business confidentiality and normal competitive advantage issues.

"This ought to scare the hell out of all of us in this deal with legitimate intentions. I haven't told Mo about this because I want to give him more than I have given you. That's where you come into this search. I need you, Hanna—with D's help, as appropriate—to find everything you can about the shell corporations. We need to know if they are all legitimate or somehow mob-related. We need to know who owns them and where their money comes from. And, if possible, we need to know all we can about the buy/sell contracts that have been undertaken on these parcels of land in the last few months.

"We may be walking into a mess that is far greater than the nearly impossible project we signed on for. And your research must be absolutely quiet and untraceable. I know you are not experienced at that, but it is an absolute requirement. I'll give you whatever air cover I can, but we need to get on this ... yesterday. Questions?"

No questions. Hanna and D left to begin their careers as top-secret double-zero agents in the world of industrial dealing.

CHAPTER 38

As the week progressed, Henry's team went about its tasks with energy and diligence, perfecting their data, polishing their models, and anticipating the tough questions likely to arise in the public meeting. Even Amanda was impressed with the quality of the team's preparation. Martin and Charles applied themselves admirably to their allotted responsibilities, and the information they acquired piled up in files that would allow the PP team to deal with anything that could reasonably be expected from an audience at a disclosure meeting.

And the sub-project was going ... nowhere. The history and vitals about the three shells were airtight. There appeared to be no way to crack the code and know who owned what or whom and on what basis. Hanna was frustrated, and D, ever the picture of cool under pressure, was becoming agitated. He had been unable to reach his CIA contact and old team mate to see if there was progress to be made on that front.

As Henry, Hanna, and D sat in Henry's office after the full team meeting, Henry slapped his hand down on the desk in a gesture of futility.

"How the hell do we find the rocks these guys have crawled under? There has to be something illicit in this structure; there just always is. Every TV show like this I have ever seen always has a minute detail that exposes the evildoers for who they really are."

The statement was interpreted as an attempt to lighten the doom with a little levity, and it was modestly successful, but the levity was not exactly permeating the subteam's outlooks.

They were startled when the phone rang, rather loudly it seemed. Henry answered to the panicked pleading of Hanna's assistant. She had to find Hanna and/or D immediately. It was urgent, government business. And clearly that meant something scary and troublesome. Henry assured her that they were both right in front of him, and who would she prefer to talk to? She asked for D.

Henry handed D the phone, and he began to listen. Nodding his head twice, and taking a couple of notes, he thanked the assistant, and hung up with a wry smile.

"Bingo!" he said. "Our first break. Adam, my old basketball buddy—the white guy, remember? He is on to something and will get back to me by tonight, but he advised me urgently to sit very tight and make myself small. This is dangerous."

Henry laughed, "And how does a six-foot-eight black guy with a seven-foot wingspan make himself small?"

D returned the laugh, "I stoop over and say 'yassuh, coach.' Magically, I am small. When Adam says that, he usually means that I need to be less of a target. It's basketball street talk."

"Maybe we should take it literally this time," warned Henry. "Very literally."

Hanna added, "Yeah, the first two shell corps on Jack's list are sort of legit. They were created by the owner of the old mine as a means of spreading the liability around if there was ever any need because of environmental problems. They are not funded to any extent, and no capital is tied up in them, but they are available if needed. They could be useful in any settlements with regulators."

"The third company is the one that is interesting or scary. No records of any US citizen in the registration or ownership records—just three other offshore entities also with no records of ownership, business purpose, asset ownership, or recent financial transactions. But several months back, there were a couple of transfers in and out of a Cayman bank account in this company's name. My guess is that this company is where any potential problems lie, but I have no hard proof."

"Good work, Hanna. Get that info into a file, and let's keep it somewhere only one of the three of us can get at. And that means especially Mo and Amanda for right now. If we get further along this string we are pulling, we will have to let them in on what we find, but for now, we need to understand what we are looking at."

"Got it, Boss," Hanna giggled. She was actually enjoying this crisis, and learning how to handle it with some skill at the same time.

They adjourned for the day.

When Henry got home, there were two messages on his machine, one from D, and one from Harper. He decided to confront the most intimidating one first, and dialed Harper.

Her machine answered, "You have reached Harper Philips, fly guide extraordinaire. I am out with a client catching fish, but if you'll leave a message, I'll get back to you as soon as they quit biting and I get home or back to the office, take your pick."

Relieved, Henry dialed D and was shocked at the shaky voice that answered.

"Hey, I heard back from Adam. It seems we have stumbled onto a major joint-agency operation to take down a ring of drug and gun smugglers. Adam didn't have any first-hand knowledge of the operation, but was just piecing together bits he had picked up in 'casual' conversations."

D continued, "It seems that one of the central American cartels is trying to establish itself as a new go-to supplier and has a lot of money to launder. They created our third owner shell in the group, and have bought part of the land in question under a buy-back agreement with the other two shells. Sort of like preferred shares. The buy-back occurs at a premium over the purchase price, and if the value goes above the buy-back price, the company is free to sell the land to someone else. That explains the recent sales of two subdivided portions of the acreage they own. It's interesting in that this is kind of an illiquid way of laundering money. That suggests to Adam that there is a lot of cash in play, even though the company is not leaving many footprints in the drug and arms markets yet.

"The ATF, DEA, FBI, and CIA are all involved, and are talking with the EPA to help out with some leverage on the land in our project. CIA is advising-only since there is possible involvement of foreign governments, but all the action is domestic for now, so the agencies that deal with US-based crimes are supplying the resources. It is a real turkey shoot, and lots of people are looking at this entity. We are in a big cesspool here and sinking fast if we can't figure how to swim out."

"Wow! Whatever happened to that nice simple statistical job I took at Mo's offer?" said Henry. "I think we know enough that we have to alert Mo. This is more than we ever conceived could be happening. Let's try to see him tomorrow morning. Have you told Hanna what you found?"

"Yes, she is fully informed."

"Then I'll make the meeting for the three of us and Mo. I'll let you and Hanna know when I've got him nailed down."

After they hung up, Henry anticipated a sleepless night. He had never been remotely involved with anything like this and wondered how he could stay out of jail if, in fact, he survived to tell the tale. He was worn out and in no mood to deal with the phone when it rang, and he remembered the message he left Harper. Maybe he'd deal with her tomorrow. He couldn't afford to botch this conversation, and his mind was anywhere but in the present right now. He let the phone ring until it stopped. And he did not retrieve the message.

His mind was already in Mo's office, figuring out how to tell the CEO that his big dream was riddled with crime and corruption, and could ruin his personal and political fortunes.

Talk about a difficult conversation ...

CHAPTER 39

After a sleepless night, Henry arrived at his office early the next morning, about seven-thirty. He was surprised and pleased to discover that Hanna and D were
already there and had his coffee ready. Before retiring
last night, he had managed to get hold of Mo and arrange
an eight-thirty meeting for this morning. Mo was a bit
confused as to the urgency, but he trusted that Henry
would not waste his time or the time of the team.

So, the three had an hour to prepare for how they
would deliver the shocking news to Mo. He was not
acquainted with the ways of the world in these
matters—to his credit—but neither was anyone else,
and they would have to guide each other through the
situation by holding on to the tail in front of them ... a
line of blind elephants trying to get through the
pending storm.

They decided that Henry would lead. Then Hanna
would present the information they had and could confirm. Then D would discuss the risks and financial/legal
implications for the firm, and Henry would summarize.
Henry would also emphasize that this wasn't going
away, and a decision would have to be made. Mo might
not respond well to that kind of pressure, but it was there.
After an hour of solid preparation, they adjourned to Mo's

office. Thankfully, Amanda was not yet in the office and would not, therefore, insist on being included.

Mo greeted them jovially with his typical expansiveness, praising them for the quality of their effort and results so far. Henry cautioned that he might change his tune after they presented the current situation. Mo, unable to conceive of that kind of bad news, frowned slightly, and invited Henry to fill him in on whatever it was. Henry felt that he still did not have Mo's full attention.

But he soon got it with a typical straightforward opening, "Mo, we have a set of issues with Parsons Point." Mo sat up straight. "There are questions about the ownership group on the land."

Mo responded, visibly upset, "Damn that Jack Morris. I knew he was going to cause trouble."

Henry jumped in quickly, "No, no. It is not Jack. We know Jack and the other local landowners well, and have vetted them thoroughly. No problems there. The problems are with three shell corporations that own land farther up the drainage. Or, I should say, the potential problems. Hanna, perhaps you could shed light on this."

Hanna picked up the pass smoothly, "Two of the three shell companies are related to the mine owner and appear to be harmless. They were set up for risk management reasons, if they were ever needed, so that the entire liability would not fall on the mine owner. The third company is neither so clear nor transparent. It has no records of ownership, business charter, any assets owned, nothing. It is very sinister-looking. And there have been some transactions with some other companies which changed the ownership of certain parcels of land in the land included in our project. There is not a public information string that we can track, and this arouses a lot of suspicion. Fortunately, D has been able to pull some bits and pieces together to get a bit better picture."

Just like going to the rim, D took the ball, and attacked the opportunity. "From what I can find out—and I cannot under any circumstances legitimately know any of this— the third company is up to its navel in shady or even illegal activities. They are under investigation by a joint-agency action involving the ATF, DEA, FBI, and managed by the CIA. Can't get much more federal than that. The CIA is leading because of suspected foreign government involvement, but all the resources are from domestic agencies because all the currently known activity is domestic US ..."

D stopped in mid-sentence as there was an urgent and loud knock on Mo's door. His frantic assistant stuck her head in. "Mr. Stearns, I'm sorry to interrupt, but there are some rather imposing gentlemen here who insist on seeing you right now. They have badges and ... credentials."

Mo, clearly shaken, advised her to show them in. He asked Henry's team to stay. As the door opened, three dark-suited, white-shirted, dark-tied individuals entered. All appeared to be very serious, and the slight bulges under the left armpits of their tailored suits enhanced that impression.

The man on Mo's right began, "Mr. Stearns, I am Special Agent Smythwick, FBI. This is Agent Downing, ATF, and Agent Allen, DEA. Officer Dunbar of the CIA is the leader of our team, but he has a conflict and could not join us today as he is testifying before a joint intelligence committee of Congress on matters relating to what we have to discuss. We need to speak with you about an urgent matter of national importance, and possibly national security impact. Can we speak privately?"

Mo recovered slightly, "My team here was just about

to inform me, I believe, on the matters you wish to discuss. If you don't mind, I would like to have them remain to hear your information."

"It's a bit irregular, sir, but we are going to need help from you and your firm, so I guess, if they are already involved, they would be the people who 'need to know.'"

He continued, "We understand that you have an option on some land which you wish to turn into a technology park for commercial real estate purposes, and that land is the primary asset of a partnership composed of eight different owners. Is that correct?"

Mo said flatly, "It is. We know five of the owners well, and have checked them out in depth. But I suspect you are going to tell me about the other, corporate, owners."

"That is correct, sir. Two of those owners cause us no concern. But the third one is the subject of a major joint-agency investigation, and we are getting close to some indictments and actions that will be controversial, and will affect your development of the tech park."

Everybody from US&G shifted in their chairs and sat on the edges of their seats. The tension in the room exceeded measurement.

Smythwick charged ahead, "This company is suspected of trying to push into drug and arms markets by seeding those markets with cash and discount prices. They are new to the market, and don't yet understand its dynamics, but that doesn't stop them from trying to disrupt it to their advantage. Their strategy is to pump a lot of money into laundered investments, with agreements from the sellers to buy those investments back at a negotiated premium in the medium-term future. Imagine, mobsters and gun runners becoming investment bankers. No offense intended, Mr. Stearns."

Mo chuckled, "None taken. After all, we are mere advisors, not true investment bankers."

We believe that we can take them down safely—meaning, without the violent reactions often seen on the people who help bring such organizations down. I'd prefer to not go into the nasty details, but I'm sure you're acquainted with some of the incidents to which I refer. So, with that background, I would like to sincerely request your assistance in this particular operation."

"And how would that work?" asked Mo.

Smythwick laid out the plan, "We understand that you have purchased a one-year option on the land from the ownership group to do all the regulatory work, site analysis, EIS reporting, and mitigation planning of any issues discovered. And we understand that you have slightly less than seven months to complete that work before your option runs out. Further, if your option expires, the landowner group's value declines dramatically. If there is no development, then there is no market value identifiable. The third owner then has no liquidity in the asset, and we confiscate it in our enforcement action. It disables them and makes a meaningful hole in their cash reserves—not to mention their credibility in the arms and drugs markets—just like real business."

Mo was on his game now. "Yes, but it also destroys the value for my local investors, who are friends and colleagues of mine. I'm happy to help you get the bad guys, but I would hate to ruin the good guys in the process. Is there any way to protect them?"

Henry was thinking, *"After all, I want to be their governor in two years."* But he kept his analysis to himself.

Smythwick responded, "I can't give you any guarantees right this moment, but we think the weight of four

federal enforcement agencies—and national security—
might be regarded favorably by the EPA, who could engineer a solution which would give the local investors
something acceptable rather than confiscating their money. Unfortunately, I am not at liberty to discuss those
details right now, but it is part of the overall plan."

Mo arched an eyebrow, "And what role do you
foresee for this firm in your plan?"

"The one you play well—dealmaker, putting a deal
together. Continue doing what you are currently doing. I
am told there is a public disclosure meeting a week from
Thursday to expose the idea of the project and attempt to
gauge public reaction. Please hold that meeting, and
make it clear that the project is one of high expectations
for the community and will bring huge benefits to the
citizens of this area."

"And what's going on in the meantime?" asked
Henry.

"Can't tell you that, but the important thing is that it is
buying the agencies time to cement their findings and
their case. Just a normal development schedule will most
likely allow us to collect the evidence and witnesses
needed to make a very successful enforcement action."

Henry was skeptical, "Didn't I see that on a TV show
where all the witnesses got kidnapped or executed?"

Smythwick became slightly defensive and agitated.
"That is TV, Mr. Hansen." (Henry was suddenly terrified
that Smythwick knew who he was.) "In real situations,
we are highly successful in concluding these actions safely for all concerned."

"Point made," offered Henry.

"Cool it, Henry," commanded Mo. "Mr. Smythwick is
just doing his job, and I believe he is acting in good faith.

"Mr. Smythwick, we will gladly assist in this matter, insofar as we are able. But I must insist that none of our people are placed in danger of life or limb in helping you do your job. It is certainly to our benefit that we not do business with people like these, but we are not enforcement agents, and have no history or skills in managing these types of risk. We'll do what we can, and our staff will support you in whatever way is available."

"Thank you, Mr. Stearns. That is all any agent could ask. We'll be in touch."

As the three agents left, all the air in the room seemed to follow them. Stunned and still, the team jointly and individually considered what was coming over the horizon at them.

Mo spoke for all of them, "So, where to now? "

Henry picked up the loose ball. "Business as usual. Mo, does Amanda *'need to know'*? It could place her in physical danger, and It might make her tentative in front of the public at the meeting. She needs to be her polished, in-command self to generate confidence and a good cover."

Mo agreed, and the four of them parted ways, pledging absolute confidentiality on matters requiring secrecy. And there were no jokes about having to kill anyone.

Henry remembered that he had not gotten back to Harper last night, and the point about secrecy made his hair stand up. How could he deal with Harper and *not* divulge what was going on? This might impose a price higher than he was willing or able to pay.

It occurred to him that he should just run for the hills and find some place to fish and play golf that was calmer and less dangerous than this town was becoming.

CHAPTER 40

The afternoon passed uneventfully. He received no secret phone calls from the CIA, or any other agency, and he heard no static from Amanda. Mo must be keeping his word on Amanda not needing to know yet. But there was one obstacle to tranquility that kept rising up before him ... Harper.

He remembered that Jack expressed great confidence in Harper when she is dealt with honestly. *What did he say? "When all else fails, try honesty."* Henry was not conversant in dealing with a relationship that truly mattered, so his confidence in honesty, per se, was not well established. Perhaps his trust in Jack would have to substitute for his lack of experience in matters of the heart. But he saw no other alternative.

He dialed Harper and, mercifully, she was with a client on a stream somewhere. He wished he could be there instead of on this phone, but he dutifully left a message for her to call when she returned from her business day. He would probably be home by then and finishing his third Blue Moon Ale. But at least it gained him a temporary reprieve. Could he even hint to Harper that he was one of the good guys? Would the CIA put out a contract on him if he slipped? Or the cartel if they found out? The questions chilled his spirit, not to mention scaring the bejeezus out of him.

Well, he would just have to burn that bridge when he came to it. Nothing to be done until Harper returned his call.

At eight in the evening, the moment of reckoning appeared in the return phone call. Henry cautiously answered—and, yes, it was Harper.

"Hey stranger, I thought you were mad at me. I haven't seen or heard from you since ... well, *you* know."

"No, Harper. How could anyone, especially me, be mad at you? Not possible," he smoothly responded. "I've just been busier than a one-legged man at a butt-kickin' and I am just now coming up for air."

"Well," she purred, "why don't you come over here to tell me about it? I've got that great bourbon, and you don't have to be in any hurry to get home." *What a blessing, a woman who gives very clear invitations.* "And I have a lot on my mind that I want to discuss."

Once again, Henry experienced the piercing sensation made by a cold steel knife. But he responded cheerfully, "H, that sounds like a great idea. I'll be there in twenty minutes."

On the short drive to Harper's, Henry rehearsed how he would conduct this critical conversation. But he couldn't, for the life of him, come up with a way to say what needed to be said without giving away the whole program—a failing which would undoubtedly cause him great grief with four, maybe five, government agencies. How much jail time would he serve for spilling the beans on a top-secret operation? Would it be treason? Or just mere incompetence?

No, it couldn't be that. Two-thirds of the politicians in Congress would be in jail for that. But that truism did not ease Henry's sense of stark fear as he neared Harper's home.

As he pulled up in front, he saw the porchlight come on. He knew what waited behind the door ... he thought.

As he approached, the door opened slightly and he could see Harper's smiling face. She moved behind the door as it opened and closed it when he was in.

The sensation was a taser shock. Harper stood there in a T-shirt ... apparently *only*. Henry saw a lot more of her fit, muscular legs than he remembered from before, and he suddenly forgot why he came. Harper reminded him gently but passionately with a warm, deep kiss.

"Hey, Babe," she cooed. "What took you so long?"

Henry had no answer as Harper led him into the living room and sat down on the couch. Two glasses of very fine bourbon waited for them on the table. Handing him a glass and taking one herself, she curled up beneath his arm, with a quiet toast, and sipped the pale, smooth bourbon. Henry was too nervous to easily say anything. But a couple of sips helped. He decided to enjoy this moment with Harper ... while he could. It might be a long time till the next one.

"Harper, we need to talk about some important stuff." The words were difficult to get out of his mouth, given the quivering voice and high levels of anxiety Henry was experiencing.

"I know," Harper smiled, "but that's what breakfast is for. Right now, other things are more important."

"Such as ...? "he asked.

Without a word, she took her glass in one hand and Henry's hand in the other and got up, leading him to her bedroom. "Bring your bourbon," she teased.

Once in the bedroom, Harper put her glass down by the bed, and the T-shirt magically disappeared over her head and onto the floor. Henry swallowed hard. Her body was athletic and inspiring. In fact, Henry was extremely inspired. He hurried to undress and tripped over his shorts as they came off. He was mortified, but Harper's smile quickly relieved his chagrin as she pressed her nakedness up against his in a kiss so hot that Henry's knees buckled.

So hot ... and yet so tender that he was immediately certain of a deeper meaning than he had ever known from a woman.

Oh shit, I am doomed, he thought as they tumbled into the bed. But he didn't think about anything else for the next two hours as he and Harper gently, languorously, and passionately explored each other in the most intimate and loving detail. They drifted off into a fitful sleep that neither really wanted but both required, given their lack of strength to stay awake.

Sunlight came far too quickly for them, and they groggily arose to take on the new day, Harper more certain than Henry of the promise it contained. Henry was withdrawn and apprehensive as Harper poured their coffees, and she recognized it.

"Hey, you ought to be floating like I am. What's up? Surely you are not feeling guilty?"

Henry sat bolt upright. *Did it show? Of course I'm feeling guilty, but for reasons you can't yet suspect. How the hell am I going to deal with this?*

Harper continued solicitously, "I am having breakfast with the man of my dreams, and you are looking at me like I just drowned your puppy. Help me out here. Let me know what is on your mind. Promise I can help make it better." And if as though to prove her point, she reached out to fondle Henry's thigh.

Henry bit the bullet, and charged head-on into the ultimate test of his maturity and manhood. "Harper, there is a meeting a week from tomorrow that you have probably heard about, and that I am sure you will want to attend."

Yeah," she said. "Jack mentioned it when we were fishing up on the Hattowoc yesterday. What's so important about it?"

Henry's unconfident voice came back, "It's complicated. There are a lot of moving parts. There are parts of the information that I am sure you will not be happy with. But please, don't jump to conclusions. All is not as it seems. I can't tell you the whole story, but please trust me on this. There will be a happy ending. *I think.*"

Her suspicious eyes betrayed her focus, "Henry, it's not like you to be so cryptic. You are always a straight guy with no hidden agendas. What could possibly be so bad that you would be so nervous? You can tell me."

"Harper, I honestly can't tell you. For reasons that sound like they are out of a novel, but even *that* is more than I should say. You just have to believe that I have found something with you—our fishing together, our Italian dinners, and our personal histories—that is unique in my life, and something that I value above all else, but I still can't tell you."

Now Harper's Spidey-sense was on full alert, but she looked into Henry's eyes and found something to give her comfort. "Alright, I'll trust you, but I am really unsure why it should have to work this way. We have something deeper than fishing or golf, and I am not happy about not sharing the really important stuff."

Defensively, Henry pleaded, "It's not like that Harper. Just hang on for a while, and it will become clear why it has to be this way. Believe me, this is critical to you—to us—and it's going to work out great."

"Hmmm, sounds like something Bobby Philips once said to me ... before he took my virginity. He married me and then ran off with a red-haired cheerleader six months later."

Henry cringed. "Harper, I am not Bobby Philips," he asserted, with as much gravitas as he could muster. "It's not that way."

"Okay, I trust you, at least until proven otherwise. I do love you, and I want this to work out for us. I want us to be happy for a long time."

And there it was. It had been pushing at the confinement of the chrysalis, a butterfly trying to be birthed. Now it was said and out in the open. Henry was frightened and relieved at the same time, and he dared to pronounce what he had never spoken to any woman.

"I am madly in love with you, too, Harper, and I will not place us in danger of mistrust. You are my—our—future."

That drew a smile and a huge kiss from Harper, and the world seemed right again. At least for a while.

CHAPTER 41

Predictably, Henry was late arriving at the office ... not to mention somewhat flushed. The biggest event of his life so far and he had to leave to get here and do this. Not the storybook chain of events one might imagine in a story with a happy ending, if indeed there was to be a happy ending.

His first call was to Jack's private number. When Jack answered, Henry implored, "Jack, we need to have a very private meeting. I can't tell you any more than that, but I need to chat with you about Harper. Can you help me?"

"Name the time and place and I'll be there. I've got to take care of my fishing guide and golf partner. I have a lot at stake with the two of you."

Yes, you do. More than you will ever believe.

"Lunch at Ralph's. We can get the private table and one of his knife-and-fork special pizzas," suggested Henry.

"Later, about one-thirty?" asked Jack.

"Deal."

Next matter was an update from Hanna and D. They joined him in his office within five minutes.

Hanna smiled lasciviously at Henry, "Isn't that the same suit you wore yesterday? If I didn't know better, I'd swear you have something going on that you're not talking about."

Momentarily shaken, Henry glanced up from his desk to see Hanna's smile and answered, "NOYB, Mata Hari. And besides, let her without sin cast the first stone." They both laughed, while D puzzled at the tone of the conversation.

But D did have some interesting news. He had found some additional financial transactions relating to the dealings of Company Three and sent them on to Agent Smythwick. The good agent had traced them to a bank account in Cypress and then from an account in Luxembourg. That account revealed some information on ownership that brought the FBI/ATF/DEA team closer to a prosecutable case than they anticipated, and several months ahead of expectations. From what they learned in Luxembourg, they found an aspiring young investment banker in Zurich who was the common point through which all transactions passed. When confronted, he folded like a cheap tent, and the joint-agency team felt it was now within weeks of an arrest and an indictment.

Henry was optimistic at this news. "D, why did Smythwick tell you all this? I would think it is very confidential and critical to their case. It is surprising that they would share it with mere mortals like us. I would think that Mo would be the only person they would tell, if they would tell anybody at all. Something smells funny here."

Neither D nor Hanna had a good answer for this. It occurred to all of them at once that the agencies were trying to engineer a leak so that something would happen to allow overt action. It also occurred that, if the three of them were the vehicle for the leak, they were in something more than theoretical danger. Most unprofessional of the agencies.

This new development caused Henry's mind to come

into focus sharply. He was in a new position that challenged his judgment and his instincts like never before. If this was part of growing up, it is a miracle that anyone ever survived the process, physically as well as emotionally. He had no touchstones to know who could know what—and what was real, and what was disinformation—to elicit some response from some unknown entity who might kill anyone who got in their way, or who might be a smoke screen for law enforcement. He decided the best approach was to call Agent Smythwick and insist on some transparency, especially since some lives he treasured (including his own) could be at risk.

He called the agent and made an appointment for coffee the next morning at the agent's hastily rented office space nearby. The rest of his day was spent futilely attempting to figure out why Smythwick would put Henry's team at the epicenter of a dangerous subterfuge with a planned leak. Federal agencies did not ordinarily do that without consent from the people at the center of the plot/leak/plan. The effort to figure out the leak was useless, and led to no progress or better understanding of the situation.

At home later, Henry touched base with Harper, and found it an uncomfortable conversation. She was trying to be cheerful, sexy, trusting Harper, but it didn't quite come across as Henry had remembered. Talk was tentative and changed topics arbitrarily. Henry was at a loss for what to talk about and how to lead the conversation away from controversy. He desperately wanted to be alright with Harper, but he could not assure himself that was happening. After a mutually brave effort to preserve what had been established, they hung up, neither believing that it had been their usual happy encounter.

The next morning, Henry, in his best dark suit, white

shirt, and striped tie, appeared at Agent Smythwick's office for a stern conversation. The Agent was cheerful and greeted Henry warmly. *That was not expected.*

Henry got right down to brass tacks. "I have some concerns on behalf of my team members that I need some clarification on from you."

"Okay, fire away," returned the agent. *An unfortunate figure of speech.*

"One of my team informed me yesterday of some developments in the case that I was surprised he knew. He told me that he found them out from *you*. Is it your standard practice to feed citizens information that could endanger them? Isn't this kind of information usually reserved for the enforcement agencies on a 'need to know' basis?"

"Mr. Hansen, the short answer is yes. This type of information is usually kept in-house with the agencies. But the truth is that, when my colleague from the CIA, Mr. Dunbar, testified yesterday to the joint Congressional Intelligence Committee, he discussed this information. The Senator from South Carolina has chosen to 'leak' it to the press, since he distrusts the intelligence community so much, and it is now public knowledge. If you watched the morning TV newscasts, you were made aware of the Zurich connection. Since we have the testimony of the young investment banker on unquestionable grounds, and secured from any tampering, we do not feel anything has been lost. But that is a fortunate accident. We are ready to move and the 'leak' won't affect us, and your team should not be in any danger."

Henry wanted to believe Smythwick, but discovered he had his own measure of distrust for the intelligence agencies, even though there was no 'deep state' issue in his mind where they were concerned. He was much more focused on the issue of manipulation of individuals than the presence of overarching conspiracy. He opted to accept the role of good citizen, helping accomplish a worthwhile goal, from which he would also benefit, and leave the political sparring to the pros.

"So, am I free to discuss this with other concerned parties?" inquired Henry. "That would help me save a lot of wear and tear on some very frayed nerves and some thinly-stretched relationships."

Smythwick replied, almost empathetically, that since the information was in the public domain, anybody was free to discuss it. However, he emphasized that discussion of any information *not* public, which would compromise the case, would be prosecuted vigorously. Henry took that as a yes. They both rose and shook hands, with Smythwick repeating how grateful the agencies were to Henry, his team, and Mo, for the assistance rendered so far. He reminded Henry to please continue on the current path of assembling a deal, and speak carefully. Henry gladly agreed.

As he left the FBI office, Henry turned his attention to the coming conversation with Jack, his new BFF. He could let Jack in on some of the changes in the status of the project, but he would have to exercise some discretion during their lunch. There were only so many beans that could be spilled even now.

And what could he tell Jack that could be passed on to Harper in order to save that precious relationship?

As Ralph showed them to 'Henry's table,' they ordered the knife-and-fork and soft drinks. No wine in the middle of the day for either of them. Henry asked Jack if he had seen the morning newscasts or read the papers yet.

"Yeah, both. But I sure didn't see anything interesting.

Just a bunch of speculation on the disclosures from the Joint Intelligence Committee of Congress latest hearings. Honestly, that guy from South Carolina. He changes positions more often than a lost chicken on the highway. Now he's shooting off his mouth about a joint agency thing where they have tracked down some cartel money that is being laundered through shady real estate deals."

"Jack, slow down. That thing he is talking about is *our* deal, Parsons Point. Remember the third company on the land up the drainages? That is this cartel deal. I, we—Mo and I—have been talking with an FBI guy who is involved in this 'enforcement action,' and he confirmed to me less than a half hour ago that they have been outed by the senator and I could discuss parts of this with you." Henry was very authoritative and Jack listened carefully.

"Does this mean we are not gonna get assassinated by some guy in a leather overcoat with a silencer on his Beretta?"

"Hopefully," said Henry. "But no guarantees as yet. We are supposed to have the meeting next Thursday, and still be presenting a major development deal for public comment and input."

Shifting gears, Henry attempted to address the Harper issue.

"Jack, what really scares me—and few things do after the last week or so—is how I can hang on to Harper. She is the most valuable thing in my life right now, and I think when she hears the meeting next Thursday, she will write me off and never speak to me again."

Jack donned his wise friend face and asked, "Have you been honest with her? Have you looked her in the eye and told her what is happening?"

Henry responded sheepishly, "Well, yes ... and no,

not completely. I told her she was going to hear something that would not make her happy, but there is more that I can tell her, and please trust me."

Jack frowned, "I give you fifty-fifty on that basis. It is a lot to ask, and you guys have only been together what, a month? six weeks? You don't have a long history to build on, even if it has been intense."

Henry arched his eyebrow, "How do you know how intense it has been? What has Harper told you?"

Rushing for reassurance, Jack maintained that Harper had said nothing. He had just observed how she was behaving and how she had changed over the last few weeks. He had noticed how much happier she seemed, even when not on the water fishing. When Ralph told him about the dinners after days of fishing, Jack had figured out that Henry had something to do with Harper's new outlook.

Jack pushed for more, "So, what happens next? Or do you have to kill me if you answer that?"

"Not right away," Henry answered slyly. "But if this doesn't work for Harper and me, you're on the top of the list. No pressure though."

Henry recounted what he could about his visit with Smythwick.

"They are ready to move, and they think the information already acquired and secured will be enough to allow warrants and even indictments. That sounds overconfident to me, but maybe I watch too much TV. He seems genuinely grateful for our help. But, we still cannot allow any of this to be known outside you and me ... and my team. Maybe not even Mo—not sure on that one."

Jack jumped in again, "Okay, let's get this show on the road. I will speak with Harper and try to keep her on this continent where you are concerned. You get about making this whole enforcement deal come together so that we can all take a breath. And, if luck prevails, we will all have something to celebrate come fall."

CHAPTER 42

One week and a day to go before the big meeting. *Would that also mark the lifespan of his enthralling relationship with Harper? Would his developing love of fly-fishing survive the next week or the few months after that required to bring the enforcement action to a conclusion? Would he and Jack just survive at all?* It was difficult to know whether there was real danger or if this was all just imaginary terror fueled by too many FBI TV shows with predictable plot lines.

He tried to distract himself from negative thoughts by concentrating on his responsibility to Mo and the firm, his team's efforts to prepare for the meeting (either real or fake), and his possible role in the intermediate-term future of the firm. He did not invest time pondering how he would relate to Amanda in any of these instances.

Mistake.

On Thursday morning, Amanda appeared at his office door, resplendent in bright orange (a jumpsuit, exceptionally well-tailored), and red slings showing toe cleavage. Her sexuality, while clearly evident, was not emphasized ... except for her natural presence being in the same location as the clothes. There was obviously something on Amanda's mind.

"May I have a word?" she requested respectfully.

"Of course," Henry answered cautiously. He was now able to read Amanda's intentions quite well, and he knew when to be on his guard with her ... which was almost always.

Amanda, in her best teamwork and goal-oriented voice asked, "Is there something going on that I should know? I am seeing lots of activity surrounding the Parsons Point project, but I am not seeing a lot of new information brought forward. And when I ask questions, I get answers that some would characterize as evasive.

"If I am going to get ambushed at the meeting Thursday, I would, at the very least, like a heads-up so I can prepare and perhaps find an effective way to deal with it. Frankly, I am expecting a lot of community support, but I am also expecting some strong and emotional pushback from the naturalist and outdoor community. You got my back on this?"

Henry demurred, slightly, but then came back strong.

"Absolutely, Amanda. This is a good project, good for the community, good for our firm, good for the land-owners. It works well for everybody involved, and I'm pretty sure we can work this in a way that will be acceptable to the naturalist groups that are interested. We've got some high-powered help in this one."

That statement raised Amanda's eyebrow.

"So, there *is* something that I am not being told? I should raise hell with Dad and get that fixed, but if you tell me that you got my back, I trust you. You have proven to be a person of substance."

"I am keeping Mo fully informed and up-to-date on all the developments concerning Parsons Point, and I'm confident he can deal with all the issues that we are identifying. You will be well prepared for the meeting, and you will do great. You seem to be developing some *sub-stance* yourself."

Amanda liked that; she had not heard anything so positively pointed at her from Henry before. But she wasn't sure of his reference. She had always possessed that quality in her own eyes.

Henry continued, "Hanna and her team have all the numbers; best, worst, most likely, and a couple of extreme contingency cases built and modeled in case of an emergency question. Martin has assembled a great potential site plan with development needs and plans to address them. They make great conversation points, so long as we don't have to implement them right away. And we have done a ton of environmental homework on the infrastructure needs, the development issues, and the long-term impact of the old mine and its problems.

"We have initial support from the EPA, and we will be using a tested method of remediation that is currently working successfully in a community that has been historically ravaged by mining and the acid tailings problem to the point of uninhabitability. Right now, everyone is happy, and it is a great role model for us. What more can you ask for?"

Amanda was cautious, "Sounds too good to be true. There has to be more to it." She was probing, trying to uncover what she had not been told.

Henry saw it and reassured her sufficiently to cause her to stop probing. "It won't be a rainbows-and-flowers meeting but we are in good shape on the concerns that matter the most to the most people," he said.

Amanda nodded and retired from the field gracefully.

Henry and the team continued to polish their prep for the meeting, and to make sure Amanda was prepped as well.

Thursday's session with Amanda and Mo was a concise, competent demonstration of just how well a team could ferret out the important questions in any potential conflict situation, and derive answers based on real information that could satisfy a variety of individual agendas. Henry was quite pleased at the ingenuity and command of the relevant data that his team offered to the possible questions. Based on what they knew, and could extrapolate out of the known, it looked like the presentations would be delivered in a way that would generate widespread public support for the project. *It almost was a waste to make all that effort, achieve such command of the information, present it so authoritatively, and then have everyone discover that it was all a fake just to catch a bunch of cartel bad guys.*

While the meeting prep moved along at a quick pace and looked like it would be fruitful, Henry worried about how the meeting would affect Harper. He had not talked to her for a few days, and there was a nagging thought in his head that there was something that he needed to know about her, and her attachment to Parsons Point, but did not. So, to avoid absolute panic, he put his head down and charged, trying to get the red cape before the matador pulled it away. He remained focused on the project-related tasks, and tried to put his personal concerns on hold.

Harper, on the other hand, was plowing blithely along, taking care of her fishing clients, tending to Rex, and wondering why she had not heard from Henry. Their last conversation was strange and kept echoing in her inner ear. *Why was it so important that Henry be assured she would trust him no matter what she heard?* She wondered if he had another woman, or if he was involved in something illegal, or if he was just caught up in his work and this big project.

It was difficult to go through a whole week without fishing with Henry. Even though he had turned into her romantic interest, he was still great company on the river, and watching him learn the art of fly-fishing was—as with all great practitioners of an arcane art—a joy for her. The entire weekend passed with no word from him.

Now she didn't know whether to be worried or pissed.

As it happened, Henry and Jack played some more golf and liberated a couple of new sandbaggers from the oppression of their money through a series of unlikely birdies and very intelligent team golf. They had to be careful or they would build a reputation that would make it hard to get an honest game. Henry had begun to think that a membership at CCC would be something he could enjoy, and he looked forward to reestablishing his once-proud golf game.

CHAPTER 43

On Monday, as Henry pulled out of the company parking area, he noticed a car he had not seen before sitting across the street. It was occupied by a man in a 1930's newsboy-style cap who appeared to be waiting for something or someone.

Henry knew it was a car he had not seen before since it was a bright orange Porsche 911, probably one-model-year old. As Henry turned to go home, the Porsche followed; Henry noticed but paid no mind ... until the car was still trailing him when he turned into the parking area of his condo. The Porsche kept going and did not follow him into the multi-story garage. But it was a strange feeling for Henry.

Perhaps Agent Smythwick should know about this.

A call to the good agent revealed nothing. His office had, indeed, spotted the car two days ago, but so far nothing negative had turned up. It was registered to a stud farm in Kentucky. It was natural to Henry that such a flashy car would somehow be expected for a horse racing business. No information was yet available on who the driver might be, but the FBI was following through. Smythwick advised care, but no panic. There was no reason yet—the agency was tailing the Porsche even as it was tailing Henry. The Porsche appeared and disappeared several times over the week leading up to the public meeting.

Nothing happened.

Harper was frustrated, still no word from Henry. Maybe they would connect at the meeting. Jack said it involved Henry's firm, so surely he would attend.

Jack and Henry had breakfast on Thursday morning at CCC. Henry was pensive and Jack was nervous. Henry asked, "Have you seen or talked to Harper?"

Jack replied, "No, we didn't fish this week. Have you been straight with her?"

Henry squirmed, " I haven't talked to her in a week or more."

"Not good, birdie man. You are in deep trouble, unless I miss my guess."

Henry shuddered, "I guess we'll find out tonight."

The rest of Henry's day creeped by at a glacial pace. The dread rose in his throat like a bad fish dinner. But it did go away when he remembered the orange Porsche and its driver in the newsboy cap. *He was probably a hit man from the cartel and was going to eliminate some obstacles tonight.* He hoped Smythwick and his colleagues were up to the task of protection and prevention.

He checked in with the team and found them ready and able to deal with the data, the concepts, and the questions. He hoped that Amanda could deflect all those, and his team would not have to get involved. He personally wished to stay as far in the shadows as possible.

The meeting was held in the town hall—a modest but comfortable building which housed municipal offices, the small police station, the town council room, and a larger auditorium-type room for meetings and small events. When Henry's team arrived it was already packed, and tension was high. A number of people arrived with signs and attitudes, while others looked like they were going to a string quartet concert and had no idea of any possible controversy.

The parking lot was full, but the team managed to find a place to park their van that wasn't really a parking place, but would not be a problem to get out of … unless they were in a hurry. Henry did not see the orange Porsche anywhere, but he did see Harper's CJ in the first line of parking spaces. The dread returned. The team entered and took seats along the side of the auditorium as unobtrusively as possible. Henry noted the three joint-agency men at strategic points in the back of the room. They were very official and dressed in their standard government suits, shirts, and ties. The bulges under their left armpits were prominent, if you knew where to look. The crowd was restive and growing impatient.

After a twenty-minute delay, Mo appeared to a smat-tering of applause, more polite and less voluble than a normal golf clap but sincere in its intent. A large portion of the room remained stonily silent and near hostility. Henry identified Harper sitting in that part of the room with Jack beside her. He hoped Jack was there to protect Harper and keep her from doing something drastic.

"Good evening," Mo began, with his customary com-mand of all that surrounds him. His size, his huge smile, and his outsized personality lit up the room. "I am Mo Stearns, the CEO of Ursa, Stearns and Giacana. We are a banking and advisory firm founded in this community thirty years ago by people just like yourselves, and I am one of them. We help investors acquire capital for funding growing businesses, and for community development to the benefit of all its citizens, and we have been privileged to grow with this community for those thirty years.

"When we started the firm, the aluminum plant was

the economic heart of this town and area. It provided for the workers who filled its facilities for three shifts, turning out the raw materials which supplied one of the greatest industrial expansions in the history of the world. We helped get the funding for many of the businesses who supplied the plant and many that provided goods and services for its employees and their families. Our efforts contributed to the building of a sound economy and a strong tax base, which allowed the development of an excellent school system, and the creation of many first-rate municipal services.

"That plant is no longer the economic engine it once was, and our community is caught in between stages of economic progress. We need a shot in the arm to inspire new growth, new employment, and new opportunities. US&G has always been a critical ingredient in that growth, and tonight we want to share with you a plan to reestablish and nurture the transition to the next level of economic health for this area.

"I'd like to introduce my daughter, Amanda Stearns, the Chief Operating Officer of our firm, to tell you that story. Amanda ..."

At the edge of the room, Henry and the team sat quietly, amazed as always at Mo's ability to capture the room, no matter what size. Even the potential opponents seemed spellbound. Henry was certain he had just heard the kickoff to Mo's gubernatorial campaign.

Amanda entered, stage left, attired in effortless elegance. She wore a simple blue business suit and a pale blue silk blouse. Navy pumps, and nothing to suggest the tigress that stalked beneath the proper and demure suit. But she, too, captivated the room.

"Tonight is the first night of the rebirth of our local

economy," she opened. "May I present Parsons Point Technical Park."

A curtain behind her rose to expose an enlarged version of Martin's site map with artist's renderings of the various parklike areas, the buildings, people at lunch, and some people in canoes in the small bay off the Blaine River that fronted the site. There were prominent logos of industry leading firms in software, AI, cloud services, telecom, entertainment, electronic medical devices, and IT services, all the proper names for the occasion. All of them assured the audience that this would not be a vulgar manufacturing park but a headquarters park, filled with the executives and specialists that brought big salaries and heady lifestyles to the community, the certain driver of growth that Mo had referred to.

The intake of collective breath among the audience was noticeable. No one could accuse US&G of not dreaming big.

Henry, scanning the audience, noticed that Harper was animatedly talking to Jack. From Jack's body language, Henry did not think that Harper was happy. His analysis was correct. Harper was furious, and Jack was working hard just to keep her in her seat.

Looking further along the back wall Henry saw a new face. A man, clad in a leather overcoat and ... a newsboy cap ... stood about halfway between the federal agents observing the proceedings. Henry was pretty sure that an orange Porsche 911 currently decorated the parking lot also. *Curious, wonder who he is.* The federals made no move to close in on him or surround him in any way.

Amanda continued, "US&G, in cooperation with a group of local landowners, has created an option for the most advanced, environmentally sound, and ecologically sustainable major development project to be undertaken in this country in the last thirty years. We have defined areas of focus in all the critical disciplines to assure that all regulatory and infrastructural requirements are met in a manner consistent with low pollution, a low carbon footprint, and clean water. Parsons Point is, after all, a renowned fly-fishing location, and we intend to maintain and enhance that reputation."

A sneer came from the audience. Henry was certain it was Harper, but did not look around.

"Furthermore, we have entered into discussions with the EPA and other federal environmental entities to clean and mitigate some historical issues at the old mine in the hills above the Point, so that the pristine nature of the site will never be damaged by contaminated water or silt from the mine. We are employing the very successful technology and solution used in Anaconda, Montana, to remedy long years of land abuse. In Montana, today, a beautiful public golf course sits on that land in Anaconda. It is enjoyed by thousands of outdoor enthusiasts every year, and has been a model for years cited by the EPA."

"I think you can see that we are going very deep into the detail of this development to guarantee that it is something that we can all take pride in and enjoy every day of our lives in this community. Great National and Global firms to enhance the business flow in our economy. Great firms committed to social and environmental health of all the stakeholders and citizens in the community. And great staffs of highly educated, highly paid technical experts that will raise the levels of income, the tax base, the values of our homes, and improve the quality of our lives.

"Let me walk you through the various phases of our thinking and project planning."

Amanda spent the next hour going through the site map and the list of potential owners and tenants in the various buildings on the map, as well as the 'human' features of the site (parks, child care centers, stores, restaurants, municipal services, transport maps and routes on the campus, and landscaped areas that would add tranquility and peace to the development). She discussed Hanna's financial models and demonstrated to the crowd the beautiful economics the park would generate, and how that money could flow into the city, county, and individual pockets.

Her presentation was well received and the crowd was, for the most part, supportive. They had been snowed by the prosperity and economic benefits Amanda promised.

As she completed her presentation, Amanda pumped up her enthusiasm a bit. "And, to complete the introduction of Parsons Point Technology Park, I'd like to introduce you to someone very special at our firm. He is a local guy known to many of you from his years of work with the Pirates, helping them build performance metrics to improve the quality of their team efforts and the baseball futures of the players. Please welcome the Project Manager for Parsons Point, my favorite guy, Henry Hansen!"

Lightning shot through Henry's gut. Not only was he introduced as the PM, he was tied closely to Amanda. Neither of those would sit well with Harper at all. He tried to hide, but Amanda was insistent.

"Henry. C'mon up here and help me answer these folks' questions."

His rook was pinned and there was nothing he could do about it. Henry mustered what bravado he could find, and ascended to the stage from the audience. He did not look at Harper but he could feel the confusion, anger, disappointment, and resentment radiating from her. Jack was trying to appear nonchalant, but Harper's heat was driving him to seek shelter. Henry shared that desire.

The questions were pretty predictable and mundane. One asked how the numbers were derived and if there were any contingencies included. Of course, there *were*, and Amanda ran through them quickly, not so well that anyone could actually understand them but well enough so that everyone was aware that the process had been thorough.

Another question came up about the old mine and its potential hazards. Henry explained the Anaconda model and how it had brought the community together and sustained itself for several decades. He managed to work in a golf story and related it to the course now flourishing in Anaconda.

A third question focused on phasing of the project and projected start date. Amanda slid through that with the explanation that there is so much preliminary environmental and infrastructural study to be done, it was difficult to predict accurately, but the target was early in the following spring. Her answer assumed that the public support and the regulatory agency support were forthcoming and strong.

And that was it. An hour and a half from the beginning. Done. No riots, no confrontations. Apparently, the crowd of antis had decided that it just wasn't important to raise hell yet. They wouldn't get support until they could uncover corruption or deception large enough to make people mad.

Henry started to leave the stage (ASAP) but became aware of Harper storming the podium where Amanda stood. Jack was scurrying behind her, trying to prevent a murder, and showing eyes of absolute terror. As Harper reached the podium, she shot Henry a deadly glance and turned to Amanda.

"Thank you for your detailed explanation of your plan tonight," she said politely if frigidly. "I just wanted to introduce myself. I am Harper Philips."

Amanda shook her hand looking bewildered.

Harper continued, "Philips—does that ring a bell? How about Bobby Philips?"

Amanda flinched, "Yes, I think I dated Bobby Philips in college. Quarterback, pre-med? Right?"

"That's right," Harper responded with obvious malice. "He was also my husband when he ran off with you."

Oh, shit! Henry wanted to crawl under a table, but there weren't any.

"And furthermore," Harper went on, "Craig Parsons— as in Parsons Point—was my grandfather. And I'll be damned if I will allow you to steal both my husband *and* my grandfather's favorite place in the world without one helluva fight. Buckle up, lady. You're gonna need your seat belt for this one."

And with that Harper turned on her heel and strode aggressively off the stage.

Henry was dumbfounded. Jack just shrugged. Amanda blanched. She had never had to confront the result of any of her frivolous dalliances before in her life. She was heavily shaken and had nowhere to find a clever way out of this discomfort.

Henry was gasping for air and turned to try to catch Harper. No way. She was gone in a flash. Only Jack understood what was in Henry's mind, the desperation he felt at that moment. And Henry was not about to be consoled by a golf buddy. He was only fearing a great loss.

CHAPTER 44

She was gone, perhaps for good. Henry was as close to heartbroken as he had ever been, although it was not clear to him that was what he was feeling.

As he turned back to the auditorium to find Jack, Leather Overcoat approached him and blocked his path. "Mr. Hansen, we need to talk. Very seriously."

Henry mumbled, "This really isn't a good time. Can you call me tomorrow?"

"I think not. If you'll join me for a drink, I think you will see just how important our conversation is."

Henry suddenly focused. The voice was incredibly familiar but the face and overall appearance was not. His fight-or-flight sense was on edge, and his caution button had been pushed repeatedly and hard in the last few seconds. He agreed to Overcoat's suggestion.

"Let's meet at Ralph's. Do you know where that is?"

Leatherman replied that he did, and would be there in twenty minutes. He and Henry left separately for the trip to Ralph's. When Henry arrived at the restaurant, the Porsche was in the parking lot, and Ralph showed him to the usual table. The overcoat was off and the wearer still seemed familiar to Henry.

As Henry sat down, Leather Overcoat presented his card: "HoHan Studs and Training, Morrisville, Kentucky." Henry was taken aback, but focused.

Leatherman spoke, "You haven't recognized me yet, have you?"

Henry nodded, "Not yet, but I feel like I should know you."

"Yeah, you should. My current given name is Maxwell Stendahl. But HoHan stands for Horace Hansen."

Henry's mouth gaped in disbelief. "You work for Uncle Horace?"

"Sort of, but not exactly," said Max. "Although I am using a name given me by the witness protection program, I am Uncle Horace. And I think you have figured out by now that it is much more than 'uncle.'"

Henry was unable to fashion a response in words, so he sat while Horace continued.

"I have lots of news that is important to you. Let's start with your mother."

Uncle Horace launched into the story. "Your mother was not the ill-adjusted psychopath everyone thought she was. Helene had a serious medical problem—a series of tumors in her frontal lobe—that affected her behavior over the years. Our mom never told anyone. I knew because I was the only one in the family that could get Helene to respond in a reasonable manner. When she was eighteen, I volunteered to take her to her prom. I wanted her to have some semblance of a normal experience. She picked up on what everyone else was doing, and convinced me to give her that same 'experience.' Shortly after, we discovered she was pregnant ... with you. I nursed her through her tumors and her pregnancy, and when you were born I took on the role of father—discreetly and very quietly. Most people just thought that I was being the captive little brother taking care of the evil lesbian's daughter. We never let them know anything different."

Henry sat, stupefied.

Horace went on. "Do you remember when you were growing up? Who taught you baseball? took you hunting and fishing? showed you how to figure all those baseball stats? I wasn't just being a good uncle; I was trying with everything I could muster to be a good dad. And I had a helluva lot to learn with no role model to teach me. Didn't mind the hunting and fishing so much, even the baseball, but the rest of it was hard—real hard—since I had to learn how to be a man at the same time I was teaching you to be one."

Henry's whole understanding of his childhood was flashing before his eyes, followed by images of a new story that he had never encountered. It was a frightening experience, and he recognized that he was being forced to reconsider everything that he had regarded as truth for the last twenty-odd years. He returned his attention to Horace.

He spoke, with a quavering voice, "Horace ... Dad ... why didn't you ever let me know? I found out from a devious woman who had me vetted for a job ... and she found out easily. Then she used it as a tool to try to manipulate me into something that she wanted me to do for her future. It was a very distasteful experience."

"Henry, the answer is simple ... and complicated, all at the same time. I guess I just never had the courage to face you and let you know that I had done something so outside the bounds of 'normal' society. I liked what you and I had shared, and I didn't want to take the chance that you would always avoid me and write me off. I know you sort of did that with your mom. But I do understand that one. You didn't have the data."

So that's where it comes from. You gotta have the data. I am not wrong, I just need to make sure that I live by that no matter what. Search, and the data will set you free, so to speak.

"So, how come I haven't heard from you all these years?"

Horace flinched noticeably, "How much time do you have? It's a long story, but worthy of a good whodunit or spy novel."

Henry perked up, "So, fill me in."

"When you were in elementary school, I somehow developed a fascination for various forms of gambling. I never had a lot of money, so I couldn't get into too much trouble. When I was about twenty-six or -seven, I had some cash that I had saved up from several employment situations that were not entirely legitimate, and I decided to risk it all in an effort to get out of our situation, and maybe make Helene's life and yours better. I got into a card game and won $85,000. One of the guys in the game was distraught, and, in an attempt to try and recover, he bet his prized colt—a runner with good prospects. I knew about him through some 'contacts' who were involved in racing and had heard of the horse, including some rumors about its value at auction. I decided the bet was attractive and dealt the cards.

"We were playing Texas Hold 'em. I dealt myself two aces as hole cards, and I wasn't cheating. It was a legit deal and I just got lucky. I dealt the other guy a king and a small one but didn't know it. The flop was a king and two tens, not good for me, but I figured two more cards to go, I might come up with something. Turn was an ace. I now had three. He had two kings and two tens with one card to go. He was convinced that he could get a ten or another king and be in control with a full house. He had no idea that I had three beauties already and could beat him even if he got a good card on the river. Then I dealt the river card, another ace. Now I had the hand won, 'cause the best he could do was two pair—kings over tens, and I had four aces. He never knew what hit him. When I turned up the two aces in the hole, he just collapsed. And I had a race horse.

"A horse, I add, that I had no idea what to do with. So, I pondered for a week or two, using up a lot of poker winnings from that night for hay and feed and training fees, and decided to run him in one of the lesser stakes races. He won by six lengths and never sweated. Decided to do that again in a higher stakes race. He won by three lengths with a come-from-behind charge at the eighth pole. I kept going. Six more starts and six more wins, by comfortable margins, and clearly the best runner in the state that year.

"I started getting calls about syndicating the horse and putting him out to stud, a move that would make me a lot of money. I decided to do that. Good decision."

Henry could not imagine what he was hearing. *You can't make this stuff up.*

"I took that syndication money and invested in a lower tier stud farm and training service, changed the name to HoHan, and began booking clients and owners as my horse's success became broadly known; the money rolled in. I had never conceived that there was so much money to be made in the entire world. I put some aside for you, college money. I endowed that first scholarship you won to ensure that you got off on a good foot. And I kept making money on the farm. Then I started housing other successful runners that were being put out. My fees and my percentages just kept multiplying, success I certainly had never anticipated. I managed to take care of Helene's medical expenses, fund your undergraduate university, and get myself a reputation for being a sharp business guy."

Henry's hard-earned but not entirely well-founded

self-esteem took a major hit at the news of the "scholarship." In a shaken condition, he asked Horace, "Please be very clear here. Are you telling me that I did not earn that scholarship? That it came only out of your guilt and largesse?"

"Hang on," countered Horace. "I provided the money, but the university insisted that you meet the requirements of other scholarship competitions in their portfolio. So, you didn't compete with other scholarship holders, but you achieved at the same or higher levels. You belonged, without any doubt whatsoever."

Henry was still uncomfortable with this 'data' but decided that, since it confirmed his own feelings about his success, he would not argue with Horace's statement, and he would accept that he belonged in the elite company of scholars that he had become accustomed to.

Horace continued, "When you were developing into an outstanding student and scholar, I was being approached by the FBI—Agent Smythwick as a matter of fact—to help them with some strange circumstances they were investigating in the industry … money laundering, related to some drug operations by a new cartel. The FBI thought that I could move more freely in the industry than their guys since I was becoming accepted as a player, but did not have ties to law enforcement. I was very reluctant. Then something happened that changed my mind.

"Helene's tumors began to grow more rapidly. They were too far advanced for any kind of treatment. But there were some drugs available on the black market that might have a beneficial effect. They were available through the new cartel. These guys didn't mess with street drugs; they were going after the big money that came with the desperation of wealthy people who had relatives with untreatable problems. I took a chance and established a connection for Helen's medicine, exactly what the FBI wanted me to do, but I didn't know that. I did it on my own."

Henry squirmed in his seat. *So, not only did I not win my scholarship, but my Dad was mixed up in illegal drugs to try to save my Mom. This is a soap opera.*

Horace filled in some more blanks, "I was to buy the drugs and be an informer for the FBI. If it all worked out, I would not be charged, and I would be protected. This went on for about five years, up until a few months ago. Your mother survived but worsened; the inevitable became clear. We talked about you, and she made me promise to find you and explain the history that I have told you tonight.

"But the good news. A couple of months ago, the FBI came to me and told me that they were ready to take down the kingpin of the cartel. If I could just make one more transaction, they would be in place to nab him and take him to trial. I agreed. The transaction was shaky but the Feds got there in the nick of time and I didn't die. They got several of his leaders, but the big guy got away, and I got a promise from Smythwick for witness protection, which is where I am now.

"So, you have to keep tight about this conversation tonight. It is dangerous for me. But as a man, I had to find you and give your history to you; it seemed like my obligation as your dad."

Tears streamed down Henry's face.

All the years he had used up in anger and delusions about his skills, personality, self-esteem, value as a person … all that now in question. How could he live with the new stories of his mom and dad in a way that would allow him to continue to survive in his professional and personal worlds? And how would he ever tell Harper? Would he ever be able to span the gap and recover the feelings that had been growing between them?

Horace saw the reaction and sensed the conflict that had to be tearing Henry up inside. He continued with a degree of reassurance. "During all this, I have developed a high level of trust with Smythwick. He has a letter for you in case anything happens to me. It will no doubt request your assistance with the conclusion of the case against the cartel and provide some options for you. My attorney has a copy also, along with a copy of the will which leaves everything to you—the stud farm and a significant amount of cash, and some suggestions as to how to deal with Smythwick. But I don't see that as a necessary precaution right now. I think the FBI has everything pretty well covered."

Henry sighed, relieved. "I don't know what to say. This is all stretching my capacities to process, and I feel like I have to start living a brand-new life. That is not necessarily a bad thing ..." *if it will help me get Harper back.* "I need to think about this and sleep on it. Let's talk tomorrow morning and figure out next steps."

Horace replied, "Good idea. Tell you what, let's meet at Smythwick's office at nine-thirty, and we can discuss all this with him. It will give you some comfort, and we can make some concrete plans."

"Great ... Dad. I'll see you then." For the first time ever that Henry could remember, they hugged, shook hands, and started toward their respective cars.

Henry could barely walk, but he managed to start his car and get it in drive. Then he pulled out of Ralph's parking lot and started home. He had gone about 400 yards when the flash of light in his rear-view mirror and the loud "whump" behind him caught his attention. There was a huge fireball, and pieces of what Henry was certain to be an orange Porsche were still flying through the air. When the shock wave hit him and the car, it also hit Henry as deep in his soul as it could go.

He felt lost in that sense as someone who has just found a way through the wilderness—only to have it snatched away—might feel. Annihilated, crushed.

As he turned around to go back to Ralph's, he knew what he would find. The Porsche was obliterated, and, Henry was sure, his father along with it. His entire life to date no longer existed. He was on his own.

Henry picked up his phone and called Smythwick to tell him what had happened. He was already en route to the restaurant. Ralph had called the police and they had called the FBI. *How the hell did the police know to call the FBI?*

Henry gave his statement to the police, carefully side-stepping the witness protection stuff to protect Smythwick's case. As he turned to leave, Smythwick arrived, offering his condolences. *How could he know so quickly?*

The agent suggested that they meet at his office at nine-thirty tomorrow to go over all the data points and information concerning Horace, his role, and available steps for Henry. Henry agreed, and slinked off home, exhausted. He called no one, and did not sleep well. *Was he next?*

CHAPTER 45

Eight o'clock arrived far too early and gleefully from Henry's alarm clock. His mood had no room for the happy chirping that he had programmed into the device. He knew that he had a big, sad, anxiety-laden day to face. And then he had to go to the office.

After a minimalist breakfast of coffee—he had considered reinforcing it with brandy, but did not—Henry dutifully addressed Smythwick's assistant at nine twenty-seven, "Henry Hansen to see Mr. Smythwick. We have a nine-thirty appointment."

"Just a moment Mr. Hansen, I'll let him know you're here," replied the uber-efficient young man in a dark suit, white shirt, and dark tie.

Shortly afterward, the door to Smythwick's office opened and Henry was invited in. Smythwick oozed empathy and understanding, but also competence and focus. Henry wasn't sure whether he was being used or comforted. He also knew this meeting was going to be neither simple nor transparent. *But there has to be a pony in there somewhere.*

As Smythwick eloquently expressed the FBI's sorrow at his loss, Henry detected what he analyzed to be the first small indication of insincerity and façade. He waited for the rest. And he wasn't disappointed.

"Your father was a valued informant and colleague for the Bureau. We held him in the highest regard and respect," Smythwick began. "He had worked with us for several years in some matters of the highest sensitivity to help identify and close one of the most sinister money laundering operations in our history. We are at a severe loss as a result of last night."

Wow. How sensitive the government can be ... when it has purposes to be served.

Smythwick continued, "We were about two weeks away from having an ironclad case against the cartel on its money laundering. They were supplying lifesaving but rare and expensive drugs to families with life and death needs. Naturally, they were getting even more premium prices and generating a lot of cash. The operation was being run like a business. Accountants, operations managers, delivery teams, supply chains, and a very astute CEO who looks very much like one would expect a Wall Streeter to look, three-piece suit and all. If we can get him, we have the cartel, and we can shut them down."

Henry was skeptical, "So, go get him."

Smythwick flinched a bit, "Not that easy. We have nothing that connects him directly to any of the transactions in the money laundering chain. He has been 'investing' the cartel's money in undervalued real estate, and then liquidating it when the money is needed for expansion, or the product line, or entering new markets. Just like a real business.

"One of his investments was the land that is now part of the partnership that Maurice Stearns' firm is proposing to develop. The FBI was conducting a sting to buy the land from him—legal transfer of title and everything—so that there would be a hard link between him and the laundered money. Before, the land has passed from one lightly-documented shell company to another, and its true ownership could not be fully established. If he transferred the ownership legally to get his profits and original capital out, then we would have the documentation we needed."

Henry was alert now, "I understand, but what has that to do with my father or me?"

"Your father, because of his connection with us, was going to be the buyer. He was going to pay the cartel about seven million for clean title, and the Bureau was then going to seize the money and the CEO, thus shutting down the cartel operations. Unfortunately, that possibility no longer exists."

"I see that," said Henry, "so what does it all mean, Batman?"

"I have a letter here for you from your father. He asked me to give it to you … if anything should happen. It explains most of what I just told you in greater detail and requests you to help us finish off this beastly organization. He wanted to do it in honor of Helene, and to be a part of doing the right thing."

Ah. Now for the close.

Henry read the letter. Smythwick had described it accurately. "So now you want me to step in, somehow, as my father's deputy, to close the transaction and enable the capture of the cartel leadership?"

"Lock, stock, and barrel," agreed Smythwick. "This will shut them down. And our intelligence sources tell us that the other cartels/families want these guys gone so badly that they will make sure that they never resurrect their business, and those who took them down remain safe, just as a good business practice of limiting competition."

"And you believe them. Why would they help the FBI?"

"Not totally clear, but they have taken steps like this in the past to control the proliferation of competitors. They seem to feel like they can handle the FBI so long as they don't have too much competition. Too-many-cooks-in-the-kitchen kind of thing."

Hmmm. That says a helluva lot. I bet Smythwick doesn't want to unpack any of that.

Henry cautiously advanced the next question, "How will all this work? What are you asking me to do? I am not exactly experienced in this undercover stuff, and frankly it terrifies me. I believe that I am at significant risk." *That nice job calculating baseball stats looks a whole lot better than it did a few months ago.*

Smythwick began slowly, "We have another letter for you from your father. It appoints you as administrator of the HoHan Trust, which was created for the benefit of the Hansen family and its heirs. You have full authority to manage the Trust assets—buy, sell, develop, or transfer, any or all of them—for any legal purpose you deem worthy."

Henry quietly peed in his shorts.

"H ... how much is the trust worth as it currently stands?"

"Approximately thirty-two million, six hundred and twenty-nine thousand dollars," Smythwick calmly announced.

Henry peed again.

"Uh, so my father anticipated that he might not make it through this. And now he is asking me to put my life on the line to complete his work so far. And what happens to the trust after the 'transaction' is completed?"

Smythwick replied, "You, as administrator, will conduct

the Trust's business, according to the terms of the letter, and the assets become the property of the Hansen family."

Third time. "Which, as of now," Henry sighed, "is me."

"Correct."

"Oh, God." *What do I do now?*

Smythwick shed additional light on the next steps, "The cash position of the Trust is approximately ten million, with liquid assets of eight available if needed. The price of the land is seven million. We suggest that you close the deal at seven, and then you have a valuable piece of land to include in the family Trust. We have the cash, the cartel assets, the CEO, and his leadership team. Problem solved."

"And how do I know that I can actually do something with the land?" Henry inquired perceptively.

"We have support from the EPA that they will 'assist' an environmentally sound use of the land as much as possible. And we will, as part of that agreement, make the proceeds of the sale—which we confiscated—available to them to finance their contribution to such a project. You and the Trust will be in a very good position to do something meaningful."

"If I survive to tell the story," groaned Henry.

"We can assure you of that," smiled Smythwick.

Did you assure my father too? "Who can I talk to before committing to this scheme?"

Smythwick became less friendly, "You can enlist the help of US&G under an NDA, which we will draft—which we have already drafted, in fact—and you must get Mo to sign it before going into any details. You are going to need his help to do anything with the land, as he has the option, and then you and he will have to go to the landowners to ensure that you can do whatever it is you decide. Of course, I point out that you and Jack Morris will now be the primary owners, and that should give you some workable alternatives."

Henry perked up a bit. *There might actually be a realistic and worthwhile deal here yet.* "Can I include Jack in the conversation with MO?"

"Yes, if you get him to sign the same NDA, but no one else until we have the cartel people behind bars. For your safety as well as the security of our case."

Henry replied resignedly, "Okay. Got it. Can I have a copy of the NDA?" And Smythwick handed him two certified copies awaiting notarized signatures from whoever executed them. "Is there anything else we need to cover this morning?"

Smythwick seemed to breathe in relief, "I think not. Obviously, I am available if you need answers on short notice. You have my cell number. And, Mr. Hansen, I sincerely thank you on behalf of the FBI. You are considering a great service to us and to your country. Please let me know as soon as possible."

They shook hands and Henry left. He felt trepidation, confusion, some sense of duty—and yet, for the first time since the big meeting, a sense of optimism. The optimism arose not from the enhancement of his personal fortune and stature, not from his sense of justice for his parents, not from his personal pride in being a key part of a major solution. It arose from his hope that he might be able to tell Harper and regain her confidence. He had not confirmed with Smythwick when he could bring her in on the events, but he did see a possibility that it was closer than it had been after the meeting. He had a chance that he did not have last night.

Maybe doing the right thing was really the right thing.

CHAPTER 46

When he returned to his office after leaving the FBI, Henry closed his door to try to buy some time for sitting and thinking. He had to have some critical conversations, and he had no idea in what order.

He needed to talk with Jack for help with Harper, and possibly with something that would be of value to Mo and US&G that Jack might have some ideas about. Then he needed to talk with Mo about how to preserve the value of US&G's option while avoiding the cartel—and keeping straight with the multi-agency enforcement team. He should probably talk with Amanda, since she would have to manage the firm and any project they came up with as Mo was set to take off and run for governor.

He wanted to talk with his team and get them steeled for the onslaught to come with all the confusion that would ensue. He would have to have a meeting with the cartel CEO so that the FBI could conclude their work and start the wheels moving toward a long-term solution. And, he had to spend some time convincing Harper that the world was alright—he was alright, and they were alright. *That would be the toughest conversation of them all.*

Well, if it was easy, anybody could do it.

First, call Jack. Make some progress, then build on that with Mo and Amanda. Small steps to lead to a win.

Henry picked up the phone and dialed Jack's private number. Jack answered quickly—psychically almost, like he knew it was Henry. "I heard about the explosion last night. Was that the guy who stopped you when you were trying to catch Harper?"

"Yes, and it is a long, long story. I want to tell you all about it, but not over the phone. It is a mystery-spy-mob thriller and demands quite a bit of security. Can we meet somewhere that is very secure and quiet? I'll spill all the beans, because I really need your help, and I have permission to tell you a lot."

"Sure, Henry. Come by my office after hours. I'll make certain everyone has gone by six-thirty and we can talk in my office. It's soundproof, and I have a secure telephone line if we need one. I've never been in a spy novel before; this could be exciting. See you then."

Yeah. Exciting ... or fatal.

Next, a touch-base with Mo, asking for a meeting the next morning at nine. Invite Amanda for nine-thirty in order for Henry to properly prepare Mo for the news that he would be losing his pet project. It would take some time to convince both of them that it is in the best interests of the firm to take a different path on this one.

Then Henry needed to make the call to Smythwick to commit himself and the firm to the close-out of the deal and a proposal that the EPA could support in lieu of the tech park. He hoped Smythwick and a team of agents would be available to protect him at the final transaction.

Just like the movies. The docs are signed and the wire transfer of the cash confirmed, and the good guys step up, flash their badges, and put cuffs on everybody in sight. I hope.

Risking life, future, and fortune so far—no problem. The next event in the sequence was the most intimidating of all. He would need Jack's help getting that one on the books, and Henry would definitely talk with Jack about that tonight.

After recovering Harper, he would have to put forward an interesting alternative program that would complement Mo's gubernatorial ideas, and make Amanda's efforts profitable in her first major project as CEO. Henry had no idea what that would be yet. He and Jack would have to come up with something that would keep everybody on the ranch and support it going forward.

Do I have enough moxie, creativity, and skill to pull this off? I am way outta my league here.

Somehow, the team had to be enlisted to make whatever was going to be "the move" actually happen. Henry felt like they would give it an all-hands effort, but this would be totally new ground. None of them had ever seen anything like this. He would talk to them, in spite of the FBI restrictions, after talking with Mo and Amanda. The conversation would be 'hypothetical' and in concept only, just to see what creative thinking could be brought to bear. If that effort was successful, then the firm would be off to the races again on a new project that could support Mo as candidate for governor and Amanda as the farsighted new CEO. It would be nice to have a win-win out of all this.

In sequence, Henry. Keep things in sequence. Do what you have to do first, and then let things fall into a natural sequence of order. Give the opportunities time to be converted into matter.

With that in mind, Henry turned to the highest priority, at least in *his* mind—his meeting with Jack, and how he could leverage that into regaining Harper's favor. He finished the day, although his concentration was not really sharp. Instead he was focused on what he could tell Jack and how he could convince him to remain on board with the land he had in the partnership now.

Henry appeared at Jack's silent-and-soundproof office at the appointed hour and was surprised to see that the dealership was truly deserted, except for Jack. They had utter privacy and security for their discussions. As Henry entered Jack's office, Jack extracted a bottle of eighteen-year-old small batch bourbon from his desk, along with two glasses.

"This is really great stuff," he said. "You can only drink a tiny bit at a time, so it lasts longer—and it makes you smarter as time moves along. I've had many of my best ideas after a couple of hours with this stuff, and limited hangover the next morning. It's a pity our politicians don't seem to be aware of its magical powers."

Henry chuckled at the time worn joke, though it was actually tinged with truth, and quickly moved to the matters at hand. "Jack, I am in deep shit, up to my chin, and I need your help."

Jack got it. "Henry, just tell me what I need to do."

Henry took a deep breath and sighed. He took out the NDA from Smythwick and said to Jack, "I can tell you everything, but if you breathe a word to anyone, I'll have to kill you. And I need you to sign this document before I can say anything."

Jack was shocked and flustered, but—trusting his golden-puttered partner—he signed and gulped hard. "Okay, let's roll. Tell me what I am signing on for."

Henry unloaded the entire story of the cartel, Jack's partner in the land owner partnership, the contract with his father, the FBI, the potential help from the EPA, the short timeline, his fear of having to tell Mo about the death of the tech park deal, and his fear for his own life—and possibly Jack's and a dozen others.

Jack turned pale but put on a brave face, "Hey, if it was easy ..."

"Yeah, I know," Henry cut him off in mid-cliché. "'Been down that road already."

Jack changed directions. "Do you trust the FBI? Can they deliver what they are promising? Can you be confident that everyone will survive?" His concern was clearly for himself as well as 'everyone.'

Henry nodded, "I think so."

Jack added, "Is it the right thing to do? Will everyone be better off if you do this and it works?"

"Yes, unequivocally."

Jack accepted the assent. "Then it seems to me that we ought to find a way to do it."

And the die was cast, the Rubicon crossed, and the cards dealt—all the famous gambles of history merged into one moment for Jack and Henry. But, like Lee at Gettysburg, operating without his cavalry for two days, Henry didn't know what he didn't know. The path to a win was not clear. And Henry's version of Pickett's charge was coming sooner rather than later.

"Jack, between us, we control some very valuable and crucial land in this deal—*assuming we are alive*. We can give some drive to a project that will ease Mo's despair, and maybe even create some community support. Any ideas what that could be?"

Jack could only think of a conversation he had at the golf club recently, "Some of the people at Cottonwood are willing to invest in a second location for a new course with a more modern design—you know, target golf and all that—in an effort to get a PGA tournament scheduled here. But I'm not sure how that could be leveraged into what you need. Let me think about it. Don't worry, I won't talk to anybody about specifics that would get us in trouble—more trouble—with the FBI."

"Thanks, Jack. You could be a big help here. But, please, think fast. The FBI is ready to move on this. And ... Jack ... there is one more thing."

Jack smiled knowingly, "Yeah, I figured. Harper?"

"Y'know, I have never felt this level of pain in my life related to a woman and a relationship, and I need to get this right."

"You are, truly, in trouble with Harper. But it is because she has invested emotionally in you, too. And she doesn't want to write off that investment. So, there is some common ground for the two of you to find each other and find satisfaction in that relationship again. Trust me, you just have to be honest and trust her to participate in your troubles as well as your successes. Have you told her any of what you told me?"

Henry cringed, "No, there hasn't been a lot of time, and I am concerned that she just won't listen. So, I have been trying to resolve all of this in order to show her that it was not a scheme to cheat on her attachment to Parsons Point, and that I am a man to be trusted."

Jack offered that he could always arrange a fishing trip for the three of them that could sort of be a neutral platform to begin a reconciliation. Henry liked that, and told Jack to hold on to it until Henry could call him to confirm a date.

As Henry left Jack's office, he thought he saw a non-train at the end of the tunnel for the first time since the meeting.

As Henry arrived home, his phone rang with a message from Mo. Tomorrow morning was not good but the next morning would be fine and Amanda was available. *Not perfect, but it'll have to do. Maybe I can make progress with the team tomorrow.*

Henry's energy returned, and, although he slept fitfully, he awoke the next morning ready to slay some dragons. As soon as he got to the office, he gathered the team.

"Guys, we have a challenge in front of us that is like nothing you have ever seen. And if I tell you too much about it, your lives are in danger. From me, the FBI, or some nefarious characters who cannot be named. You in or out?"

The office burst into laughter from all the team at once. Henry was not laughing.

"Uhhh, no shit. This is serious and it requires some very clear and creative thinking if I am to survive, figuratively and perhaps literally. I really need you on this. Let me fill you in on the events since the meeting the other night so you will know what you're dealing with."

Carefully, leaving out no critical events, but protecting the guilty, Henry recounted all the strange happenings—beginning the moment he noticed his tail in the orange Porsche up to the moment he left Smythwick's office. Details were judiciously communicated, except where they were clearly too risky.

After forty-five minutes of storytelling and question answering, Henry summarized. "So, here's what we have. Control of two critical parcels of land. A pledge of cooperation from the EPA, if we choose a worthy project. Support and protection from the FBI. The possibility of strong community support. The embarrassment of canceling the project that we announced with such fanfare at the meeting. I am open for ideas. Gimme your best shots."

He was met with stony silence from the group. Not a hint of any creative ideas or public admission that there was any hope at all. It was depressing.

After a full five minutes of silence, Hanna very slowly raised her hand, "What about a PPP?"

Henry looked at her quizzically, "What is one of those?"

She brightened and responded, "A Public Private Partnership. A Public entity—say, a government agency or development agency funded by public money—combines with private investors to create an SPV, Special Purpose Vehicle, to accomplish some public-benefit type project. The private side contributes equity; the public side contributes equity that is paid back in some defined period, not unlike preferred shares bought back at a premium over a contractual period. The private entities are allowed to acquire additional funding, either equity or debt, to accomplish the SPV purpose and use proceeds to implement or to pay back the public entity."

Henry brightened. He began to see the path that had, so far, eluded him.

Hanna continued, "We have the public support from the EPA. We have the equity from the two pieces of critical land, and some local investors who probably would be able to come up with financing for the project. And we have an IB firm who now holds the option on the land and would be able to facilitate additional financing if needed. A very public beneficial project would certainly look good in Mo's run for governor, and the project could be structured with enough ownership by local investors and citizens that it could be done at advantageous rates. Everybody wins. That's all oversimplified, of course, but it fits."

Henry was overjoyed, probably prematurely. "Hanna, I could kiss you. But then I would get in a lot of trouble." He sneaked a sly glance at Charles, who smiled at the joke.

Hanna giggled.

"I think you are on to something. What homework do we have to do in order to start discussing this with Mo and Amanda?"

"I can give you our copies of the regulations with a summary in an hour, and you can take it with you. It is pretty clear and has been done often in other locations. In fact, unless I am mistaken, this vehicle is similar to the one that was used in Montana, but don't bet the ranch on that."

D also had heard of the practice and offered an example of a situation where the vehicle was used to construct a venue for a G-League basketball team in a small city, "in the public interest."

Martin joined in that he had seen examples of similar projects scattered around the technology corridors for infrastructure improvements and public facilities to encourage tech companies to invest in various locales.

Henry was now looking not just at a light at the end of the tunnel, but at the full-fledged end of the tunnel.

But he wasn't seeing deals, or money, or politics, or even successful arrests of a crooked boss and his team. He was seeing Harper, smiling at him.

CHAPTER 47

The team broke up the meeting and went about their chores for the day while Henry prepared to convert Mo and Amanda from fearless corporate profit mongers into high-minded public interest seekers. He knew that Mo could be convinced to take the high road in favor of his campaign, but he was uncertain how Amanda would react to having the giant development project killed for the benefit of the smaller PPP that seemed to be the better path all around. So, he carefully built the arguments with as much data and factual support as he could muster.

He looked at success rates for similar projects which included large amounts of public agency support, investment recovery and pay out rates for office development projects, ultimate return figures for three carry periods, and a couple of disaster scenarios, to temper the natural optimism that normally pervades these kinds of proposals in the first place. He got D to run some simulations of overall economic impacts—given three of the scenarios—and an estimate of the economic value of the benefits under a successful PPP project. The only thing he could find that would swing the scales in favor of the PPP was the probability of Mo's elevation to the governor's office. Uncertain economic value, but high political status value to Mo.

As he reviewed the options he had prepared, fully believing that he would be talking to Mo and Amanda in the morning, and also fully believing in the power of data, his phone rang. Henry thought it had an ominous sound although he had no idea why. He found out as soon as he answered.

"Hansen."

"Henry, It's agent Smythwick. Things are moving a bit faster than we had anticipated. We need you to be available for a 'closing' on the land tomorrow morning at ten. I'll give you the address and the procedures. You are to be alone, but you can have one associate there to help you manage the payment technology. We will be nearby, ready to intervene if things don't seem to be working. An FBI team of ten will be hidden within steps to protect you."

Henry's skepticism was not well disguised. "And how will you know if things don't go well? I certainly will be searched for a wire, and I assume that the facility will be blocked against wireless listening devices."

"We have drones that can hover, undetected, and penetrating radar-type tech that can show us what is happening behind thick walls and ceilings. We will have virtual eyes on you. And we know the layout of the building well so we can get to you quickly. They will want you to transfer money by automated transfer order, and will have a laptop computer there to execute the transaction. We will give you a bank routing number and account under our control that will look like it is one of yours, so that you can actually fund the closing. It will be, for all practical purposes, a legitimate transaction—at least from our side."

Henry's pulse quickened, not quite to the level of panic,

but noticeably. "And I can take one person with me to operate the transfer tech? OK. I got that figured out. How do the logistics work?"

Smythwick took twenty minutes to explain how the admission to the room would work, the wire checks, the gun searches, the hard-nosed attitudes Henry would encounter, the likely conversation with hardened criminals, the transaction itself, and the exit. It was not reassuring, but Henry was in.

When the conversation ended, Henry called D. "I need some big-time help, and it has to be very street smart. Maybe smarter in the dark arts than you are comfortable with. Can you come to my office right now and discuss this?"

Forbidden by Smythwick to give Mo any details right now, Henry made his excuses with Mo's assistant for missing the morning meeting. He promised to get back to Mo asap with a new time. He was relatively certain that would not keep Mo happy, but it was the best he could do.

True to his respect and genuine regard for Henry, D was there in minutes. "Alright, Fearless Leader, what is this huge problem that requires knowledge of the dark side of street smart?"

Henry filled him in, further expanding the circle of risk, and in mild defiance of the FBI's recommended procedures. D's eyes lit up and he showed visible excitement. "I had to deal with some druggies in high school, but nothing this sophisticated. I do think, though, that I can read the room pretty well, and understand instinctively what is going on in tough situations. And it might not hurt you to have a very big black man walk in with you—kind of raise your stature, y'know." And he smiled confidently.

Henry acknowledged the point but was unable to return the smile. "I'll need you to look pretty menacing. Can you do menacing?"

D became very calm, "Opposing power forwards used to think I was menacing. Of course, they didn't have guns. But I am not as pretty as you see here; I can do menacing ... from experience."

Henry took a deep breath, "Okay. I don't know anyone else I would trust to do this, but I do have to be honest. This is very dangerous. You could be hurt ... or worse."

"Look," D injected, "I'm no gangbanger, but I've been around a lot of them, and still managed to keep my cool and my menace. I am the best person you know to have with you in this."

Henry believed him. "I'll pick you up at 8:00 a.m. tomorrow morning. We'll have a cup of coffee to get under control, and then our meeting is at ten. Here is the routing number and account number that Smythwick gave me—oh, and the password. Memorize them, and don't forget 'em under pressure. It is our only ticket out of that room, and the ticket to a lot of other things that are waiting for us."

D smiled, again confidently, "See you then."

Mo and Amanda would have to wait, *hopefully not forever,* for the alternative deal proposal that Henry still had not manufactured out of dream cloth. He had no idea how he was going to present an idea that would satisfy them. But if he was successful, they would be riding the crest of a wave of admiration—even perhaps heroism—forward. Maybe he could lever that into something they would go for.

Given the real pressure and danger of the land closing,

and the less lethal but still real pressure of Mo and Amanda, Henry almost threw up. At least he didn't pee his pants. That was an improvement. He knew he couldn't back out, but that didn't stop his rising bile or stem the abject fear that made him unsteady.

Why the hell am I doing this? And why is it worth it? Harper, you better understand it was for you when you're holding my bleeding body in your arms.

CHAPTER 48

At the appointed hour of 8:00 a.m., Henry picked D up at home and they went to have a coffee and steady their nerves. At least Henry did. D seemed to be working on familiar ground, a thought that scared Henry a bit. But it also gave him some confidence that D had his back.

Henry's phone rang and Smythwick confirmed that the FBI team had been in place for a couple of hours so as not to show any suspicious activity near the time when Henry and D were scheduled to arrive. He reassured Henry, again, that the FBI had his back. Henry had more confidence in D.

As they sipped their coffees, D explained what they were likely to encounter. To Henry it sounded like all the television clichés he had ever seen. People would be dressed in black; there would be a lot of tough talk, most of it sincere; there would be an insane amount of suspicion and distrust—that's how these guys stayed alive, after all—and if anything out of the script occurred, guns would be pulled, and, in all likelihood, used. Henry and D carried no guns. Henry and Smythwick had agreed on a code word for "Help, get my ass out of here!" It was "elephant in the room." If Henry said that, the FBI would immediately intervene, hopefully in time to rescue Henry and D, and apprehend the CEO and his team.

The inevitable became the immediate, and the two of them left to go to the vacant warehouse where the transaction was supposed to be completed. As they arrived, Henry thought again how much this reminded him of any FBI/cop thriller he had ever seen on TV. D was far too relaxed for credibility ... unless he was more practiced in this discipline than Henry could imagine. That he might be was a good thing from Henry's perspective.

As they approached the rusty and neglected-looking door, it opened in anticipation of their entrance. Just as D had warned, the conversation was rough, tough, and largely one way. The wire searches and gun searches were conducted with little respect, and the three factotums in black tactical gear conducted the two acquisition advisors into the presence of Mr. Granato—an imposing though almost elegant figure who would fit in any board room in the world. Immaculately tailored suit and shirt, very expensive shoes, ultra-expensive silk tie, and coiffed to a degree that would shame Hollywood.

Granato eyed them with suspicion. "You guys are awfully young to be doing such heavy business."

"A tribute to our capabilities and our rapid rise up the corporate ladder," snapped D.

Granato growled, "He speak for your side?"

"When I wish him to," responded Henry. "He is my technical guy, and can manage the logistics of the transfer and closing documents. Here is the letter of authorization from Max with the proper and agreed authentication code."

"He looks very familiar," grunted Granato. "I seen him before, but I can't place him."

Henry and D kept their mouths shut on that one. "Can we get to the business at hand?" asked Henry. "We came here to complete the purchase of the land formerly owned by the mine owners up the Hattowoc River. The price is seven million and we have completed our due diligence—we are ready to close. But we want it properly established that we are the legal, lien-free owners. You have a deed of trust that meets those conditions?"

"Yeah, yeah, keep your shirt on. We got all that," groaned Granato. "We'll need a wire transfer to close. Bank routing number and account number. You got that?"

"Got it all, and a password to ensure that we control the final confirmation," Henry proclaimed with more confidence than he felt.

Granato smiled, "Here is the pile of documents for you to look at. I'll give you fifteen minutes. Then I expect a transfer."

Henry and D exchanged glances and each took half the pile to review. They weren't too sure what to look for, but Henry knew that the primary document—the deed of trust—had to have the right names and the legal description. There had to be a contract of sale which gave the proper amount, and the absence of liens had to be specifically assured by the seller, with recourse if it turned out to not be true.

He and D took the allotted fifteen minutes and agreed that, from what they could tell, the documents were okay. Henry desperately wanted to have something that provided leverage for an enforceable threat in case there were irregularities in the papers, but, having none, he decided to drop that strategy. He glanced at D, and with apprehension D stepped to the computer and accessed the transfer system at the bank Smythwick had indicated for them.

As he entered the routing number, Granato came to life and yelled, "Now I got it! I know where I know you from. You are that basketball player who disappeared from the draft a few years ago. You're from Marquette, and you beat Nova in the famous tournament game, and then you disappeared. I lost a lot of money on that. I had you picked to go to the Lakers in the first round. That did not make me happy."

D calmly replied, "Yeah, I decided that I wanted to make some real bucks. I could have joined a gang in the old neighborhood, or take an offer from a Wall Street firm. I made up my mind that I could do better going with a lower profile investment banking firm, and work my way into the inside of some deals. So, here I am."

Granato stiffened, "I don't think I like this a bit." The three henchmen all pulled Austrian pistols and racked the slides. Henry knew there were no safeties on those pistols, and realized that the stakes had become very high.

"Look," he said with exasperation, "the *elephant in the room* is that he has the codes to get you your money, and only *he* has them. If those guns go off by accident, then you don't get paid, and your deal falls through. You want that?" *Geez, I hope Smythie has his ears on for that one.*

Granato hesitated. D had stealthily entered the remaining information to complete the transaction except for the password. He waited for the word to go ahead from Henry.

Granato continued to hesitate.

"What'll it be?" inquired Henry. *Thirty seconds had passed. Smythwick had said forty-five max.*

Granato angrily blurted, "Finish the damned transfer." D complied, entering the password.

At precisely the moment that D entered the final information, all hell broke loose. The door was smashed in, six guys yelled "FBI" in unison, and one government-issued Sig Sauer snapped twice when one of the three henchmen turned and appeared to level his Glock at an agent. That was unfortunate … for him. He fell, mortally wounded, to the floor. The other two quickly dropped their pistols and Granato raised his hands. The remaining henchmen were quickly subdued with flex ties, and Granato was handcuffed as Miranda rights were recited for all of them.

Henry realized it had been some time since he had breathed and relieved his body's need for air accordingly. D smiled, "Piece of cake."

Smythwick came into the room, smiling, and shook Henry's hand.

"Well done. We got it all and the transfer has been confirmed, so we have direct, documented involvement of this team and their organization. Unbeatable case, thanks to you, Mr. Moffat, and the rest of your team. I would suggest that we have a couple of agents hang around you for a few days just to make sure that everything is copacetic, and you and the team are safe. You okay with that?"

Still starved for air, Henry could barely talk, but he did agree to the protective agents for a few days. D also agreed, and seemed in command of the whole scene.

Then a remarkable event occurred. Agent Smythwick seemed to soften noticeably and the Bureau-installed demeanor became decidedly more human. In a muted side-conversation he said, "And as a demonstration of our sincere respect for Horace and our gratitude to you, the Bureau would be pleased to assist in a small memorial service in Horace's honor, if you would like. It can be done here or back in your hometown, wherever you think best."

Henry was quite taken aback, but it seemed like a good thing to do. Maybe clearing the air would be a good thing for everybody involved, himself included, and especially those nosy busybodies back home who made Horace and Helene's lives so miserable when they were growing up.

"Thank you Agent Smythwick. I think that is a grand idea, and I will get back to you in a bit on that offer. I'd really like to do that, but I need a little recovery time right now."

One of Smythwick's agents escorted D and Henry outside to their car. The remaining agents from inside and outside corralled the cartel members into a van and hauled them off to lockup, pending indictment and trial.

As Henry and D drove slowly and carefully back to US&G, Henry contemplated the conversations he had just completed and the ones he still required in order to bring this whole affair to a conclusion. Mo and Amanda. Smythwick, to get ownership of the land squared away. Jack, to get a plan in place for their two parcels, and how it might relate to Hanna's PPP suggestion. And, the big one, Harper. If she would see him and talk so that he could explain all the events and outcomes, he might have a chance.

When they arrived at US&G, they managed to get back to their respective offices without incident. Henry, pale and shaken, was still contemplating the priorities of what lay before him when his phone erupted. *I have a bad feeling about this call.*

His bad feeling was confirmed. It was Mo in a thunderous fit of temper.

"Hansen, where the hell have you been this morning? I need to talk to you. And what have you committed this firm to without my agreement? That kind of shit could cost you your very lucrative job. Get your ass in my office immediately!"

Henry was weary and out of energy, but he knew that he still had the advantage over Mo because he had the data and the results. It was just a question of whether Mo would realize that Henry had the advantage.

He trudged to Mo's office only to find that the facts of the situation were far worse than Mo's call had indicated. To say that Mo was furious was an understatement of titanic proportion. It was miraculous that the roof had remained in place.

Man up, Henry, we all gotta pay the piper sometime. And besides, if you go down for doing the right thing and saving everyone's ass, then you go down for a good cause and you can be proud. Henry really tried to believe that he felt that way, since he knew his resolve and manhood were about to be severely tested.

Time to face the Inquisition.

CHAPTER 49

As Henry entered the Chairman's lair, he was aware of a hush in the room. And he was surprised to see Mo, Amanda, Hanna—and *Smythwick*—already in the office. His sense of dread began to exceed the space available. *This is going to be very ugly.*

Mo opened—as in opened fire.

"What were you thinking to commit the people and reputation of this firm in such a hair-brained and dangerous plan as what you just did this morning? You have placed me ... and Amanda ... in a very difficult position. What if something went wrong and you and/or Moffat had gotten hurt or killed? The potential liability would have killed this firm, and a lot of other people would have 'died,' economically at least."

Henry had little defense to offer. Amanda sat quietly, and it was impossible for Henry to tell if she was gloating or laughing.

But then Smythwick stepped in. *How did he get back here so fast?*

"On the other hand, the FBI, ATF, and DEA are incredibly grateful for the unbelievable dedication and courage that you, Henry, and Mr. Moffat have demonstrated to get this case closed and moving toward trial. You placed your lives, personal resources—not a small amount of money—and personal credibility at substantial risk to help rid our country of a grave menace and possible security risk. I cannot say enough positive about your conduct and fortitude."

Mo smiled and continued, "Yeah, you whippersnapper. That took balls, and, even though it scares the shit out of me, I have to admire your decision-making and execution skills. I don't know anyone else in this whole town who could have done what you did. I would be right in firing you, or at least being pissed off enough to bury you in some nondescript job for life—or until you got fed up and left."

His rant continued. "And you have totally screwed up my lifetime dream project. What are we gonna do with the money we have invested in the tech park preliminary EIS, and related work? What use is that expensive option that I paid for? Just because you are nearly a hero doesn't mean that we solved all the problems associated with this fiasco. Maybe I should make you pay for the money that I and the firm will lose because of your courage. What do you think?"

Henry felt his resolve return, "Mo, I saved your ass from the embarrassment of being tied up with mobsters. I gave you a big win that will allow you to run for governor on a stronger platform than any other candidate, and I have some early thoughts on how to make wonderful, clean, popular use of the land and your option that will actually work."

He didn't yet, but he did have some ideas of baby steps into uses that could still be profitable and civically very attractive for a potential governor. He just needed a little time to flesh them out ... sort of ... maybe. Geez, he needed to talk to Jack.

Mo sat back in his chair, a look of surprise on his face

at Henry's feisty response. Amanda quietly smiled into her hands as she concealed her face from the group. Hanna giggled. The other men remained stolid.

When Mo recovered, he glared at Henry, "Okay. That answer bordered on insubordinate, but there is just enough that is of interest that I think it should be followed through. I'll give you thirty days to convince me ... and Amanda ... that your ideas are worth pursuing on behalf of this firm. You can use your team to build and 'prove' your case, and I—the firm—will consider it from all perspectives. If you're good enough, we might even consider investing our own capital. But mainly I want to see something that will get some useful mileage out of the money we have already spent. Got it?"

Relieved, Henry spat out, "Got it." *I feel like I should be requesting permission to be excused.* But most of all, he wanted time to breathe, think, and consider next steps. He had encountered enough pressure for a lifetime today.

He headed for his office but detoured to go to the coffee room. He clearly needed caffeine to get through the rest of the day. Back in his office, he was interrupted by a knock on the door. It was Amanda. As she entered, Henry saw that she was upbeat but subdued. She sat down and smiled at Henry in a way he had not seen from her since he had known her.

"Wanted to tell you, that was magnificent. I have never seen any living person have the balls to stand up to my Dad like that ... and make it stick. Anyone else he would have fired on the spot—and he has—no questions, no severance. Do you have any idea what that means?"

"I guess it means that he sees some promise in other possibilities," Henry shrugged. "He wants to see what I'm talking about."

Amanda sighed. "You nimrod. It means that he respects you, Henry. Nothing less. And that is a first ... *ever*. It means that he is ready to turn over the reins, or a big part of them, actually, to you, to me, to us ... if you're willing to consider what I have been talking to you about. We are a natural team. Brains, charisma, glamor, technical skills, people skills, and we look damned good together—a power couple like none in the history of this town. We can both be quite proud of us. Get it?"

Henry suddenly wearied, "Amanda, you are class and glamor, and you're damned good at what you do—PR, marketing, and operations. You are the princess in the royal family and *the* natural choice to be the firm's leader when Mo is governor. I can only play a supporting role, ever, in that. I am a rookie, have some valuable skills, and a good mind. Plus, I am becoming far more experienced in some disciplines than I ever wanted to."

Henry let out a long breath, then continued. "But I am not your natural mate; I am an excellent resource for you to utilize in leading this firm, and I am happy to be that. I am not a good fit to be your spouse, mate, love interest, significant other, consort, or anything other than a professional advisor. I am flattered, as I have told you previously, and even honored, but I am not right. I won't put us in that potential position of discovering, after a short while, that Camelot doesn't reside here. But thanks for the compliment."

Amanda's disappointment showed in her bittersweet smile. "Henry Hansen, you have remarkable courage and integrity. I respect the hell outta that. Yes, I wish you could be a bit more mercenary and unrealistic about me, but, in the long run, I have no doubt that what you say is fair and true. You are the most substantial man I have ever known, and can I at least be proud to be your colleague and friend?"

"Deal," said Henry with some relief.

"And," she continued, "is there a woman who has whatever it takes for you to think long-term about her?"

"Oh, yes," he replied. "But that is far from accomplished, and I have a lot of work to do there. When the work is done, successfully or not, you'll know.

"Now I have a lot of thinking and case building to do if I'm going to do right by my boss, Boss. And I need to get going. I've got meetings to arrange, agreements to acquire, models to build, finances to plan, and a whole shitload of imagining to undertake. If you'll excuse me, I'm feeling the pressure to do some serious work."

Amanda laughed in a friendly, supportive manner.

"Okay, get to work, minion. Put your back into it. I'll leave you alone to work your magic."

And she left, not fully satisfied, but content. In her mind, this was going to work out well.

Henry, on the other hand, was a bit lost—he had need of some creative thinking that required help from his golf partner. He and Jack controlled the two most important assets in the potential PPP Special Purpose Vehicle, and they had to figure out how to make best use of the assets in a way that got Mo elected, provided prestige and income for the firm, assured benefits to the community, and ... got Harper back in Henry's life with a long-term future—*especially that*.

He picked up the phone and called Jack's private number.

"Looking for a money game against some padded handicaps?" Jack asked when he answered.

"Not just yet," said Henry, "but I do need the wise

insight of a good businessman as to how we can use our respective land holdings to do something really spectacular. Interested?"

"Wondered how long it was going to take for you to call. I've been looking at this for a couple of weeks, poring over some possibilities. When can we talk?"

"ASAP," said Henry, "but in a very private setting. This has to be you and me putting a plan together that will save my ass and your investment."

"Breakfast tomorrow morning at CCC? I'll get us a private room."

"Seven-thirty," said Henry. "See you there."

CHAPTER 50

As Henry and Jack sipped on their first cup of coffee the next morning, Henry voiced his consternation at the present circumstances.

"You and I control two very useful and potentially valuable pieces of real estate. But they are not valuable unless we can find a use for them that takes advantage of their unique qualities. Given that the EPA is not red hot about required approvals for the tech park, what can we do that will use our land holdings well, profitably, and for civic benefit?"

Jack showed the beginning of a sly smile. "Remember how I told you about those CCC members who thought a second golf course would be a good thing for the club? I looked at it and I don't see how it could support itself ... unless it would become a tourism generator. You know, 'famed Cottonwood creates a new modern Cottonwood Hills Course fit for tourney play on the PGA tour' kind of thing. Turns out, that is not all that far-fetched. I and some of the guys have some contacts in the industry who have expressed interest in such a project.

"Three design firms would be interested in taking a look and having preliminary discussions. The topography is good, but the threat from the old mine is significant. I figure that the EPA already has had good experience with the project in Anaconda and would be willing to help with another similar project, and our potential economics are far superior to Anaconda's. Bigger community, larger economic base, broader diversity of population, good prospects for tourism. Not a lead pipe cinch, but a good basis to explore."

Henry shrugged, "Okay, I like that, and there may be a good possibility to go that way. But, that doesn't do anything for your land, the former tech park location. What can we do with that?"

Jack's smile grew, "Like any good golf or business partner, I have some thoughts about that, too. But there's a catch. You have to involve Harper in the discussions and planning."

Henry brightened noticeably but kept his business cool, "I have no basic problem with the idea, but two problems—one, Harper is totally pissed at me for some time now, and two, we need business connections, and Harper is not a business-connected person. In fact, she is quite anti-business."

Jack cautioned, "Hold on, partner, don't think that just because she isn't networking like crazy for deals her Rolodex does not hold some potential jewels for the right purpose. And, if you're willing to eat a little crow—and I'll admit that you haven't really done anything wrong, but crow is the price—I think we can resolve the other problem in a most reasonable manner. I have a fishing trip booked with Harper day after tomorrow. Maybe I should bring a guest who just happens to be a competent fly fisherman?"

Henry brightened again ... more. *Tunnel, light at end, no train.* "Jack, you are a better and better golf partner every day. I like the way you think. How do we go about this?"

"Meet me at my office at seven on Sunday. We'll go in my car, and I'll tell Harper I'm bringing a business guest so that she will have boots and waders for you. When we get there, you let me soften her up for the shock, and then you appear. She won't cancel the trip since I have already paid, and maybe she'll agree to listen and consider our plan, such as it is."

"I dunno, Jack," mulled Henry, "I am not confident that she will go gentle into that good night. I expect some fireworks."

"Hey," Jack corrected, "It is what it is. You got to work with what you got and make it happen. Intelligence, charm, good looks … well, one outa three ain't bad. Gotta do the best you can. Sincerity might help, too."

"Okay, Jack. If you read Harper as well as you read putts, we have a fighting chance—or, rather, I have a fighting chance. You might want to run for cover and hope she'll let you pay her to take you fishing in the future."

Jack quipped, "I'll take my chances, smartass. You just make sure to bring your A-game."

Biscuits and gravy tasted a whole lot better after the conversation. Jack was teaching Henry how a good partner can always help make the best of a difficult situation … so in life, as in golf. Henry was more optimistic than he had been for weeks.

Henry returned to his office and sought an audience with Hanna and D. He needed some economic assumptions and the modelling that could be built from them.

"Jack Morris and I have a skeleton of a plan that could use his land and the land that I own as a result of the FBI takedown of the cartel. But we need to be able to support it with some semblance of data. Hanna, can you find statistics on the financial results of PPP projects focused on tourism and recreation development in mid-sized cities? Golf and fishing focused if possible. And I need to know something about the permissible capital structures of SPV's under active PPP's. Can they be owned by individual public shareholders, or do they have to be 'qualified investors'?

"D, I need you to take Hanna's info and build three realistic models—best, worst, and most likely case. We need to know how rapid growth can be managed and what happens if there is no growth, as well as a normal-development timeline—complete with operating statements and balance sheets and cash flow if possible. If you can, identify the ancillary tax revenues that come off the economic activity in the three cases, and, if you can, summarize the public infrastructure costs of each case. No prob, huh? Oh, and I need this by Monday morning."

Dr. D laughed out loud. "Sure Henry, the difficult we can do immediately, the impossible takes until … apparently, next Monday. On it!"

Hanna supplied her usual giggle, signifying excitement to be doing something challenging, worthwhile, and enjoyable.

Henry used the rest of the day to organize his feelings and planned rhetoric when he next saw Harper. He was ecstatic to have the chance, but terrified. Interesting, since he felt no guilt at having wronged her because, in his mind, he hadn't. But he felt emptiness at not having her with him when he was facing danger, or confused about how to proceed, or just lost in the tangle of events. He also was painfully aware that Harper thought he had betrayed her on Parsons Point for the sake of mere profit— an unpardonable offense to Harper. He decided to pitch his redemption on the secrecy, FBI, dangerous-for-you-to-know platform, with the hope that she would see that he had her best interests at heart. Surely any woman could understand that?

Yeah, but ... Harper Philips is not just any woman.

After processing his feelings about Harper, he remembered that he needed to talk to Smythwick and accept his offer for the memorial service for Horace. He dialed the agent's private number and got an immediate answer.

"Agent Smythwick, I would very much like to take you up on your kind offer for the memorial service for Horace. I think it should be done in Nacogdoches, Texas, where my grandparents lived for a long time, and where my mom and Horace grew up. My Grandmother used to attend a small church there that has a bit of local history to it. It should be able to handle the 'crowd,' which I don't anticipate to be heavy. But that would put a nice touch on tying the loose ends of this whole incident together."

And maybe the loose ends of my whole life as well.

Smythwick responded that he already had the Gulfstream 280 available for Saturday morning, and would publish a notice in the local paper tomorrow morning for an eleven o'clock service. He would arrange catering for after the service, and then get Henry back on the Gulfstream to be home by dinner time, with perhaps a nice calming cocktail or two on the flight. Henry was astounded at Smythwick's efficiency and planning capabilities and thanked him profusely.

Smythwick put the final touches on the conversation by saying that an agency car would pick him up at his home at seven on Saturday and they would depart Stearns Field International by eight-fifteen.

Hmmm. That's one I need to ask Mo about.

Henry agreed, the details were set, and he made a

note to draft some remarks for the service. He had one
more day to get through in the office and then the trip to
Texas—returning in time to fish with Jack and Harper on
Sunday ... he hoped.

CHAPTER 51

In his later years, Henry was to remember the next day as little more than a blur. He had no memories of the day being a buzz of activity, chasing the information he had demanded of Hanna and D. But chasing it they were, and effectively.

A morning meeting between the three of them shocked Henry in that Hanna had already located the basic data from three applicable projects, and boiled down the common elements into a small table which D could then use like a database. He had detailed out some assumptions, created a couple of algorithmic if/thens for each assumption, inserted some best/worst type of data from Hanna's research, and built the skeletons of three models to be reviewed.

Miracles only come from motivated people, and these two gave new meaning to the term.

Henry's motivation was directed entirely differently. Though he knew he had to address Mo's challenge, he was far more concerned about how to address Harper's challenge. The truth would be a good start, but even Henry was not sure the truth was believable. Jack would have to provide a lot of backup to sell the true story of events. But the fact that Jack and Henry had a plan to develop a new approach might get Harper's attention—

especially if she could play a central role and end up with a project that *she* wanted and that would make her proud.

What would that be? Yeah, like what the hell would something like that be?

At the end of the day, Hanna and D had made enormous progress. They had data and models which suggested that a project of smaller scale than the tech park could be financially rewarding to the firm. If there were an equity offering and a project with investment requirements to accompany participation, it would generate some decent revenue. If the firm could then structure a secondary offering of shares to individual investors, there would be fee opportunities—and, maybe, in the case of potential US&G warrants, a trading gain for the firm. Pieces could be made to fall into place.

There was a big question, however. What would the project be? A hotel, a shopping area, a resort and conference center, a civic center? They all had possibilities but they all also had infrastructure challenges, roads, parking, soil composition issues and stability questions, green belt considerations. Just to name a few. And none of them had that pizazz, that emotional hook that would build community enthusiasm and support sufficient to overcome the hurdles that were bound to be placed in their various lanes.

And how could Harper's support and participation— representing the naturalist and conservation focus—be incorporated? She has to be on board, and loudly.

Henry took that conundrum home with him, hoping to be able to sleep on it. Didn't happen.

CHAPTER 52

Saturday arrived and the Agency car—a huge black armored SUV—arrived at Henry's precisely as promised by Smythwick. The short trip to Stearns International was uneventful and Smythwick met him at the terminal building. They boarded the jet for the two-hour flight to Nacogdoches.

"So, Agent Smythwick," Henry began, "How do I rate a private jet obviously meant to transport eight or ten? This all seems like a bit of overkill."

Smythwick cautiously responded, "You and your father have rendered enormous service to the Bureau. That service is worthy of a few carefully executed reciprocal benefits. Please don't be under the illusion that just anyone gets this kind of attention."

"I am flattered and impressed," returned Henry. "How did you get to know my father?"

Smythwick smiled slyly and launched into the story.

"As you know, your dad was a fair hand at poker and he won that racehorse. Well, when he finally decided what to do with that horse, he entered a totally foreign and strange world, at least for him, and met a whole lot of 'interesting' characters, interesting to the Bureau for a number of different reasons. I first met him when he came to me because he was concerned that he was getting trapped into an illegal money laundering operation and that the inflow of cash into his horse operation—and later into his stud operation—was something that could get him into a lot of trouble. He had never operated illegally, but he had been close enough to the edge a few times that he knew trouble when it showed up at his door."

"We realized we had a very credible resource for several cases we were trying to crack that involved the racing industry. Lots of very rich, high-powered people with shady backgrounds mixed in with the honest and respectable owners and breeders who show up in fancy suits and hats at the Kentucky Derby every May. We had to have a guy who could walk the walk and talk the talk and be perceived as natural in that environment. Horace was perfect. He wasn't a natural spy or agent, but he had a very sharp nose for a plot and a strong sense of smell for fishy events. We knew a bit about where he acquired his insights but we thought he probably was not a criminal, and we turned out to be right."

The things you never know about your family.

"When we came on the Parsons Point scam—pardon, it was a scam from our point of view even though it was a legitimate business deal from yours and your firm's—Horace was the only guy we knew who could bluff his way through the machinations of the guns, drugs, and money transactions we discovered and lead us to the baddies."

For which talent he paid a significant price when the Porsche exploded.

For the rest of the flight, Henry found himself fighting a range of feelings from anger at the incompetence of the FBI for getting his father killed to the relief of knowing that the bureau valued him and his service as a true hero.

Military families at Dover air base meeting the President must feel the same way.

In just under two and a half hours, the Gulfstream was on its final approach to A. L. Mangham Jr. Regional Airport in preparation for landing at a private terminal for the convenience of the bureau and its VIP passenger. Henry's remarks had been prepared, rehearsed, and edited to what he thought would be an appropriate presentation to the audience he thought would be there to hear them—which is to say, a small and probably hostile one.

At the airport they were met by another heavy Bureau SUV for the short drive to little church that had been important to Jane. It only took about fifteen minutes to get there on a Saturday morning, but when they pulled into the church drive, Henry felt a jump back in time by a hundred years.

The church was founded shortly after the Texas won its independence from Mexico. The founders included local people and a well-known evangelist who had a hand in founding a large number of Baptist Churches in East Texas in the 1830s and 40s. It had been in operation ever since as a prominent fixture in the first town in Texas.

Nacogdoches had always been a unique small jewel in the middle of a traditional section of a large and colorfully-historied state, and the town contributed more than its allotted share to that eccentric and fabled history. The church's cemetery still contains the remains and stories of Texas settlers from 1840 to the current time.

And it was the church where Jane Hansen met Margaret Elliason—an event which turned out to be foundational in the annals of the Hansen family.

They arrived at the church around ten-thirty, and a crowd was actually gathering. Henry noticed the usual collections of pickups old and new, beat up sedans, a smattering of SUVs, and at the far end of the parking lot all by itself, a very red sports car—a convertible that had a sort of vintage look to it, but he couldn't recognize what it was.

Just your typical East Texas memorial service gathering. A lot of trucks and a car or two that make no sense at all for this parking lot.

But the outside of the church quickly fled his mind when he got inside. It wasn't jammed, but was filled with twenty-five or thirty people, none of whom were recognizable to Henry. He had expected ten at the outside. He was properly greeted by the pastor and a couple of the deacons, and he took his seat while the crowd settled in.

At precisely eleven o'clock, the pastor began the service with a proper Baptist hymn—Amazing Grace—some well-chosen scripture, and a few brief announcements, including a potluck luncheon to follow the memorial service. Then he made his remarks about the deceased in a careful and measured respectful tone—as if it was what the gathered were there to hear, and who might disapprove if he said what he was really thinking. After a few moments, he introduced Henry as the son of Helene Hansen and the nephew of Horace Hansen, who some of the congregated might remember as the children of Jane and Lars Hansen. While Henry's individual connection to the church was a bit dated and distant from the current congregation, the pastor's remarks emphasized that the Grace of a forgiving God transcends time and distance, and that the true members of God's church—and those close to them—are always welcomed in His house.

The crowd stirred somewhat uneasily; they actually did remember Jane and Lars, and Helene and Horace ... and Margaret. Apparently they were not sure how they felt about that.

Henry ascended to the podium and began to speak.

"I don't know if I know any of you. We may have met, but I haven't been here in a long time. I do remember that my mother, Helene, would complain to me bitterly about her isolation from her peers and her lack of friends for reasons she could not comprehend. She vaguely suspected it had something to do with her mother, her father, and her friend Margaret Elliason. My mother was distant and unemotional and unattached from events and people around her, and I think I missed some of those experiences growing up that bond you with others and allow you to learn and adapt to the world you inhabit. I grew up with a 'flat side,' as we say in East Texas.

"But I am who I am both because of and in spite of those events and others in my early life. And I am coming to realize that I cannot dwell on what I don't have as a result of my childhood, but that I need to understand and make use of what I *do* have. I have come to learn that not knowing what you don't know can be misleading and even harmful. Because of her erratic behavior and social ineptitude, I always thought that my mother, Helene, was a bad influence on me, and that I needed to separate myself from that history."

I have recently learned from my Uncle Horace that his sister, Helene, had brain tumors from an early age, and they affected her social skills and attitudes. While the tumors were slow to develop—and inflict the ultimate damage—they were untreatable. So my mother's life became a process of waiting for the inevitable, to die alone in a diminished state of consciousness. In her final words, uttered a few weeks ago to my uncle, she implored him to find me and tell me the whole story. She asked him to let me know that she was aware of me and my success away from the family home, and that she was proud that I was becoming a man to be admired. I had never known that she saw me that way."

Guilt hit the crowd, and there was a shift in a number of chairs as the discomfort became palpable.

"My relationship with my uncle, on the other hand, was decidedly different. He was present in my life, seeking to help me through the 'awkward' years. He taught me sports—baseball and basketball especially—and he taught me to hunt and fish. He busied himself trying to teach me to be a man, and an honorable one, while trying to teach himself the same lessons.

"Before he died, Uncle Horace had become a clever, and reasonably prosperous, businessman, and amassed some financial muscle. He had enough muscle, I discovered a few weeks ago, to assure me a good start academically, a solid platform on which to build my own real achievements and earn the next steps in my growth into manhood—a concept with which I was largely unfamiliar except through the efforts of my Uncle Horace.

"I am learning two very important facts: First, 'Nothing happens for no reason.' It is just our job to figure out why they happen. And second, there is no bigger fool than the one who doesn't know what he or she doesn't know. I now see this learning process—and it is a process that will probably never be complete—is the direct result of what I gained from Helene and Horace. It was certainly not obvious to me at the time, and I still struggle with it. But it is infinitely worth learning and embracing in one's most hallowed inner sanctum.

"I'm sure that idea will not be lost on this group of people, in this House.

"My mother died with a certain nobility gained late in

her life, but noble just the same, much like deathbed salvation. And Uncle Horace, with all his 'colorful' business dealings and habits, died a hero, helping the FBI solve a number of very difficult white-collar crimes. A man to be proud of and to emulate for his motives and intentions.

"So, for those of you who knew them, they were not who you thought. And few of us are. 'Judge not ...'

"I sincerely appreciate the chance to meet you all today and share these thoughts, even though they may be far from what you expected. I hope they will be useful to you in pursuit of your own comfort and self-esteem that you place in your family, church, friends, or society at large.

"Thank you, and may God bless you as He has me."

As Henry stepped down there was no movement, no sound, not even an inhale or an exhale. Even the pastor seemed shaken. At last he rose.

"Henry, thank you for helping us learn a great lesson today, the same one you are learning but from perhaps a slightly different perspective. As important as it is to your growth as a man, it is even more critical to our growth as humans and Christians. We are humbled.

"Now let's all sing The Doxology, and then lunch is served outside in the shade of these magnificent pine and oak trees."

As the congregation sang the Doxology, Henry and the pastor walked down the aisle and stood side by side at the door to greet the assembled as they came outside for lunch. The pastor gripped Henry's arm as if he needed the stability of Henry's energy to continue standing.

As always, the exit from a church service is a lot more light-hearted than the entrance. This one was no different. Several people thanked Henry and praised him and his courage volubly. Other just smiled politely.

One woman stopped because she had something to say.

"Henry, I am Maybelle Hawkins. Margaret Elliason was my great aunt. Many times my sisters and I would visit our cousins, and Margaret would take all the children into her parlor and sit us down in front of the fireplace and tell us stories about the old days. She told us a lot about Jane and Lars and Helene and Horace. She was direct and accurate but never unkind, and we learned about what it meant to live here in those tough times, and trying to adapt and survive. I don't know for sure what kind of relationship she had with Jane except I know that they loved and respected each other in the very best sense of those words, and Aunt Margaret helped Jane get through some terrible difficult times.

"I always got the feeling that this community was not so kind to Helene and Horace, and your remarks today have convinced me to reconsider how I relate to those people that I don't choose to bring into my circle of friends, and why. There may be some really worthwhile people out there that I have missed because, as you said, I don't know what I don't know. Thank you so much for your wonderful insights, and your character."

There was no doubt that Maybelle was sincere, and she had taken Henry's message to heart, but, frankly, Henry didn't know how to accept such loquacious praise given in such "Bless your heart" fashion.

He decided to be accommodating and smile while thanking Maybelle. That all drew a smile from the pastor.

The last person out of the church was a small, frail old man with a beard down to his waist, hunched over and walking laboriously with the aid of a cane. He also stopped to chat with Henry.

"Y'know young man, you're pretty wise for someone

still wet behind the ears. That took a lot of guts up there, and the people out in the chairs seen that. And Maybelle was totally sincere in what she said. Don't be put off by her gushin'. She's a good person, and you reached her.

"And I'll tell you somethin' else. I been around here a long time. I seen a lot of history pass through this town, even this church, and even this cemetery out back. Ain't nobody here got any call to judge Helene and Horace. I seen all them timbermen, the railroad men, the bankers, all the civic leaders, and the people who founded the enterprises and the businesses that made this stretch of the woods. They built the sawmills, they built the old Texas and New Orleans railroad that enabled the sawmills. They even had some hand in the East Texas oil business. They did all that stuff. Some of 'em still around today. And, most important of all, I knew your grandfather, Lars."

Henry listened a bit more intently.

"He was a man's man. Never seen any man could outwork him. He was able and strong and could figure out any problem he ran into while he was working. I even think he was honorable. But he was always two brick short of a full load when it come ta livin' outsida work. He just missed understandin' what was goin' on around him. When it come time ta know how to plan where he was goin', or how he was goin' ta provide for his family in the future, or how ta learn how ta do somethin' ta make a livin' when the trees were all gone, he was scared outta' his mind. So he got mad, and he drank, and he got mean 'cause 'o the booze. But he wasn't no bad man. He just got caught up in a place in time and history that he couldn't cope with. I know he did some terrible things, but down inside, he weren't no bad man. Like you said, he just didn't know … you goin' to do great things, young man. You got what it takes."

"Thank you, Mr. … "

"Smiley, Eldridge Smiley. Proud ta know ya, son. Good luck."

Smythwick appeared at Henry's elbow and said, "Better say your goodbyes. We need to make tracks to the airport—I have to get the jet back to the next user."

Henry agreed and went to thank the pastor. Then he gave Maybelle a hug and went to find Smiley. As he searched for Eldridge, he again noticed that red sports car in the far corner of the parking lot. He was very curious what such a car was doing in the churchyard of a small historic church in Nacogdoches, Texas. So he went over to take a closer look.

As he came closer, he realized that he was looking at a Ferrari Testa Rossa—about 1958, he guessed. *Who the hell in this crowd would be driving such a car? They are rare and worth millions.* It really didn't fit.

The top was down, so he walked over to look inside … and stopped cold in his tracks. In the front seat was a leather overcoat, neatly folded with a newsboy cap on top, and a note with his name on it. He was shivering while he reached down to pick up the note and open it.

It simply said, "SMYTHWICK CAN REACH ME IF NEEDED."

Henry felt his knees go weak, and wept quietly for a few moments. Then he turned, dried his eyes, and went to go find Smythwick to get back to the plane.

All the crowd was leaving, as the food and iced tea was disappearing quickly, and people had other places to be on Saturday afternoon. The Ferrari had not moved. As Henry and Smythwick walked off toward the FBI vehicle

Henry sneaked a quick look over his shoulder to see if anyone had gotten into the Testa Rossa. To his surprise, Eldridge, looking much taller now, and without the help of his cane, was standing by the car's door. He opened it gently, got in, and closed it just as gently, and started it up. As he drove away he made eye contact with Henry and smiled. Smiley, of course. And Henry smiled back.

On the flight back home, Henry was pensive and quiet, while Smythwick wore a parental smirk. On their final approach, Smythwick sat down beside Henry and said, "What you did today took courage and conviction. We are all better because of it. Those people certainly have something new to think about ... and I think you came out of it with some insight and knowledge you didn't have before. I hope your confidence in the Bureau and in me is a bit firmer than before."

"Agent, thank you. It is," Henry responded. "I have an enhanced outlook from which to move on. Now I just want to get home and get some sleep. Big day tomorrow."

After landing and taxiing to the dedicated hangar, Smythwick thanked Henry again, looked him straight in the eye, and then hugged him fiercely.

Will wonders never cease? No one will ever believe me. The Bureau is human.

CHAPTER 53

When Henry awoke next morning, he was groggy, crabby, and hungry, having forgotten to eat dinner the evening before. Some breakfast would help calm him, but too much and he would have nervous stomach. Henry's sensibilities rested on a knife's edge. In spite of his morning disarray he managed to get into some fishing clothes and clean up enough to meet Jack with some confidence that the day would be successful … with Harper—the fishing didn't really matter.

When Henry arrived at Jack's office at the appointed hour, Jack showed concern. "Henry, you look as nervous as a rookie batting clean-up. How can I help you get it back under control so that Harper doesn't kill us both?"

"Aw Jack, I just want everything to be alright between me and Harper. I am miserable with her on the outside looking in, and sort of being in limbo."

Jack consoled him, "Why don't you just tell her that? I'm sure that is as important to her as it is to you."

Henry was moved but not totally convinced.

"Remember, you're dealing with Harper, just be straight, and she will respect that."

"Okay, okay, I got it. Can't be any worse than where I am now, anyway."

They piled into Jack's new truck for the short trip to

the put-in site where they were to meet Harper. Henry liked the substantial truck, although it was physically a larger vehicle than he was used to. Jack just enjoyed the testosterone-inspired looks of the truck, and celebrated its size and power. The day's plan was to drift a few miles of the Blaine, finishing up the day about a mile below Parsons Point. The put-in site was about two miles upstream of the point, and slightly upstream of the junction of the Hattawoc and the Blaine—excellent brown and rainbow water all the way.

Conversation on the trip was, blessedly, inconsequential man-talk, golf, and fish tales. Henry was relieved to not be focused on "the moment" … until he had to be. When they arrived at the put-in, Jack suggested that Henry get out of the truck and conceal himself in the trees near the path that passed for a ramp. When he heard Jack and Harper talking, Henry could slip out and be there, ready to talk with Harper and ready to fish from the drift boat. Henry readily agreed just so he could hide for a few moments before the inevitable confrontation.

As Jack pulled in, Harper greeted him with unexpected cheer, "Hey, how's my favorite client today?"

Jack, catching the drift, replied, "Terrrifffic! How's my favorite guide today?"

Harper's bravado failed her, "Aww dammit Jack, I'm not all that great. I am so sad, disappointed, pissed off, and confused over this Henry thing that I am just off my feed. I vacillate between rip roarin' anger to utter despair. And I'm not sure which one would prevail if I saw him right now. By the way, where is your guest, for whom I brought a whole bunch of extra gear?"

"He's here," said Henry, stepping out from the brush alongside the river.

Harper's first reaction might have passed for just a flash of relief and affection ... if it had not been quickly followed by an eruption of towering rage.

"What the hell are you doing here? You are not getting in my boat! I only allow trustworthy people in my boat! You used me, abused me, misled me, and then betrayed me ... trying to steal the most sacred spot in the world from me and a lot of other fine folks ... all for profit in a freakin' real estate deal. You got in my waders and I even showed you my girl guide wet-nylon-shirt trick, and you blew it off for money! And then you didn't even try to call me and set things straight or tell me to get lost or whatever! Why would I ever want to see you again?"

Henry was intimidated by the range of Harper's vitriol and anger, but he held his ground and didn't retreat.

Jack jumped in quickly, "Harper, there are circumstances that dictated what Henry had to do, and a talk will clear things up very easily if you will just hear Henry out. Lord knows I have been lending him a crying shoulder long enough because of his desperation over you and this whole situation."

"Circumstances, huh? Bullshit. I will not be reduced to a circumstance. I am someone who thought you were special and let you know it. How could you just ignore me?"

"Well," Henry began, "If I hadn't ignored you, you might not be here now. You might even be dead."

Harper, for all her emotion and anger, was brought up straight by the finality of that statement.

Henry went on. "The whole Parsons Point development—even though it started as a real deal for Mo and Amanda, turned into a sting led by the CIA, involving the ATF, DEA, and FBI. There was some money laundering, drug dealing, and even some arms dealing—and one of the companies that owns land in the project was a target of the investigation. I was approached by the FBI through my father, whom I had not seen in fifteen years. I had to respond to the FBI, and I didn't even have time to bring Mo up to speed as to why I was killing his dream project. That was almost as scary as facing the mob."

Harper sat down on a big rock, obviously shaken. "Why didn't you just *tell* me? I would have understood and even supported you."

"I couldn't tell anybody except a few people directly involved in the sting operation, which involved mob thugs with expensive suits and very lethal guns. You would have been in grave danger, and the mob could have generated leverage over me in the business deal that the FBI set to trap them. I couldn't involve you or inform you.

"Two days ago, we concluded the sting, captured the bad guys, and seized their money—which was actually my money, inherited the day before from my dad ... who the mob eliminated. The FBI set up the sting, and handled me through the ordeal. I now own a piece of land up in the hills above the Hattowoc that is critical to the former project, and Jack owns the primary land where the main project was to be built. Mo has nothing but an expensive option, and I have limited time to put something in place that will meet a huge array of requirements from a number of sources.

"But Jack and I have some ideas as to how to pull the chestnuts out of the fire and make something useful, appealing, and profitable out of all this. But, Harper, we need your help."

"What? A couple of high-rollers—big-time money golfers on the sandbag circuit—need help from a li'l ol' girl who fly-fishes better than any man within fifty miles? How does that work?"

Henry demurely answered, "I don't know, but I do know that I am as sincere as I can be, and our need for your help is very real. We need a vision that can be transformed into a plan that is executable and makes a lot of diverse groups happy to support. You are probably the best voice for those groups, given your outspoken statements at the tech park meeting. Will you help?

"You dimwit, of course I'll help, as long as I am convinced that your intentions are honorable, and will benefit more people than a huge real estate development meant for the Barons of IT would have."

Jack was elated, "Fan-effing-tastic. I'm glad that's settled, now let's go fishing!"

Harper was more circumspect, "Jack, it's far from settled, but fishing is the best way I know to settle it. Jump in the boat. Henry, get your gear on and let's see what's happnin'. There is a lot of wind today, so that will mean terrestrials on the water and hopper fishing. And then there is a potential pale morning dun hatch late morning or early afternoon, so some traditional eastern-style dry fly action. It could be a great day."

For any number of reasons.

Henry donned his waders and boots and Harper arranged the two men in the drift boat.

"Okay, guys. Rules of the road. Jack, you take the front seat as the most experienced angler, Henry you're behind me in the back seat. We fish sitting down when the water is a bit rough—gotta keep the center of gravity low in choppy water. You can stand up for casting and landing fish when the water is smoother, but stay in the knee braces for stability and safety.

"We'll stop once in a while and I'll drop the anchor on a sandbar or two so we can wade and fish some special spots thoroughly. And when we finish, there's a good chance we will have caught a lot of fish and maybe even a trophy. Any questions?"

None. So, the boat was loaded and Harper pushed off, grabbing the oars on her way in. Harper had tied a size ten hopper pattern on Henry's nine-and-a half-foot five-weight rod to match to a nine-foot tapered leader and a five-x tippet. Jack was fishing a size six big black bug that resembled a cricket, but he announced that he might add on a nymph as a dropper if the cricket got no takes. His rod was a nine-foot six-weight and his tippet was a bit heavier at three-x.

Harper pulled them into mid-stream, and they both cast toward the left shore. Numerous hoppers, crickets and other flying insects of size were seen in the air on the bank, and some inevitably blew into the water. After about two minutes of preliminary casting that got them used to the wind and the drifts of the large flies, Henry and Jack both had their first fish. Simultaneously, the fish swirled underneath their dry bugs and took off in opposite directions. The fish were not large, but feisty, and they strained the leaders and bent the rods sportively. But both men were adept and easily brought the fish to boat quickly—Jack, a two-and-a-half-pound rainbow, and Henry a two-pounder. Henry was a lot happier now, and Jack was ecstatic.

Sunshine and dry flies are a powerful combination, capable of making grown men smile and laugh uncontrollably.

They floated on for about a mile or so, catching fish every fifth cast or so, an exceptional day. Henry's best was a three-and-three-quarter pound bow, and Jack managed to boat a four-pound brown after he tied on a nymph dropper.

As they were approaching a sand bar, Harper announced that she was going to drop the anchor and they would wade fish a bit. Henry was standing in the back of the boat fighting a fish on the right side of the boat. Jack, also fighting a fish, was slightly left of the boat's centerline. Harper, making a statement, shifted her weight quickly to the left and the boat tipped left just enough to send Henry tumbling into the water on the right. The river was shallow here, and Henry got his shirt and his pride wet but no lasting damage was suffered by either.

Harper looked at him with an air of superiority and pointedly stated, "And don't forget who is in control of the boat the next time you want to go off on some hairbrained, dangerous, life-threatening adventure. I am still the person with the oars in my hands!"

Then she jumped into the water beside Henry and planted the largest, wettest, Frenchiest kiss she could muster on him. "And don't you forget it. You make sure that I come along with you *all* the time, and that kiss is just the beginning." Huge smile.

Henry's heart leapt, and his fishing technique was forgotten ... for the moment. The world was right again, even though there was still a lot of ground to cover. Harper made sure the wet shirt trick played again.

Jack was discreetly overjoyed for them both.

After a few moments of deep and genuine affection, Harper announced, "Back in the boat. We have serious fishing to do and limited time to do it in. Onward!" As she sat down on the rowing seat and pulled the anchor, she informed her "clients" that they were in for a special treat. She had been experimenting on Parsons Point for a while and had discovered a new way to fish the Point that seemed promising.

When they approached the sacred spot, Harper dropped the anchor—anchored the drift boat above the normal wade-fishing spot—and tied up an eight-weight rod with a size two sculpin on a 345-grain sinking tip, and a level ten-pound leader/tippet about six feet long. Both Henry and Jack were surprised to see the Point fished in this manner as they had never heard of anyone trying it previously.

Instead of casting upstream, Harper cast across and quartering down. The heavy sink tip line whizzed past Henry's ear and he watched it settle in the water. Harper did not make any upstream mend, and just let the fly find its depth. Her line drifted naturally with the current, and the deep fly found the right location of a big fish. Harper's line straightened and came tight. No fish could be seen.

"Ha! A big brown," she said. "I'll bet that one will go six-and-a-half or seven pounds."

The fish ran for a few seconds and the rod straightened ... and the line went limp. Harper disappointedly reeled in to find that the fly had broken off at the knot but the line and leader were intact. "Jack, you take over while I re-rig."

Jack began casting a similar rig in the same manner as Harper but drew no action. He kept casting as Harper re-rigged a rod with a number four Spruce fly in front of the same sink tip line and ten-pound leader. Jack was still not getting takes, or even interest, apparently.

Harper injected, "Okay, Henry's turn. We can't spend too long here because we want to be further downriver when the PMD hatch starts. But take a few casts, Henry."

Henry picked up the heavy rod and sink tip and had trouble making it cast accurately for the first few tries. He could get the drift alright, but the cast was a chore with the heavy rig. After a few minutes he got the semblance of a helpful casting technique under control and was able to place the Spruce fly where Harper had directed. He let it drift slowly in the swirling current on the point and watched it, realizing that he was holding his breath. Just as he was ready to pull the fly in and cast again, the bright yellow line shot forward.

"Raise your rod tip and set that hook! That is a monster!" Harper was more excited than Henry had ever seen her ... about a fish anyway.

Henry did, and the fish took off. Harper pulled up the anchor rapidly and put oars in the water to follow the fish. It almost pulled the light craft behind it. Henry had no idea that a fish could be so strong. Harper instructed him to keep the line tight but not to put too much pressure on the fish as it seemed large enough to break even the ten-pound leader.

The fish never jumped, it just ran. A couple of times it turned around and swam straight at the boat, leaving Henry to scramble as fast as he could to get on the reel and retrieve the slack fly line. If the fish got an inkling that he had slack line to play with, Henry would lose him immediately. This game went on for a full ten minutes as the boat drifted steadily downstream toward the take-out point. Henry was not certain he could land the brute at all. Harper told him he had less than a minute to land the fish or they would float past the take-out point and the next one was four miles further down.

No pressure, Henry.

In the last fifty yards before the take-out, the fish

seemed to tire. Henry could make some progress. He managed to keep the fish from taking more line and move him a little closer to the boat. Harper, for her part, was trying to get the boat positioned to get to the shore and the take-out point. She managed to put the nose of the boat into the shore, jump out, and tie it to a log. Henry was now free to fight the fish from in the boat or, if need be, the stream.

Fortunately, the great fish was tiring, and Henry gently nudged him toward Harper on shore. She had the big fish net out so she could net the trout safely. The fish would try to make a run as he neared the net, but he was just too tired. Harper got the net under him leaving the fish in the water but raising the edge of the net out of the water, a fish corral. She was practically in tears.

"Henry, that was magnificent! You were terrific; not many guys would be patient enough to bring that fish to boat. Let's weigh him." She brought out her trophy scale and tenderly clamped the big brown's lip and lifted it out of the water. "Nine point nine pounds. Wow, that may be a record on the Blaine."

She placed the fish back in the net where it measured thirty-one inches against the tape in the centerline of the net. She held the fish there for five full minutes to allow it to recover from the fight. Jack had been running around snapping pictures because he knew no one would believe the story. Henry was just breathless.

When Harper at last released the trout from the fish corral to swim away, she was very quiet. "I guess we may have to change the name of this place to Hansen's Point. You seem to have mastered it well."

"Harper, we both know that, both times, I could not have landed the fish without you there ... here. You were more responsible for this success than me; if you hadn't handled the boat, getting it going, keeping it in the right place in the river, and then getting it to shore so we didn't pass the take-out, I would have been just another almost-lucky rookie …

"Now, I am famous!"

All three were laughing raucously.

Jack confirmed Henry's credit to Harper. "Harper, I have never witnessed such able boat handling. You were fabulous, and Henry is right. He could not have done it without you. You were a great team."

"Were?" slyly inquired Harper. "I think 'are' is more appropriate."

Henry teared up and hugged Harper tightly. "Okay, dinner. Jack's buying." They all set about getting the boat organized and stashed on Harper's trailer, left graciously by the transfer service. As they piled into Harper's truck, she sank in feigned disappointment.

"Damn," she said, "We missed the PMD hatch." Laughs, boos, and Bronx cheers followed until everybody was exhausted.

"Let's go to Ralph's," said Henry. He had mixed feelings about that place, given his recent experience, but he still knew of no place he'd rather be to celebrate this day with his two best friends and partners. So, to Ralph's they agreed to go.

Inside, Ralph was overjoyed to see them all, even though he offered his condolences to Henry. Henry said, "C'mon. Let's go to the table and order some expensive Italian wine and I'll tell you the entire story."

Through the course of a two-hour dinner and three bottles of very expensive Italian red wine, Henry filled in all the blanks—beginning with his last dinner at Ralph's.

It was a story of very high highs and unbelievably low lows. In fact, it was more than Harper could grasp and her emotions ran the full range of despair to joy. Jack had known the outline of the story but had not heard the full details. He was moved. And he felt very good about his golf and business partner—a brave, mature, insightful man, with depth and even charm, when needed.

Their conversation covered a lot of project options also, and as they talked, their excitement grew notably. The ideas flowed freely, and, given the appearance of sufficient money to finance them, and the promises of the FBI and the EPA, the issues quickly centered around how to attract key merchants and professionals and sites to the project so that it could serve a broad customer/client base, be profitable, and become a source of civic pride.

Even Harper was caught up in the enthusiasm. And she had some solid business ideas to contribute to the discussion. The final unsolved matter was how to get name recognition in the project to attract other investors and tenants. No one quite knew who to approach or on what basis. Finally, Harper lit up.

"Let's put this discussion to bed. I want to make a phone call or two that may bring all this together, and we can get back together to finalize when I have my phone calls behind us."

They were all worn out from the fishing, the wine, the rich food, and the excitement. They left with Harper in her truck and trailer and the two men in Jack's truck.

They set off for Jack's office, where Henry shook Jack's hand, thanked him profusely, and hugged him. Then he drove home.

CHAPTER 54

Henry arrived home emotionally and physically ground down to the merest resemblance to his normal collected self. He had experienced the maximum degree of joy, grief, relief, excitement, enthusiasm, and love in the last few hours. There was no room left for any more emotional experiences ... good ones, bad ones, interesting ones, no room.

And the phone rang.

"Henry, it's Harper," the phone stated. "We have a lot of ground to make up, and I have some very good stuff to tell you. Can I come over and brighten your minimalist condo with my brilliance and happiness? Not to mention a good deal of good old-fashioned lust?"

Henry found it difficult to justify refusing such an offer. "Harper, it would really make my day, my week, perhaps my life."

"Great answer," she said, "I'll be there in fifteen minutes. Warm my side of the bed for me."

Henry smiled, but was also aware that he was operating at the edge of his limits and he didn't want to screw this up. This is the outcome he had been searching for, and he wanted Harper to be in his life permanently on every basis he could imagine. He didn't really care if he was not at his best as long as Harper didn't care. His

mind returned to the image of the wet guide shirt cling-
ing to Harper's fit, muscular body, and her intention in
making sure he noticed. What a perfect pairing of
discretion and desire. Could there possibly be a better
woman … in the entire universe?

The few minutes prior to Harper's arrival were spent
in making the 'minimalist' abode at least reasonably presentable. After all, Harper deserved better than a pigsty
from her chosen man. Success in making things presentable was limited—by Henry's lack of energy, and by the
lack of true options. When one's furniture consists of a
sofa, a rug, a chair, and a sixty-five-inch TV, the choices
for arrangement and ingenuity are not plentiful. But she
had seen it before, so Henry's energy was not further di-
luted worrying about her reaction.

When she did arrive, Henry immediately saw what
she meant when she referred to her brilliance and happiness. Harper glowed, and the glow spread throughout
Henry's cave. The atmosphere was enhanced by the
warm, passionate embrace Harper and Henry shared.
There was nothing desperate or lustful in the embrace,
just sincerity and confidence that this is the right path for
each of them.

"Got any of that good scotch left?" Harper inquired.

"Maybe we've had enough spirits for tonight," offered
Henry.

"Oh, c'mon and man up," teased Harper. "Surely you can
keep up with a woman who hardly ever drinks." Her sly
grin sufficed to "inspire" Henry to "man up" to the challenge
and pour them each a shot of the 50-year-old potion.

As they slowly sipped the liquor, Harper related the
story of her calls.

"Well, I figured this out," she began mischievously.

"What we need is a small settlement dedicated to fly-fishing, conservation, outdoor recreation—like hiking and mountain biking—and ecological soundness. I have secured a commitment for a hotel with restaurant to be called Parsons Point Lodge and Resort. It will have a conference center and education facility, small offices for guide services, the headquarters for two fine bamboo rod builders, a dealership for a leading drift boat brand, and near future additions of fishing and outdoor specialty retailers.

"I'm sure you and Jack have some significant ideas too." The sly grin reappeared.

"Harper! We just discussed this a few hours ago. How could you possibly have gotten all that done in the time since?"

"Hey, no problem. After all, Bob's my uncle!"

"But," she continued, "I'm worn out, and I want to curl up with my head on your shoulder and your arm around me and sleep like a rock ... maybe among other things."

"Deal," said Henry, relieved at the prospect of sleep ... but considering that it might be delayed slightly. And he led her to his bedroom joyously and full of anticipation of so many things in their immediate and longer-term future.

They awoke early the next morning so that they could go by Harper's place and get her dressed appropriately for a day of corporate work. Henry was taking her to the office. Harper had neither idea nor comfort with how to operate in this environment, but she managed to piece together an outfit of simple tan tailored slacks, an unwrinkled light blue guide shirt, blue blazer, and navy-blue low-heeled slings that would certainly be corporate enough for US&G on a casual day.

Harper asked playfully if she should bring a fly rod to

the office to complement the outfit. They decided that was overkill and the rod stayed in its case.

On the way in, Henry left messages with Hanna and D to meet him as soon as he arrived with as much data and progress as they had made on his requests. They would be there and ready, Henry told Harper.

And Henry warned Harper that they might turn some heads when they arrived together, so it should not surprise her to be inspected carefully. Harper wasn't sure whether to enjoy or be offended by that possibility. She decided that she would just be whatever she felt appropriate when, and if, it happened.

It happened.

Both Harper and Henry noticed the turning heads that Henry had anticipated. No catcalls, or lewd remarks, as Henry was too well respected to have that greeting bestowed on his female colleague. But, a lot of interest, and the buzz, spread through the firm quickly. An intriguing blend of surprise and respect seemed to dominate the buzz which, naturally, drifted back to Henry as soon as he and Harper had their morning coffee.

Hanna and D had heard the buzz and were waiting with more than their usual curiosity and enthusiasm. Henry made introductions and the group seemed immediately comfortable in this context. Henry took charge, and they got to work.

Hanna and D laid out their data and preliminary models first, grabbing Harper's interest quickly. She didn't understand it all, but she was agile enough to recognize critical points and ask perceptive questions.

When D and Hanna had finished, Harper explained her concepts, and the conversations with "uncle" Bob. Hanna and D were impressed, and immediately saw how to fit Harper's vision into the framework of the PPP and SPV that Hanna had put together for D's models.

Harper supplied details, and D charged off to put them in the models and produce complete project financials for three cases. Hanna, Harper, and Henry continued to discuss structural things—like ownership, capital needs, future operations, and the overall umbrella under which the project could be successful. About forty minutes into this discussion, there was a knock at the door and Charles stuck his head in the room.

"Is this a private meeting or can I horn in?" he asked carefully.

Henry, realizing that Charles was there under strict instructions from Amanda, sensed value in his influence with Amanda and graciously invited him into the "circle" of planners. Charles was particularly interested in the lodge and resort ... and the restaurant that it would include. He got excited as the discussions revealed more of the overall plan.

"Not to exceed my reach here," he injected, "but I have an idea about the resort. Let's keep it simple and all American. Keep the supply chain short and basic so that we are protected from shortages or single-source suppliers, and broaden the appeal of the resort to a wide range of client bases—just good marketing principles.

"We can call the restaurant 'The Iron Skillet' and specialize in good old-fashioned comfort food from the four corners of the US. Fried chicken, chicken fried steak, Yankee pot roast, Maine lobster, Pacific northwest crab and salmon, Tex-Mex and Santa Fe Mexican dishes, Gulf of Mexico shrimp, burgers, fresh veggies, and all kinds of potatoes, for example. And I happen to know an excellent chef to oversee this cuisine."

Hanna giggled, "And I can vouch for Charles's talents ... in the kitchen, too." And she giggled again.

Harper smiled knowingly, "Hanna, I understand you completely."

D returned with his financial projections and a huge smile. "Nothing is certain, of course, but these are looking quite good. Even the worst case is sustainable if we have a decent capital base, and if we don't go crazy with the operating expenses. Naturally, everything is driven by the occupancy rates of the hotel and the average room price actually achieved, as opposed to the posted rates on the advertising tear sheets."

Charles pointed out that the lodge would need something to set it apart from all other such locations around the US. "You can go fishing anywhere. Why come here?"

Harper jumped in quickly, "Because this lodge will be 'Bob Dorffman's Parsons Point Lodge and Resort,' honoring the greatest fly fisherman who ever lived, Craig Parsons, my grandfather. The development will be called Craigston Township, and touted as the epicenter of the fly-fishing world."

Charles was impressed. "You seem to have a feel for marketing, Harper."

"Well, "she said, "I was raised *near* a barn, but not *in* one. I have been exposed to the fly-fishing business since I was eight years old, and I have developed some insights and a lot of contacts. This comes naturally to me."

Henry was catching the rising tide of possibilities and beginning to feel like this was not only a good idea but perhaps the foundation of a successful business venture. His phone rang; it was Jack with good news.

When he hung up, Henry was beaming.

"Jack has firm commitments for twelve million to build a

new CCC golf course on my land in the Hills from members and friends of CCC. The new course will be called CCC Hills Course, and actively seek a PGA tour spot within two years of its completion. Three design firms will provide letters of interest after a preliminary inspection, and they are ready to start on the letters within the next four weeks if we can get ready. Add that as an attraction for Craigston Township.

"I asked Jack to join us in Mo's office this afternoon," Henry added. "Oh. Maybe I'd better ask Mo to join us in his office, too."

Henry called Mo to set the scene for the meeting. Mo was not overjoyed to have such short notice, but he understood the need for speed and made time available at two-thirty. He promised that Amanda would be there also.

Jack was arriving at one-thirty, so the team had time to prepare information. Henry asked D to prepare a slide deck with the concept, the basic confirmed information— including probable tenants—the nature of Dorffman's commitment, the outline of the golf course idea, and the possible sources of income and trading gain for US&G.

D chuckled good naturedly and said, "I was wrong. We don't have till Monday for the impossible. We only have until two-thirty." And he charged off to do his PowerPoint thing.

Henry ordered lunch in for the team, including D, and they continued their preparations. Harper rose to the occasion and demonstrated solid business acumen in organizing the presentation section concerning the lodge and resort. Like everything else in her life, she was a natural at it. The team was flying and actually making progress, given the short deadlines Henry had imposed.

Sometimes good leaders expected the impossible because they knew it wasn't.

CHAPTER 55

When Jack arrived at one-thirty, he walked into a messy office littered with the remains of the buffet Henry had ordered. He immediately asked if he could munch on the leftovers as he had skipped lunch tying in the CCC guys who were eager to develop the Hills Course. Henry allowed as how he had earned some lunch.

In the next hour they reviewed D's slides, changed the order of some key sections, and assigned certain sections to D, Harper, Hanna, and Henry. No time for the luxury of a full run-through, but they got the idea organized and logical so that they could encourage rational discussion and build some support from Mo and Amanda.

At the confirmed hour, the team made its way to Mo's lair, and was admitted.

Amanda was waiting for them and was shocked to see Harper among the team. Her memories of the confrontation with Harper at the public meeting were still quite vivid, and she would have preferred not to experience them again. But, Amanda thought, ice was called for to subdue the temper and emotions. Amanda was not going to ruin the meeting for personal reasons.

After Harper was introduced—with special emphasis on *Dr.* Harper Philips—and Jack's presence explained briefly, Henry led off.

The lead-off man's job is to get on base. Don't try to hit a home run. Even take a hit by pitch, but just get on base. Give the team something to work with.

But Henry was ambushed before he could start.

Amanda stared straight into Harper's eyes and said, "Dr. Philips, I'm sorry we got off to a bad start, either last week or in college. While I am not happy with the state of our interactions so far, I am perfectly willing to hear what you have to say that will support this team and their recommendations. My focus is on the future and welfare of this firm, and we have substantial investment in the Parsons Point project that we intend to recover. Just so we all know the rules of this encounter. That, and only that, is my interest."

"I understand very clearly, Ms. Stearns," Harper replied. "And just so you know the rules from my side, I have no problem with this firm doing well out of the project which we have identified for today. But I do want to be a part of something that is of sound ecology, sound conservation, available to all citizens, and promotes civic pride for its quality of life impact and its social value, not just its profitability. Henry has represented your firm's interests quite well, and I think, if you will hear us out, our ideas have met the tests you require ... *and that I require.*

"We are an accident of circumstances, but we are in this together, if you are interested."

Henry flinched, but then he relaxed. *Go Harper. Brilliant response.*

He then began by recapping the details of the Parsons Point saga and how it got diverted into a sting operation for the government agencies. Mo and Amanda had heard this part before. But then Henry diverted into his personal story, the conversation with his father, the impact of the cartel on his childhood, his father's connections with the FBI, the explosion, and the transfer of his father's assets to the trust which Henry controlled and was currently the sole beneficiary.

That point was not lost on Mo, as he now had to regard Henry as a member of the investor class rather than only a competent technician and enabler. Henry's words automatically carried fifty percent more weight now. Add the fact that he might be an important campaign donor and supporter, and that proportion doubled.

Henry finished with, "And so, in order to take advantage of the important land holdings of Mr. Morris and myself, create income opportunities for US&G, work cooperatively with the community interests represented unofficially by Dr. Philips, and create an asset that will be a source of civic pride and tax revenues for decades to come, we have come up with an innovative plan that will be unique among American communities and interest groups.

"Hanna, would you please educate us as to the possibilities presented by a public private partnership and a special purpose vehicle."

Henry read the reaction from Mo and Amanda and felt energized.

Got it! Line drive double. I'm on second in scoring position.

Hanna took over with no loss of momentum. Just like Dragnet, she stuck to the facts. Jack Webb would have been proud. Her careful explanation of the principles, structures, and capitalization of the PPP and SPV grabbed Mo's attention … and appealed to Amanda as a good way to begin her reign over the kingdom. Hanna pointed out that the PPP gave US&G opportunities to get paid for creating the documents and structure, to earn fees for any additional capital or debt that was needed, and to take warrants for shares which could be sold after a holding period to generate a trading gain. All ground that the team had anticipated and covered before being asked.

Henry quickly confirmed Hanna's points, adding that his land and Jack's would constitute a large portion of the required equity. Additionally, the FBI had agreed to transfer the seized purchase money—ultimately from Henry—to the EPA to pay for the mitigation process on the old mine land and the upper drainages surrounding the property that Henry now owned. Henry outlined the Anaconda project where the EPA and community had worked together to deal with the eco-effects of the tailings and hazardous waste from the copper smelter. The EPA had issued a preliminary endorsement of the proposed Parsons Point project with final parameters and procedures to be agreed by the parties. Not a conclusive status, but certainly a big positive step.

Henry then introduced D to present the financial projections and conditions on which the project would be executed.

Now Mo and Amanda were sitting up straight ... and listening.

Runners on first and second, no outs. The meat of the lineup coming to the plate and the power in the on-deck circle.

No rookie at looking formidable opponents in the eye and holding his own, D employed all his physical stature and intimidation factor to his advantage as he began his erudite examination of realistic financial outcomes. He presented all three cases, carefully exposing all the variables and some rather extreme outlier events, while deftly analyzing their potential impacts. Mo and Amanda were no longer casual observers. They were blown away ... and beginning to be true believers.

Base on balls. Bases loaded. Nobody out.

Henry took over after D astounded and amazed the Stearnses. "Now there is a question that must be foremost in your minds—and if it isn't, it should be. How do we attract the necessary businesses, facilities, vendors, investors, customers and tourists, and all the other people necessary to make a successful project like this? Such a project requires recognizable names that the targeted markets can relate to, trust, and accept advice and endorsements from. Thanks to the efforts of Harper Philips, we have established such links with individuals who have both money and reputation they are willing to put at risk in this project. Harper?"

Harper opened with strength. "When I was small, I was the youngest in a family of five, the only girl. Coincidentally, I was the only one interested in sports and the outdoors, my brothers all preferring intellectual and artistic pursuits. My dad and grandfather taught me everything they knew about every sport I was interested in, and then I did the rest when I discovered what my true loves were—fly-fishing and golf. And I have been skilled at each over my life. Right now, I am focused on fly-fishing and the related conservation and ecological issues because I believe, as do many others, that the outdoors is something that is an ingrained part of our character. If we lose or abuse it—our clean water, our stewardship of natural resources in field and stream, our access to life away from the office or factory or trading room—we have done ourselves irreparable damage, and will never recover. Yes, emotional commitment—a dangerous idea. But, especially in this case, a deserving one."

Harper then went on to detail the history of her relationship with Craig Parsons, her grandfather.

Then she introduced her relationship with Bob Dorffman. "Bob was my Grandpa's best friend and fishing buddy. When Grampa passed, and the fly-fishing world mourned the loss of the greatest fly fisherman ever, 'Uncle' Bob moved in to fill the hero gap for fly-fishermen everywhere. He is now regarded as the greatest living fly fisherman. He is sponsored by fourteen leading sporting companies, a leading brand of bourbon, several outdoor clothing and gear companies, and a bush airline in Alaska. He has amassed a large fortune through his globally-syndicated television show, 'The Drift, with Bob Dorffman.' He has been my best friend since Grampa died. And he has been sitting on a pile of cash looking for a worthy opportunity.

"After Henry, Jack, and I came up with this idea over dinner, I called Bob and told him what we were thinking. I couldn't even finish before he asked, 'How much can I invest?' as though he was fearful that I would limit his involvement. I asked him his comfort level, and he said, 'As much as you need.' No further questions.

"We propose that his investment be the cornerstone of Craigston Township—Bob Dorffman's Parsons Point Lodge and Resort. Bob is willing to finance the entire lodge project as his equity contribution to our SPV. He is that confident that it will be successful. But that's not all. He committed three other tenants for the village—two fine bamboo rod makers, and a world-famous fly-tying company in which he has an investment. He feels confident that he can secure further tenants for the village—including a drift boat dealership for the current leading brand and several outdoor related retailers—and he is willing to subsidize the rents of guides who wish to headquarter in the village to promote the area's fly-fishing possibilities. It's not enough to make the project cash flow positive immediately, but it is a strong foundation from which to market the village to other interested parties. And I have a few fishing-related contacts to throw into the pot also."

You could almost hear Mo and Amanda shouting "Amen, put a dollah in the plate, and be saved!" They were hooked.

Bottom of the ninth. Walk-off grand slam. Game over.

Henry then introduced Jack for the coup de grâce.

Jack described how he and Henry had become friends, and how Henry was establishing himself as a serious competitor at CCC.

Mo reminded them that Henry had a membership in whatever club he selected due him as part of his package at US&G. Jack took note of that.

Jack continued, "A number of members at CCC have risen up and expressed interest in updating the club. You may remember that CCC has some place in the history of the game and is reputed to be one of the best maintained courses in the US. However, because of limited land and advances in golf technology, CCC has become a members' club, not really well positioned to host major amateur or professional tournaments.

"So, these members are campaigning for a new course which can be designed and built to modern standards, and regularly host major events and tournaments. They have money, but no land available … until Henry and I looked at the possibilities … and Henry decided that he is willing to commit his land under a ninety-nine-year lease for the purpose of a championship caliber CCC to be known as the CCC Hills Course.

"We have three major architecture and course development firms' interest in submitting proposals as soon as they can get a look at the land. With the support of the EPA in the ecological issues, and the history of the Anaconda project—which has a magnificent course on the tailings of an old copper smelter, including black sand in the bunkers—we think we have a unique opportunity to check a lot of boxes in the valuable-and-responsible-development-of-golf-courses agenda. We would propose that the CCC Hills course would be available to all guests of the Parsons Point Resort as part of their standard guest package. It would also be available to other tourists and players as part of an effort to open up championship golf facilities for non-country-club players who are serious about golf and its history. Details of that have to be worked out, but we are confident it will happen."

Henry stepped in again to deliver the closing argument. "Mo, Amanda ... you can see that this concept is not casual, nor off-the-cuff. We have the resources and the contacts and the money committed to make it successful. We need a local firm to provide the underpinnings to actually execute. US&G is well positioned to do all that work, benefitting from substantial fees, consulting income, and trading gains available. And It sure as hell isn't a bad platform to run for governor from. Craigston Township is, in the truest and most time-honored sense, a win-win-win.

"We ask for your support and commitment to this project and the capital/debt raising needed to make it a reality."

Mo and Amanda exchanged glances and quick nods. Mo, in the tradition of long-winded political candidates began to respond eloquently, but then cut himself off in mid-sentence.

"Screw it. Henry, deal! Jack, set up a meeting for the community like we had for the original Parsons Point for next week, and let's get this thing out in front of the public. Build some support."

Especially for the candidacy of the next governor.

There was much handshaking and congratulating around the room, and smiles abounded on all faces. The meeting adjourned and Henry's team 'readjourned' in his office. Henry thanked everybody for their efforts and shrank into his chair, drained but pleased, and knowing that he and Harper had come a long way in a very short time. Hanna, Charles, and D returned to their offices, and Jack left to go close the dealership and begin setting up the next public meeting—leaving Henry and Harper alone in his office.

"Well, my dear, what do you think of corporate life?" said Henry.

But before Harper could answer, there was a knock; Amanda stuck her head around the door edge. "Am I interrupting anything?" she asked mischievously.

Henry, wise to her ways, replied, "No, come on in."

Amanda entered and looked straight at Harper. "That was really well done. I could say amazing, fantastic, world-class, but that would all just be hyperbole. It was just straight, good, effective, and infectious. Everybody is a believer now.

"And you two are extremely fortunate to have found each other. I am supportive and happy for you, but also a bit jealous."

"Sorry, Amanda, I don't follow," said Henry.

"Bullshit, Henry. I see the way she looks at you. And more importantly, I see the way you look at her. You told me I would know when you found someone. Henry, I *know.* Harper, you are a formidable woman, and one to be admired. We got off to a bad start, but I hope we can agree that we are on the same page together now. And if you can do that, I am proud to be your friend and colleague." And she embraced Harper warmly with respect and affection.

"And Henry, you are one lucky son of a bitch. Don't you dare screw this one up." And she hugged Henry in that respectful manner of colleagues who like each other but feel awkward hugging in public. Henry knew it was sincere and accepted it graciously.

Wow. Sometimes the good guys win. And sometimes there are more good guys than you thought.

Amanda left the office and Henry looked at Harper. "You never answered my question. But stop. Don't. Let's move this party to some place more private and get to know each other better."

Harper smiled and flirted, "If I was Hanna, I would giggle. Let's go to my place and pretend to create some heirs to that family trust of yours."

Just pretend?

EPILOGUE

The three days after the breakthrough meeting in Mo's office had allowed Henry and Harper time to make strong progress on the heir-creation project, and the two of them were now forged into a formidable force for anyone who sought to take them on ... in all the best ways.

Jack had set up the new Parsons Point disclosure meeting, which would also serve as the kickoff announcement for Mo's gubernatorial campaign and Amanda's elevation to the CEO position at US&G. The business community was abuzz at the changes and the not-officially-confirmed-but-still-well-known news surrounding the FBI sting involving the former tech park project. Jack, as emcee of the next meeting, would make heroic reference to Mo and Henry and the US&G staff as key elements in this successful law enforcement effort which protected the community and led to the next great opportunity.

On the day of the meeting, Henry gathered his team and thanked them all personally while explaining what would happen during this evening's meeting. They were all invited and strongly encouraged to circulate in the crowd and make contacts for themselves and for the firm, and, naturally, for Mo's political benefit. Jack would give "full" details and then announce the structure. With any luck there would be no surprises or bad news, and a grand time would be had by all, especially at the post-party being hosted by Mo's campaign at the Metropolitan Hotel's grand ballroom after the meeting.

At precisely seven-thirty, Jack convened the disclosure meeting.

"Ladies and gentlemen ... we are gathered here tonight to hear a remarkable story and discuss a remarkable project that will benefit this community in economic, environmental, and recreational ways, placing us in a small population of unique communities in these United States." And with that dramatic introduction, Jack launched into the backstory of US&G's original project presented in this same room only a short time ago. He relayed a lot of details, but not so many that he would make problems for himself with the FBI. Agent Smythwick stood in the back of the room to assure that circumspection was adequately observed.

Jack, the masterful storyteller, wove the elements skill-fully, including the evil of the drug cartel and its history, the tragedy of Henry's father and his "death," the challenging requirements of the EPA in managing possible environmental issues, and the courage of Mo Stearns to take these issues on for the purpose of making the city a better place. He detected a slight whisper of skepticism that moved around the room. But when he told the story of the sting and the personal risk undertaken by the exceedingly brave Henry Hansen, one of Mo's most trusted executives, the crowd quickly turned his way; he had them on his side now.

Then he turned to the good news. "As a result of the sting and the elimination of the cartel from this community, we now have a proposed project that will put us on the map in a manner to make us proud." The curtain rose and a slide of the artist's rendering of Craigston Township showed in its most radiant glory.

"Craigston Township will be the very heart of fly-fishing in the world. Its anchor feature will be the Parsons Point Lodge and Resort, a traditional American fishing lodge with luxury appointments and connections to the outdoors and fly-fishing. Patrons of the lodge will come here for the fishing, hiking, mountain biking, and, in a short time, world-class golf on a PGA Tournament-quality course.

"The Resort will be managed by Dr. Harper Philips, granddaughter of the great Craig Parsons, and the best fishing guide in this part of the US. Dr. Philips will be ably assisted by Dr. DeMarius Moffat as Chief Financial Officer and Director of Operations. The resort will contain a conference facility and what we might call FFU, Fly-Fishing University. There will be office space for a dozen guides who wish to be associated with Craig Parsons and … Bob Dorffman, Parson's favorite fishing partner and family friend, who graciously is supplying the capital for the Lodge.

"A major part of the resort will be 'The Iron Skillet,' a first-class white-table-cloth restaurant specializing in the finest array of regional comfort food available in the US. It will be led by Charles Cameron, currently Director of Marketing at US&G. I would now like to introduce Dr. Harper Philips, the person who brought most of this opportunity to the investment group and US&G. Dr. Philips …"

Harper came to the podium—a confident, self-possessed woman, totally in command of the moment. She thanked all the right people—Mo, Amanda, Hanna, D, and especially Henry. "The project will be carried out under a PPP, Public Private Partnership, and a Special Purpose Vehicle, consisting of an investment group of Jack Morris, Henry Hansen, the Environmental Protection Agency, and three corporate investors who have interests in the old mine in the Hills above the Hattawoc River. This remarkable coalition came to pass through some extraordinary circumstances, and has resulted in a very strong, well-capitalized, and very well-conceived entity, with the strength to create, maintain, and sustain this world-class resort.

"It will eventually be available for investment from individuals who are interested in owning a piece of a very unique property. Craigston Township will serve as a model—the first of its kind—for a whole generation of environmentally-oriented, conservation-directed, profitable investments to address our crying need for steward-ship of our outdoor heritage. I am proud to be a part of this endeavor, and I hope you will be as enthusiastic about it as I am."

When Jack returned to the stage, he was beaming, in his best car-dealer face. "Now, there is a giant party to follow this meeting, but we are not through here just yet."

"I want to introduce one more person to you, who, in the classic sense, requires no introduction, Maurice 'Mo' Stearns."

Mo entered the stage and greeted everyone. "Thank you for attending our meeting tonight. I think you will agree with me that what you have heard so far is truly remarkable. And it is due mostly to the efforts of some remarkable people: Henry Hansen, Harper Philips, and Jack Morris. I am profoundly in your debt."

"In light of the developments around the development, so to speak, I am retiring from my role as Chairman of US&G, and will be succeeded by my daughter, Amanda, who will become CEO effective thirty days from now. I will retain my seat on the board of US&G, but I will spend my time in other pursuits.

"I want to bring my business and civic experience to the table for the benefit of the citizens of our state, and help us realize the future of which we all dream. And the pursuit at the top of my list is that, tonight, I am announcing that my hat is in the ring for the Office of Governor."

The crowd exploded into applause and a roaring cheer.

You will hear a great deal more about this in the near future—and even tonight, if you are unfortunate enough to get trapped in a conversation with me, or with Jack. I hope you will all find me a strong candidate and support my campaign with your votes, your efforts, and, of course, your campaign contributions.

"Thank you all for being here and hearing all this wonderful news. Now let's go celebrate. The party is at the Metropolitan Hotel in the Grand Ballroom. I'll see you there shortly. Thanks again. Meeting adjourned."

The audience did not have to be invited twice to the party. The exits to the meeting room were suddenly quite crowded. As Henry and Harper jostled their way through the melee, Henry spotted Smythwick and tipped his imaginary newsboy cap. Smythwick smiled and gave Henry a thumbs up in return. The smile was more important than the thumbs up.

As the crowd gathered at the Metropolitan, the atmosphere was electric. All the business and community representatives in attendance were jubilant. A huge scandal had been avoided, with the outcome being a valuable and widely beneficial project.

Mo was circulating happily, no doubt lining up contributions for his run. Jack was back slapping, supporting Mo's efforts and probably selling a few cars, not to mention looking for some new unsuspecting sandbaggers that he and Henry could rescue from their money. Amanda was radiant since she was now identified as the heir-apparent to the work of her father in establishing US&G as a quality, reliable, and extremely competent investment bank.

Henry and Harper were quietly celebrating in a corner surrounded by their friends, Henry's team, and a couple of aspiring young hangers-on in the statistical community. Harper and Amanda even smiled at each other across the room. Henry avoided eye contact with Amanda, and was locked into Harper's eyes, totally enamored as he had been for months.

After trading smiles with Harper, Amanda continued to size up the crowd from a distance.

A tall, muscular young man in a very expensive suit came into the sweep of her radar, one she had not been aware of previously. He caught her eye at the same time she discovered his. A spark ignited.

He began to amble over to her, and she instinctively primped just a bit to make sure she was in control of the situation when he arrived at her feet.

"Hi, Amanda, congratulations. And how are you these days?" he offered.

Amanda thought he sounded quite familiar with her and it took her aback. "I'm doing great," she chirped happily. "An evening full of good news, and a lot of excitement for the future of the community and a lot of good people."

"You don't recognize me, do you?" He asked, laughing.

"Please forgive me, but no I don't. I am thinking that I should."

"Amanda, it's Ari. We haven't seen each other in months and I have been wondering what you are up to," he said.

"You're right, we haven't," she agreed. "You look like you have been using the time well. What are you doing?"

"Well, I quit my job at the insurance company, and the Pirates hired me for Henry's old job. He gave me an introduction and a great character reference."

Amanda was interested. "You know, you have had a major hand in the events we are celebrating tonight. You first introduced me and our firm to Henry. And what are you doing for fun in these months?"

"Well, as you can probably tell, I've spent a lot of time in the gym. I just decided that I needed to be healthier and more fit. And I decided to try to add a bit of muscle mass at the same time," Ari proudly pronounced.

"Time certainly well spent," Amanda noted. "You look terrific."

"But while improving my body, I haven't neglected my brain. I am about three point five feet into the Five-Foot Shelf of Harvard Classics. Gotten through all the Greeks, and I am now trying to get a grip on Locke and the social contract school. It's even fun, and I'm gaining both knowledge and confidence. It is *really* a revelation for me."

"Ari, that's terribly worthwhile. You are truly becoming a man of substance."

He smiled modestly, "Well, I'm trying."

"Let me buy you a drink, "Amanda offered. "What are you having?"

"I'm enjoying a really fine local craft beer from the Riverbend Brewery. And I'd enjoy another ... if we can keep talking."

"Yes," she purred, "*of course* we can keep talking. I am really interested in everything you've done in so short a time.

"Tell me, how do you feel about very dry martinis ... ?"

ABOUT THE AUTHOR

T. A. Parrish is a seasoned business executive, consultant, and avid fly fisherman. A native of Texas, he has lived and/or worked on five continents, fished widely in North America from Alaska to Pennsylvania, and golfed from Washington State to Scotland, Continental Europe, and South Africa.

Raised on sports and educated in academically challenging institutions, he has been indoctrinated with ideals of fair play and skill development. With wry humor and biting insights, he creates an accurate though sometimes prickly version of maturing. His skepticism is balanced with an unrelenting optimism which does not retreat from hard observations, but also refuses to submit to the cynicism which often accompanies them.

Mending is his first novel and explores concepts and characters not often associated with each other. He writes from experience in worlds that he has inhabited. Set in a universal place which many will find familiar, *Mending* sees and observes events in an indistinct time which are just as relevant today as they might have been half a century ago or will be half a century in the future.

9 781665 301022